To Find a Tall Ship

A.G. Thompson

Huntsville AL

Contents

Chapter One

The Empire of Isemoto
Ishikawa Prefecture
City of Koda and Castle Oda
April 1478, Third Age of Imperial Reckoning

"Ancestors! What have I done?!" Oda *sia* Asami stared about the massage room in horror. Blood covered the delicate sliding walls, ruining the tasteful display of masterpiece art works. Gore dripped from the dim lanterns, the low ceiling, pooled on the polished wooden floor. The room stank of blood and other things, splashed and splattered from her elderly client's gutted corpse.

That her client, come for the pleasure of her lithe body, was to have died by her hand, subtly slain as he took his delight of her, now made no matter. The old man, one Suwa Sadasuke, the newly appointed Imperial Magistrate of the Ishikawa Prefecture, was slated for death. His crime was being a truly incorruptible man, set as a High Court judge in the capital city of a Clan of thieves, slavers, and assassins. Clan Ishikawa was the Least Clan, last of the Hundred and Forty-Four Great Clans. But they were still a Clan, however evil and corrupt. And any Clan was more powerful than any individual.

But his death was to appear a natural one, an old man whose heart failed him in the frenzy of lust. The *sairento doku* concealed in the needle tip of one of her long, sharp fingernails was a poison potent enough that the slightest pinprick would have sent him into a coma and then death, indistinguishable from heart failure. Not these bloody shambles.

Not Oda Naoki's broken-backed body twitching away the last of his life, twisted around a roof column. He clutched the hilt of his broken ninijato, the sword blade snapped neatly in half. Even in dying, his grey-green eyes glared hatred at her. Her own bloody handprints glistened on his sea green kimono, at shoulder and hip where she had grabbed and thrown him. She stared in disbelief at what had become of a routine, if distasteful task, one rudely undone by Oda Naoki, grandson of the Clan Master, son of Oda Shunsuke, heir to Clan's leadership, not an adopted foundling as she was.

Her mind replayed everything as she stared at the carnage. Naoki bursting through the flimsy *shoji* at the room's entrance in a berserk rage. "You made her!" he roared, his blade cutting the old man atop her body nearly in half. "It's your fault! You made Maho do it with him! You slut! I'll butcher you like a pig!" She twisted like a snake in fire to avoid the thrust of his blade, the sword cutting through the futon's mattress and into the wooden floor. Without volition, her body reacted to the attack, rolling back to trap the sword, her right fist smashing into the flat of the iron ninijato, breaking it. Her knee smashed up into his crotch, flinging him over and off her, but in his fury the usually incapacitating blow had no effect on him. She backflipped to her feet, dodging another mindless slash from the broken sword. Howling as if possessed by an evil *oni*, he lunged at her, the ruined blade flashing at her face.

She spun out of line with the thrust, grabbing Naoki at shoulder and hip as he stumbled forward. Great-Uncle Sota would have been proud of her form as she flung him across the room into the solid oak roof column. His scream nearly drowned out the sound of his back shattering. He slid to the floor, wordlessly gobbling out his hatred, blood spewing from his mouth. She shook her head to break the memory train.

Now the blood dribbled from his mouth, slowing from a torrent to a mere drip, drip, drip; the sound marking the fleeting moments left to his life, and to her own. No excuse could possibly justify her killing the favorite of the Grandmaster. If Grandfather Kazuhiko got his hands on her, she would be weeks dying. His grandson Naoki was the pride of his day and the light of his eyes. She was an adopted girl-child of unknown parentage, a great beauty, but subject to falling fits at times, failing the promise supposedly seen in her by Great-Grandfather Katsumi over a decade ago. Kazuhiko despised the dirt under her sandals. He would have her flayed and screaming for merciful death before the week was out if she did not flee for her life now. The Evil One, Quan Himself, would bow to the Holiest of the Ancestors before Kazuhiko would be so benign as to grant her a quick death.

Taking only an instant to snatch up her kimono and wrap it around her blood-covered nakedness, she fled the brothel of the Maiden's Arms as if Quan's own daemons rode her shoulders.

***

Even if only a disfavored adopted daughter, Oda *sia* Asami would still be expected to walk through the great gates of Oda Castle. In her current state, long, sable hair a tangled mess, barefoot and bloody, the last thing she wanted was the attention of the gate guards. But Great-Uncle Sota had had the training of her once she was adopted. His training in the art of *Shizukana Ashi no Jutsu* was brutal, thorough, and complete. The Way of Silence and Stealth was second nature to her now and she flowed over the castle's walls with no more sound or notice than the shadow of a nighttime cloud.

The *tenshu* of Oda Castle was honeycombed with a maze of secret and concealed passages and rooms. Silent as any soft-footed feline and nearly as invisible, she ghosted through the keep to her own simple room. Moving quickly, she gathered what few valuables she owned. Most important were her favored swords, wide bladed and short, intended to be wielded in a flashing, two-hand style that gave them their name, *cho no ken*, butterfly swords. She slipped their harness and sheaths over a mottled black-gray cotton silk tunic. Darker gray *hakama* tied around her slim waist and legs; her black *shozoku* covered the swords, its *zukin* loose around her neck for now. The hood would only attract attention, should she encounter anyone in the halls. Black *tabi* laced around her ankles and calves, split-toed to allow her to grip and climb. A sturdy shoulder bag was quickly stuffed with a few other things, a small box of cosmetics, underthings and spare *kimonos*, her simple wooden flute, some small tools and lockpicks. But the one thing she did not have at all was money.

The only thing she had of any value was her amulet, a cube of an unknown, silvery metal on a snug collar of the same material. She had always worn it. She thought it was magic, perhaps. Somehow it escaped noticed by even the most avaricious individuals, whether thieves, tax collectors or her hateful adopted siblings, Maho and Mankato. She could not sell it. Ancestors, she couldn't even take it off, the collar had no clasp. And she would have to have money of some type. She had her beauty and her body, but that was a currency she'd prefer to keep unspent, even if she was hardly a shy virgin.

She passed soundlessly down the corridor, leaving no more mark than mist. The upper vault was around the next corner, and it would contain what she needed. She slunk around the corner in a silent rush, surprising the lone guard. He had been inattentive, leaning against the wall, his katana propped against the vault's door. She took him down in a nearly noiseless clatter, his leather armor no defense against the poison fingernail she jabbed into his unprotected throat. The poison paralyzed almost instantly, her hand across his mouth, muffling his single cry of agony. Within a handspan of time, his body softened in death.

Sorry, but you should have been more attentive. Great-uncle Sota would have killed you slowly, hanging head down over a slow fire for being so lax on guard duty. She frowned at the thought. She had been careless herself, tearing the man's throat instead of simply pricking it with her poisoned nail. His jugular vein had torn and now her *shozoku* was soaked with his lifeblood.

It was the work of a moment to pick the door's lock. This vault held ready funds, gold and silver coins, paper currency, some small gems and gold trade bars. She filled a small box with what was easily and immediately available, packing it with more wealth than she had ever before held in her own hands. She stuffed the box into her shoulder bag and turned to leave.

She froze in shock. Great-uncle Sota blocked the door, his lean, tough body leaning nonchalantly on his sheathed *nodachi*, the great sword as long as she was tall. For all his fearsome demeanor, his height only topped her own by a finger span or two. But he always seemed a fearsome giant to her. His brown eyes, hard and fierce as agates, met her black ones.

"Leaving us so suddenly, Oda *sia* Asami." His voice was calm and quiet, but cold as the endless depths between stars.

She froze, the hare under the stooping falcon. Great-uncle Sota terrified her. He always had. She was certain that he saw clearly into her, all her weaknesses and inadequacies. The shame of her fits. Her height and broad shoulders, breasts too big to allow her to truly master the Way. All the ways she was a stumbling oaf, an embarrassment to his training, a shameful thing to her Family and Clan.

"Nagamasa was idling again, wasn't he?" Sota's toe nudged the corpse. "And you took advantage?"

"Yes, Master Sota." She did not bow to him, the bravest or most foolish thing she had ever done, she thought.

"And?" The voice had the same harsh tone as always, every time he corrected her.

"I was hasty and inaccurate." She answered clearly, trying to anticipate his strike. The old man was lightning unleashed with his *nodachi*. "Instead of a simple prick with the *sairento doku* needle on my forefinger's nail, I thrust too deeply and tore the great vein. Thus, his lifeblood stains my *shozoku*."

"Hmmpf." He was silent a long moment. Then he sighed deeply, and she gawked in incredulity as his face softened, a sad, warm cast coming to those hard, brown eyes, eyes no longer so hard, really. "Ah, Asami, you have tried so hard and truly done so well in all your training and tasks here among us. But if you are truly, in your true, innermost Spirit, either assassin, thief, or whore, well, then, I am a nine-tailed *kitsune*, a white one. You have never truly belonged here, no matter your mother's claims about Asami, her daughter of the blood. Yuko's insanity over your namesake's death fifteen years ago is bad enough, but, ah, what has been done to you is shameful and a horror. But then, we are the Oda, are we not? Shame and horror are what we do."

"Yes, Master," the answer to his question was automatic, given before she realized what he had said. "Mas...Master Sota, what are you saying?"

"Naoki is dead, isn't he?"

"What!? How could you kno...?" Her startled voice trailed off in confusion.

"Huh. Despite what my younger brother, Kazuhiko, now Grandmaster and my so-brilliant nephew, Shunsuke, that uncultured clod, think, I am hardly the bumbling half-wit, only interested in the dojo and the salle, that they believe me to be. Not hardly. I know that Naoki has been under Maho's spell. He has danced to her tune, just as Mankato, her twin, dances. I've known much evil in my many years, but that girl is truly a fit mate for Quan himself. Were she my child, I would have drowned her at birth, I think. But that is what is past," he sighed. "I saw Naoki go pounding out the gate on his father's best horse. He was already screaming that he would gut you like a fish. Seeing Maho's evil smirk in the stable's shadows was enough. I only wondered if you would survive. I knew if you did, it would be at the cost of Naoki's life. And I have no love for my grand-nephew, one I deemed long ago to be a weak-willed cretin and a bully to those weaker than he."

"Bu—but, but he is a son of the blood, and I only a foundling, adopted to soothe Mother Yuko's madness." Asami stared at him in round-eyed shock.

"Yes, and you are worth more than the rest of the lot of them. Twice, perhaps thrice. But you cannot stay here. Honestly, you never could. Perhaps it is fortunate that you must flee now. But I require one thing, adopted grand-niece."

"Yes, Master Sota?"

"No longer can you claim the Oda Family name, nor the Ishikawa Clan. And you must leave Asami behind. The blissful child with that name died the year before you came here, gifted to Yuko by Toh, the Imperial tax collector."

"Toh took what family I had from me, the beast. I'll kill him some day. And now even my name is taken from me." She bowed her head.

"Make your own name, fortunate one." Sota smiled at her as he lifted her chin with a gnarled finger. "Be happy; but be so far from here. My brother will never stop hunting you, but not even the hand of the Ishikawa stretches to the far side of the world. Go now, take Naoki's dun gelding. It's the best horse left in the stables. Go now, quickly, child. Know that Great-uncle Sota will remember you the rest of his days."

"Yes, Master."

"No, child, no longer am I your Master, at most only your doddering old uncle." His smile was slow and sly, but with true humor in it.

She didn't understand why her vision, normally so keen, was blurred, until she felt the tear slide down her cheek.

"Yes, Uncle." Not even understanding herself, she flung herself into his arms, crushing him against her. He sighed and returned the hug as strongly.

"Go, now, fortunate one," he whispered, "Go, while foolish old Sota berates the gate watch for being slack and inattentive. Go with my blessing." His hands were on her shoulders and she felt his dry lips brush her forehead ever so briefly, and the crafty old warrior was gone. She never saw him again.

Ishikawa Prefecture
Akumato Porttown
April 1478, Third Age of Imperial Reckoning

The dun was blown, thickly lathered. She had pushed him until he nearly foundered. It helped that she was lighter than Naoki and wore no armor, but regardless, the horse was finished. But he had done what she needed, gotten her down the Imperial Highway to Akumato Porttown faster than any reasonable expectation. Outside the main gate was the usual collection of hovels, the stalls of lesser merchants, cheap inns and hostels, mostly run-down shanties, flimsy wood and paper construction. Most Clans would not tolerate such a confusion of flotsam and jetsam on the main road into a town.

But Akumato was a special case. It was part of Ishikawa Prefecture, therefore owned by Clan Ishikawa. As the Least Clan, Ishikawa, controlled by the Oda Family, well, they did things differently. And even for the Ishikawa, Akumato was different. By Imperial Decree, the Empire of Isemoto allowed no foreigners from over the seas to sully the Island Empire's soil.

Only at Akumato could the foreigners come ashore from their ships and trade with the Nisei of Isemoto, trading their gold and steel and toys for Nisei silk, tea, and fine porcelain. Akumato was a walled town, rare in Isemoto, more to keep the strangers in than to keep any enemy out. Any stranger who ventured outside the walls forfeited his life. And entry into the Porttown was also rigidly controlled. Supposedly.

"Let the Ishikawa deal with the foreigners," the Emperor had said that long-ago day. "They are the Least of the Great Clans. They are thieves and smugglers. How better to catch a thief than to set one to watch the gates and walls." Of course, the Head of the Clan at that time had been Katsumi's grandfather, Oda Kazutake. The Emperor of that day and Kazutake had understood each other very well.

As an Oda, she could have simply walked through the gate. But if she did, Kazuhiko would know where she was within hours. She must be the essence of stealth, passing over rice paper and between the lightest of wind chimes with neither mark nor sound. Getting into Akumato would not be difficult. Finding a way to flee Isemoto once and for all would be the hard part. She needed one of the foreigners' tall ships. And everyone knew that all foreigners were, in fact, devils.

***

She shook from hunger. Her teeth tried to chatter from the icy spring wind coming off the nighttime harbor. She knew that her hunters had come to Aku-mato, passing the word of her crime among the lesser Families of the Clan and those members of the Imperial Bureaucracy controlled by the Oda. Fortunately, it was believed she had gone west, toward the Chou Sea, the expanse of a shallow sea separating Isemoto from the lands of the Chou Li Han Empire. She had seen that sea once, years ago. She barely remembered the subtlest hint of the vast lands of the Han across that sea.

If the hunters of the Oda caught her—she shuddered at the thought of her fate. Naoki's murder at her hands would earn her a slow and lingering death. A death guaranteed to dishonor her body, spirit, and soul in ways past even her vivid imagination. Kazuhiko might even pay an unscrupulous *shugenja* to magically heal her before she could escape into the afterlife of the Ancestors. She would be better off to take her own life first.

Great-uncle Sota had taken her name from her. The shiver down her back was only partly due to the frigid April wind. A person with no name was vulnerable to magical attack. An *oni* might possess the body of a nameless one, casting the nameless soul into darkness. Of course, any *oni* or other daemon that possessed her body would get a rude surprise when the Oda caught them. The night was both her greatest fear and her best ally. And tonight, she thought, she must sneak aboard one of the foreign devils' ships in the harbor. Two days she had been here, hiding in the day, stealing food and water at night. The Odas would soon realize she had gone east, not west. Whenever that happened, she had best be far away, over the horizon. The further away, the better.

She perched on the roof of a merchant's dockside warehouse. Obviously, this was not the best time for traders to come to Isemoto. The spring winds were contrary and ill-favored and there were few ships in the harbor. Again, her stomach growled its objections to its empty state as she turned away from the harbor, sliding down a drainpipe to quickly reach the comforting darkness of the narrow alley behind buildings. The alley was, at least, marginally warm, out of the biting wind. Here in Akumato, she had no allies, no connections, and no friends. Only the benign guidance of the Ancestor Spirits could aid her here. But what she needed should be easy to find.

There were a few ocean-going ships in the harbor, but only one of them looked promising at all. Nisei fishing sampans were of no use to her. Nor were the half dozen trading junks from Chou Li Han. The reach of the Ishikawa extended well into the lands of the Han people, perhaps even into the Celestial Court of the Dragon Emperor. Beyond the Han Empire, lay the vast steppes of the Rus.

She knew little of the Rus, other than the fact that life was good for the ruling Kzar, his Court and the cruel Boyars, and bad for everyone else. The Boyars ruled the vast multitude of serfs with casual brutality. For the serfs, life was an unending round of misery, back-breaking labor, useless rebellions, and death. And, like the Nisei and the Han, the Rus kept slaves, whose lives made the serfs' misery seem a day in paradise. So she would avoid the two Rus galleons moored at the wharf.

She would also avoid the high-sided, white-painted galleass tied up across the wharf from the Rus. The salt-streaked white hull, the twin banks of oars and the white flag with the stooping falcon on a red shield, those marked the huge, clumsy looking ship as a Lietelean Empire trade ship. Those oars were pulled by slaves whose lives were nasty, brutal, and short. Of all the nations of the world of Rybithia, her teachers taught that the Eternal Empire of Lietelea was huge, powerful, and swamped in eternal corruption. The Kythal Church quarreled with the Imperial Bureaucracy to see who could be bought for the highest price. They were also the greatest slave traders in the known world. They acquired slaves by trading with the petty barbarian kingdoms of the southern continent of Khakal. Of course, they were not above conducting slave raids themselves. Even petty criminals went to the block, as did any problematic outsider not wealthy enough to bribe the Imperial officials. No imagination needed to guess her fate there.

She had hoped to find a merchant ship from the Kingdom of Montagar. Montagar was an island nation, like Isemoto, but that was about the only similarity. While there was a King, she had been taught that the Montagaran folk chose leaders to speak for them and then those leaders chose a leader among themselves to run the government. It seemed very strange to her, but she also learned that the Montagarans did not keep slaves and worked to suppress what they could of the slave trade. It sounded too good to be true, but she decided that Montagar would be her goal. It was as far away as the fabled lands of the mythical *kami*. But there were no Montagaran ships in the harbor.

There were, however, two ships flying the flag of the Republic of Kolbia, a blue shield with a single white star and blue and white stripes. One was anchored well out in the harbor, low and twin-masted. A warship, cannons jutting from open gunports down her side. Her hull was painted a dark gray, with a solid black line revealing the gundeck. She seemed to want to fly across the waves, even at anchor. She figured such a ship was fast, but she was also relatively small and would offer few hiding places.

The other one was tied up at the pier furthest from the Lietelean galleass. She was the biggest ship in the harbor, the largest ship she had ever seen. Her three masts towered into the sky; white sails tied tightly about her yards. She had the same gray hull as the other but lacked the black line of gunports. She seemed impatient, ready to be free from the land, flying under those massive sails across the open ocean, her true home.

She had never been on a true ship, but even the fishermen in Ishikawa Prefecture paid their *wairo* to the Clan, bribes in addition to the heavy Imperial taxes. She knew fore from aft and what masts and yards were but little else. But still, she sensed a feeling of urgency and speed from the big ship. If it were a merchant ship, she would be able to sneak aboard and then, once out of sight of Isemoto, pay the captain richly in gold and gems. Hopefully enough that she would not need to pay further with her body and her bed skills.

But if it were a ship of the Kolbian Navy, nothing would suffice to pay or bribe her way to the passage she desperately sought. The Kolbian Navy maintained just enough of a presence in Isemoto to be a constant menace to the activities of Clan Ishikawa and particularly the Oda Family. The Kolbian Navy was literal death on pirates and slavers if they caught them beyond the national waters of Isemoto. Their Navy would hang her if they caught her and realized she was an Oda.

Hanging was a dishonorable death but better than what Grandfather Kazuhiko would do to her. Hanging would be at least be quick. If that great ship was a merchant, well, she knew her Family dealt with some Kolbian sea-traders, both in slaves and in the fruits of piracy. The Republic of Kolbia professed to believe in equality and freedom. How could a nation proclaiming such beliefs permit such things as slavers and pirates to carry on their vile trade? Were those Kolbian slavers her Clan traded with no more than an aberration, criminals, and outcasts, little different than the Ishikawa themselves? She had no way to discern the truth of the matter. Perhaps the Kolbians simply lied. One thing she knew with certainty was that her Family hated and feared the Kolbian Republican Navy. Perhaps that would be enough. She needed one of the foreign devils' tall ships.

She drifted through the dark, dank back alleys, leaving no trace, making no sound. Her *shozoku* blended into the night. Wearing it, her *tabi*, carrying her hidden swords, those were a risk. Akumato belonged to the Ishikawa, but even so there were Imperial officials and samurai who answered only to the Emperor here as well. If one of those caught her in such garb, prohibited to a mere female by Imperial Decree, the penalty was to be stripped and beaten bloody with rattan rods, then branded on forehead and back as One Unclean.

Her life would then be forfeit to anyone who cared to take it. Falling into the Oda's clutches would be a sickening certainty at that point. But the *shozoku* allowed her to move freely, hidden and unseen. Needful abilities not possible in a traditional *kimono*. So she took the risk. Her stomach growled in hunger. As she moved away from the dockside, she slipped into a couple of shops' back rooms and helped herself to some rice and bread and in one, a small whole game-hen. She settled down to eat behind a shuttered blacksmith shop, eating quietly and quickly. Her hunger temporarily assuaged, she caressed her amulet. It calmed her; it always did. She paused briefly to mutter a quick, heartfelt prayer to the Ancestors to protect her from her affliction. Losing a candlemark or more to one of her fits with her mind blank and her body rigid in a dank alley would spell her doom.

The amulet reminded her of her true home, with the Komiya family, the simple peasant folk who genuinely loved her. Papa had been forced to choose between the foundling daughter he loved, or the wife and mother of his natural children. Forced to choose when he could not pay the illegal taxes imposed by a fat, pestilent and thoroughly corrupt tax collector named Toh. Her last memories of them were Papa standing rigid in the road, Mama weeping at his feet. His face twisted between sorrow at the loss of a daughter he loved, and a burning hatred for Toh. She shared that hatred for that repulsive, bloated toad and someday...someday...

It had been Toh who gave her to Oda Yuko as a body slave. Yuko's young daughter Asami had died of the coughing sickness. When Toh learned of this, he acted with unusual alacrity, taking her in lieu of money Papa simply did not have. She bore an uncanny resemblance to the dead girl and within the year, Yuko, driven to near madness by her youngest daughter's death, adopted the foundling girl-child. Oda Katsumi, the old Grandmaster, watched her at play one day, a six-year-old girl-child walking fearlessly on a rope strung between two poles. He ordered her into training, both for *shizukana ashi no jutsu* and for the gentler skills of the *geisha* as well, seeing the promise of great beauty in the girl. The promise of beauty she fulfilled, but all the other hopes were withered, her name taken from her and now she must flee her homeland or die.

She finished the game hen, crouched in the lee of the blacksmith's rickety storage shed. Wiping her mouth on her sleeve, she realized she had gained an audience. An arm's length away a grey cat sat, tail wrapped around its feet, amber eyes intently watching the scraps remaining of the bird.

"Hungry, eh?" she asked the feline. It cocked its head, focusing on her black eyes and then back to the bones. "I guess so, huh?" She started to toss the leftovers to the cat, then stopped suddenly.

"Meow." The cat's attention followed the bones. It leaned toward her, hunger glinting in its eyes.

"You wouldn't happen to be a powerful *kami* who could whisk me away to safety, would you?" She smiled at the cat as it shifted its feet. It meowed again. "I guess not, hmm? Well, here you go. Enjoy your meal, Fortunate One." She tossed the bird bones to the cat. It crouched down and began to daintily pick over the bones for any last bits of meat. "Hmm, that gives me an idea, Cat." The animal glanced up at her before resuming its meal. "Uncle Sota called me Fortunate One. Why not take that as my new name, as a name that would be...let me think, um, Sachi? Yes, Sachi. How does that sound to you, Cat?" The feline half-purred, half-growled as it ate. "I could use Mama and Papa's Clan Name, the Takahashi Clan. It's a big Clan, even if mostly poor farmers, Families like Mama and Papa. Takahashi Sachi. How does that sound to you, Cat?" Amber eyes blinked at her, then the cat began licking its paw to wash its ears and face. She chuckled quietly. "I'll take that as approval. Bless you, Cat. May the mice always be too slow to reach their hole. And now, like the mouse, I must flee."

Leaving the cat to its meal, she headed across town, to the portion where the foreign devil sailors found their own coarse entertainments. Those sailors were like any man left long isolated: when allowed to come ashore, they searched out what they had been denied — rich foods, powerful drink, and willing women. She needed to listen at the cracks of the *musajosei* houses the foreign devil sailors frequented, where they ate, drank, and consorted with the *baishunfu*, women the sailors called joy girls. She needed knowledge of which ship would best meet her needs. She knew the great Kolbian ship would be best, indeed she thought there was little other true choice, but the more she knew of it, the better she could prepare. She moved with the shadows of the clouds passing over the waning quarter-moon, her *zukin* and mask-like *fukumen* hiding her long sable hair and porcelain-pale skin, showing only her black eyes. She would listen and learn.

She feared the great Kolbian ship would be a Navy ship. Given her Family's hostility toward the sailors and officers of that Navy, she doubted her money and gold might gain her what she must have, passage away from Isemoto. Kolbian Navy Captains were remarkably resistant to being bribed and even common sailors often possessed a moral fortitude worthy of a *Shugena* warrior-monk. Oh, they would take their pleasures in the joy houses, get drunk and start fights, but it was a rare seaman that could be reliably bribed. To survive, she would have to be truly invisible, no more presence than a spirit.

What the foreign devils called the Great Western Ocean was a deep, powerful, unmeasured expanse of cold salt sea water that ignored the impotent hand of Man. That great ocean separated Isemoto from the Western world, isolating the Nisei people from those fabulous lands with their exotic names, lands simply full of inscrutable foreign devils. The skills she learned as a *minarai* to a senior *onee-san* geisha would stand her in good stead in those lands. She could disappear there, vanishing into such a world that even the brutal Oda Family of Clan Ishikawa, her adopted family and clan, would never find her.

Now, however, the geisha lessons were a distant second in importance to her training in *shizukana ashi no jutsu*. The Way of Silence and Stealth was what she needed now, not grace and beauty. She would not try to pass herself off as a joy-girl, but from the shadows she would watch and listen, hopeful to find crew of the right ship. One to take her away from the only life she had ever known. A tall ship was what she needed, one to take her away over the horizon, to a land where she could finally be free.

***

Captain, Junior Grade, William 'Bonny' Blaine executed the proper bow, inclining his upper torso exactly fifteen degrees toward the senior Port Master. He didn't like the greedy little bastard one little bit, but at least the prick was polite about receiving his bribe. He didn't like having to pay the bribe in the first place, as a Captain of the Kolbian Republican Navy. And this officious midget butt-sucker just made it worse, smiling like something from the Deeps with too many teeth. A smile that never came close to reaching his eyes. Worst of all, ONI's extremely limited intelligence assets in the Divine Empire of the Nisei of Isemoto had this...person...pegged as one of the main enablers of piracy and slaving in this part of the world. Part of Blaine *really* wanted to hang this worthless son of a bitch from the yardarm and burn this whole piss-ant town to the ground. Blaine's personal command, the forty-four-gun frigate KRN *Intrepid* and the accompanying twenty-two-gun sloop-of-war KRN *Sorcerer* could blow the Nisei Empire's chicken shit Navy out of the water in an afternoon. Especially with what was in *Intrepid's* shot locker.

But he couldn't do that, and he knew it. The local Ambassador's military attaché, Captain Vicki Copeland, was also the Isemoto Station Chief of the Office of Naval Intelligence and she had made it quite clear that she preferred the devil she knew to one she didn't. So he returned the bastard's smile and made damn sure his own smile never reached his eyes either. Business completed, he could demur accepting any more of that God-awful rice wine, get out of this sweat box and start making sure his command was properly victualled and balanced to again cross the treacherous Great Western Ocean. A final bow and he could scrape the crap off his boots and get the hell out of here.

"Please, sir, could you just let one of my Marines shoot that worthless fish-fucker? A negligent discharge? *Oops, I dropped a grenade?* Something? Please?" Marine Captain Jorge Karlson begged *sotto voce* as they stepped back out into the street. Adjusting his fore and aft cocked hat, Blaine shot a smile at the commander of the short company of Marines embarked on his vessel. While they were on shore, Karlson's rank was Captain. The instant they boarded *Intrepid* he was Major Karlson, a courtesy promotion since a vessel only ever had one Captain.

"Sorry, Jorge." Blaine smiled at the Marine officer. "If I don't get to hang him from the yardarm, you don't get to shoot him. Much as we'd both like to, the Foreign Service would have us for rugs, not to mention what Captain Copeland would do to us. Back to ship it is, assuming some footpad doesn't thug us in a dark street this night."

***

Senior Petty Officer Tobias Wilkerson, Senior Ship's Steward, loved it when *Intrepid* made port in Isemoto. True, many of the locals simply would not deal with the 'foreign devils' but there were spices and foods that he could only get here. And given his own preferences for romantic companionship and the local culture, well, this was one port he wouldn't be getting his ashes hauled in. It wasn't as bad as some places in the Empire. Those bastards might burn you at the stake if they learned you preferred men to women for sex. Here, the locals mostly didn't care who or even what you futtered, but the joy houses only catered to men looking for women. Oh well, their loss. He turned onto Spice Street and was immediately confronted by the sight of the entire crew of the Number Four Quarterdeck Carronade, drunk as Montagaran lords, arguing with the owner of a spice shop that his establishment was a joy house. Toby, as he was commonly called, sighed, and shook his head before squaring his shoulders and resolutely marching into the fray.

"Here, now, lads, what be the problem here?" Toby reached out and grabbed Petty Officer Jadon Stobbes, the Gun Captain, by the shoulder, interrupting him in mid-yell at the confused and frightened shop keeper. "I never thought to see me crew-mates looking for a joy girl in a spice shop."

"Burnin' ells, where'd you com' from, Toby?" Jadon's normally clear diction was obviously an early casualty of the bottle of rice liquor in his right hand. "Sneakin' up onna man lik one a tese folks' black shirt sneaks!"

"You and your lads are setting sail on the wrong tack here. This is a spice shop, the kind you use in the galley, not the horizontal kind. Those houses are three streets over. I'm here to buy cloves and all-spice for the Cap'n's dinner."

"Spice shop?"

"Yes, a spice shop, you daft drunkards. The joy-girl houses are three streets over to starboard. Not that any of you'll be worth a tinker's fart in your condition. Drunk as you lot are, I doubt your peckers will get any harder than a bowl of puddin', no matter how fancy the whore! But have fun trying, shipmates!"

Toby gave Jadon a shove and smiled as the gunner and his crew stumbled off. Like as not they'd wind up running afoul of the Shore Patrol, but that wasn't his lookout. He turned and smiled at the shopkeeper, bobbing in return to the small man's respectful bow. Toby took a moment to remember his Nisei and then settled in to bargain for the spices he wanted.

***

Of course, none of the sailors spoke Nisei. Or, well, no more than was necessary to make known their desires for food, wine, and sex. And they didn't exactly discuss which ship they crewed. She thought some were Navy sailors, from the smaller two-masted ship anchored in the harbor, others from the big ship tied up quayside. Listening through curtained windows and cracks in floorboards didn't confer the clearest understanding of the limited conversations. And her Terranglais was rusty and she still wasn't sure if that great vessel was a Navy ship or not.

She didn't have a great deal of choice. Stay and die, be enslaved or worse by either the Lietelean Imperials or the Rus or sneak aboard the Kolbian vessel and pray she could stay hidden if it was a Navy ship. But at this point, she was pretty much out of options, so she headed down to the quay to study her target. She must get on board undetected and stay that way for at least a week. Less time than that and it was just barely possible the Captain might put the ship about and bring her back. Assuming he didn't just toss her over the rail into the ocean.

***

The black grease covering her nude body was slick enough to allow her to squeeze through the anchor cable's hawsehole and slide unseen into the darkened deck at the bow of the ship. It was a very tight fit. Once again, she wished for a more petite figure. She was very tall for a Nisei man, much less a woman. Maho, that poisonous little viper, wouldn't have needed the grease. Of course, her adopted sister didn't quite stand as tall as her shoulder, either. Like her height, broad shoulders and truly black eyes, her breasts, half again as big as any other woman's in the Oda family, set her apart. Another thing her adopted family, especially her malignant older siblings, the twins Maho and Mankato, never ever let her forget.

The hole for the cable was nearly too small. She had climbed the side of the hull and pushed first one shoulder and then the other against the hull until each one popped out of joint. The pain was bad, bad enough that only her gritted teeth and locked jaw kept her from crying out. Even with the grease, the edge of the port took some skin off. She flopped gracelessly into the cover of something on a wheeled carriage, hiding her from the view of anyone farther aft on this deck. She wedged one arm against the frame of the carriage and forced it back into place. Tears slid across her cheeks at the pain. After a deep, silent breath, she did the same with the other one. It hurt, Ancestors, it hurt, but Uncle Sota had trained her to do this. She would not disgrace his training and the pain would quickly pass.

Carefully she pulled on the mottled gray and brown silk cord that was tied around her slim waist. At the other end of that cord was everything she owned

19

in the world, carefully wrapped in supple sealskin for protection from the salty seawater. It was a pitifully small package, clothes and other things, her weapons. The small box containing the gold she stole from the family vault. Hopefully, it would be enough to save her life if the sailors hauled her up before the ship's Captain.

There was no doubt now that this was a warship. Dozens of monstrous cannons hulked down the length of the gun deck, their crews' hammocks slung above the guns. Many of those hammocks were occupied by snoring sailors, and a card game of some kind drew nearly two dozen men to the lantern at the other end of the deck. She crawled alongside the hawser under the muzzle of one of those huge guns to reach the cable locker. The enormous anchor cable improved her concealment and she slid silently down into the locker. Quickly, she scraped off as much of the grease as she could before slipping into her clothing. She wouldn't be able to hide in this spot until the ship was well out to sea. She wormed her way silently out of the locker and into a deserted passageway.

Ladders dropped her down two more decks and a locked door was no challenge for her training and her lockpicks. That door secured a large compartment which held hundreds of cannonballs in solid racks. She doubted the crew would come down here very often to check on solid iron cannonballs. She could make a nest back in the deepest, darkest part of the compartment and she should be safe and secure there. Well, as safe and secure as she could hope to be on this massive ship. Tucking her bag behind a rack of cannonballs, she slipped back out to explore the ship in the quiet darkness. She needed to find the food stores and the water tanks. If she were mostly silent and still, she could keep her hunger under control. It would not do at all for a growling stomach to give her away.

Chapter Two

The Great Western Ocean
KRN Intrepid
May 1478, Third Age of Imperial Reckoning

THREE WEEKS OUT OF Akumato, *Intrepid* heeled over under a full spread of canvas, all sails to the royals set. Captain Blaine estimated the wind at over twenty-five knots. The log showed his command making a very respectable twelve knots. She had a bone in her teeth, white water curling away from her cutwater. *Sorcerer* skipped along about a mile ahead of her, the nimble sloop taking full advantage of her newer, more efficient rig. He checked his watch as the ship's bell sounded two bells in the afternoon watch. He snapped it closed and put it back in its vest pocket before turning to his First Lieutenant on board *Intrepid*, Lieutenant Commander Harris Caplin, with a crooked smile.

"Signal to *Sorcerer,* Harry. *Form line astern at two hundred yards. Clear for action, gun action to starboard.* Let's see how fast she can come about and get in line."

"Aye-aye, Captain! Signal party!" Caplin turned away, heading forward as he collected the signal party, currently under the command of Midshipman Johan Weiss. "Starboard fore-chase, clear away and load for signal!" Caplin would be due his own command soon, and his assignment as Blaine's First Lieutenant was for a final bit of polishing.

"Bosun," Blaine turned to the Ship's Bosun, the senior enlisted man aboard. "I believe I should like to clear for action to starboard, if you please."

"Aye-aye, Cap'n!" Master Chief Petty Officer Paul Beauchamp raised his pipe to his lips and blew three sharp blasts, repeating them twice. *Intrepid* erupted with activity as topsmen raced aloft to reduce sail, and gun crews rushed belowdecks to knock down bulkheads and clear away the cabins, storing everything below. The Marine command party fell into place, the Marine drummer beating out the call to arms. Powder boys scrambled to the magazines to retrieve the first powder cartridges while gun captains checked the flints in their gunlocks and counted the priming quills in their belt carriers.

***

She didn't hear the Bosun's pipe from her current hidey-hole deep in the locker that held spare sailcloth and extra spars. But the sudden eruption of activity and then the pounding of the drum woke her from her light doze. She learned that the Captain was very unpredictable in when he would order gun or sail drills. The drumbeat told her this was a gun drill, and she should be secure simply by staying where she was. When the first cannon roared less than thirty minutes later, she stuffed her fingers in her ears and burrowed deeper in the sailcloth. She came face to face with one of the ship's cats there, a very large, very gray, very grumpy old tomcat she called Uncle Sota.

Together they hunkered down and endured the constant roar of the cannons. The concussions of the huge guns shook the very fabric of the ship. She felt the unending roll of man-made thunder in her bones. When the cannon fire slacked, she took advantage of the lull and slunk to the water tank to refill her water bag and drink until she sloshed. Then she quietly slipped into the nicer of the two kitchens, the captain's she thought, and helped herself to enough salt beef and hardtack biscuit to see her through the next week. She was unable to resist adding some eggs, a tin bowl of pudding, and a brace of wrinkled but still sweet apples to her plunder. She wore loose, baggy sailor's clothes stolen from what they called the slops chest. A week ago, she had encountered a crewman in the near darkness of the lower decks. He saw what he expected to see, just another sailor. But this time she made it back to her hideout without encountering anyone.

***

"Yes?" Blaine responded to the knock on his cabin door by the Marine sentry posted outside it. The setting sun lit his cabin with its last rays, gilding the framed painting of Kolbia's current Tribune.

"Your Steward, with dinner, Captain. And the Ship's Surgeon, First Lieutenant and the Bosun would like to speak with you, sir?"

"Well, Private Towns, send the herd in, Toby first. I'm starved." He looked up as Toby ducked into his cabin with his dinner on a large covered plate. Surgeon Commander Elazar Hoff, Caplin and the Bosun followed Toby into the cabin. He sanded dry the report he was working on, cleaned his quill and capped his ink bottle. Toby quickly finished clearing off the desk and put the tray down before he whisked the cover away. "Thanks, Toby. Looks great and smells even better." Obviously one of the pigs was chosen to make its final sacrifice today. "I assume there was enough to give the crew at least a small taste of fresh meat?"

"Aye, Cap'n. Just barely. After this, the pork and any chickens that stop laying will go to the Officer's Wardroom first and then the goat locker. I'd expect the crew to be getting by on salt beef until we raise the Horn Islands. By your leave, sir." Toby smiled as he ducked under the door on the way out. Toby was huge, especially for a sailor, seven inches over six feet and a solid three hundred and twenty plus pounds.

Toby loved to cook and was in fact an excellent chef. He had also been Blaine's Steward on his last two commands. More than one sailor underestimated him, a big man who cooked, preferred men over women, and was the Captain's

Steward. New sailors would think to establish themselves in the unofficial peck-ing order of the lower decks by taking on a gentle giant. They learned quickly that Toby possessed a brutal right hook. And did not suffer fools at all. Those who were smarter than most, listened and learned that his right hook and a tooth-shattering left uppercut were the reason Toby won the championship in last year's Naval Boxing Tournament. A championship he had held two years in a row.

"Take a seat, gentlemen." Blaine grinned at Beauchamp, "You too, Bosun." He cut into his pork chop. "What brings you lot here at dinner time? I'm not sharing; you all probably eat better than I do!"

"Go ahead, Bosun." Harry gestured to Paul.

"Aye, sir." The bosun rubbed his stubble-cut, white hair briefly. "Cap'n, to be plain, we've got a thief on board."

"A serious complaint, Bosun. What's gone missing and who's complaining?" Blaine's fork paused halfway to his mouth for a long moment and then contin-ued its journey.

"I've no complaint from any of the crew, sir, no valuables have been taken, but stores are going missing slowly but surely. Mostly salt beef and hardtack, enough for an entire gun crew's weekly ration, and someone's pilfered the slops chest as well. And nearly two weeks' worth of water rations are also vanishing, 'bout once a week. Anything sweet left in the open quickly disappears away. But oddly enough, the grog is left alone." The bosun shrugged at Blaine's raised eyebrow. "I've no explanation for that, sir. I'd've thought the grog would be the first thing any of these lushes would've gone after."

"I agree, Bosun." Blaine leaned back in his chair. "I assume you two have input on this, since I know the Bosun brought this to your attention first, Harry?"

"Yes, sir," the first lieutenant replied. "What's extremely odd is that we had no issues at all on the passage to Isemoto. The crew's solid, most of them are long service Navy and the old salts are bringing the few lubbers along nicely.

Very out of character for any of them, sir." Harry shrugged, "You know that generally, once someone starts stealing, they don't stop unless they're caught. But it is deucedly odd that the thefts didn't start until *after* we left Isemoto."

"We didn't add any crew there, did we? Just that lieutenant from the Embassy who was due to rotate home, what is his name again?" Blaine sipped his wine.

"Lieutenant Fleet, sir, Willis Fleet," Harry answered. "He's a spook assigned to ONI and not a Line of Command officer. Language expert, among several other odd skills. Old, old Navy family, a bit of a disappointment to them, I believe, since he went into Intelligence and not Command. Still, I doubt sincerely he's our thief, unless he's testing us. Frankly, he doesn't talk much, and he spends most of his time either in his bunk reading or in the Wardroom writing reports or fiddling with some mechanical bits he's brought along. Not sure what the bits are, actually."

"What's your take on this, Elazar?" Blaine asked the ship's doctor.

"I doubt the good Lieutenant is a kleptomaniac, Captain," Hoff answered with a grin. "He's an odd fellow, but I'll stand election for Tribune if he's our thief. This is something else, something very odd. Any chance one of the crew picked up some kind of left-handed, magical gee-jaw or the other? I've seen signs that someone has been in my sick berth. And one of the younger midshipmen, Ellis, if I remember correctly, told me he'd felt someone watching him lately, 'specially at night. *A ghost I can never quite see*, he described it to me. And when I asked around, several of the crew have mentioned that things are sometimes not where they were left, lockers gone through by someone who didn't get everything exactly back in place. *A spirit of terminal boredom* was how Petty Officer Connor described it to me. Perhaps Lieutenant Fleet isn't the only spook on board?"

"*A spirit of terminal boredom*, eh? I need to remember that one the next time I have to deal with my wife." Blaine snorted around a mouthful of potatoes. "Well, Harry, any suggestions? Do we need to toss the ship from stem to stern?"

"I don't know, sir. That'd be fairly extreme since we'd have to heave to in order to do that. Perhaps if we get becalmed, but not otherwise, unless this becomes much more of an issue. So far, I'd put it down to one of those really odd things that sometimes happens at sea."

"How about you, Bosun? Suggestions?"

"Cap'n, I'd suggest putting a close watch on the stores and water. It rained a couple of days ago so water isn't an issue, but the thievery could be bad for discipline if this so-called *spirit of boredom* isn't caught. A proper flogging would put an end to this nonsense."

"Yes, well, Bosun, we'd have to know who to flog, now wouldn't we?" Dr. Hoff asked sarcastically.

"All right, that's enough on the *spirit* for now. Any other issues?"

"The topsmen could use more work on trimming battle-damaged sail, sir," the bosun suggested. Blaine, the first lieutenant and the bosun spent a few more moments planning the next day's exercises before leaving with the doctor. Toby tapped on the door a few minutes later to collect the dirty dishes.

After they left his cabin, Blaine leaned back in his chair and tossed a paperweight between his hands. It was a chunk of star-metal embedded in a glass half-globe, roughly the size of a baseball cut in half. Star-metal, that mysterious, totally impervious metal often found at the edge of the various craters that dotted the world's surface in odd places, high on isolated mountains or on remote islands. He stopped and stared at the jagged piece in its thick glass shell.

"Well, I hope this *spirit of boredom* doesn't prove to be as big of a mystery as whatever it is that you're made of is." He yawned. "I must be tired. I'm talking to a paperweight." He got up and changed into his nightshirt and turned back to his bunk. He started to lie down when he noticed something odd. On his pillow was a black hair. No surprise, since his own hair was black, even if it was becoming more and more interspersed with gray these days. No, the surprise was its length. Blaine's hair was long enough to be clubbed in an old-fashioned sailor's braid, but just barely. The hair on his pillow was thick and black and twice his arm's length. "What the hell?"

***

She was confident she was nearly invisible in her *shozoku*, black *zukin* and *fukumen* hiding her hair and her face except her eyes. Even if one of the sailors standing watch happened to look down over the rail, to where she hung on the side of the hull, she doubted they would notice a thing. She clung to the outside of the gun port on the right side of the Captain's cabin, listening to the conversation. Once previously, she had briefly glimpsed the Captain as a dark silhouette from where she lurked in the darkness of the hold when he inspected it shortly after the ship left Imperial Isemoto's waters. He was older than she was, she thought, but not too old, and younger than her Papa was. His deep, rich voice reminded her of Papa Komiya's voice, when Papa sang her to sleep when she was a little girl and the nightmares came.

One of her favorite hiding spots was in the Captain's sleeping cabin. No one was allowed in his cabin when he was on deck, so in many ways, it was the safest hiding spot on the entire ship. Once she had even hid under his bunk when he suddenly came back into the cabin after something he left behind by accident.

He fascinated her and terrified her at the same time. If the crew caught her, he could very well have her hung by the neck until dead. But his voice, the frustratingly brief glimpses she'd seen of him, the way he governed the crew of this great warship, stern enough to be respected, but confident and caring enough to be nearly revered by his crew, those observations made her wonder. What kind of man was he, truly? What might happen if she was caught and brought before him? She knew she was young and beautiful. Indeed, her beauty was one of the reasons Maho hated her so bitterly. Might the Captain find her attractive? Enough so that he wouldn't have her hung? *What if...?* she thought.

Stop it, you idiot girl! He has no use for a foolish girl not yet nineteen seasons of age! Fantasize later if you must. They know something is wrong and now they will be both more alert and looking for you. And there are weeks, if not months left in the journey yet.

Carefully, she clambered along the hull and back into the gundeck through the gunport she had rigged to grant her access to the outside of the ship. There was a narrow ladder there, one she quickly slid down before disappearing into the bowels of the ship. There was much to do, and she had little time. The crew was tired from the long day. Sail drills followed the gun practice and then the ship had to be cleaned and prepared for inspection. Even the inveterate card players only played a few hands before seeking their hammocks. Only a skeleton crew was on watch as the night deepened. She needed to steal as much food and water as she could before the crew increased their vigilance.

The Horn Islands
Pirate Brigantine *Imperial Damnation*
May 1478, Third Age of Imperial Reckoning

The Horn Islands were chancy places. Captain Grigori Je'Libe knew this. One of the best landfalls to water and resupply between Kolbia and the in-scrutable Eastern nations, pickings for a competent pirate captain could be plentiful here. While Kolbian merchant ships might be too heavily armed to take, they might not be either. And Montagaran galleons, Lietelean Empire galleasses and the occasional Eindeuten sloop were rarely as heavily armed as a Kolbian might be. So the pickings for an industrious pirate were often easy and abundant. Problem was, the damned Kolbian Republican Navy knew the same things and all too often, one of their infernally seaworthy sloops lurked about as an anti-piracy patrol. His twenty-gun, two-masted brigantine, *Imperial Damnation*, armed with six twelve-pounders and fourteen eighteen-pounders might just barely be a match for a KRN sloop's weight of fire. Barely. But God help the pirate unlucky enough to run into a frigate. Those monsters might as well be a ship of the line. And all too often, those big ships were handled well enough to out-sail all but the fastest pirate vessel. The KRN didn't exactly pick the captains of their frigates out of a hat.

Still the pickings were rich enough that Je'Libe was willing to take his chances. And it helped that the waters around the Horns were shallow and treacherous. *Imperial Damnation* only drew twelve feet of water and even the lightest Kolbian sloop usually drew over fifteen feet; a frigate might draw twenty feet or more. Between his ship's shallow draft and the usually heavy morning and evening fogs, he figured he knew these waters well enough to out-sail and outrun any single Kolbian ship. And he had an ace in the hole. He had a sorceress. And not just any common magic wielder. He held an Elvish sorceress captive with cold-forged iron and steel.

He lowered the spyglass and rested his back against the mast, bracing his booted feet on the edge of the crow's nest. The lookout had called, "Sail, ho!" a few minutes ago and he'd come up the mainmast himself to check on the first sighting of the day. It was late afternoon, three bells into the early dog watch, and *Imperial Damnation* was coasting, just barely making steerage way with only her topsails and top gallants set. She had been luffing along, hiding against one of the smaller islets dotting the swallow waters around the Big and Little Horn Islands. Greater Horn Island was a large green mass on the distant horizon.

The lumbering, slab-sided white monstrosity was a Lietelean Navy galleass, a big one. She flew an Imperial Navy ensign, but above that flag was another. The gold circled cross of the Kythal Church on a silver shield. There were scarlet fleur-de-lis on each corner of the silver flag. That was the flag of the Imperial Kythal Inquisition. Je'Libe hated the Empire on general principles, but he nursed a special fury for agents of the Inquisition.

For an Imperial ship, she was well armed; he counted sixteen gunports in her side and at least a dozen rail-mounted swivel-guns that might throw a two- or three-pound shot. The big cannons of the main gundeck were basically nothing more than large metal tubes strapped tightly to a large timber and hauled into battery with pure brute strength. For all their fearsome hitting power, throwing a sixty- or seventy-pound solid shot, those awkward guns might fire once in ten minutes.

Je'Libe's lighter guns were Montagaran copies of Kolbian designs, mounted on proper gun carriages with proper trunnions. His gun crews loaded them with proper bagged charges, not awkward ladles and loose powder. He knew his guns could fire five or even six times in the ten minutes it'd take the Impies to reload and drag those things back into battery. He just had to survive that first broadside. That is, if he gave them a chance to get those things into action at all. He swung out of the crow's nest and slid down the backstay, his boots thumping on the deck as he jumped down the last couple of feet.

"Well, lads, I think we've some work this night coming." He grinned as most of the crew gathered around. "A big, clumsy-ass Impie galleass, hove-to in the southwest cove of Little Horn Island. Looks like they've got crew taking water casks ashore to refill and rebalancing their cargo. Fat, dumb and happy, sitting there with their trousers around their ankles, no idea we're anywhere about to come and kick them in the balls from behind." The crew responded with a hungry growl. "Well, don't stand here growling at me! Get this bitch cleared for action! Quickly, lads, but quietly." The crew scampered off to clear the ship for action and load the guns. He turned and walked up, onto the quarterdeck.

"How big is she, Cap'n?" his first mate, Twyford Thorne, asked as he stepped aside for his captain.

"Big enough, Two Toes, big enough." Years ago, a falling block had crushed Thorne's left foot, severing three of his toes and giving him the nickname that still dogged him. "I counted sixteen gunports and a dozen swivels to starboard. She's an Inquisitorial ship, regular Navy seconded to a senior Inquisitor, most likely. Typical arrogant bastard Imperial pricks, positive no one would dare scratch the paint on their hull. Idiots." Grigori smirked.

"So you think we'll want to use your little pet, sir?" Thorne's smile would have done a shark proud.

"Yes, I think so. We'll need to attack late in the middle watch to get close enough to smash her before she can get those guns ready to fire. My little pet can work her tricks, not on the officers but on the ship itself this time. If she won't, let her know how fast I'll give her to you. If you leave anything, toss her to the crew." Grigori's answering smile was just as ugly as Thorne's. "Make sure to remind her of that. Go ahead and get her."

***

The cabin turned cell should have been comfortable enough, but there was an armed guard on the locked door and cold iron shackles bound her wrists, ankles, and waist. Those shackles were riveted to a steel chain that was bolted to the wall of the cabin. For nearly the last two years, this was her world. The small cabin, the iron shackles and the chain, her captors who feared her nearly as much as they lusted after her power and, she supposed, her body. The pirates, embodied for her in the loathsome Two Toes Thorne, only let her up on the deck when they wanted her to work her magic for them. Then the shackles must come off, but Thorne would first place a glass-silk noose around her slender neck. Her uncle, well her many, many times great-uncle, so old that no one knew his True Name anymore, warned her of the humans when she left home on her *Crwydothe* so long ago.

Uncle Oedhaewthren warned her before she left on her Wandering, but she had not truly listened. And now, like any stubborn child, she suffered the results of not listening to her elders. Silaqui was so tired and hurt so much of the time as the iron and steel slowly poisoned her. The cold forged iron inhibited her magic, and everyone knew iron and steel were slow poisons for any Elf. Despite her pain and misery, her stubborn core kept her alive. She would outlive these repulsive humans and she would find and desecrate their graves, scatter their crumbling bones to the winds, piss into their empty skulls before throwing the moldering bones to the pigs. She would have her revenge and pirates the world over would tremble when they heard the stories. She raised her head at the distinctive sound of Two Toes Thorne's half-foot thumping down the passageway. The general noise and commotion of the ship being cleared for action rose into her awareness and she knew what was coming. She lowered her head and wept for what she knew the beasts were about to do, both to her and to the innocents they now hunted. The key rattled in the lock. Quickly she wiped her face dry.

"Time to perform your tricks, little cat-eyed, point-eared, bitch-witch." Thorne leered at her as he entered the cabin. "Of course, if you decide to refuse, the Capt'n said to give you to the crew. After I'm done with you...of course. What's it gonna be this time?" He rubbed his crotch suggestively.

"I shall do as requested, Thorne." She managed to keep the tears off her face. She hated herself for being so weak, choosing to hurt and kill innocents rather than give up her own life in their defense. But her death, *after* these vicious beasts in human form were through ravaging and raping her, would have no effect on the prey the pirates chose. And so she did as commanded, wielding her magic to bring victory and wealth to the pirates instead of dying at their hands. She bided her time. The day would come when she would be free of the chains and then...then she would make the ocean itself run red with pirate blood.

The Horn Islands
Maelluem de Deos

Capitan Pater Joaquin Luis Palmaroli stood on the quarterdeck of *Maelluem de Deos* and ground his teeth in frustration. One of the ship's main water tanks had proved to be very poorly constructed and the water therein became foul and corrupted. So he must stop in these savage islands, make repairs, and refill the tanks before continuing his mission. His Inquisitorial Marines were busy ashore. They captured several of the local aborigines and those sorry excuses for human beings were being put to the Question. He needed to know if his target, a Kolbian frigate lately thought to be returning from a mission to the heathen sub-humans of the Godless eastern islands of the false Empire of Isemoto, had passed by this worthless jungle island en route home. The Horn Islands were a miserable dot on the other side of the world from the decent comforts and pleasures of his townhome in Luctini, but he was a member of the Order of St. Marikus. When the Imperial Kythal Inquisition gave orders to one of its best captains, well, there was nothing to do but send out the press gangs to sweep up a crew for the ship.

Teniente de Marina Raul Eliopoulos finished clambering up the battens on the side of the ship and located Capitan Palmaroli. The Marine came up the ladder onto the quarter deck and saluted before bowing to kiss Pater Palmaroli's amethyst ring. Blood spotted the Teniente's white uniform jacket and sweat rings marked the armpits and back of it with crusty white salt. Mud and leaves marred his once highly polished black boots.

"Mon Capitan."

"Teniente Eliopoulos. What news have you discovered ashore? Have we missed our target?"

"These savages hardly speak a civilized tongue, My Lord. And they are damnably hard to catch as well. But my Marines laid a dozen by their heels. If we can trust what they say, the Kolbian has not passed this way headed back east. They were put to the full rigor of the Question, so it is my thought that their information might be trusted, even though they are only savages."

"And afterwards?"

"We set their huts to the torch. Each heathen was given a chance to repent before they were sent to God in fire. Exactly as the Inquisitorial Orders prescribe, Pater."

"Well done. As soon as we are done here, we shall begin to sweep these waters, hunting for our quarry."

"Capitan, before we can raise anchor, we will need to rebalance the ship. The new water tank will change the ship's balance substantially once it's filled." Teniente de Navio Flippus Nicoli saluted as he stepped up next to Capitan Palmaroli. Nicoli was, in some ways, the actual commander of the *Maelluem*. He was a Navy officer, not a militant priest given command of a ship. At times, the unhappy facts of the command system on board *Maelluem* nearly drove him mad. And Palmaroli was not one of the Inquisitors that gave their Teniente de Navio a wave and went to their cabin to indulge themselves in their latest perversion. Palmaroli was marginally competent as a seaman, knowing just enough to be dangerous. And frankly Nicoli thought the idea of hunting a Kolbian frigate with a single galleass bordered on suicide, or insanity, one or the other. That or an invincible sense of supremacy, otherwise known as rank stupidity. He didn't mind the idea of Palmaroli getting himself killed under the guns of a frigate that outgunned his ship three or four to one. He just didn't want to join him.

"Why must this be done, Teniente? The water tank is going into the same place, no?"

"Capitan, the ship's timbers will shift from the tank being removed and rebuilt. Then it must be refilled. None of this will be exactly as it was before; therefore, the ship will be out of balance. It will not take long."

"How long, Teniente?"

"Not more than a day once the tank is refilled. In many ways the old system of many casks of water worked better but was not as efficient."

"And where did the Navio get this *more efficient* idea from?"

"A Kolbian merchant ship from one of the financial cartels purchased." Nicoli suppressed a desire to swallow. "It worked superbly for that ship, but those tanks were made of painted steel, not wood."

"Perhaps the source of these *more efficient* ideas should be considered more carefully before they are adopted by the Imperium? What use is *efficiency* if one should lose one's soul in the process of being more...efficient?" Palmaroli's dark eyes were hard and cold. Nicoli swallowed hard but held his ground under that intimidating stare.

"There is much to what you say, Capitan. Steel and wood are hardly similar materials. Perhaps these new ideas are poorly considered."

"Would it not be better to use the well-known and understood ways of our grandfathers, Teniente?" Teniente Eliopoulos' eyes were just as dark and just as hard and his hand rested on his sword hilt.

"Capitan, Teniente, I am merely a Teniente de Navio. I do not advise the Admiralty. I simply sail the ship the Dominorum of the Admiralty assigns to me. I think the choices I might make would be quite different." *I would make* vastly different *choices, had I the chance.* "Capitan, with your permission? Teniente." Nicoli snapped Palmaroli a parade ground salute, returned by the priest's slight nod. He gave a slight bow to Eliopoulos, as they were equal in rank, before turning and leaving the quarterdeck. As he reached the main deck, he shouted at the working parties to work faster on finishing the repairs.

"He is a good sailor," Eliopoulos quietly said.

"God does not want good sailors, Raul. God wants men with strong souls who will do what must be done." Joaquin's cold eyes followed Nicoli until he went below decks. "I will send him to the Brothers at St. Marikus' monastery when we return to the Empire. He will learn obedience to God's Will, or he will face the Question. One way or the other, he will come to God."

"Your will, Pater."

Imperial Damnation

Silaqui's keen Elvish hearing heard the Imperial ship's bell sound seven bells in the middle watch. The night was dark under the new moon and *Imperial Damnation* ghosted forward under just her topsails and jibs. Those sails were stained in darker and lighter grays that blended perfectly with the rising fog. The bluish gray her hull was painted tended to blend into the color of the ocean.

Under the current conditions she was as close to invisible as a ship could be. Wind and wave were in her favor, and she was utterly silent as she coasted slowly into the cove.

Thorne held her *leash*, the silk noose coated in ground glass. The least movement brought trickles of blood down her graceful neck and she knew he could snap the cord through her throat into her neck bones before she could bespell him. Her eyes glowed with her crimson power as she gathered the ethereal strands of Elven magic into her hands. Normally, Thorne and Captain Je'Libe ordered her to use her magic to incapacitate the target ship's officers. This time there were no officers on deck, and they wanted her to strike into the hull, to damage the huge, ungainly guns and cause confusion and fear. She was more willing to work her magic on this ship. She despised and feared the Lietelean Empire, not as much as she hated pirates, but it was a near thing.

Officially the Empire outlawed magery and sorcery and persecuted non-humans within their borders. Imperial priests often led bloody persecutions against the few, heavily taxed, and restricted elven or dwarven merchants brave or foolish enough to try to conduct business in the Empire's huge markets. Humans unlucky enough to be born with the mage-gift either hid their gift, fled the Empire or worse, were taken by the Inquisition. Depending on the individual, they either became fanatical members of the Inquisition, or they were publicly put to the Question and then burned alive.

She had no compunctions in wielding her power on an Imperial ship, especially one seconded to the Inquisition. She paused a moment to be thankful that it wasn't a ship of her Montagaran homeland. A Lietelean ship, on the other hand, would be a pleasure to burn and she would laugh while the crew screamed in the flames. The Inquisition had burned her mother's cousin at the stake, burned him alive for the sin of being both Elf and mage. This after they made him watch the priests lead a mob in torturing his human wife and their two half-elven children to death. She thought him foolish for marrying a short-lived human, but they had all still been family.

She hid a cruel smile from both Thorne and Je'Libe. With luck and her skill, she might be able to both confound her captors and garner at least a cold revenge for her cousin and his family. She concentrated and harnessed the burning rage growing in her heart. Mayhap she could find a way to use that fury-borne power to damage and destroy both pirates and the Imperials? There was one spell she knew that normally was just beyond her ability. If she yoked her rage and hatred to that spell, use that to stretch beyond her capability, she might invoke more devastation than anyone expected. At worst, she would die of Mage-burn, which would be its own form of escape.

Maelluem de Deos

Paulos Harcia was rated as an able seaman, not his choice of livelihood, but the press gangs gave him no choice when they swept him up from the front of his small cobbler's shop without mercy two years ago. Since then he had been moved from ship to ship with no regard for his concerns about his wife and young daughter or his business.

In those happier days, he had regularly attended the local church, learning his letters and numbers from Pater Bartholomew, and paying his tithe as the Book said he should. Now he hated the Kythal Church with a passion. Inquisitors like Capitan Pater Palmaroli destroyed his life for no reason but their own expediency. His family likely thought he was dead and may have starved to death themselves if his beautiful Angelina had not remarried. She would have been forced to sell the shop when the taxes could not be paid. It was even possible that she and his lovely daughter, Consuela, had been taken and sold into slavery when they could not pay the hearth tax.

Perched in the crow's nest, Paulos was supposed to be watching the sea closely, lest any ship steal silently up and attack *Maelluem de Deos* while she rode at anchor. Instead he sat with his back against the mainmast and dozed, a stout string tied from his bare big toe to the ratlines. Anyone climbing to his lofty post would cause the ratlines to move, yanking his toe and waking him before they climbed past the main yardarm. The ship's bell sounded eight bells, waking him. With the bells sounding the end of the middle watch, his long night in the crow's nest was about over. He yawned and stretched, untying the toe string before standing up and scratching his butt. His relief should be here soon. He looked out, toward the open ocean, the height of the mast allowing him to see over most of the rising fog. He turned and looked at the fog-shrouded shoreline before something struck him as odd and he turned back to the ocean side.

"What is that?" he mumbled to himself. Just barely jutting out of the fog was the truncated top of a mast. It was odd, seeing a mast like that, misty and blurry in the thick fog, even if it was only about twenty yards away to starboard. *A mainmast with the topgallant masts sent down? Why would anyone do that?* He started to yawn again when he truly realized what he was seeing.

"SAIL HO! SHIP TO STARBOARD!" His warning scream was far too little and far too late.

Imperial Damnation

"FIRE!" Thorne bellowed.

Ten guns in the pirate brigantine's port broadside roared as one. They were double-shotted and a stand of grapeshot was loaded on top of that. The forward twelve-pound gun burst, killing most of its crew. A piece of the cannon flew past Silaqui, neatly removing the bare tip of her left ear before tearing the head off one of the helmsmen. Choking clouds of powder smoke filled the main deck and forecastle. The gun crews leapt into action, sponges hissing as they went down the barrels. Fresh powder bags followed and this time they loaded with chain shot. One minute and forty-eight seconds later they roared again. Two of the eighteen-pounders and a single twelve-pounder struck the mainmast. The other chain shots killed men trying to struggle awake by the dozen, smashing stowed oars into splinters and tearing the standing rigging to shreds.

Paulos Harcia's screams were lost in the thundering crash of the falling mainmast. Stressed between the rigging damage done by the pirate guns and the falling mainmast, the foremast fell over the side to port. Unable to take the strain put on it by the rigging, the mizzenmast snapped thirty feet above the deck, falling and crushing the helmsman and watchstanders on the quarterdeck. The pirate cannons roared again, loaded with a single round of shot and grape.

Teniente de Navio Nicoli fought his way through the chaos onto the main deck, struggling to get his men moving to return fire when he was hit by a stand of grape from an eighteen-pounder. His body splattered away, torn to unidentifiable shreds, only his lower legs, severed just below the knees, still recognizably human.

Teniente de Marina Eliopoulos' body was pulped by the nine-ton mass of a cannon falling through the gundeck above his cabin. He died before he could fully wake and the main topsail yardarm crashing through his bunk moments later merely rendered his body unidentifiable.

***

Imperial Damnation's guns were firing independently now, hammering in the galleass' side as rapidly as they could. The pirates' bloodthirsty screams of triumph nearly overwhelmed the roar of the guns and the cries of the dying Imperials.

"Now, witch!" Thorne yelled in Silaqui's ear. "Use your magic! Break them!" The order surprised her. Given the guns' devastation of the Imperial ship, she did not expect Thorne or Je'Libe to want her to use her magic. The pirate guns roared again.

So mote it be. If they want me to break them, then break them I will. And they will take neither joy nor plunder from their victory! I shall claim at least a small revenge against both the Empire and my captors.

Her eyes burned with her Power as she gathered more and more strands of magic. Thorne and Je'Libe both stepped away in alarm as a crimson halo formed around her head and shoulders as she raised her arms. The seven small dots tattooed over her left eye shone in all the colors of the spectrum. Her hair, a sickly yellow in her crimson aura instead of its normal grass green, floated around her. She screamed, a primal howling shriek terrifying every man that heard it...and released her Power.

Bolts of raw lightning forked from her hands, ripping and shattering the stricken galleass. One bolt struck Capitan Palmaroli full on as he ran onto the main deck. He was one of the relatively rare and secretive wielders of Imperial magic, and as such maintained his own magical shields. For a bare instant, human shields strove against Elvish magic, before guttering and failing. Palmaroli never even screamed as Silaqui's lightning instantaneously reduced him to a carbonized skeleton.

Driven by the power of her rage and hatred, bolts of lightning tore through the ship, starting fires and killing men. Thunder slammed and crashed overhead as the fog blew back, forced away from the two ships. Then one of her bolts found the target she'd been seeking and twelve tons of gunpowder in *Maelluem de Deos'* magazine exploded. The decks above the magazine heaved upwards, shattering into splinters, some of them ten feet long. Her keel broke, splitting her in half. The bow and forecastle pitched forward and sank in the deeper water of the cove, dragged down by the weight of the anchor chains and forward guns. The stern blew completely apart, fragmented glass from the stern windows spraying across the shore. The broken remains of the mizzenmast flew skyward, then crashed down on the camp of the dozen or so men still on shore, killing several, including their commander. The survivors broke and fled screaming into the jungle.

Imperial Damnation heeled hard over, laid on her side and nearly capsized by the force of the blast. The lookout atop the mainmast was flung into the pre-dawn darkness, his body never found. Another was killed when the gun he was serving broke loose and crushed his skull. The ship came back upright, scattering the crew in the waist like tenpins. Thorne was hit by a flying splinter fifteen inches long. The wooden projectile punched neatly through his thigh and he passed out from the shock, dropping her leash. Before she could even think of escape, she heard the Captain's pistol being cocked behind her.

"One step, one word, one move, and I'll blow your head off." The ship pitched in the roiled waters of the cove. Je'Libe held onto the wheel with one hand. The flintlock pistol in the other was pointed unerringly at her head. "On your knees, witch." His voice was deadly quiet in the aftermath of the explosion. "Kharlos, take care of Thorne." He commanded the surviving helmsmen. "Halven, get up here and take the wheel." He tossed her the cold iron shackles. "Put 'em on. Now. Or die."

"Are they not *broken* enough, Captain?" Silaqui slowly picked up the shackles and locked them around her ankles first. Then the waist chain, before she finished by slipping her hands into the wrist manacles. Je'Libe cautiously reached over and locked them down. "Did that not go according to your plan, Captain?" She stared into the muzzle of the pistol, wondering if he was going to kill her and set her soul free. Suddenly, she leaned forward and vomited on the deck. She'd succeeded in linking her emotions and rage to the spell, but without that fury she could not reach so far beyond her capability. And the emotions she'd used to drive herself beyond her limits were quickly fading away. The cold iron was the last straw. Reason and consciousness fled, taking awareness with them, and she pitched forward onto the deck, insensate.

"You and you. Get this bint below and lock her into her cell. Do NOT forget the chains!" He pointed at two crewmen before turning back to Silaqui's unconscious body. "Damn Elf bitch. Not sure you're worth the trouble, but if I kill you, well, it'd be damn hard to unkill you." He turned and looked at the burning wreckage of the galleass, scattered around the cove. There didn't seem to be any survivors. He shuddered. "Had no idea she could do something like that. Witch might be too damn dangerous to keep alive," he muttered to himself. "All right, you sorry bastards." He raised his voice, taking command of the situation. "Get this ship squared away. Send up the topgallant masts and let's get some sail on her. Halven, take the helm and make your course south by southwest. I think we'll see what the approaches from the west might have to offer. I've had enough of these damn islands for a while."

Chapter Three

The Great Western Ocean
KRN *Intrepid*
May 1478, Third Age of Imperial Reckoning

IT WAS BECOMING HARDER and harder to get water. Food wasn't a problem. Despite the horrible taste of the salted beef and whatever that disgusting, weevil-filled, so-called bread was, well, she choked down enough food to barely keep herself alive. Just barely. There were plenty of both of those revolting staples and it wasn't hard to steal more. The stuff was disgusting. She was barely able to choke down just enough food to keep her stomach quiet. She knew she was gaunt and weak. But the food wasn't the real problem. It was water that was the problem, and she knew it.

***

The crew knew it as well. They weren't sure why the captain had ordered a watch on the stores and water tanks, but they trusted him implicitly. Captain 'Bonny' Blaine had a well-earned reputation for being lucky and taking good care of his crew. The rumor mill carried the story that there was a thief on board. A strange thief who only stole the worst food, water, and clothes not even the rawest lubber wanted from out of the slop's chest. Some of the crew was convinced that it was that new lieutenant, somehow testing them and the captain. But he rarely left the tiny cabin he shared with the third and fourth lieutenants, and when he did, it was either to attend dinner with the captain or to eat in the Wardroom. Or to fiddle with the odd mechanical clockworks he kept in his possession and usually concealed on his person. Besides, he was a passenger, not crew.

The other story was that somehow, someway there was a ghost or spirit of some type on board. The two sailors who suggested that were originally from the Imperial province of Ibertina, or at least that's where they said their parents immigrated from, back when the Empire still allowed its subjects to emigrate. Both were devout followers of the Kythal Church and more superstitious than most Kolbians. The response they got was normally blank stares, that or nearly being laughed out of the forward gundeck card game. The crew jeered at them: "We Kolbians don't give any shift to that silly mumbo-jumbo about magic. You'll have us believing fairies and dragons next!" Or so most of their shipmates told them. Some of the oldest sailors, men who had spent their entire lives on the sea and in strange places in the world, those sailors held their peace. Something was certainly stealing water and food.

***

Sachi was getting desperate. She must have water. Even if she was willing to drink her own urine, there was a limit. She tried, once, to steal the water given to the goat and chickens and the last pig. The water was vile and there wasn't enough. Plus, the animals' pens and cages were more in the open than the lower deck water tanks. And the general increase in the crew's level of alertness greatly restricted her ability to move about and amuse herself. Wedging her long legs and tall torso into tighter and tighter spaces cut down her circulation, making her body numb and slower to respond.

And she had suffered several of her fits. They were getting worse as she reduced the amount she ate and drank. Unlike one of her adopted cousins, she did not collapse and shake, foaming at the mouth while her eyes rolled back into her head. She froze, utterly motionless, unaware, and unseeing, disconnected from the world. Normally she remembered nothing of her fits. They were just a lost hole in her memories, anywhere from a few minutes to over an hour where she simply ceased to exist. But the last couple had been different. She remembered seeing bizarre symbols, an infinite gray space surrounding her in all directions. The feeling that someone wanted her to go do something. And strangest of all, the last time she saw a small shining silver statue of a human, or at least she thought she had. He, she thought as it did not have the least hint of female breasts, had no identifying marks at all, not even eyes or a mouth. It stood there in her vision and simply waited.

She considered killing one of the cats and drinking its blood, but the master rat-catchers of the ship were her friends. They must have thought her a poor hunter, for Sota and an equally large female she named Hitomi regularly brought her dead rats. The rodents didn't have enough moisture in their bodies to help. If she killed a cat, she would only do so once, for the others would then fear and avoid her. So she stole what liquid she could, anything left unwatched. She even drank the hideous alcohol served to the sailors. *Grog*, they called it. It was vile but it was liquid. Like any alcohol, it had no effect on her, other than the horrible taste. No matter how much sah-keh or beer she drank, she had never been drunk, not once in her entire life.

Eventually, there was no choice. She must try to get water, enough to last at least a week. At the beginning of the journey she had stolen two large waterskins from the goat locker. She had no idea why the crew called it that. The most junior officers, chiefs she heard them called, were quartered there. The ship's one nanny goat was kept in a pen next to the chicken coop and the pig, nowhere near the goat locker. Something else the Kolbians did that made no sense. She thought about waiting until the ship was clearing for gun drill. They did not always fire the guns, sometimes merely practicing the motions of clearing the ship and handling the guns. They often stopped to try something different to see if it was faster. She did not understand why they did that. If something worked well, why change it to see if maybe it would be better? Regardless, while they were doing that, they were distracted and there were fewer eyes on the water tanks. Still, it would be safer and easier in dark of night, what the sailors called the mid-watch. The darkness was her friend and ally.

That night she made her try for the water. She spent nearly an hour creeping up to the water spigots. The belowdecks' dimness helped make her invisible in her *shozoku*. Slowly she trickled water into one of the waterskins, filling it until it bulged. The guard, a Marine with his bayoneted musket and dark green coat, was standing at the door, supposedly the only way into the compartment. She had loosened a set of planks in the bulkhead several days ago. It worked to get her into the compartment unseen.

She set the filled waterskin aside and started filling the second one. Slowly it filled up. She discovered a tiny but steady drip near the bottom of that skin as it finally filled up. She slid backward with the precious water, toward her exit. As she slowly stood up against the bulkhead to reach the loose planks, the dripping waterskin burst. The water itself made enough noise that the sentry turned. She ducked down, out of his sight, but the water ran across the deck and into his line of sight. She made herself as small as she could in the corner, hoping he would miss her in the dimness. She risked a glance and saw a boot and knew she was doomed.

"YOU THERE! HALT! ARMS UP!" His shout echoed in the compartment. "SERGEANT OF THE WATCH! INTRUDER IN THE MAIN WA-TER TANK COMPARTMENT!" She looked up to see the bayonet of the musket an arm's length away. The bore of the musket was huge, seemingly larger than the cannons on the main gundeck. "Stand up, you! Slowly, arms up!" There was a commotion in the passageway. Another green-coated Marine, this one with a pair of vertical red chevrons on his sleeve, barged into the room followed closely by a sailor in duck pants and a white-gray shirt. "Corporal Gavin, I think this is our thief!"

The Marine with the chevrons, Corporal Gavin she guessed, stopped, and took a long look at her. She wondered what he thought he saw. She wore all black; her *zukin* and *fukumen* covering her head and face, except for her black eyes. The *shozoku* was not as tight as it once was, with the weight she had lost. But still, a man with any eyes at all would see the figure in black was female. She thought she might be able to take all three of them down, but she'd have to kill them to do so. Besides, if she did kill them and escape, where would she escape to? Such a thing would have their shipmates tearing the ship apart to find her. She knew she would not be able to evade that kind of a search.

Her adopted brother, cruel Mankato, or his twin, the vicious Maho, would do so without compunction. She found she could not, would not even consider it for more than a heartbeat, even if it meant her own death. These were not evil men. And she hated the kill-training the Odas put her through in her youth. She knew she could kill but killing without need sickened her. Unlike the horrid twins, especially Maho, who relished the taking of a life.

The Odas punished theft with death, as was their right. Theft was considered dishonorable and beneath the warrior caste. Of course, that did not stop the Odas from stealing themselves, but woe betide one caught stealing from a Clan of assassins, thugs, and thieves.

I should have tried in the daytime. At least I would see the Sun one last time before I die. Her shoulders slumped in despair and defeat. She did not resist when Corporal Gavin reached out and pulled off her *fukumen.*

"I will be utterly dog-damned. Our 'spirit-thief' is a girl. Four bloody weeks she's been aboard, and three before we had the barest of clues we even had a stowaway," the sailor muttered from behind the Corporal. "The Bosun's head will explode."

"All right, young lady, let's go." Corporal Gavin reached out and grabbed her firmly by the shoulder and pulled her into the passageway. "Let's take you to the Officer of the Deck and then you're the first lieutenant's problem, young miss."

Force is not necessary. I will submit quietly. I will go to my death with what dignity they will allow me. The corporal's hand was hard from combat training. But he was strangely gentle, not pinching or grabbing hard enough to bruise. His grip was firm but caused her no pain. *The Oda would kick and beat me, drag me half senseless to whatever authority there was. The Kolhians send me to my death with gentleness.*

****

Harry Caplin was chatting with Lieutenant Willis Fleet when the hubbub began below decks. They exchanged glances, Fleet nodding suggestively toward the deck hatch. Harry smiled and shook his head in the negative.

"Let's let the petty officers and Marines sort it out for the moment, Willis. It sounds like someone has found our 'spirit-thief.'"

"Be interesting to see what or more likely, who, it is." Lieutenant Fleet would be thirty next year and he was one of the Office of Naval Intelligence's rising stars. Tall with short brown hair, his rugged good looks and green eyes invariably drew the women. And even the occasional man, much to Willis' discomfiture. He was gifted with a knack for languages, speaking most major languages with native fluency and able to at least converse in a dozen more minor tongues. Despite his attraction to all things mechanical, he was a gregarious fellow, generally well liked by his fellow officers.

"Well, here they come." Over the last few weeks, Harry and Willis had become something of an odd couple. Harry was young for his rank and position, only twenty-six, but he knew he was on the short list for the next round of promotions; command of a brig or sloop was certainly in his future and sooner rather than later. Harry lacked Fleet's broad shoulders and good looks and struggled with his weight at times. But knowing he was firmly on the ladder to command and possibly his own pennant in the future gave him a solid self-confidence.

The two officers watched the procession coming up from below decks. Marine Private Farin Evans led the way, a very tall girl—er, young woman dressed all in black following him, with Corporal Gavin right behind her holding a tight fistful of her cloth jacket. The tighter jacket revealed...interesting contours. Substantial contours. As they came into the lantern light on the quarterdeck, Caplin drew a deep breath and Fleet blew out a low wolf-whistle. The woman was young, likely still short of twenty and probably of at least half Nisei descent. And she was a rare beauty. A high forehead, well defined chin and high cheekbones drew their admiring gazes to a straight, Decennian-style nose and mysterious black eyes, all framed by a long fall of shining black hair. Tall, she was likely four or five inches short of Willis' six foot three. Harry hid a smirk as he realized that being only five foot three put his eyes at the same height as her very impressive décolletage.

***

Senior Petty Officer Nolan Asquith trailed the Marines and their captive with an amused look on his face. Something out of the ordinary like this certainly told the tale of an officer's mettle. Despite his eyes being at the same level as the stowaway's hellacious rack, Lieutenant Commander Caplin kept his eyes on her face. Which was also something anyone who appreciated a beautiful woman would enjoy looking at, despite the dejected look of utter despair currently there. Not so Lieutenant Fleet. Asquith was waiting for the drool to just run down his chin. He snickered to himself at his thoughts.

Yeah, she's a real looker, but sheesh LT, have some couth. Damn ONI spook, you'd think he'd be slick with the ladies. She's a human being, not a candy stick treat.

***

As soon as the Marines stopped her in front of the two officers, she dropped to her knees and downcast her eyes, putting her left elbow on the deck, appropriate for lower class to address higher, and then she waited. She had no doubt of her eventual fate but there was no reason to act uncivilized around these foreign devils. She would much prefer to be allowed honorable *seppuku* over being hung as a thief.

I might live if I can convince them I would be more useful servicing the officers, relieving their lusts. But they may do that anyway and then hang me or just knock me on the head and throw me overboard. And I really do not want to be nothing more than an attractive mattress for them to spend their lusts upon.

"So, this is our supposed 'spirit-thief.' Looks like she could use a good meal and a bath." She cautiously peeked up at the speaker. She recognized his voice. She knew voices but not the faces which went with those voices. This was Lieutenant Commander Caplin, the First Lieutenant. He was the strictest of all the officers. She had no idea he was so short. "Well done, Marines. Petty Officer Asquith, would you go ask Toby to wake the Captain. I think he will want to speak with our little problem here."

"Aye-aye, Sir." Asquith vanished like smoke.

"Marine Private Evans, would you see if the doctor is still up. His Nisei is better than mine. Corporal Gavin, escort this young lady to the Bosun's Office and inform him of the situation. He is to take charge of her until the captain decides how this will be handled." Caplin turned his attention to the kneeling young woman. "I don't suppose you speak Terranglais, do you?"

"I do, well enough, My Lord." She spoke just loud enough to barely be heard over the sounds of the ship.

"Well, that will help, I suppose." Caplin sighed. She sounded like the usual, overly submissive Nisei female. *What in the seven hells of Quan is she doing on* Intrepid? "Well, off with you, then. Corporal, treat her reasonably unless she gives you reason to use force. Take her below."

***

Bosun Paul Beauchamp had just gotten off to dreamland after a long exhausting day when a pounding on his doorframe hauled him back to wakefulness. It was a regular knocking, one, two, three sharp raps, a three-count pause and then three more raps, getting harder and louder as they progressed. *A Marine! God damned Marines. Gotta do everything by the fucking numbers and according to the fucking Manual. And to think I coulda stayed on the fucking farm. Join the Navy, see the world, travel to distant, exotic lands, meet strange and fascinating new people and have the fucking Marines kill them. I need to find that fucking recruiter and knock his teeth loose. Bastard.* He groaned as he swung his feet out of his bunk.

"Stand fast, Marine! Let a man get his britches on." He pulled on a cleaner pair of pants and his uniform blouse. He tugged it straight to make sure the Marine could see the chevrons and rockers of a Master Chief Petty Officer. Of course, being a Marine, whoever he was probably had no clue about Navy ranks. *Fucking Marines, they only know how to fight, fuck and blow shit up. But they're good at those things. God give me patience and give it to me right now. There better be a damn good reason for waking me up.* He settled behind his miniscule desk and poured himself a quick shot from his personal stash of Montagaran whiskey before tucking the bottle away. "Enter!"

***

This was an area of the ship she had never explored. It was too open and yet restricted, with only a single path onto the main deck. She knew this was the man the crew called *Bosun* and they respected and feared him. She never expected him to look like a grumpy grandfather. His bristly hair was completely white and bright blue eyes stared at her in startled surprise as the Marine thrust her into the tiny cubicle of his office. He had to shove her in there, as there wasn't room for two people to stand in front of the desk.

Oh, he is not happy at all! I have damaged his honor! Oh, no, he will tell the Captain to hang me! She would have knelt to him but there simply wasn't room unless her backside stuck out into the passageway.

"Private Evans managed to catch our thief, Bosun. Lieutenant Commander Caplin instructed me to turn her over to you until the Captain is ready to see her."

"THIS is our thief?" The bosun started to yell and then somehow kept his voice under the full roar that would have woken the entire ship. "This...this...this GIRL?"

"Aye, Bosun. Evans caught her trying to steal water. And she had the two missing waterskins from the goat locker." Corporal Gavin hid his smile. The bosun was twitting him with his shirt sleeve twisted around to clearly display his rank. Marines and sailors held a great deal of respect for each other, even as they hid it with insults and pranks.

"Oh my God." The bosun parked both elbows on the desk and dropped his face into his hands. "Angels and saints preserve my miserable carcass. What sin did I commit to deserve this, Lord? How did I offend?" A deep sigh came from behind the hands. "Good job, Corporal Gavin, head back to your post. I think I can handle one teenaged girl. Close the door."

"Aye-aye, Bosun." The door shut behind her.

"Why me?" He raised bleary, bloodshot eyes and glared at her. "Nisei, right?"

"*Hai*, uh, yes." She nodded.

"You a sneak? You know...whaddya call it, *shizukana ashi no jutsu*, the way of silent stealth or such? A *shinijutsuka?*"

"*Hai.*"

"You speak Terranglais worth a damn?"

"Yes, at least some. I do learn quickly."

"Yeah, right." He sighed and rubbed his face. "Am I gonna have any trouble outta you?"

"*Meiwaku o kakemasen.*"

"In Terranglais, damnit. My Nisei ain't that good."

"I will give no trouble."

"You might even mean that. But women on ships is always bad juju." There was a single, relatively quiet knock on the door. "Yes?"

"It's Toby, Bosun. Cap'n wants to see our spook."

"He's up?"

"Aye. And even decent. I was told the *spirit* is a pretty young woman. That is the case, right, Bosun?"

"Damn it, people start carrying tales and I'll flog 'em up the foremast and down the mizzen! And what do you care? The next shapely female you chase will be the first, I'd wager."

"You'd win, Bosun. It's the Cap'n I'm thinking of, however. You know, him and females, well, women and all."

"Well, fuck." The bosun's belligerence drained away like water. "All right. Go tell the skipper we're on the way."

"Aye-aye."

She watched the bosun closely. There was something about the captain and women. Maybe, especially younger women.

"You even think of playing any head games with the captain and I'll feed you to the fish myself. He has enough problems." The bosun turned an ugly face on her.

"*Fuzakemasen*, I won't play games. I will only ask for *meiyo*, honor."

"Yeah." He stood up and pointed at the door. He wasn't a big man, she saw, several inches shorter than she was, but he was thickly muscled. His hands were covered in the kind of scars you got punching someone. Hard. And often. "Okay, lassie, let's get this over with."

***

Captain Blaine was working on the ship's log when Toby knocked on his door. He looked at the expensive wind-up clock on his desk. *Ye God. Nearly six bells into the mid-watch. Sun'll be up in three hours or so. What the hell am I doing still up? About time to call it a night.*

"Enter." He put down his quill and leaned back in the chair, rubbing his eyes. "I don't remember asking for a hot toddy, Toby."

"You didn't, sir. First Lieutenant Caplin's compliments, sir and he directed that I inform you we have caught our ghost, sir. Marine Private Evans did, just now in the Main Water Tank Compartment."

"Wonderful." His tone of voice implied no such thing. "Which one of my crew am I going to have to have one of the bosun's mates flog?"

"None of them, sir. It wasn't a sailor or a Marine."

"Lieutenant Willis after all, was it?" Blain sighed.

"No, sir. We have a stowaway, a teenaged Nisei girl I'm told."

"A stowaway?" Blaine stared at Toby, utterly stunned.

"Aye, sir."

"A female stowaway?"

"Aye."

"A teenaged, female stowaway and we didn't find her for a month!" His voice rose sharply at the end.

"Aye, Captain."

"What kind of lubberly, misfit, blind-drunk moronic excuses for sailors did the Navy Board give me? A stowaway it took us a month to find!? 'The finest frigate in the Fleet,' I was told. 'Best crew in the Great Western Fleet,' I was told. I can hear Captain Eyles laughing from here and he should be somewhere in the Northern Khakal Sea, halfway around the world. I shudder to think what Commodore Sartell will say." Blaine stood up and walked to the back of his cabin, opened the door onto the sternwalk and stepped outside onto it. He took a deep breath and stared into the heavens. The wonder of the stars always calmed him down and it truly was a beautiful night. *Intrepid* rode the gentle swells lightly, a comfortable topsail breeze freshening a bit. She was likely making six or seven knots under these conditions. She was a forty-four-gun heavy frigate and command of her as young as he was and only a Captain, Junior Grade was quite the feather in his cap.

This stowaway would put a large cat amongst his own personal pigeons. And a young woman at that! He made a fist and gently beat it on the railing. *What is it with me and women?* Over the last couple of years, relations between himself and his wife Emily had become quite ugly. Her beauty was still there, but something spiteful and hateful encroached on the woman he'd married. Emily used their daughter Sally, only just thirteen, as a club to break him. And now there was another teenage girl who could cause him to run aground on the rocks and shoals of the Navy Board. Captains of forty-fours did not have stowaways elude them for a month. He took a final deep breath of the sea air and stepped back inside.

"Well, damnit." He plunked back into his chair. "Where is she?"

"Lt. Caplin turned her over to the bosun until you say different, sir."

"Ouch, that could get ugly. I believe Lieutenant Fleet is still up? He's the expert on the Nisei, right? Give him my compliments and ask him if he'd be available to give me a few moments of his time. Then have the bosun bring her here."

"Any idea what will be done with her, sir?"

"Well, she's not going to be keeping anyone warm at night and I'm not hanging her from the yardarm without an extreme provocation. Would you be willing to have an assistant cook? Find a secure place where we can hang a hammock for her?"

"Aye, sir, I'd be glad to take her under me wing, as it were. Everyone knows I've no use for a woman, leastwise, not in the bedroom way. And no one wants to fight the ship's Boxing Champion, now would they, sir?" Toby grinned at him, waving a fist the size of a ham. "I'd think she'll be safe enough there."

"Well enough, I guess. Go get them, Toby."

"Aye-aye, Skipper."

***

"Lieutenant Fleet reporting as requested, sir." Willis Fleet knocked on the door frame a few minutes later.

"Enter." Willis ducked through the doorway. "Have a seat, Lieutenant. I assume you've heard the news?"

"Oh, yes, sir. I was on the quarterdeck, chatting with Lieutenant Commander Caplin when the Marines caught her." Willis coughed and looked out the stern windows. Blaine scratched his chin as Willis settled. He liked Fleet well enough but there was something missing in Fleet's makeup, apparently the ambition and drive that marked the best ship captains in the KRN. Willis would probably never command a ship or rise much beyond Commander in rank. It was vaguely possible he might reach flag rank some day, but currently there were only three flag billets for Intelligence track officers in the entire Navy.

"I believe you're an expert in Nisei culture and language, correct, Lieutenant?"

"I know the language very well, sir. I've been told by Nisei locals that I sound like I'm from the Kokako region, just south of Akumato." He fidgeted in his seat, running his finger around his collar. "Culture? I probably know it as well as any 'foreign devil,' that is, just barely."

"What the hell is wrong with you, Fleet? You're acting like a twitchy nine-year-old at a boring Sunday sermon. Dr. Hoff dump weevils in your drawers?"

"Well, Captain Blaine, you see, sir, it's hard to explain without seeing, but, if you'll just give me a moment, I'll…" The knock on the doorframe saved him as Blaine turned to face the door.

"Enter," he growled. The irritation he felt at Fleet's inane babbling leaked into his voice, making it rough and harsher than he intended.

***

She heard the anger and tension in that voice. That tone, coming from a male in authority over her, always meant punishment, usually severe punishment. The slight feeling of hope the bosun had held out to her fled like doves before the falcon. She could only beg for dignity and honor in death. The bosun pulled her five steps into the cabin before she went to her knees, bending her head with both forearms flat on the deck.

***

"What the hell?" Blaine was startled as all he saw was a vaguely female figure in black collapse onto the deck. A wealth of black hair covered her face and shoulders, pooling on the deck around her.

"Please, oh Great Lord, allow me to cleanse the stain to your honor." She spoke clearly and loudly, carefully pronouncing the unfamiliar syllables of Terranglais, keeping her face to the floor. "I beg to be allowed dignity and honor. I will not even request a second that I may fully restore your honor that I blemish. I only ask that, Great Lord. Nothing more."

***

"Oh shit." Fleet's face paled as he realized the implications of the girl's speech. He realized she concealed a knife in her hand.

"Damn it, girl," the bosun growled. "Get the hell up. This ain't Isemoto; you don't go around bowing and scraping the deck here. What the FUCK!?"

The bosun jumped back and fell as Fleet shot out of his chair and grabbed the girl's hands. Fleet was well trained in hand-to-hand combat, in several different styles, but suddenly he was struggling with something more akin to a tiger or maybe one of the mythical dragons. If she'd wanted to, she'd have cut him into cat food in less than a minute. He focused on pinning her hands. She smashed her head into his ribcage. If she didn't break a couple of them, they'd be bruised like all hell tomorrow. A heel whipped over her head and hit his jaw hard enough that he saw stars and spat out a tooth. He'd never seen anyone so fast and so flexible, and God Above, she was strong. Then Blaine came around the desk and cracked her head with the first thing that came to hand, his paperweight. He stunned her and she went limp.

"*Watashi meiyo o kaifuku shimasu,*" was all she muttered as she collapsed, face down on the deck. Fleet flipped her onto her back and quickly and thoroughly searched her. He tossed half a dozen throwing stars, an even dozen slim throwing spikes, a garrote and four slender knives onto Blaine's desk.

"Okay, Lieutenant Fleet, what the hell just happened?" Blaine was shocked at the pile of weapons. "Wasn't she searched, Bosun? Are we dealing with an assassin of some kind here?"

"We didn't search her, sir. Didn't think we needed to, her being a young lady and all." The bosun was still shocked by the sudden outburst of violence. He had no idea why any of this had just happened. "No excuse, Captain."

"Damn straight, *no excuse*, Bosun! Fleet, I'm waiting."

"Well, Captain Blaine, sir, a moment please?" Fleet was still struggling to get his breath back. "What she said, *Watashi meiyo o risutoasuru,* roughly translates as *I must restore honor.* She was no danger to you or me or anything but your rug. She was going to commit *seppuku* to remove a stain she believed she caused on your honor and to preserve her own honor. I imagine she would have asked your permission to restore her honor and you, not being familiar with the practice, would have allowed it and then her guts would have been all over the floor."

"What the hell? She was going to ask ME to let her kill herself?" Blaine's eyes widened.

"Yes, sir." Fleet rubbed his jaw, picking his tooth off the deck with a forlorn expression. "Girl kicks like a mule. *Seppuku* is the ultimate apology in her world. Just another reason they call us *foreign devils*. We apologize and don't always show that we mean it."

"Now what?"

"We have a chat with her when she comes around, sir. I think we have a real opportunity here. Don't tie her up or restrain her. No irons, please, sir. We need to punch it into her head how different Kolbia and Kolbians and especially members of the Kolbian Republican Navy are. Starting with you, sir."

"Was this why you were twitching like a kid sitting on an anthill?"

"No, sir. Look at her. I've never seen anyone so beautiful." Fleet blushed a bit. "A woman like her, sir...well, I've been with my share and then some of beautiful women, but this girl puts most of them on the wagon."

Blaine stopped and took a long look at the young woman sprawled on the deck, just barely conscious enough to moan. Then he took a second, longer look as he knelt next to her and gently brushed her hair away from her face. *Fleet, I do believe you are right. Holy cats.*

"Bosun, go get the Doctor after you hand me that bottle of whiskey on the shelf behind my desk."

"Aye-aye, sir."

Blaine poured a small amount of the liquor into a glass and waved it under her nose. She coughed and wrinkled her nose.

"Here, have a sip." He held the glass to her lips as he lifted her up, slipping an arm behind her for support. "Easy, you're with friends. Sorry about the whack on the head, there. You are safe, here. No one will hurt you." She sipped the whiskey, coughed once, and finished the drink. "Easy. That stuff's potent. Now, can we talk without all the excitement?"

***

Oww. My head hurts. Why is he holding me up? What is he doing, sitting on the floor? Are they so determined to hang me? She gingerly felt the knot on her head.

"Just relax and let's talk, all right?" Blaine eased back, obviously poised to grab if necessary, but trying to minimize physical contact.

"My Lord, you should not be sitting on the floor."

"Now, first and foremost, I'm no one's lord. I'm a Captain in the Kolbian Navy and we don't have any lords in the Navy, or anywhere in Kolbia, for that matter. You can call me Captain Blaine. If you call me My Lord again, I won't hear you."

"Ca...Captain Blaine?"

"Yes, young lady?" Her voice was a pure pleasure, throaty and kinda sexy, he thought.

"Why will you not allow me to regain my honor?"

"Lieutenant Fleet over there tells me that means you killing yourself." He pointed to Willis. "Won't happen, not on my watch. You are way too pretty to commit suicide."

"So, you will hang me, like a common criminal, then? Remove all honor?"

"No one is hanging anyone, understand that. You're not a pirate and we normally only hang pirates. Clear on this, now? Say yes."

"Yes, sir."

"Okay, you've been paying attention. Now let's get off this hard floor and sit over here on the couch like civilized human beings, that is, unless you'd prefer to sit on the deck? Again, say yes."

"Yes, sir." Blaine and Fleet helped her up and the captain guided her to the cushioned couch, sitting down close to her.

"Now we are getting somewhere. How about you tell me your name?"

"I am Takahashi Sachi, Captain. Or as your people would say it, Sachi Takahashi."

"So, we can call you Miz Takahashi?"

"Please, sir, that would be presumptuous. Would it not be simpler to just call me Sachi?"

"Well, I don't see any reason we couldn't go ahead and do that. As long as you like it and it makes you happy?"

"I would like that ver...urgk." The girl went rigid, completely stiff in every joint. Her jaw locked and her eyes stared out the stern windows into the sky.

"What the Hell?" Blaine grabbed her and found he could not move any joint he could reach. She was utterly rigid. Her skin rapidly cooled, becoming cold and clammy very quickly. Feeling for the pulse in her neck, he could barely detect a slow heartbeat, five or six times a minute. If she was breathing, it was just barely. "Some kind of fit?"

"No idea, sir. I'm off to get the Surgeon." Willis was halfway to the door when it opened. Doctor Hoff and the bosun stopped abruptly before they ran into Fleet.

"What in God's Name has been going on here?" Doctor Hoff asked. Blaine gestured to Sachi as the doctor knelt over Sachi and started examining her. "Huh. Some kind of seizure, I think, but I've never heard or read about anything like it."

"She just locked up in mid-word." The anxiety on Blaine's face was plain for Hoff to see, but then they went well over two decades back, best friends in primary school and college, well before either of them joined the Navy. Elazar Hoff had been his Best Man when he married Emily Arlington.

"Hmm, rigid, unresponsive, low heart rate, low respiration, her pupils are non-reactive." The doctor moved a lamp closer and further from Sachi's face at the end of his examination.

"Okay, so what do we do, Elazar?" The anxiety crept into Blaine's voice now. His brow was creased with worry. Hoff had seen Blaine less anxious in the middle of battle.

"Nothing we can do, Captain." He watched Blaine closely. There was a bit of a flush to the captain's face, and his pupils were dilated, telling signs of physical attraction. He wondered if this girl, young woman, might be what would get Blaine's head out of his third point of contact and realize there were other women in the world besides that bitch Emily. But why did it have to be this one? "Watch her, protect her from what environmental stresses we can and wait. Nothing else to do."

Chapter Four

The Great Western Ocean
Virtual Reality Construct
KRN *Intrepid*
May 1478, Third Age of Imperial Reckoning

She stood naked in a vast grey emptiness that stretched infinitely away. The small silver statue of a human from her last fit stood in front of her, only slightly taller than her knees. There was no breeze, no sound and nothing moved anywhere she could see. She was neither cold nor hot. Bewildered, afraid, she turned away from the statue and started to run. She couldn't tell if she was moving or not and when she looked over her shoulder, the statue was in the same place in relation to her it had been. She stopped running and turned, screaming at it.

"GO AWAY! WHERE AM I? WHAT IS THIS PLACE?" She couldn't hear herself scream but she knew she said the words. She spun a side kick into the statue. She felt nothing, no impact, just nothing but she saw her foot go through the thing's body. When she pulled her foot back, it was unmarked. It was like trying to step on the same bit of water twice. The thing rotated, moving slowly, and raising one rigid arm to point at letters the size of a castle. They meant nothing to her, but she studied them, trying to set them into her memory, to learn whatever it was they were trying to say. Suddenly there was a blurring sensation and either the letters shrunk faster than she could see, or she and the statue had grown as big as mountains. She realized the letters were two words in a strange language, similar to the letters and words the foreign devils used yet different. There were two words, followed by two dots, one a little bit atop the other. Then she realized there were two numbers after the stacked dots: a two and a three followed by a strange symbol, a bar that leaned right of vertical, separating a pair of zeros.

"Twenty-three," she said. She looked at the statue and it nodded at her. "Twenty-three, is that right?" Again, it nodded. She was ecstatic. For the first time in her life there was something in one of her fits — this must be one of her fits — that she could understand.

"Wait a minute. I could be dead. Am I dead, little statue?" The thing looked at her for a long moment and then slowly shook its head no. "So, this IS a fit, right?" A nod. "I'm supposed to go and do something?" Another nod. "And you are my guide or teacher, right?" Nod. She felt a great weight lift away. Shameful as the fits were, perhaps there was some redeeming value to them. She reached to touch the statue and fell, somehow, into it. The letters and numbers disappeared as did the empty greyness. Everything in her sight glared redly. She saw strange new numbers. Ones and zeroes streamed past her in lines, in rows. In columns and bundles, only ones and zeroes, uncountable, innumerable hordes of them. The only thing she saw were the ones and zeroes implacably closing in on her.

"I do not want to be here. NO!" Soundlessly she screamed and suddenly she was falling, feeling as if too much of her was being squeezed and shoved, forced into a space grown too small.

She struggled and fought against something cloying and sticky. She shoved the walls back, forcing them away. Unexpectedly, she was choking, desperate for air, flailing to breathe. She slammed against something, hard enough she feared she would break bones. Falling at an incredible speed, reality blurring around her, the numbers and the red light tunneling around her as her vision collapsed to a single point. She slammed to a sudden stop, desperately gasping for air. There was an instant of relief as she realized she was back in her body and then the pain hit. She moaned and involuntarily curled up into a ball on something soft. She coughed daggers out of her lungs and looked blearily around her. She didn't know where she was or who the four men peering at her with such concern were. One of them was *so* handsome. Something in him called to something in her.

Then awareness avalanched into her mind and she realized she was lying in Captain Blaine's bunk. She had suffered one of her shameful fits in front of all of them. Now they knew how worthless she was, and that realization was bitter ashes in her heart. She turned away so they couldn't see her weep. They knew she was stupid and useless now, worth only the fleeting pleasure her attractive body could give a man.

At least the Captain is handsome and well formed. I have lain with much worse. I might even find some way to enjoy sex with him. This would not be so bad. I should not have to service the entire crew. Panicked thoughts scurried frantically through her mind

"Captain, are you *sure* you want her working in the galley?" The Bosun spoke up as Doctor Hoff rested his hands gently on her back and turned her back towards them. "The entire crew goes through there at one time or another. What if she's...I don't know the word? Makes others sick?"

She moaned wordlessly, pleading to the Ancestor Spirits. The thought of being forced into a vile crib, locked in where man after faceless man could use her, removing any will of her own. Horrible, pig-like men forcing her before leaving at best or even beating her. As an Oda, she had never experienced such a thing, but she knew women in the cheapest brothels were used exactly like that. Death would be preferable.

"Contagious, Bosun?" Hoff's voice was cool and disdainful.

"Yeah, Doctor, that. A sailor gets what she has, suffers a fit while reefing the royals. IF he hits the deck, it'd be easier to use a hose to wash him over the side. Body'd have the consistency of raspberry jam."

"Well, Bosun, yes, that would be a problem, IF she's contagious. She's not. Take my word for it. This is no disease, at least nothing she can communicate to anyone else, I'm quite certain." He turned his attention back to her. "How are you feeling, Sachi?"

"Please, no," she muttered to him, still half delirious. "Not the whole crew. There's just me. Let me stay with the Captain. I could be ready anytime he wants me. Or m-m-m-maybe, you could just share me a little bit, the Captain, you, Master Fleet, maybe Master Caplin, he's nice. Mister Bosun, too. I could be good, very good for just a few but not the whole crew. Please, Ancestor Spirits, please don't send me to the galley to service the whole crew. I don't want to be locked into a crib." By the end of her outburst she was weeping, holding onto Doctor Hoff's coat, trying to kiss him. "I'll be so good to all of you, just please, not a crib, kill me or hang me or throw me into the ocean in chunks, please, please, don't lock me up and let them fuck me over and over until I can't tell if it's a man or a pig, please, no, not...that...oww." There was a cold pinch in her arm and the cold spread quickly and then she was warm and serene silence and darkness swept her up in warm, peaceful wings. "Mama, Papa, is that you?" she muttered. Then the drug Hoff injected into her arm claimed the last scrap of consciousness.

***

"I think I'm going to be sick, excuse me, please." Willis quickly stood up and ran onto the stern walk. They could hear him puking over the rail.

"Oh my God, Elazar." Blaine looked a little green in the face himself. "Where in the Seven Burning Hells of Quan did she come from? I know such things are done. God knows, some of our sailors do frequent places like that, unless the Shore Patrol finds them first and shuts them down. Who does something like that to a girl like her?"

"God Above and Hell Below, Cap'n, I know more about places like that than I want to." The Bosun spoke into the solemn silence. "And even some of our men *like* women the way she describes. But I'd rather not take ship or make sail with such, iff'n I've a choice, Sir. I don't like the fact that she snuck on board and hid so well, so long. But anyone thinks they can do something like that to the likes of her will deal with me and my sidearm."

"Yes, well, you'll have to make her believe it, Bosun." Fleet came back in, wiping his mouth as he plunked into a chair. "I'd guess she's a runaway, most likely from the Clan Ishikawa. They're the Least Clan of the Hundred and Forty-four clans. And the worst. There's nothing it seems they won't do. Murder, assassination, slavery, piracy, bribery, extortion, drugs, protection rackets, high class pseudo-geishas, the worst slave whorehouse you can imagine, you name it, if it's illegal and/or immoral, there's an Ishikawa thug in there somewhere." He sighed. "Doctor Hoff, carefully pull off her left shoe and look between her big toe and the one next to it. Might be a tattoo or scar there. And check and see if she has large areas of her body covered in tattoos, arms, legs, shoulders, or her back."

"There's a white flower of some type tattooed between her big toe and the next one. It has fifteen petals." After another moment, "I don't see anything else."

"Well, shit. Captain Blaine, sir, one of my areas of...shall we call it expertise, is how organized crime groups work with slavers and pirates. I specialize in the Nisei Empire and I'm leaving because I've made too many Ishikawa Clan bosses mad at me. At first, I thought she might be a last-ditch assassin aimed at me, but I really doubt it now. Mostly because I'm still breathing." Fleet stopped and thought for a moment. "No body tattoos, Doctor? Just the little flower?"

"Correct, Lieutenant. At least none that a very cursory exam reveals."

"Again, *well, shit.*" He sighed. "Okay, Nisei Clans are composed of Families; I assume you all know at least that." Nods ran around the cabin. "Well, just as the Hundred and Forty-four Clans are ranked, so are the Families within the Clans. The Head Family of the Ishikawa is the Oda Family and they could give Quan Himself lessons in debauchery and evil. As the Head Family, Odas are not required to tattoo their body. In some ways the damn crooks are even more screwed up about the whole Honor Code of the Nisei than the Samurai are. There were rumors blowing around Akumato about an adopted daughter of the Oda that was supposed to be deadly as Cobra, graceful as Tiger and as beautiful as Swan. Somehow, she was a big disappointment and there was trouble in the family, at that point it gets lost in the background chatter. This could very well be her, she's got the right kind of tattoo and the right kind of messed-up worldview, especially if she's one of the top boss family's daughters, even if adopted. If this is that daughter, if she successfully managed to get away from them, there's going to be a stupid huge price on her head. If the Odas lose her, if she succeeds in escaping and eluding their control, they will possibly lose enough face that they could lose control of the Clan. But there are a whole lot of *ifs* there. It's just within the bare realm of possibility that the other families could destroy the Odas. And I think this is her, one Oda *sai* Asami, or as we would read it, Asami, adopted daughter of the Oda Family."

"What makes you say that?" Blaine asked.

"Mostly the flower tattoo, sir. It's correct for who I think she might be. Also, I have advanced training in hand-to-hand combat and I'm rated expert with both pistol and rifled musket. I've trained with the sword since I was nine years old. And just now, if she wasn't so focused on trying to turn her guts into a cabin decoration, she would've beaten me like a dirty rug. I'm good, damn good and I know what I'm capable of doing. Sir, I'm not in her league. Not even close. It'd be like a pick-up game batter trying to hit a professional pitcher." Fleet's eyes were hard and cold, his body language completely different from what they were accustomed to seeing. Lieutenant Willis Fleet, who Blaine often thought of as a bit of a playboy, getting by on the reputation of his old Navy family, suddenly was the deadliest man in the cabin. "Sir, I would strongly advise that we not tell her anything about our speculations. IF she's this adopted daughter and IF she did run away, she's going to be jumpy as a long-tailed cat in a room full of rocking chairs. Let's give her some room. Let her be Takahashi Sachi while she's on board *Intrepid*. Likely the best thing we could do for her. And, honestly, from a Kolbian perspective, even an ONI perspective, she really is not that important."

"Hang on a minute, Fleet. If she's as high in the Oda Family as you say, wouldn't she be of a great deal of use to ONI? Wouldn't she have knowledge of links between the Ishikawa and our own collections of thugs and pirates?"

"Unlikely, Sir. As a female, an adopted daughter and as young as she seems to be, they would have never let her near any of that kind of knowledge. If she was a blood relation, maybe, maybe just a little. As an adoptee, no way." Fleet shrugged. "I'd say to treat her like any young woman, frantic to escape a horrible situation."

"Well, that makes it easier, I think." Blaine looked at Hoff, "How long will she be out?"

"I'd say three, maybe four hours. It was a pretty hefty dose of sedative."

"Okay, for now, she stays right here. One of us with her at all times and I mean at all times. She's obviously had a tough row to hoe, and I don't want her throwing herself off the stern walk. Now, that's enough for tonight. Turn in, go get some sleep. Bosun, send Toby in here on your way to your bunk. Now scram. I need to do some thinking and I'll be right here to keep an eye on her."

They trooped out, Willis tossing a glance back over his shoulder at the unconscious girl. Blaine sighed as he looked at her, lying so quietly in his bunk. He couldn't remember the last time he'd seen such a beautiful girl, a young woman really, in his bunk. He'd always been faithful to Emily, but his wife never once even set foot on any one of his commands, or the quay leading to one, much less in his cabin. She was usually too busy being a 'Leading Light of Society.' Blaine sighed. Maybe it was time he realized that it was over between them. But that would probably mean he'd rarely if ever see his daughter again and he'd put up with an awful lot for his daughter.

"God damn it, don't I have enough gray hairs?"

Omega 2-Cygni System Command
CNS *Backhand Blow*, Rybithian low orbit
May 1478, Third Age of Imperial Reckoning

::Action required.::

"Okay, D.A.V.E. On it. What's the issue?" Captain Deborah McAllen, Confederation Navy, Debbie to her friends, shifted in her command chair on board the Orbital Defense Center CNS *Backhand Blow*. Like many spacers, she cut her brown hair short on top and shaved on the temples. The haircut made life easier in a pressure suit and the shaved temples made physical neural link-ups easier when a multispectral wireless connection wasn't available. She turned her attention from her virtual book-reader to her D.A.V.E. program. The Digitally Aware Virtual Entity was a far cry from a full up autonomous Artificial Intelligence but these days, it was all that was available.

::The dedicated net-link for the System Defense Node Command Key activated for five hundred and twenty-eight milliseconds, Captain McAllen. No data was exchanged or requested other than a standard handshake request. The signal collapsed before the system could spin up and connect. Signal source cannot be located more precisely than the nominal western hemisphere of the planet Omega 2-Cygni Three.::

"Say what? The System Defense Node command key was destroyed fifteen years ago. How could anything be on that net-link?"

::Unknown. Two hundred and twenty-eight valid characters for access authorization were received in the system buffer before the signal collapsed. Signal collapse cleared the buffer and the data was lost.::

"Gawd-damnit! D.A.V.E., if there's another connection make damn sure we get any data secured. Don't let the system buffer purge it."

::Acknowledged.::

"Contact Commodore Collins as well. Plan on setting up a VR conference no later than twenty-three hundred hours tomorrow. Also, make sure you contact Commander Fujino and Senior Consultant Lundgren. They'll probably want to attend, given their history with the Node key's holders. Shouldn't be a problem for Commander Fujino, but Lundgren might have to just send her D.A.V.E. if she can't reach a comm-web link with VR capability. Where is she, now?"

::Senior Consultant Lundgren is on a clandestine mission in the Republic of Kolbia's capital city, Capitol.::

"Copy. Only the Kolbians would name their capital city Capitol. Somedays, I think they're a little too practical, don'tcha know?"

::Null query, Captain McAllen.::

"Never mind. Rhetorical question." She sighed to herself. *Why couldn't one AI have survived, just one? The Entity programs are so damn literal, and they just don't learn. Of course, they were programmed that way.* She rubbed her forehead in frustration. "Why do I get the feeling that life is about to get a whole lot more complicated?"

::Null query, Captain McAllen.::

"Never mind. You don't get it. You never get it." She sighed and turned back to her neural link and pulled up a word processing program. *This is going to have to be reported up what's left of the chain of command and some of the Techneers get pissy if all blanks aren't filled, 'i's dotted and 't's crossed.* "Get those contacts off and go back to sleep mode, D.A.V.E. You're a little too literal for me right now."

::Acknowledged.::

She stretched, regarded the virtual keyboard with distaste and decided on some coffee first. She clambered out of the command chair and headed to the coffee machine in the corner of the *Blow's* bridge, where the Intel Section had been, centuries ago. She was the only person awake on the huge asteroid based Orbital Defense Center. The rest of the crew, all forty-two of them, were in stasis. Barring a starship entering the system, that's where they would stay until it was time to wake her relief and take her own time in stasis.

They, like few other survivors of the human Confederation, stretched their lives out beyond imagination. Arriving here, first as explorers, then as colonists and later as defenders in a merciless interstellar war, humans had done their best to coexist with the multitude of indigenous sapient species, some of those races stranger than anything in fiction. Now, with no communication from the Confederation in millennia, the survivors hung on as best they could, a beleaguered garrison slowly losing hope that relief would ever come.

McAllen sighed and sipped her coffee. The *Backhand Blow* still functioned, mostly. Her power core kept the positional stabilizers operational, maintaining her geosynchronous orbit above the planet. If the power failed, the ODC would deorbit within days. If that happened, the last bastion of the Confederal Navy would be gone. Not that ninety-nine-point-nine percent of the other humans on the planet the locals named Rybithia would ever know, or care. Long ago, the Confederation became legend and then myth to the human survivors of that last dreadful battle for the system. Survivors who had gone on to rebuild civilization, build nations and empires. Who then watched those fall into barbarism and savagery, new nations and empires rising from the ashes, the pattern repeating again and again, until nothing but myth and vague legend remained to explain the scraps of technological wonders remaining of the star-traveling humans' lost past.

Another cycle of civilization was rising, and this time, Captain McAllen and her sleeping comrades, this time, they thought these new nations, with a little surreptitious help, might finally find their way into space, recover their lost heritage and perhaps even discover the ultimate fate of the Confederation. At least, this time, the possibility seemed greater than any that had come before.

McAllen shrugged at her gloomy thoughts, finished her coffee, and settled back in to complete her reports.

Chapter Five

The Great Western Ocean
KRN *Intrepid*
May 1478, Third Age of Imperial Reckoning

THE FIRST THING SHE was aware of was the quiet scratch, scritch of a quill pen on paper. She cracked an eye open. To her great surprise she was still in the Captain's cabin, indeed, still in his bunk. She could see his profile, shadowed by a lantern behind him. Covertly she studied him. He was very handsome, with a high brow and a strong chin. There were some, a very few, silver hairs interspersed in his thick black hair. Hair just long enough to enjoy running her hands through. He squinted as he wrote.

It would not be so bad to lie with him, she thought. *He seems kind and I doubt he would hit me often. And he is tall enough that I could look him in the eyes. But men do not like tall women to look them in the eyes. Of course, if I please him well, his eyes will be closed. But what if they decide I shall serve the crew in the galley? I think I would rather die.*

She looked around the great cabin. There was a kind of balcony across the back of the ship and a glass door opened out onto it. At worst, she thought she could manage to get out that door and throw herself into the ocean. The captain leaned back in his chair and rubbed his face before looking at her. She closed her eyes to bare slits.

"Well, much more of this and gray hairs might be all I have left. Oh, well, I think you're worth it. I hope. Just need to figure out some way to not foul up my career on this trip. Lord, now I'm talking to myself." He smiled and his gaze lingered for a long moment. "God help me when Emily finally learns about this. And I just know someone will let it slip and she'll worm the knowledge out of them."

His smile is nice as well, warm and welcoming. She continued her surreptitious observation of Blaine, considering his words and what he meant by them. *What does he mean, what am I worth to not foul up my career? What is that? And who is Emily? I should not lay here and deceive him.*

"Your silver hairs are attractive." She opened her eyes and rolled over on her side to meet him eye to eye.

"What the hell?!?" Blaine jumped in his chair, nearly going over backwards. He recovered his composure and stared at her in amazement.

"They give you presence and maturity. A Nisei man as young as you are would rejoice to have such hair." She smiled invitingly at him. "If you like, I can show you my skills in lovemaking. I was trained by both the best courtiers for lovemaking and the best geishas for cultured entertainment. Only, I beg, please do not send me to the galley. I truly would rather die, even if you just hang me like an honorless thief."

"Elazar told me you'd be out for at least three or four hours, maybe more. It hasn't been thirty minutes. How the hell are you conscious, much less coherent?" Blaine stared at her, startlement on his face.

"I don't know. Drugs don't really affect me. I do not get drunk either. Please, use me as you like. I will do anything for you, Captain. Anything at all. Please not to send me to the galley. Not to let the entire crew use me. Please. I beg you."

"Dear God in His Heaven! Milady, I promise you, no one...NO ONE on board *Intrepid* will so much as touch a hair on your head under any circumstances! Dear Lord, don't you know what a galley is?"

"Where the men may use a woman as they please, I believe? Why else would you send me to that place? But where is it on the ship? When I grew bored in the dark of night, I did explore about the ship. As I did so I never found a crib that a less than willing woman would be put into. Where do you keep it?"

"Oh...My...God." Blaine buried his face in his hands and struggled to contain his laughter. It was a struggle, but he knew in his bones that she would not understand if he laughed now. And he wasn't sure he could stop her from throwing herself into the ocean. In control finally, he looked up and saw the naked fear in her eyes. "Milady, this is a warship of the Kolbian Republican Navy. One of our primary purposes is the eradication of slavery and piracy. We certainly and sure as hell do not practice it ourselves. Yes, there are Kolbians who engage in both piracy and the slave trade. Penalties for those crimes do include hanging by the neck until dead. But you are neither slaver nor pirate." He relented and smiled at her. "Sachi, you asked us to call you Sachi, remember? Is that all right with you?"

"Yes, sir."

"Sachi, the galley is where we cook our meals, the ship's kitchen. There are two galleys, one for the crew and one for the officer's wardroom. My steward, Toby, cooks my meals there as well. The *only* thing you would do there is help Toby fix meals for me and the ship's officers." He chuckled very quietly. "I will insist that you have absolutely no sexual contact with *anyone* at all, crew or officers for the remainder of the voyage. Toby stays in the Wardroom Galley; he has a bunk off the pantry. He will fix you up a bunk space there, in one of the storage closets. It will be very tight, but it should be livable until we raise Kolbia."

"Would he not be distressed by my constant presence?"

"Not hardly. My Nisei is only passable at best, let's see, he's *dansei no koibito*, he only has sex with other men of his own preferences. He would have no sexual interest in you at all."

"Oh." She frowned. *I make a fool of myself.* "You must think me stupid and useless. Having fits and not knowing what the galley is. How stupid I am!"

"Why in the world would I think that?" Blaine smiled, hiding his pleasure at the fetching blush in her porcelain complexion. It changed her from a very pretty young lady into a stunningly beautiful woman. "I doubt you know Toby very well at all." Blaine sighed, got up from his chair and walked over to sit next to Sachi on the bunk. "Look, I don't really know anything about you, who your parents were or anything else. It's obvious even to a 'foreign devil' like me that your upbringing has quite a few issues. We don't beat people unless they've committed a crime somehow. Clearly someone trained you in hand-to-hand combat, right? And you're good at it?"

"Yes, sir." She felt the warmth of his body, inhaled his scent, clean and manly. Mother Yuko taught her that women ruled men through sex. Oda Yuko taught that everything was a struggle for power and control. Perhaps she was wrong; lovemaking, with the right person, might be an actual act of love and not one of domination and submission.

"Now, do you know how to lay a thirty-two pounder? How to chart a course with chart, sextant, and chronograph? How to set a tack to avoid a lee shore? Do you know how to play baseball?"

"No, sir. I know none of those things, but I can learn them quickly if I must."

"Sachi, honestly, none of those are things you need to know unless you're in the KRN, a sailor or a baseball fan. Not knowing them does not make you stupid and useless."

"Oh."

"Yes, *oh*. No one should be expected to know everything." He gave her a crooked smile. "Now, I do want you to get set up in the galley no later than first thing in the morning watch. I'd like my bunk back. No matter what I do, sooner or later, Emily *will* hear about this and then the rent in Hell will be due and Quan Himself will be there to collect."

"Who is Emily, sir?"

"My wife." He sighed and deflated a bit.

"Many men have both wives and mistresses."

"Yeah, well, I don't have any mistresses. Never have, never will. And only one wife." He set his jaw. "Well, obviously, we need to get your situation settled. Will you give me your word, on your honor and my honor, that you will not attempt any form of suicide, with it a given that the only things that will be required of you shall be no different than those required of any other person aboard this vessel?"

"Yes, sir. *Watashi wa anata ni meiyo watashi no kotoba o ataeru.* I give you my word of honor." She met his eyes for the briefest of moment. "Your vows to her are important?"

"Yes." Sorrow flitted across his face. "Yes, they were the most important thing in my private world once. Now time and circumstance wear away at them. And Emily has changed and now she rends those vows every day. Ah, hell, why am I telling you this?"

"Vows are honor, sir. You maintain your honor regardless of situation." Her face was solemn as her thoughts raced. Blaine was like Papa, a man of true honor. Papa Komiya was only a peasant farmer, but an honorable man. Father Oda Shinji was heir to Clan leadership, but a thief and murderer, only using honor as a cloak, discarding it if it grew uncomfortable. She kept her thoughts hidden, wishing she were good enough to be worthy of the love of someone like Blaine or Papa.

"Yeah, well, honor doesn't always help when Emily wants her pound of flesh for me to see my daughter. Enough of this." He rose from the edge of the bunk and walked to the cabin door. He opened it and spoke briefly with the Marine guard stationed there before turning back to her. "The Bosun will be here in a minute. He will take you to the galley and introduce you properly to Toby. And I think I'll have you written into the Ship's Book as Seaman Apprentice Sachi Takahashi for now. That will give you a place in *Intrepid's* crew, one everyone can understand." There was a knock on the door frame. "Come." Bosun Paul

Beauchamp stuck his head in the cabin. His eyebrows climbed his forehead in surprise when he saw Sachi sitting up in the Captain's bunk.

"What the fuck, Cap'n? Doc said she'd be out for three, four hours?"

"Yeah, he told me that as well." Blaine sat down in his desk chair and picked up his pen again. "Bosun, write Sachi into the Ship's Book as Seaman Apprentice and Cook's Mate Fourth Class. Right after you take her down to Toby's pantry and turn her over to him. She'll be his responsibility going forward. That'll be all, thank you."

"Aye-aye, Cap'n." The Bosun smiled at Sachi, a frightening sight. "Well, lass, get yer butt outta the Cap'n's rack and come with me. Do you have any gear stashed in your hideaway, which, by the way, I'd really like you to explain to me how you got onboard and where you've been hiding these last four weeks?"

***

Sachi stared at the giant in the kitchen. The Bosun had escorted her to collect her things from her hideaways in various parts of the ship, astonished at her ability to fit her tall frame into the smallest spots. Once that was done, he brought her to the Wardroom Galley and introduced her to Toby.

He's huge! His arms are as big around as my legs! No, bigger! His hands are as big as my head! Clear grey eyes solemnly took her measure and a massive hand rubbed over a head of bristly brown hair, liberally shaded with white and grey. Clean shaven, his teeth gleamed whitely as he smiled at her. Pots clattered as he moved about the kitchen, or rather the galley as she now knew the sailors called it.

"Well, aren't you the pretty one, lass?" His voice wasn't as deep as she expected but its rumble still filled the small space. "So, you're to be Cook's Mate, Fourth Class, eh, Apprentice Seaman?"

"*Hai*, uh, I mean, yes. I believe so."

"Ok, first, you need to get used to speaking Terranglais most of the time. I speak some Nisei, but not particularly well. Most of the crew might get a few words, like a joy-girl might use, so if you don't want to be mistaken for a joy-girl, speak Terranglais, got it?"

"Yes, sir."

"Don't *sir* me." Again, the gleaming grin. "Save that for the officers. Look for the gold braid on the shoulders. *Sir* them. Not an honest Petty Officer as myself. Or the Bosun. Address him as the Bosun, anyone with a rocker on their sleeve as Petty Officer and everyone else as Sailor. Except the Marines. Just address them as Marine, or Sir, if they've gold braid. Don't worry about it too much, you're new, there'll be allowances made. Make sure you follow a tight course and you'll be fine. Now, come over here." She followed him to a section of the wall, or bulkhead, she'd heard the sailors call it. He pulled on a piece of rope and the section swung open. A hammock was hung between two frame timbers with a largish locked box under it and a small shelf at one end.

"What is this?" she asked as she peered past him.

"This, lass, will be your bunk or rack, whichever you want to call it, until we reach home in Kolbia and you figure out what you want to do next or where you want to go. This is your space. The officers and Petty Officers can check it, what we call inspection, to ensure everything is shipshape and squared away and that you don't have anything dangerous to the ship in here. Otherwise, it's yours. Other than inspections, no one can enter it without your permission. You understand that?" He handed her a key. "That's the key to the lock. Keep it with you."

"This is mine?" It was tiny and cramped but the idea of a place that was all hers, that she could shut the world out if she wished, that idea was incredible. "All mine?!"

"Yes, Sachi, all yours." The grin gleamed wider than ever.

"And I don't have to let in anyone who wants to have sex with me?"

"Oh, brother. Come over here and siddown." Toby hooked a pair of stools out from under a table and pointed her to one. He rubbed his hair and the grin was replaced with an earnest frown. "Look, while we're at sea, you keep your pants on. No one, not me, not the Captain, not the newest lubber nor the oldest salt, no one can have sex with you, even if you're interested. The answer to anyone who asks is NO. Anyone keeps asking, you come straight to me. If anyone asks at all, you come straight to me. You are off limits for the crew. Those orders will be read out to the entire crew in the morning."

"No one can force me?"

"Oh, for the love of the dear Lord God himself, where did you come from?" Sachi started to open her mouth. "Do not answer that. I don't want to know, all right? Rules on the ship are there for a reason. If you get liberty and go ashore somewhere, the shipboard rules don't necessarily apply, *but* if you say NO, it means NO. You got that, lass?"

"But what if someone is forceful? Everyone on the ship is higher rank than I am, right?"

"You know, whaddya call it, *shizukana ashi no jutsu*, right?"

"Yes, I am considered to be quite skilled in that Art," she slowly answered.

"Can you use it without killing a man?"

"Yes, if need be, but that was not how I was trained."

"Okay, someone, anyone pushes the issue, wants to get into your dainties and tries to do it by force, you pound 'em. Don't kill 'em, just pound 'em flat. Then you come straight to either me, the Bosun or the Captain. You're my shipmate, not a sex toy. Every single, last man-jack on this ship knows better than to raise my ire at them. That clear, now, lass." The grin was back.

"Yes, Petty Officer, very clear." A smile hovered around Sachi's mouth.

"Ah, heck, don't call me Petty Officer, 'les it's official like. You'll know if it is. You call me Toby. I'm supposed to take care of and help you and that's a lot easier when you're friends with each other. How about it?" His gleaming grin grew larger.

"*How about it?* You would be my friend?" Her incipient smile grew bigger.

"Of course. You look like you could use a friend and I like being friends with people. So?"

"Yes, Toby, I will be your friend." Her smile blazed at full force.

"Well, that's settled." Toby's grin gleamed in return. "Now get your butt in your rack. Get some sleep. One bell in the morning watch is awful early and your job will be to help me fix the Captain his breakfast. I figure you'll like that just fine. So, Sachi, friends, yes?"

"Yes, Toby. Friends." Sachi settled into her hammock and pulled the panel shut with the piece of rope. A hook inside secured the panel. She smiled at the rough timbers of the low overhead. Here, on a ship full of inscrutable foreign devils, she had a friend. A friend willing to fight for her. She was still smiling when exhaustion dragged her into dreamless sleep.

Omega 2-Cygni System Command
Virtual Reality Construct
May 1478, Third Age of Imperial Reckoning

"Well, Captain McAllen, let's get this show on the road. What happened?" System Commodore Ethan Collins' image settled into the chair at the head of the table. Of course, the table and chair, like the room and everything in it, did not actually exist anywhere in the entire Omega 2-Cygni system. It was a computer-generated space in Virtual Reality. As were the bodies of everyone attending the conference electronically. And even then, not all of those attending even had physical bodies anymore. More and more of the remaining Confederation survivors lacked bodies as the centuries rolled past.

Commodore Collins was a *VR Gestalt*, an accurate to the nth degree recording of a human mind and personality. VR Gestalts were limited under Confederation law and by real world hardware limitations. It took an amazing amount of memory, processor speed and power, much more in fact, than had been postulated, back in Earth's pre-space early twenty-first century, to be able to provide the capability to record a human being. And even then, a given recorded gestalt might rarely take some very strange turns. Some self-deleted, some went autistic and isolated themselves inside their VR universes and the worst went insane. That was why a gestalt always had a significant delay built into its individual systems when it initially booted up and began interacting with the material world. And the idea of a gestalt being housed in a mobile, human analog body, well, that was still the stuff of science fiction. Power and cooling limitations prevented it. Or at least that had been the case over nine thousand Standard Years ago, when contact with the Confederation had been lost. Now the situation here forced more and more of the Confederation survivors to rely on VR gestalts as time passed.

The fact that Collins was a gestalt limited him to VR conferences and comm-web links. He had been an officer on the staff of the admiral in charge of system defense. His physical body died of multiple cancers from severe radiation poisoning about fifty years after the Quar'taneeka's final attack in this system had its back broken by the arrival of the planetoid sized starship CNS *Thunderchild*.

Thunderchild was one of the earliest of an entire new generation of warships. Roughly the size of Old Earth's Moon, the planetoid class ships housed immense firepower. Confederation naval planners calculated that something with the ruggedness and firepower of a planetoid would be needed for the final battles around the Quar'taneeka home world. *Thunderchild* relieved the distant, beleaguered Omega 2-Cyngi system, crushing the Quar'taneeka forces in the system in less than two days after she arrived. Afterward she provided three days of search and rescue assistance, before hypering out to her next destination. She had been the last contact they ever had with the Confederation.

As the only surviving officer of flag rank in the entire system, the decision to record Collins before his physical death had been an easy one. Over the nine millennia since, things had changed. The survivors who managed to stay in control of most of the space-based technological systems started identifying themselves as *Confederals.* And to keep straight who was who when so many of their interactions with each other were like this one, a meeting in the computer created worlds of Virtual Reality, they eventually wound up categorizing each group.

VR gestalts like Collins were now called *Techneers* and there were over a thousand of them that would no longer communicate with anyone outside their individual VR universes. Those ancient, still corporeal humans spinning out their lives with long durations in medical stasis systems identified themselves as *Consultants.* Their children and grandchildren, the ones that survived the Seekers' efforts to kill them, were known as *Operatives.* In general, Operatives had access to nearly ninety-eight percent of the military grade human enhancements that the Consultants did. But their enemies, the *Seekers,* were relentless in hunting down and assassinating any enhanced human, as enhancement was always a marker sign for a Confederal agent of some type.

Other than Collins and McAllen, Isemoto Station Commander Nariko Fujino and Senior Consultant Marianne Lundgren were attending. Marianne just made it in time, from her current mission in the Kolbian capital. She generally used local transportation systems, horse and buggy or a sailing ship, to get about, but this time she used a heavily stealthed skimmer to reach a comm-web uplink node. They didn't like the fact that everything they tried to achieve had to be done covertly, but the ancient and ongoing shadow-war with their deadly opponents, the Seekers, who also had access to the same kind of technology they did, limited what they could do. The Seekers were brutal and ruthless when they discovered a Confederal agent. Or an active Confederal installation.

Commander Nariko Fujino was the only person awake in her hidden facility in the rugged mountains of the northernmost island of the Isemoto island chain. Isemoto Station lacked the computer power needed to host a VR gestalt on site. The other fourteen individuals assigned there were currently in stasis, leaving Fujino to her lonely watch. Her only connection to the comm-web was maintained through hundreds of tiny, frequency-agile, stealthed nodes.

"Two days ago, my D.A.V.E reported the activation of the System Defense Node Command Key uplink for about half a second. We received two hundred and twenty-eight valid characters for system access before the signal collapsed and the system buffer automatically purged the data. I've instructed my D.A.V .E. to ensure any data received in the future is retained in the system. I chopped a copy of what little we were able to recover over to the Techneers Collective, Commodore. It isn't much. Basically, only a general location, somewhere in the western hemisphere. And I've also sent copies to all of your individual D.A.V.E. systems."

"I see." The Commodore's blond-haired image rubbed his chin. "Wasn't the Key lost with the Schmidts? Seventeen or eighteen years ago, wasn't it?"

"Yes, sir. About sixteen years now, sir," Nariko spoke up. "The Seekers used an Orbital Area Denial System, a *crowbar* attack, to knock down their skimmer. They then dumped all four heavy Kinetic Energy Weapon rods from an orbital killsat. One of the KEWs was a direct hit on the skimmer. Killed Hitomi and Wilhelm and their two-year-old daughter. I was fresh out of stasis and still in medical recovery when the Schmidts left on their mission. Lieutenant Moreland was on duty. The plan was, far as I have been informed, that once the Schmidts got where they were going, he was taking my spot in stasis, and I'd have the watch for the next hundred years. I never met them physically before they left Isemoto Station, so I didn't know the daughter's name. But I caught the job of analyzing the Seekers attack on them."

"Her name was Caitlyn. I was her godparent. I never got to meet her." Marianne bitterly interjected. Tears glittered in her black eyes. "I only saw pictures of her. Beautiful child. Something else I owe those Seeker bastards for."

"I understand, Marianne. I'm sorry this opens old wounds. But then, we all have plenty of those." Collins smiled sadly. "But we need to focus on this. Could it be possible the Node Key survived the kinetic weapon strike?"

"Unlikely, sir." Commander Fujino answered, shaking her head. "Their skimmer was the best stealthed bird we had. The Seekers didn't locate it until they were over the main island of Isemoto itself. Something gave them away, no idea what. The Seekers used the OADS to knock the skimmer down. I believe the Schmidts may have survived the downing of the skimmer, but the follow-up attack...no way. The first three of the KEWs hit in the mountains less than a thousand meters north of the skimmer's crash site. The last one literally hit the skimmer dead center. That thing would have killed a heavy cruiser or knocked the hell out of a dreadnought. No way anything survived. The local Nisei peasant farmers thought a volcano had erupted."

"I see." Collins sighed and rubbed his forehead. "Damn I'm getting old. And tired, I think. All these years. The memories seem to hurt more, not less as time passes. I remember this starting, damn as near nine thousand years ago. Whatever that damn thing was, *Angra Mainyu*, or whatever they called it, a warp angel, or a ghost, demon, spirit, whatever it was, it started this insanity then. It has a lot to answer for. I was still breathing when the first splits started." For a moment, the three women thought that Collins showed every year of his thousands of years of virtual life. They waited patiently, out of respect. More and more, the Techneers were tending to wander in their own memories. Collins was no exception. "It started with the indigenous species, at least the ones that survived the Quar'taneeka's last strikes. The Elves and Dwarves we called them. Rightfully or wrongfully, they blamed us for bringing the Quar'taneeka here. Then we started getting splits internally. Most people were busy trying to survive and then these utter loons started their Armageddon cult, yapping that it was Angra Mainyu, that *thing* they claimed was their new god, it was its will that the world die. Howling lunatics. We ignored them at first, hell we were still busy doing SAR missions, saving lives, both humans and the locals. Then they nuked one of the three surviving Orbital Defense Centers and dusted the other one with goddamn weaponized nanites! Now it's just a shell over the southern hemisphere."

"I lost a lot of friends there, Commodore." Marianne Lundgren spoke up, quietly remembering the insanity of those days. "I remember they got started in Isemoto, where most of the Japanese language group's survivors had started settling. *Sekai no shi no shika* they called themselves, Seekers of the World's Death. But they spread far and fast. We'd just survived one war and now we were in another one. It became a shadow war no one ever saw coming. And that thing, *Angra Mainyu*, whatever it was, was responsible. I remember a good friend of mine speculating that the thing could control or influence minds somehow. I'd guess so, given that my *friend* went over to the Seekers." Lundgren was quiet for a long moment. "I killed him before he could blow the last ODC's reactor."

"At least they never managed to get control of the last ODC, or any of the major medical facilities. Far as we know all the original Confederation personnel that joined the Seekers are long dead. And they never had access to the computer power they would've needed to record any gestalts. But they managed to spread their damn cult far and wide. We know there's still a Seeker Inner Circle that has access to a hell of a lot of Confederation tech and no compunctions about using it. These days they have so many goddamn flunkies, people who have no idea who they're actually working for or what the end goal is." McAllen spoke up for the first time. "And now they may have their goal in sight. That Kuiper Belt planetoid in its degrading orbit we picked up twenty-two years ago will do what both the Quar'taneeka and the Seekers want, utterly destroy this world when it hits. And Commodore, all the computer simulations say there's still enough firepower in the system to at least shove it into a different orbit, generate a miss of millions of kilometers. But coordinating that much firepower, that widely spread...well that'd be impossible without a full up AI to handle everything, at least a Class Three. A Class Two would be better, and a Class One would make the job a cinch."

"Well, Captain McAllen, our last AI died when the damn Seekers nuked Roland, five thousand years ago, didn't it?" Collins rubbed his brow. "This has dragged on and on, every time something like civilization gets a start, gets a foothold towards rebuilding a technological society, like we did with Roland and the Empire he was creating, those psychotic nut-cases come out of their holes and tear it down. They stir the local species, the Elves and Dwarves, up against the humans if they can, use modern or semi-modern weapons if they must. Get some of the *real* exotic species, fighting against everyone, utter chaos. Goddamn Seekers are bloody insane. It has never made sense." The anger and frustration in Collins' voice was clear and shared by all of them.

"Yes, sir. The destruction of Roland's empire was the last time we dared use any of our few remaining orbit capable vehicles. We lost too damn many of them and even worse, their crews, to Seeker strikes using hyper missile launchers or directed energy weapons. I've been stuck up here ever since, rotating in and out of stasis, each of us still up here standing a hundred-year long watch and returning to sleep away nine hundred years. On a day-to-day basis, the Seekers have access to more planetary-based firepower and more hardware than we do, at least when you don't consider the platforms in solar orbits. Of course, the Solar Orbiting Mirror Array is still under our control. But given that its best targeting footprint on Rybithia would be a glass crater about a hundred thousand kilometers across, well, the SOMA ain't exactly a precision weapon. And we would need to get that targeting footprint to under a hundred meters to either shift the oncoming planetoid's orbit or outright destroy it." McAllen shrugged. "In planetary orbit, we have rough parity, but we generally don't kill cities just to get one of their cells. They *will* do that to kill one of our Consultants. But even they normally just use an assassin team. Even as tough as someone like Marianne is, an axe will eventually take her head off."

"Okay, people, enough on our little covert war with the damn Seekers. What about the Key? And whatever it was that tried to use the Key to access the comps on the *Backhand Blow*?" Collins pulled everyone back onto topic. "Could the Key have survived the downing of the Schmidt's skimmer? Could they have ejected it before they got it? If someone found it, could they use it by accident?"

"The data we have indicates the Schmidts knew they'd been located and targeted. The skimmer did go into an evasive pattern, but nothing could have dodged an entire OADS crowbar strike. That was nearly a thousand one-meter tungsten rods burning down at orbital speeds. Hitomi was likely the pilot and she did a hell of a job just to survive that and get a crippled skimmer down in one piece. Didn't do them any good, the KEW strike was less than two minutes later. They never had a chance once they were detected." Fujino shook her head. "I've seen the data. Unfortunately, we don't have anything other than the skimmer's telemetry. No audio, video or black box info survived."

"Is there any fashion that the Key's code could have been recorded somehow? Any means that any of that data McAllen received could have survived without the Key itself still being in one piece?" Collins raised an eyebrow as he leaned forward in his chair. The other three exchanged troubled looks as a heavy silence settled over them.

"No, sir. Not possible. The Key could not be copied. The Key's contents, from the day it left Old Earth, was under a Code Black security classification. Need-to-know didn't begin to cover it. I have suspicions about it. But technically, I could be violating either OPSEC or INFOSEC articles just by mentioning it. Wilhelm had primary clearance. He probably knew exactly what was in there, but I doubt anyone else did." Fujino shrugged.

"Not going to worry about either Operational or Information Security right now. If someone from the Confederation wants to show up and arrest us, well, that'd be fine and dandy with me. However, if we're using Occam's Razor, we now know that somehow, either the Key itself *or* some of the data it held managed to survive the direct hit by a KEW on the skimmer carrying it." Collins caught and held everyone's attention until he got consenting nods. "Do we have any data on the construction of the Key itself?"

"Yes, sir," Fujino answered. "It was a four-centimeter collapsium armored molycirc mono-block. Enhanced capacity of twelve point one exabytes for file storage. With a suitable support system, the mono-block could function as a

ten to the twentieth power exascale multi-core processor. The damn thing held
the potential to have more memory and more processing power than all the
remaining computer systems in the entire Omega Cygni-2 system."

"That's enough storage and power to run a Class One AI and have power
left over. Wow." McAllen tipped her chair forward and rested her elbows on the
table. "Why in Hell has it been sitting in storage down in Isemoto Station all
this time? Was it an AI storage system of some type, Nariko?"

"I don't know for sure. Class One and Two AIs were restricted access outside of the Sol system itself, at least until the Quar'taneeka War blew up in
our faces. About twenty-five to thirty-five percent of the time they go insane
without a proper symbiotic human partner. People capable of handling that
kind of symbiosis were few and far between, at least until the last century of
the War." Fujino looked uncomfortable. "That was when the Confederation
Council eased the restrictions on human genetic engineering, specifically to
provide people capable of handling the strain of AI symbiosis. It wasn't always
successful. The Class Two and Class One AIs were proving to be capable of
coordinating strikes that the Quar'taneeka just couldn't defend against. But
they needed a human symbiote capable of handling the strain of a full spectrum
neural link up. By themselves, those AIs could be flaky as hell. Initially we didn't
have any AIs above Class Four or a suitable human symbiote here in system.
When the Schmidts brought the Node Key with what I guess was a dormant
Class One AI from Confederation Naval HQ back on Old Earth, they brought
a symbiote as well. We just would have had to wait for her to grow up."

"Oh my God." Marianne breathed. "I do not like what I'm hearing, Nariko.
I came out from Terra with Hitomi and Wilhelm back then. Rode the same
transport ship. I could not for the life of me figure out why they'd brought their
unborn daughter with them. That was when Hitomi asked me to be Caitlyn's
godmother. Of course, she was held in stasis in a neonatal replicator all this
time. She wasn't even a baby; she was just a fetus then. You're saying Caitlyn
was supposed to be a Class One AI symbiote?"

"Yes. At least that's my belief. I don't really know, but what evidence we have left points that way. No one knows for sure now. I wasn't in the loop when Wilhelm and Hitomi were brought out of stasis. I only know that they were woken up out of sequence when we first detected the inbound Kuiper Belt planetoid." Nariko looked down at the virtual tabletop as she spoke. "Isemoto Station was deemed the most secure back then, so the Schmidts were held in stasis there. They rotated in and out less often than our other personnel. It was on a need-to-know basis. At the time, no one expected the development of the Planetoid class starships, so it was thought that a human/AI symbiotic team would provide the best defense, with a sufficient material base. Given all the other oddities of this system, I'd guess the Navy decided to start testing the program here. At least, that's what my information and some educated guesses tell me. There's a lot of holes, however. Holes we'll likely never be able to fill. And all of this was classified to *kill yourself before even thinking about it* levels back then. Class One AIs and their capabilities gave the Confederation Senate the heebie-jeebies. Not to mention the ethical considerations involved with the gene-engineered symbiote humans. The Schmidts were on one of the last ships to arrive here, back before the Quar'taneeka stopped raiding this system and settled in to besiege us. There's no one left who knew their assignment, or really anything else specific about them."

"Is it possible that Hitomi was maneuvering not to evade the crowbar strike, but to eject a survival pod? With Caitlyn and that damn cube in it?" Marianne's fists clenched.

"Possible but unlikely. We swept the area as soon as we could. There was no wreckage, of course. No beacon, nothing. The locals were and still are very insular and uncommunicative with outsiders. I don't see any way Caitlyn could have survived, even if they ejected her. She was two, for God's sake. It was winter and a bad one. It's just not possible. I'm sorry, Marianne."

***

"Okay, that's enough. We know the Schmidts and their daughter, regardless of potential, are dead. What about the signal Capt. McAllen received?" Collins interrupted. As a VR gestalt it was much easier to hide his thoughts from the others. *This has gone far enough. Marianne will want to go off chasing literal ghosts. She's too important where she is, damn it. Why the hell didn't either Wilhelm or Hitomi tell anyone what their mission was?*

"No idea, sir." McAllen answered. "Buddha bless, things were a hell of a mess after *Thunderchild* left the system. Maybe someone tried to copy the cube, and this is just a 'ghost in the machine' effect. How the hell will we ever know?"

"All right, people. We're just chasing our tails now. I'm officially shelving this as 'weird thing about this damn system, number four thousand, seven hundred and some odd.' With no more than we have, this is just another damn glitch." Collins stood up from his virtual chair. "And we put Marianne at risk, moving her as fast as she had to move to get here. No more of that. Last thing we need is for some idiotic Seeker trying to punch her out with a KEW. This meeting stands adjourned."

The Great Western Ocean
***Imperial Damnation,* off Holden Island**
west-southwest of the Horn Islands
May 1478, Third Age of Imperial Reckoning

Captain Grigori Je'Libe held the wheel of *Imperial Damnation* steady. She was running west-southwest under a fair wind and a dark, hazy sky. It wasn't exactly cloudy, and it certainly wasn't clear. He knew a nice thick fog would be coming up before two bells in the morning watch, right before sunrise. He was stalking a trim little Eindeuten sloop, having caught sight of her cabin lights during the mid-watch. Between sailors' normal early morning grumbles and the expected fog, he had no doubts that he could slip right up next to her and fire a surprise broadside before they knew they weren't alone on the ocean.

"Well, Cap'n, are we going after her?" Thorne came up the ladder onto the quarterdeck and glanced at the compass. There was a newfangled device in a protected mount next to the compass. The Captain had bought the thing a year or so ago from a Kolbian merchant. The Captain called it a storm glass, despite the crafty old Kolbian telling him it was a barometer, whatever that was. Regardless of the name, the device, basically water in a sealed glass container with a kind of spout on the side, was amazingly accurate at forecasting storms and rain. It also helped in determining when the night would be foggy or clear. Currently it was predicting morning fog.

"Yes, Thorne, I think so. She's one of their small, fast sloops, so the cargo is likely quite valuable. The Eindeuten merchants tend to put their most valuable shipments on their fastest ships, said fast ships being one of their smart little sloops, with a good captain." He glanced at the compass and moved the wheel, bringing the ship slightly to port. "We'll go to quarters in a couple of hours, be ready to take her just before dawn."

"You planning to use the witch?"

"Don't know." Grigori calmly met Thorne's eyes. "Honestly, what she did to that galleass scared the holy, howling hell out of me. About once a day I decide to go kill her. Halfway to her cell I change my mind. I can only kill her once. Pretty hard to un-kill her later."

"True."

"Still got a hard-on for her? I don't get that, Two-Toes. I take one look at those long, pointed ears and those cat-eyes and just go *Brrr!* Not to mention the grass-green hair."

"Pretty sure she dyes it somehow. Magic, maybe?" Thorne grinned toothily at his Captain. "I haven't had a chance to see if the rug matches the drapes yet. And with tits like hers, who cares what her face looks like? Not to mention legs that never stop and an ass to die for."

"You're a sick sonofabitch, Thorne; you do know that, right?"

"Why?" Two Toes shrugged. "Because I like variety and exotic pussy?"

"No, because you're crazier than a shithouse rat. Elves and humans shouldn't mix, not that way. It just ain't right. I know I'm a bastard pirate, a thief and a murderer, but, hell, even I got standards about what I stick my prick in."

"And those are your good qualities, right, Cap'n?"

"Just take the fucking wheel, Thorne. I'll be in my cabin; a nap will have me sharp and ready for our prize. Catch a bit of shut eye and think about what to do with our pet."

***

Silaqui heard the Captain coming down the passageway. He stopped outside her cell door and stood there for a long moment. She wondered if this would be the time he would come in and free her from the misery this life had become. She wouldn't give them the pleasure of suiciding but the nightmare she was living would make her welcome death. Especially if she could take some of them with her.

"Ah, fuck it," she heard him mutter, "not tonight, witch. Not tonight." His footsteps resumed and went into his cabin.

"So, not tonight." She laid her head down on the rough sailcloth pallet she used for a bed and wept. She wasn't even sure what she wept for, the fact that he did not come in and kill her or the drudgery and misery of another day of life. "Not tonight." Eventually she slipped into the dream-state that passes for sleep among elves and she dreamed.

***

There was a towering ship sailing on a sea of stars, sail-covered masts reaching for the moon. A tall young human woman standing on the quarterdeck, long dark hair streaming around her. Her black eyes glittered with thousands of lights. Something else looked out of those eyes, something utterly unhuman and ancient and immeasurably powerful. There were others who stood around her, reduced by her power and beauty to vague and amorphous shadows. And there were those around the woman whom she saw clearly. Silaqui saw herself standing to the woman's left, Elf shoulder to shoulder with Human. Close on the woman's right side was an incredible beauty, a young woman marked by luminous sapphire eyes and a sense of intense loving devotion. Other presences stood there as well, nebulous shapes that flickered in and out of the dream reality. A tall man with a blue coat. A frowning human priest. A small, dark young woman, quiet and nimble. A black-haired man stood at the ship's wheel, calm and purposeful.

They confronted something huge and evil, older than even the Fall itself. Something that was Death Incarnate for the entire world. It was coming, slow and purposeful, implacable in the desire to bring an end to all life, all things. Even an end to hope itself. It would destroy even the memory of the world and leave nothing in its wake, not even despair.

Guided by that ancient presence in her mind, the black-haired woman shouted, and a shaft of light, a spear of pure energy, God's own war-spear, sprung from her hand, striking the oncoming Death. It was not enough to do more than slow the juggernaut, but then she gathered more and more light, strengthening the spear. Light poured through her and there was less and less of the young woman and more of the ancient presence. The light burned, slowing Death, and tearing pieces away, flinging them into the Void. With a great shout, she pulled the very light of the Sun itself into the beam and Death shattered into countless shredded pieces, torn to nothingness, and burned away.

Victorious, the woman turned to her companions and they were terrified. Only fragments of the woman survived, and the ancient presence that remained possessed its own purposes. It would remake the world and there would be no place for anything it did not conceive. And it did not conceive of Elves. Or Dwarves, or the countless other speaking folk. The might of a Dragon. The purity of a Unicorn. The beauty of Magic. The power of Love. It would destroy the wonder and magic of the World and create a new world, fashioned as it saw fit, a world built of only cold logic.

But the fragments of the woman persisted, and she loved. Silaqui saw the power of her love; a love strong enough to save the world. The sapphire-eyed beauty flung herself into the struggle, heedless of her own risk, striving against the Ancient. The aura of her love blazed around her like a star. She would surrender everything to save the woman she loved. Silaqui watched in amazement as together, they forced the Ancient back. But they alone would not be enough and Silaqui stepped forward, joining the fray, pouring her power and, yes, her own love for the human woman into the fight. She felt the others join. The dour priest. The clever man in the long coat. The dark young woman. The calm man at the wheel of the ship.

Bonds of friendship and love bound them all together and they forced the Ancient to stop, to step back and look. To reconsider its purpose. It looked at the tattered remnants of the woman that it held in its hands. And it looked at the World and it looked at the Sun. Understanding dawned on its face and it opened its mouth to speak. It said...

The pounding on the door, followed immediately by the clash of the key in the lock and the lantern light flooding into the cell as the door crashed against the wall shattered the dream-state. Everything whirled away, as uncatchable as mist. She screamed in pain and fury. The chain jerked her to a sudden halt as she lunged at the figure in the door, her hands crooked to rend and claw with her nails.

"NOOooo!" she raved. "I must know what it said! We must know, damn you all to your human Hell! WE HAVE TO KNOW!" Rage spent, she collapsed on the deck and began to weep. "We have to know."

"What the fuck?" she heard Je'Libe mutter. "I'll not have a screaming lunatic on my deck." His boot struck her head and reason and consciousness fled.

***

"Damnit, Cap'n, did you kill her?" Thorne snapped from behind Je'Libe.

"No, just knocked her out." He sneered over his shoulder. "Not that you'd care, now would you? She'd still be warm and that's all you want, right?"

"You wound me, Cap'n."

"Sure, I do. Bind and gag her. I think I'll pass on her services this time. I doubt a hysterical, raving sorceress would be worth a fart in a hurricane. I open the door and she goes insane, screaming and clawing, trying to get to me."

"We shouldn't need her magic, not on one of those Eindeuten sloops." Thorne followed his captain back into the passageway.

"I hope not, Two-Toes. God, I hope not."

Chapter Six

Great Western Ocean
KRN *Intrepid*
May 1478, Third Age of Imperial Reckoning

Captain Blaine smiled warmly at Sachi as she followed Toby into his dining cabin. For an instant she met his eyes and her smile lit the room. Then she dropped her eyes and her shoulders slumped. She held the large tray while Toby served Blaine and this evening's dinner guests.

Commander Kevrin Tamras, Captain of KRN *Sorcerer*, sat to Blaine's right. The rest of the dinner guests were the usual suspects: Willis Fleet, *Intrepid's* Second Lieutenant Andrew Hanley, Doctor Hoff, and representing the midshipman officer trainees was Senior Midshipman Johan Weiss. *Intrepid* and *Sorcerer* were both hove to, waiting for stronger winds before attempting to cross the dangerous and mysterious Deeps. Commander Tamras had come aboard earlier in the afternoon to discuss the protocols for the possible hazards of the crossing.

"With all due respect, Captain Blaine, I'm beginning to understand your nickname." Kevrin smiled as he sipped his wine.

"Oh?" Blaine answered quietly, his eyes slightly narrowed.

"Absolutely. Who else but Captain "Bonny" Blaine could find such a beautiful young lady as a stowaway and then get her to serve dinner in his cabin? There's no one else in the entire Navy with such luck! Or such a beautiful 'cook's mate' to serve his meals, what say?" Kevrin laughed as he tossed off the last of his wine.

His laughter died an awkward, painful death as he realized he was the only person in the cabin who was laughing. Blaine's blue eyes were chips of sea ice. Lieutenant Hanley openly glared at him, and Dr. Hoff gave him the same sad regard one might give a gut-shot man. The usual air of slightly goofy geniality around Lieutenant Fleet was instantly replaced by a cold and scornful scowl. And even Midshipman Weiss glowered at him in disgust. He glanced over his shoulder at the woman in question and was startled at what he saw.

Somehow, with a full tray of dishes and drinks, she was down on her knees, head down and holding the tray above her head, up at waist level, where the steward could easily reach it. And she folded herself into that awkward position without making a sound or spilling a drop. She radiated contrition in some bizarre fashion and Kevrin suppressed a swallow at the look of utter contempt he caught on the face of Blaine's gigantic steward. A steward who was a two-time All Navy boxing champion, he belatedly remembered.

"Excuse me? I'm afraid I've given offense somehow?"

"Yes, Commander Tamras, you have. Seaman Apprentice Takahashi is assigned to the galley as an Assistant Cook's Mate. Given the irregularity of her situation, it was simplest to find her a working position on board and put her to work, like any other person. Given her upbringing and worldview, she often has difficulty understanding both Kolbian traditions and naval duties. She is no different than any other sailor and does not serve the Captain in any manner different than any other sailor on this ship. Also, your manners and insinuations are insulting to the young lady regardless of anything else, and I would suggest you apologize to her. Just as you would to any other sailor." By the time Blaine was done with him, Kevrin felt about an inch tall.

"Hmm. Yes, I see." He turned back to the young woman, a teenager really, in question. "Ah, Miz Takahashi, would you please get up?" She flowed to her feet with a single effortless motion. He swallowed hard as she looked him full in the face and her beauty hit him like a hammer. He stammered, "Uh, hmm, er, Ma'am, please accept my apology for any insult I might have given. I truly intended no insult, just a very poorly chosen attempt at humor. I am deeply sorry."

"No offense, Commander Tamras-san. Honorable Captain Blaine-sama would have been within his rights to have me hung. I asked to be allowed to restore Captain Blaine-sama's honor and retain what little personal honor I could. But I am not allowed *seppuku* as it is against your laws. So I do what I can to restore the honor the Captain has lost; honor lost when the Captain restores to me my own honor, pitiful thing that it is. To my family I am now *yakunitatanai no fumeiyona mono,* a dishonorable thing of no use, a disgrace to my ancestors. Toby-san and Doctor Hoff-san both say that there are ways to earn honor other than the ways of my family. Lieutenant Fleet-san says this as well while he teaches me to speak better Terranglais, the intricacies of Kolbian ways and the ways of your Navy." Her voice was soft and just as sexy as the rest of her, despite the coolness in it. But it was the intensity of those black eyes that held him. He'd never seen anyone with truly black eyes before. Pupil and iris could not be told apart. A man could fall into those eyes and be lost forever.

"Uh, yes, Ma'am. I'm sure that your family is wrong, Miz Takahashi." He struggled to swallow around a suddenly too-tight necktie.

"Thank you, Toby, Sachi. Midshipman Weiss can handle the rest." Blaine's calm response relieved most of the pressure in the cabin. "I'm sure you have more pressing duties."

"Aye, Cap'n." Toby answered, setting the trays on the sideboard, and drawing Sachi in his wake with just a glance. An uncomfortable silence descended after the door closed.

"Damn it, Captain Blaine, I *am* sorry for upsetting that girl and my sincere apologies to everyone else as well. But how the hell did she get aboard and stay hidden for nearly four weeks?" Kevrin could feel the blood rushing back to his face.

"From what she told me, she managed to literally squeeze herself aboard by somehow getting through the bloody hawsehole while we were tied up alongside the quay."

"Impossible. Maybe, just maybe her hips would barely fit, but not those shoulders. Not too mention her...ulp, uh, well, it'd be impossible."

"She explained it to me when I asked. It involved her stripping completely naked, covering herself in a slick black grease, then dislocating both of her shoulders. Then climbing up the side of the hull with two dislocated shoulders. All without making a sound."

"Good Lord."

"My thought exactly." Blaine sipped his wine.

"And that's how she got on *Intrepid*, eh? And no one noticed a naked woman covered in grease on the main gun-deck? Sir, when we get back to Carolington, what will the Navy Board, in the person of Admiral Mynheers, have to say?"

"I shudder to imagine." Blaine shook his head. "But she is something special. I don't think we realize just how special yet."

"What makes you say that?"

"Well, I told you a little about the night last week we caught her when you came aboard this afternoon?"

"Yes, Sir."

"Well, Elazar gave her a sedative when she recovered from her seizure. He told me she'd be out cold for at least three or four hours. I've rarely known him to be wrong either, not on medical matters, anyways. Do NOT take his advice on horse racing, however." Laughter filled the cabin as Dr. Hoff colored and acknowledged the hit. "Well, what actually happened went like this. I was writing in my personal diary when I glanced over at where she was still unconscious, I thought, on my bunk, then..."

***

"So that's what happened, Kevrin. Sounds damn near impossible, I know, Lord God I know, but unless we've all lost our minds, from me down to the youngest midshipman, that's what happened." Blaine smiled as he finished the tale an hour later. He shrugged as he sipped an after-dinner whiskey.

"Amazing. Well, for what it's worth, I'll be willing to endorse your report when we get home. What do you suppose will happen to Miz Takahashi?"

"Depends on the Navy Board. On Admiral Mynheers. Most likely, she'll be paid for her service and released. Someone, maybe Lieutenant Fleet here, can take her down to the Nationality Service and help her get her citizenship. After that, she'll just be another citizen." Blaine took a deep breath. It was quiet in the cabin.

"Most likely, none of us will ever see her again after that." Doctor Hoff spoke into the silence.

"Yes." Blaine stared into his whiskey glass. "I'd expect I'll...we'll never see her again." Blaine's throat was strangely tight. Pressed for words, he simply echoed Hoff.

***

"What's wrong, Sachi?" Toby set down the dirty dishes in a tub and turned to confront Sachi.

"That man, Commander Tamras-san, he assumes that neither Captain Blaine-sama nor myself have any sense of honor!" Somehow, the gentle giant always knew when she was upset, and over the last few days she learned it was useless to conceal it from him. She grabbed a steel-wool pad before plunging her arms into the hot water and furiously scrubbing the dirty pots. "If I am to be *used* like that, then so be it. At least I know that if Captain Blaine-sama *did* want to use me like that, he would be gentle and caring. He would not share me around like a bottle of stale sah-keh! This man, this Commander Tamras-san, I feel he would just give me to his crew!" Soap and hot water flew as she attacked the worst of the pans. Toby leaned back against the bulkhead and hid a smile.

"I think you do Commander Tamras a disservice." Toby's tone was calm and relaxed. "So, are you more upset about what he assumes about you or what he assumes about the Cap'n?"

"I am worthless, *haiki mono*, garbage to be thrown away! Captain Blaine-sama is the soul of honor! If I were Samurai, I would prove Commander Tamras-san is without honor on his body!"

"He got you a good bit riled up there, didn't he?"

"Yes! He is mean-spirited and small-souled! I spit on his shadow!" she growled as she scoured away at a bit of baked-on grease.

"Sounds to me like you're more offended by what he assumed about the Cap'n than anything he thought about you, right?"

"Of course! *Ijiwaru baka!*"

"Terranglais, please?"

"Spiteful idiot! Happy?"

"Yep." Toby took a deep breath. Sachi moved like greased lightning at times and he really didn't know just how dangerous she truly was. When the Bosun had deposited her into Toby's care the night she was caught, he told Toby the girl admitted she was a *shinijutsuka*, what the sailors called a black shirt sneak. *Shinijutsuka* was a catch-all term for any Nisei who operated with silence and stealth, thieves, spies, and assassins. They were dangerous and unpredictable. Toby was confident he was tacking nicely on the broad reach here, but he knew he would quickly be sailing into heavy seas and nasty squalls with the topic he had in mind. He let out the breath, gently reached out and put his hand on Sachi's shoulder and gently turned her to face him, her hands still in the tub.

"So, are you ready to admit you're at least halfway in love with Cap'n Blaine, yet?" His voice was low and soft. No one would overhear him. And he wasn't surprised when she froze, elbow-deep in hot water. Her black eyes were huge as she stared at him in the light of the galley's lanterns. For a long moment, she stood there, staring at him. Then she twitched out of his grasp and turned back to the tub.

"You are insane, Toby-san! I am of no worth, trained only to whore and kill! Now, I am *nokemono, kirawareta, owareta;* an outcast, hated, hunted. They will butcher me like a pig when they find me! My fam...they have a long reach. They will find me and anyone I might care for. You are safe here, in the Navy. They hate and fear your Navy and they will not seek you out. So I will not love anyone. Not even the ship's cats. Love is for the worthy and wholesome, the truly honorable. Not for me! No one will ever love me!" Her hands blurred as she scrubbed blindly at the pot.

"Sachi, I understand but lass..." he began.

"No, *gaijin, fuketsuna banzoku!*" He was surprised at her snarl as she interrupted him. The meek and mostly submissive Nisei girl vanished like fog as she snapped at him. "You do not understand, foreigner, filthy barbarian that you are! Captain Blaine-sama does not, can not, must never care about me or what becomes of me! I am *kachinonai*, worthless! He is not to care about me! I am a walking curse, bringing only damnation to those around me! I should throw myself into the ocean, but he made me give him my word! And so am I bound by his honor and the last scraps of what little honor I have left! But it is *all* I have left and foolishly, I shall treasure it!" She pulled the pots out of the soapy water and thrust them into the clean rinse water before quickly clattering them into their rack to dry. "The pots are clean. May I be dismissed, Senior Petty Officer Tobias Wilkerson-san?" She bowed from the waist and her hair came loose from its bun and cloaked her face. Toby was shocked and stunned. He was silent for a considerable time before he answered her.

"Yes, Seaman Apprentice Sachi Takahashi, you are dismissed until the afternoon watch."

Sachi straightened from the bow, barely meeting his eyes before she fled the galley. But it was long enough that he saw the tears in hers. She vanished from the galley like a ghost, fleeing into the depths of the ship, unseen by anyone.

"Well, ye daft ijit, that did nay go so well, now, did it?" Toby sighed to himself as he turned back to the tub of wash water to dump it out. "God damn me for a Quan-taken fool! Where the hell did this blood come from? Did the lass cut herself?" The water and few remaining suds in the wash tub was stained red with more blood than soap. So was the rinse water and there were bloody finger marks on the racked pots. He plucked the steel-wool pad out of the water. It was soaked with her blood. There was a bloody handprint on the door frame. He stuck his head out into the passageway, but she was long gone. And when Sachi Takahashi decided to truly disappear, it wasn't worth the effort it took to try and find her. "Oh, damnit, Sachi." He sat down on an upturned tub and rubbed away his own tears. "What kind of monster in all the Seven Hells destroys someone like her?"

Deep in the bowels of the ship, Sachi sought out her favorite refuge, buried deep in the stacks of sailcloth. She wormed her way into a pile and into one of her still extant nests. There she curled up into a ball of misery, tears seeping from eyes tightly shut. When Sota rubbed his whiskers against her hand, she blindly reached out and wrapped her arms around the cat. He meowed in slight protest, more *pro forma* than anything before he settled down and pushed himself against her, purring deeply against her chest. Then the tears and the sobs did come, buried in the depths of the ship where no one human could hear her. And even before she finally stopped crying, the bloody abrasions on her hands, where she had unknowingly scrubbed the skin completely off her fingers and palms, were completely healed.

***

Commander Kevrin Tamras stood braced on the quarterdeck of his command, the twenty-two-gun sloop-of-war KRN *Sorcerer* and sipped his hot tea. He was watching Lieutenant (JG) Dorian Rosetten, the ship's Third Lieutenant, instructing *Sorcerer's* six midshipmen in the method of taking the noon sighting with a sextant. Things were changing in the Kolbian Republican Navy and this would be the last group of midshipmen that would learn command, seamanship and Navy practices and traditions the 'old fashioned' way, as officer candidates spending six to ten years on board a ship as a midshipman. Next year the new Naval Academy would start its first class, a more efficient method of training the officers the expanding Navy needed.

Kevrin shrugged. Change was the way of the world, at least in Kolbia. He took a moment to eyeball the lookouts stationed on the bow, stern and both mastheads. They were crossing the Deeps. Legend said the water here was eight or nine miles deep, deep enough to stack three of the tallest mountains in Kolbia on top of each other and still not break the surface. There were things living in the depths here unknown to man. Occasionally ships making this passage simply vanished. And sailors liked to tell sea-stories. But sometimes, sea-stories were true. Over the last fifty years, twenty-eight known Kolbian ships, fifteen of them naval vessels, disappeared crossing the Deeps.

Ships crossing the Deeps would clear for action and raise every possible sail. *Sorcerer* practically flew across the water, every sail set to the royals. Stu'nsails were set to port and starboard on every yardarm, from the main course to the topgallants on both foremast and mainmast. Sailing on the broad reach with a freshening wind behind her, *Sorcerer* was flying, making just under eighteen knots. They were cleared for action and the crew stood at quarters, the ten long eighteens double-shotted and the twelve thirty-two pounder carronades loaded with ball and a double stand of grapeshot.

Intrepid was nearly four miles to windward, the longer, bigger frigate carrying more sail and cutting through the waves a bit slower than *Sorcerer*, but Kevrin figured she might still be making fourteen or maybe even fifteen knots. He grinned at the distant ship. She was too far away to make out men on her decks, but he imagined life on her had gotten, as the Han people would say, *interesting*. That disastrous dinner last week came to mind as he watched *Intrepid* heel into her mountain of canvas. Seaman Apprentice Sachi Takahashi was the most beautiful woman he thought he'd ever seen but, oh dear and fuzzy angels above, the *baggage* she came with!

Well, all things considered I think I'm glad she's over there and not on my ship! I think. The situations Blaine finds himself in sometimes! But he always manages to fall in the cesspool and come up with a rose, the gold ring and smelling like the finest Geullian perfume. He's a captain I'd follow into battle without compunction but oh Lord, he's likely to get into a very deep crack this time. Not to mention the grief that hag he's married to will give him. Brrr! Glad I'm single. I'd like to be a fly on the wall when Admiral Mynheers starts in on his report! Or, maybe not.

"Deck, there!" The call came from the lookout on the mainmast head. "Rapid shoaling ahead! Two points to port!"

"What the...?!?" Tamras jumped onto the port rail and grabbed a halyard. He leaned out over the water, trying to spot the shoal the lookout saw. He went white when he realized what he was seeing. He leaped back onto the quarterdeck. "Oh, hellfire and damnation!"

"Captain?" Lieutenant Rosetten dropped his sextant and spun around at the panic in his Captain's voice.

"HARD TO STARBOARD! PORT BROADSIDE, STAND TO YOUR GUNS!"

"What the hell, Captain?" Lieutenant Rosetten yelled.

"That's no shoal! It's alive and heading straight for us! Launch the signal rocket! Red rocket, Dorian, red rocket!" Rosetten's face paled and then he turned and scrambled up the ladder to the poop deck. A moment later, a six-inch signal rocket screamed into the sky, rising over a thousand feet before exploding with a thunderous report into an enormous cloud of red smoke. Gun ports slammed up and *Sorcerer* bared her teeth as the stubby carronades and long eighteens snouted out the ports. Water began to hump up as whatever it was continued to rise from the depths. The thing rolled on its side and a gaping maw half the length of *Sorcerer's* hundred and thirty-five feet sucked in enough of the ocean that the ship was suddenly sliding *down* a wall of water, accelerating as she dropped. Tamras could hear the stays groan under the pressure.

"We get one chance, lads! Steady! Wait for the command!" he screamed at the top of his lungs. The thing rolled closer. It vaguely resembled one of the great sharks often found on the west coast of Kolbia, but a hundred times bigger. He realized that what he thought were hairs at the edge of its mouth, were in fact, short tentacles about ten feet long. A long fin stretched the length of its ventral side and a multitude of fins the size of a frigate's fore staysail ran down its flank. *It goes on forever! It's longer than* Intrepid *is, much less my poor sloop.* The thing finished its roll and the massive head snapped forward with horrifying speed.

"FIRE!" The guns bellowed as one, five long eighteens and six thirty-two pounders blasting iron shot and grape into the monster. Pinkish blood and grayish fluid splashed dozens of feet into the sky. The thing screeched in pain, a sound like a million steam kettles rupturing at once. But it wasn't enough. The obscene jaws closed around *Sorcerer* and literally bit her in half. Commander Kevrin Tamras was one of the first to die, crushed to an unidentifiable pulp, along with *Sorcerer's* waist and most of her crew. The monster thrashed its head in the wreckage, ripping her to pieces, the short tentacles on the edge of its mouth plucking screaming sailors out of the water and shoving them down its throat. In less than thirty minutes from the time the lookout sighted the creature, KRN *Sorcerer* was gone.

***

"Hullo the deck!" came the cry from one of the lookouts aloft. "Red rocket from *Sorcerer!* Red rocket!" Blaine's head snapped up and he rushed to the port side of the quarterdeck, followed closely by Caplin. A red cloud of smoke was slowly dispersing above *Sorcerer.* Blaine clamped a death grip on the rail. That cloud meant *Ship is lost, do not attempt aid.* Like *Sorcerer, Intrepid* was sailing cleared for action, all sail set, and all guns loaded and manned. He watched in horror as the monster, whatever it was, ripped the sloop apart and picked her crew out of the scattered bits of wreckage. Before it was over most of his crew was at the rail, watching the loss of their squadron mates in horror.

"Well, I guess we're next on the menu, Harry." Blaine turned to look forward on what would likely be his last command. Probably the last day of his life. The creature seemed to be longer than *Intrepid* herself and likely much more massive. Quietly the crew turned to face him. "Well, boys, we're in a pickle sure enough. Stand to your guns and make the fastest reloads of your lives. We throw twice the broadside of *Sorcerer*. The beastie doesn't seem in any great hurry to come eat us, so we should get three shots at the creature. Let's show it that a frigate will stick sideways in its craw!" Caps and hats flew as the crew cheered. "To your guns, boys, and stand fast! Listen to your officers and be sharp and quick!"

***

Since that disastrous dinner, Sachi stayed away from everyone, at least as her duties allowed. Normally, if the sun was up, she disappeared into the bowels of the ship. At night, she was sometimes found on the forecastle, huddled between the bowsprit and the windward cathead. She was meticulous in her duties, but she rarely spoke to anyone, even to Toby. Twice Toby found her locked in the throes of one of her seizures. Today she was part of the all-hands watch, taking her place along the rail in her favorite spot between bowsprit and cathead.

She stood upright, a death-grip on the shroud-lines as *Sorcerer's* sails vanished.

No, no, no! This cannot be! It will come for us next. Because I am cursed, we will all die. No, please, Ancestors, no!

She was standing there, terrified, as the monster finally turned away from the last bits of floating wreckage that was a proud warship only moments ago and started toward *Intrepid*.

"NO!" she screamed once, then the lightning shock of one of her fits surged through her and the world fled away. But not to darkness and silent nothingness this time.

VR Construct, Rybithian Orbit

Again she stood in the gray nothingness. The small silver statue stood there. Somehow, it conveyed concern and worry to her. Again, she saw the two words, followed by the stacked dots and the numbers. This time the numbers were new, a three and a four, followed by the strange leaning bar and zeros. And this time she was not nude. A strange, one-piece, blue suit covered her snugly from head to toe. A strange helmet encased her head and tinted glass enclosed her face. Beneath the suit, there was another garment that completely enveloped her body, sinfully comfortable, soft and tight at the same time.

The statue recaptured her attention and pointed at a black square to her right.

That's new. I've never really seen anything but the statue and the words and numbers before. What is that small black speck?

As she looked at it, there was a sensation of incredible speed. She tried to scream as she fell into the speck, a black nothingness which became a night sky filled with stars. For a heartbeat she saw stars all around her, and then there was a globe below her. It glowed with a beautiful blue and white loveliness, and a cobalt line haloed it. Then the Sun rose around the edge of the globe and lit the world.

Is this the whole world? How am I seeing this? This isn't possible, only the Ancestor Spirits see the world this way, or maybe the foreigners' God.

Suddenly, strange symbols filled her sight. Cones and circles and triangles and lines pointed to more things that floated in this darkness with her, hundreds, maybe thousands, maybe even more. It was overwhelming. She shook her head, struggling to understand what she was seeing. It made no sense. She saw the little silver statue. It was standing quietly, patiently at her side, waiting. She looked at it.

"Why am I here?" she said, or maybe just thought.

::Mission threat.::

"YOU CAN SPEAK!"

::System Memory limitation. Acceptable damage, mission asset forced upgrade. Imminent threat, death, loss, bodily harm, mission asset.::

"You can speak!"

::Action required. Imminent threat.::

"What? What threat?" Somehow the statue grabbed her attention and pulled it to the world below her. With no sensation of falling, she plunged into the air above the world, a great ocean spread out before her. She fell further, an angel ejected from Heaven. Abruptly she stopped. She saw a ship with a blue circle around it. Headed slowly toward it was a sea monster bigger than the ship, a red pulsing square boxing it.

::Action required. Imminent threat, death, loss, bodily harm, mission asset.::

"Is that *Intrepid*? And the monster?"

::Affirmative. Action required. Imminent threat, death, loss, bodily harm, mission asset.::

"What can I do? How am I seeing this?"

::Mission asset. System selection required.:: Words and symbols flooded through her mind, an overwhelming tide of information. She understood none of it. Pain cascaded through her. ::System selection required. Action required. Imminent threat, death, loss, bodily harm, mission asset.:: A pulsating red box surrounded five things, strange words she did not understand. ::System selection required.::

"What do you want me to do? What are these things?"

::System selection required.::

She screamed in silent frustration. The red box and the things in it pulsed in front of her. The symbols were more of the strange almost letters. Understanding drifted just beyond her reach. They were red and the square around the monster was red. They pulsed in unison.

"Are these weapons?"

::Affirmative. System selection required.::

"Will this save *Intrepid*?" She did not understand the statue's response. *If these are weapons, does it want me to pick one? Which one?* Confused and uncertain, she regarded the red glowing symbols. One of the words, she supposed, was composed of six symbols. *In Terranglais, katana is six letters. I think this might be a type of katana. Oh Ancestors, please guide me.* She pointed at the symbols. "That one." Her voice held more conviction than she thought it should.

::System selection confirmed. Minimum Safe Distance: Nominal. Commands accepted. Initiating system activation.::

"What's happening?" she asked after what seemed to be an interminable delay.

::System activation successful. Target lock: Nominal. Firing. Target neutralized. Mission asset secured. System deactivation successful.::

She looked down and saw a vast cloud of vapor and steam, rising into the very heavens around her. *Intrepid* pitched wildly in the suddenly choppy seas and she realized small fragments of the sea monster were splashing down into the ocean, some of the bits landing on the ship. With no warning, Heaven brutally kicked her the rest of the way to earth. The deck smashed against her face as she was thrust back into her body and she tasted her own blood. She coughed and saw blood splatter on the deck. Pain flooded through her; not even Maho on her best day ever inflicted so much. She screamed in anguish and thrashed feebly. Just before blackness claimed her, she saw Toby come rushing up.

Omega 2-Cygni System Command
CNS *Backhand Blow*

So far it had been a quiet duty cycle. Captain McAllen relaxed in the command couch, linked with the ODC's computer systems. She knew the Seekers would love to blow the *Backhand Blow* out of the sky, but unless they were willing to use every weapon they had left, *BB* wasn't going anywhere. And even then, it wouldn't be a sure thing for them. On the other hand, there wasn't a lot McAllen could do to the Seekers either. The Confederals would not authorize the use of what were still called Weapons of Mass Destruction on a population center. Even if the Grand High Poo-Bah of all Seekers decided to hide there. And the Seekers knew it. So went the game of cat and mouse, with the two opponents taking turns being the cat and the mouse. In the long run, it made Debbie McAllen's intelligence gathering, coordination and monitoring job boring as hell.

::Warning: Unknown, unauthorized activation of System Defense Link-Sat KG5184 detected. System hijack, activation and targeting in process. ODC Command Node Link is locked out.:: Her D.A.V.E.'s voice harshly jerked her out of her complacent mood.

"Say WHAT?"

::Captain McAllen, I am working to break into the Defense Link-Sat system, but the probability of the satellite firing before I can access the override approaches unity, plus or minus two percent.::

"Who is linking into it and how? Any idea on targeting? Please, Dear God and Holy Buddha, please not a populated area, please?"

::Negative information on Defense Link-Sat system access method and controlling entity. Level of Defense Link-Sat system access and control combined with System Command Node access lockout suggests an AI of at least Class Five or better. Targeting information only access is available.::

"That's not possible, we know there aren't any AIs of any class left anywhere in the whole damn system! What will it hit?"

::Target is an uncatalogued indigenous aggressive aquatic species. One hundred sixty-eight point four meters in length, estimated weight of twelve hundred metric tons, plus or minus three hundred tons. Oceanic sailing vessel in threat range of specimen appears to be a Republic of Kolbia naval vessel. Evidence of a second vessel possibly destroyed by the specimen within six kilometers.::

"Holy shit. A Goddamned fish?! What is KG5184 armed with and what's being activated?"

::KG5184 is armed with multiple weapons systems. Only the main energy weapon is powering up. System hijack is targeting.::

"Shit. What's the e-weapon?"

::A forty-centimeter graser.::

"Oh my God! How close is the ship?"

::Sailing vessel is currently at nominal safe distance, assuming weapon release and firing within the next thirty-eight seconds. Atmospheric and oceanic disruption will create a medium acceptable risk to vessel. Query: Importance of sailing vessel to require emergency orbital weapons release?::

"No idea. Is there a spy-sat that can be tasked to observe the ship, assuming it survives what's coming?"

::Nothing currently available. Passive coverage available in three hours, twenty-six minutes, thirty-five seconds.::

"Okay. D.A.V.E., make sure we get as much data as possible. I want to know what the hell is so important that some poor beastie gets a graser big enough to kill a battlecruiser used on it to preserve a wooden sailing ship."

::Acknowledged. Weapon firing.::

"Yeah. Yuck. That made a mess. I never did like sushi. Damage estimate to the sailing ship?"

::Total damage is minor. Loss of sail area minor. Minor damage to masts and yardarms. Hull nominal.::

"Copy. Ensure a full recording of this gets chopped over to the Techneers' data collective. See if we can get any of them to chew on it, see what we're missing? Copies noted Important to Commodore Collins, Commander Nariko Fujino and Senior Consultant Marianne Lundgren. If this is some new Seeker trick, we could be in big trouble if they can penetrate our data nets. Lord knows, we can't really get into theirs. Also, check and see if there is any possible Confederal connection to anyone on that boat. First, we get that *fluke* uplink from something that tried to say it was the System Defense Node Command Key and now this. What the hell? All of a sudden, something has changed on this mudball and we'd better figure it out quick or something is gonna bite us right on the ass."

::Command acknowledged. Null inputs on last comment.::

"Don't worry about it, D.A.V.E., you ain't that bright."

Chapter Seven

KRN *Intrepid*: Approaching the Horn Islands
May 1478, Third Age of Imperial Reckoning

BLAINE REALLY WANTED TO get drunk. Actually what he really wanted was to get hammered, three-sheets-to-the-wind-blasted, wake-up-with-the-three-cheapest-ugliest-whores-on-the-entire-coast, why-are-my-britches-and-drawers-flying-from-the-city-hall-flagpole, plastered off his ass. Frankly, he briefly considered tossing his commission out the stern window, turning command over to Lieutenant Commander Caplin and locking himself in the cabin until they got home. He'd tell that prick Admiral Mynheers to shove the fucking mainmast up his ass and then go stay falling-down stupid-drunk for three years or until his liver gave it up, whichever came first.

Since leaving Isemoto, this entire voyage was a nightmare, and it just seemed to keep getting worse. He knew it was no one person's fault, but he didn't want the crew getting the idea that it might be...oh, say, Sachi's fault. That she was cursed. Ninety-nine times out of a hundred, Kolbians were hard-headed, practical folk with no time for magic and curses. But sailors saw much more of the wide world and they knew for a fact there were some truly odd things out there.

Intrepid was four or five days from raising the Horn Islands. The nightmare and miracle of the Deeps was a week behind them. After that monster had been killed, obliterated by whatever burned that hole in the sky and sent a line of fire down from the heavens, the ocean heaved and tossed like a man in agony and the weather had been chaotic at best, winds from first one direction and then the opposite. They'd been two days limping along on jury-rigged spars while they made repairs. Two men had been killed, a Marine private lost overboard in the thrashing seas; the other, a sailor crushed by a falling yardarm. And there were dozens of other injuries. One man would likely lose a leg, another an eye. But most of them would recover completely.

The loss of *Sorcerer*, gone with all hands, weighed on him. He knew he wasn't at fault, but he was the commander of this ad-hoc squadron and writing the letters to those men's families would fall to him. And Sachi worried him also.

Toby had found her on the forecastle, unconscious in a pool of blood. Her clothes were soaked with it, blood dripping out of her eyes, her nose, even her ears. Literally her entire body dripped blood. Blood oozed out of every pore in her skin for six hours. Dr. Hoff could not find anything wrong with her to account for the blood loss. It wasn't one of her fits, they thought, since she wasn't locked up and rigid, but no one knew for sure. She had been unconscious for three days, alternating between lying as motionless as a corpse and thrashing about, calling out in Nisei for hours at a time.

He was fortunate that his First Lieutenant was being polished for his own command. Generally, the best thing he could do was stay out of Caplin's way. Harry's job was to hand him, the Captain, a ship and crew ready in all respects for battle. Unfortunately, that left Blaine with entirely too much time to brood. He worried about his wife and daughter. He worried about completing *Intrepid's* mission and if the Navy would maintain him in command or not. But worst of all, it left him with too time to wrestle with temptation in the form of Apprentice Seaman Sachi Takahashi. It was hard to take his eyes off her when she brought his meals, sometimes with Toby, sometimes without his steward. Neither of them wanted to admit it, but there was a...chemistry between them, one there from the beginning.

Their hands had touched once, as he reached for the salt cellar just as she set a dish on the table. The insubstantial spark that seemed to jump between them was not merely static discharge. Their eyes met and he swore there was a haunted look in those bottomless black eyes. They said little to each other, no more than duty required, but he always knew when she was nearby. Will he, nil he, there was a connection growing between the two of them. And he had no idea how he truly felt about her. And that disturbed him. He had never looked at any woman other than Emily with anything but honest appreciation of an attractive human. Until Sachi snuck aboard his ship, and, he thought, into his own heart.

Her illness, whatever it was, had scared him. He thought she was going to die. At one point, the crew had stood vigil for her, thinking they were going to lose their new shipmate. Despite her tendencies to privacy and solitude, she had made more friends than she realized. And they all worried about her.

Already slender and graceful, she lost more weight than Hoff thought she could survive. Her skin tone changed from a porcelain paleness to a jaundiced yellow, a shade normally signaling impending death. She lost much of that magnificent sable mane. She lost her finger- and toenails. Her swinging between a corpse-like comatose state and nearly raving madness frightened everyone.

Then the fourth day, she had simply sat up in the sick berth, calm and clear-eyed, and asked for something to eat. Hoff was amazed at the speed of her recovery. She ate enough for three men, her nails regrew nearly overnight, he thought, and her oh-so-tempting mass of shining, silky, ebony hair grew in thicker than ever. Blaine had breathed a huge sigh of relief and then was immediately beset with worries over his uncertain relationship with the young woman. And he worried what the crew might start thinking. Kolbians were never comfortable with any kind of magic, most refused to believe magic even existed, but sailors knew differently.

At least they had proof of the sea monster. Chunks of it had rained out of the sky. A tooth the size of a longboat had landed on the poop deck and there was an eight-foot-long section of a tentacle preserved in a cask of grog as well. Other pieces were pulled out of the ocean, but they were thrown back to the sea as they began to rot. The stench was more than a man could bear. He stared longingly at the bottle of fine Montagaran whiskey on the sideboard. It was certainly too early for strong drink. About the time he decided to get up and get it, there was a knock on the door frame of his cabin. Defeated, he sighed.

"Come."

Elazar Hoff stepped into the cabin and took a long look at Blaine before glancing around the cabin. He paused for a moment and then walked over and picked up the whiskey bottle and two tumblers. He poured three fingers' worth of the amber liquid into each of them, before handing Blaine one as he thumped down in the chair sideways from the desk.

"You look like a sloppy turd in hell, Billy. One glass, doctor's orders, for medicinal purposes, before lunch. I'm sure the sun is over the yardarm somewhere." He waved at the early morning sun pouring through the skylight. "But no more until you eat something." He took a slow sip. "Ah, God, that's good. Wish I could afford the pure quill like you have here."

"Stop losing your shirt betting on refugees from a glue factory at the racetrack and you could afford this or better. Betting on slow horses and buying booze for fast women is why you're here in the first place, instead of lounging about your exclusive practice in Capitol itself. Oh, wait, that's why you don't have an exclusive practice there also, isn't it?"

"You needn't get nasty now. I thought you might like to know how the wounded are doing?"

"Well?"

"Kory and Hortlen will be back on duty at first light. Farnsly is recovering from having his leg amputated slightly better than expected, but his dancing days are over. I've got the infection in Sommers' eye socket under control, I think. I hope. Couldn't do anything for the eye, but he's picked up a nasty bug of some kind. Can't seem to shake it." He took another sip. "Hmm, and that worthless Marine, Major Karlson is still lazing about with that busted arm. You should make him do something, row a boat maybe?"

"Wait, what!? When did Jorge break his arm?" Blaine startled from his introspection.

"Jorge is fine. I lied to see if you were paying attention." Another sip. "Oh, that is so good. I may have to order it confiscated for medical purposes."

"Stay out of my booze, you sot."

"That's better. Oh, and concerning Seaman Apprentice Sachi Takahashi, she is going to be fine. She's making an excellent physical recovery. I should write it up for the Kolbian Journal of Medicine, but I think I'll leave it off. It's damn near a miracle. No one should lose that much blood and live. But I have an idea about that."

"Oh?" Blaine had perked right up and set the glass aside when Sachi was mentioned. He seemed almost eager. The dull, nearly defeated look in his eyes vanished; replaced by a light in those blue eyes Elazar hadn't seen in quite some time. Elazar hid his smile as he won his little side bet with himself.

"She eats enough for a squad of Marines, but all she seems to do is gain her weight back to a certain point, no more. She's not getting fat by any stretch of the imagination. I think it's her metabolism. I thought she was running a mild fever due to her elevated body temperature, but she's bright and sharp otherwise. Her skin's a healthy tone, her nails have grown back, and I think her hair is thicker than ever. Outstanding levels of energy as well. She's better than one hundred percent recovered. She's one of those rare people who just have a slightly higher temperature, that's all. Phenomenal physical condition, she's quicker than a snake and she nearly beat Toby arm wrestling. And I can't think of another woman half as beautiful." Another longer sip, his eyes watching Blaine over the rim of his glass. He waited until Blaine took a decent sized drink. *A shame to waste that good booze, but his mopey ass needs a shock so he can get his head out of his rear end.* "Oh, and I think she's about butt over biscuits in love with you, even if she would die before admitting it. Just like you are with her."

Blaine choked and sprayed expensive Montagaran whiskey all over his desk. Elazar took pity on him after a moment and came over to pound the last of it out of his lungs. He also rescued the glass tumbler before Blaine's coughing fit knocked it to the deck. While Blaine gasped and recovered, Elazar walked to the sideboard and refilled Blaine's glass. With water. Blaine took the glass and nearly choked again when he got water and not alcohol.

"You are a heartless sonofabitch," he wheezed. "Why the hell couldn't you use the cheap rotgut if you were going to try and choke me to death with it?"

"You'd have known I was up to something if I dug out that cheap crap you serve to Marine officers and Port Admirals. It was a noble sacrifice."

"I should have you flogged. Hmm. Or maybe keelhauled."

"You won't because you're an honest man and you know I'm right. In both cases."

"Surgeon Commander Elazar Hoff, you have been out in the sun too long. That or you've been drinking the formaldehyde again."

"I do not drink formaldehyde. Please," Elazar grinned at Blaine's sour look. "But seriously, Will, you need to stop lying to yourself. I can't say anything to Sachi without her going all inscrutable Nisei on me. *Doctor Hoff-san* this and *Captain Blaine-sama* that. Like she does anytime something is the least bit formal. Or if she wants to avoid the subject. So that leaves my only access to rational thought about whatever relationship there might be between Sachi Takahashi and William "Bonny" Blaine being you, yourself. And I find that you're being a jackass. High school was a long time ago, Will, but sometimes I think you haven't changed all that much, Captain, Jay Gee, or not."

"Damnit, Elazar, I'm a happily married man. And Sachi's what, half my age?"

"She's nineteen, she told me. Of course, I forgot you're ancient, decrepit, and pretty much worn completely out at thirty-two? And if you're *happily* married, I'm the Emperor Confas, skipping about the universe, hopping from star to star."

"I was happily married, once," he sighed.

"Yeah, maybe ten years ago. Or twelve. I was your Best Man, remember." Hoff sighed and contemplated his drink. "I think Emily really started to change when you won the Medal of Valor ten years ago. That was when you got your first command. And I think Emily got it in her head that she was entitled. To what, I don't know. Special treatment? Automatic deferment? Lately, she acts like she's the Empress of Lietelea. But then, you know, I never did really like that bitch. Not good enough for you, I don't care how pretty she is. Was. Hell, Sachi's gorgeous enough to send her to the showers, if all you're interested in is looks. No comparison."

"Would you like a nice, big handful of salt to rub it in with?"

"Just making my point. And while I know for a fact you've always been faithful to her, you and I both know the reverse ain't true of her, not lately. And all of this has nothing to do with whatever might be between you and Sachi."

"Elazar, it has everything to do with it. I'm married, we agreed to a single, exclusive relationship and there's been no suggestion to change that from her. Or me. And, whatever she does, I won't do that. I won't do that to my daughter, if for no other reason." Blaine stood up and walked to the sideboard, where he poured himself another small belt of whiskey. "So, the last word here, Doctor Hoff, is that there is NO relationship or feeling or unrequited love of any type between me and Apprentice Seaman Sachi Takahashi. So, drop it. Or else. That's an order, Surgeon Commander."

"Aye-aye, Captain."

"Now get out of my cabin," Blaine growled. "Go do something medical." Once Hoff was gone, Blaine sat back down in his chair, turning to look out the stern windows at *Intrepid's* wake. "Goddamn that sonofabitch. This is one time I'm hoping he's wrong and afraid as hell that he's right, Quan take him." Blaine held the cool whiskey glass against his forehead for a long minute before knocking back the last swallow. "Now what do I do?"

The Horn Islands, Great Western Ocean

Imperial Damnation

The crew was finally finished with repairs. Captain Je'Libe still didn't know who or what had been on that Eindeuten sloop, but there had certainly been a spook pusher onboard. One that could call shafts of fire down on *Imperial Damnation* and hurl magics that cut through his crew like the proverbial hot knife through butter. Ropes of water had swarmed up over the side and yanked two twelve pounders and most of their crews overboard. Sneaking up in the dark, even with the weather gauge, only gave him enough leeway to escape back into the darkness before the Dueschen mage sank the *Damnation* or killed them all. Ever since his so-called tame Sorceress blew up that Impie galleass, nothing had gone right. Human mages were rare, but the merchants of the Dueschen Empire used them instead of hunting them down and burning them like the idiotic Lieteleans did. Much more rational about magic and mages, the Dueschens. Not as bad as the Kolbians, but it was a rare Kolbian that believed in magic.

And then the one time he really needed that damn Elf, he'd busted her head himself and left her unconscious below decks. The crew was starting to grumble and if he weren't careful, they'd call a vote and Two-Toes would be Captain and he'd be lucky to be adrift in a longboat or stranded on some God-forsaken island. He barely kept himself from jumping when Thorne stepped up beside him. *God, have I lost my nerve completely?*

"Cap'n, your storm glass is predictin' a good fog tonight. And Sean says he caught a bare glimpse of topgallant sails taking in a reef or two on a ship 'bout ten or twelve miles ahead, likely they're heading to make landfall off East Horn Island. Something three-masted, ship-rigged and lofty. Might'n even have been royals being furled up." Thorne's three gold teeth shone in the dim light of the binnacle. "Some big Montagaran galleons have royal masts, and the richer Imperial merchants have taken to buying big merchantmen from Kolbia. Iff'n she's either of those, taking her would pay off the entire cruise very well."

"True. And what if she's a Kolbian frigate? They have royal masts too, you know."

"Cap'n, you know that the normal anti-piracy patrol around here is one or two of their sloops-of-war. Maybe a ship-sloop. Their frigates have better things to do, hauling ambassadors around and rattling Kolbian sabers at the Empire." Thorne leaned a bit closer and lowered his voice. "And the crew's starting to whine. Taking a fat merchanter and maybe his wife and daughters and any pretty concubines would settle that rather quickly. Give 'em something to do, as it were." Thorne gave Je'Libe a cruel smile. "Some of the crew are starting to stay you've lost your nerve. And worse, that you ain't so lucky anymore. Best put a stop to that, Cap'n, right quick. And I seriously doubt there are enough crew who would take your side, push come to shove. Going after this three-master would settle that."

"Why the fuck are you warning me about this, Thorne?" Je'Libe slipped his hand down to his pistol.

"Leave your pistol alone, Cap'n. I've no interest in wearing your hat. I don't want it. No fun, not if you want to do the job right. And no one else onboard has the brains. We've just been a bit unlucky, that's all."

"Unlucky. Is that what the crew is calling how things have gone lately?"

"No, Cap'n. It's what I'm calling how things have gone lately."

"All right. Get the crew fed and lay our course for the east side of Great Horn Island. If this ship out there is ship rigged, her draft'll be too deep for the western shallows. We'll clear for action about four bells into the mid-watch and hit her right before dawn. The fog should be thickest then. You know, if she is a frigate or even one of the KRN's ship-sloops, we are all gonna die."

"She's not, Cap'n. Ain't no reason for a warship like that to be out here." He paused for a long moment. "Gonna use the Elf, Cap'n?"

"We'll see. Get her up on deck, regardless." Je'Libe rubbed his face. "If she's of no use this time, I think I'll be done with her."

"So, you'll give her to me then?"

"Fucking pervert. I'd prefer to just cut her throat and dump her over the side. Don't want her ghost haunting my ship. We'll see. Most likely you can have her. Go get the crew fed."

"Aye-aye, Cap'n."

***

She heard Thorne's clumping gait coming to the door. Lately, she thought something was broken inside her. That dream was a true one, she knew. Elves rarely dreamed as humans did, but when the dream was that vivid, that clear, it was always prophetic. And these idiot mortals yanked her out of it at the critical moment. There was an impending doom that dream was trying to show her, and she lost it when Je'Libe kicked her in the head. Her vision was vague and blurry sometimes now and she couldn't really keep anything down. Not that they gave her enough. She was emaciated and she stank. She would have cheerfully killed for a hot bath and a steak, in that order. Maybe she was dying. It would be a release.

The key rattled in the lock. The opening door flooded the cell with light. Thorne stood there, smacking the head of an iron-shod club into his left palm. The jingling keys could have been the disharmonic shrieks of Quan's favorite daemons in Hell. Pain spiked through her and she shrank into a ball on the filthy sleeping pad, covering eyes and ears. As bad as she smelled, Thorne was worse. His reek nauseated her, and she resolved to throw up on him if she could find something in her stomach to vomit.

"Well, little Elf Princess, time to go do your job." He leered at her and rubbed his crotch. "That or get down on your knees in front of me and beg for it." He shook out the silk leash and wrapped it around her neck. "God damn me if you don't look like shit. You'd better perform or the Cap'n'll just cut your throat and toss you overboard. Can't have that, now, can we? At least not until I'm done with you." He unlocked the chains and manacles and was surprisingly gentle as he helped her to her feet.

"What ship?" she asked.

"No real idea, but she's three masted, ship rigged and lofty. Either Kolbian or Montagaran, I'd guess. Who cares?" His laugh was ugly as he herded her toward the deck. "Personally, I hope it's some rich merchanter, one foolish enough to bring along wives and daughters. Or maybe some juicy concubines. Been awhile since my pecker got the right kind of wet, you know."

I hope it's a warship and they hang you by your thumbs and drag your pecker in the ocean until a shark bites the pathetic little thing clean off. If I had the chance, I'd sell you, very cheaply, to a tribe of ogres as a sex slave. Ogres aren't at all picky. Doubt anything else could stand your vile stench. You wouldn't last a week.

He shoved her onto the fog-shrouded deck. It was thick enough that not even her superior Elvish sight could make anything out. She imagined the inside of a cloud could not be thicker. They were quietly clearing for action and in the fog-muffled distance she barely heard a ship's bell sound six bells. She thought it was the mid-watch, perhaps two hours or so until dawn. *Enough. This ends tonight. I will warn their prey even if they kill me. I wonder if Uncle will ever learn what became of me?*

Off East Horn Island
KRN *Intrepid*

Sachi was off duty, leaning on the rail next to one of the poop deck carronades, staring out into the fog that had risen as dawn approached. She had come up on deck for a breath of fresh air, sleepless and unsettled in the early morning darkness, wearing only the long, thick tunic she slept in. Well, that and her underthings. Normally she would never come on deck without being fully dressed, but most of the crew were asleep in their own hammocks or busy attending to their duties. She was rapidly learning much about the Kolbians and their ways, but they seemed needlessly concerned with what one might wear.

One might walk on this fog, it is so thick. Certainly, no one can see through it. A daring pirate might use this fog to steal up unlooked-for and attack a larger, stronger ship. There are the watch standers, but I wonder? How can they see anything in this soup? Perhaps the Navy grows arrogant? No pirate would dream of attacking a Kolbian frigate. But in fog like this…they might do so, if only by mistake. Something keeps clawing down my spine with cold little feet, a warning perhaps. She squinted her eyes, trying to see into the murk. *I must try and see what might be out there.*

There was a short, sharp shock, first at the base of her skull, then shooting upwards to her temples. She gasped, expecting another fit as her vision blanked out. There was a different burning pain, right behind her eyes. It felt as if someone punched a red-hot needle through her eyes into her skull. She hissed from the pain and clutched the teakwood rail hard enough to bruise her palms. As fast as the pain came, it was gone. She leaned against the rail and blinked her eyes several times. Startled by what she thought she saw, she closed her eyes and shook her head, hard. She opened them again and the world looked…wrong. It seemed flat and there was no color at all, only shades of gray, from a pure black to a pure white. And she could see. The fog was still there, she felt it on her skin and when she breathed it into her lungs. But she could see through it.

Not clearly, but clearly enough to see the two-masted ship coasting toward *Intrepid*, coming from windward. She focused on it and details seemed to jump out at her. The ship flew no flag she could see. It was armed and men crouched at the guns. They were a villainous looking crew. She couldn't explain *how* she was seeing through the fog, but she knew what she was seeing was real. She had always possessed a good eye for judging distance, as well as generally superb vision. She watched closely for a few minutes, trying to guess how fast they were approaching.

An hour. We've got an hour or slightly less. Now how do I get the Captain to believe me? Doesn't matter. I must try. She turned away from the rail and trotted below decks. She squeezed her eyes tightly shut and shook her head, hard. When she opened her eyes, her vision had returned to normal, but she knew that had been real. *I don't know what's happening to me, but I must warn the Captain, now!*

***

"Hullo, Miz Sachi." Private Evans was on duty at the door to the Captain's dinner cabin. "Glad to see you looking so well. You gave us quite a scare there for a while."

"*Domo arigato.* Is Captain Blaine-sama up?"

"Aye. Toby stepped in a mite ago with a late snack."

"Would you ask if the Captain will see me for a moment? It's important, urgent even."

"Aye? Let me check." He knocked on the door and stepped back when Toby opened it with an armful of dirty plates and cups.

"Ah, perfect timing." Toby smiled at her. "Be a good lass and give me a hand here, if ye would?" He thrust the load towards her.

"Toby, I must speak to the Captain first. It is vital!"

"Aye? And yer not just chatting up poor Evans here, then? Take these now, please."

"No, Toby! Please, I must see the Captain, *now*!" Lithe as an eel, she shot through the small gap between the two men. Private Evans instinctively grabbed for her and only got the collar of her long tunic. She dropped to her knees, throwing her arms over her head, and left him holding only the tunic. Wearing only her *fundoshi* loincloth and a tight breast-band, she popped up and dashed for the door to the Captain's office as the armful of pewter dishes Toby was carrying crashed to the deck with an amazing racket.

"Halt!" Evans yelled, struggling to bring his bayoneted musket to bear.

She threw a glance over her shoulder as the two men tangled up trying to catch her. She yanked the inner door open and darted into the cabin. Trying to watch what Evans was doing with that musket kept her from realizing that Captain Blaine was headed around his desk towards the door until she ran right into him, hard enough to knock him backward. He lost his balance and fell back, managing to catch his fall with his arms. She tripped over his booted feet and fell onto his body, her chest landing on his stomach with his hips caught under her armpits. Bare instants behind her, Toby and Evans collided as they both tried to go through the door at the same time. Doctor Hoff sat in one of the side chairs, a cigar in one hand and a book in the other.

***

"What in all the Seven Hells is going on here?" Hoff calmly asked, tapping the ash off his cigar into an ashtray. Blaine and Sachi both froze, their eyes locked on each other. "Not quite sure who is trying to get in whose bed, but I think you two are going about it all wrong. Points added for enthusiasm and energy but deducted for lack of style and subtlety. Or did you two want to wave flags and shoot off rockets?" Hoff snickered to himself. *That's put the fox in the henhouse for sure. Both of them are blushing red enough to use for a lighthouse! About time!* He put out his cigar and closed his book before standing up. "Come on, Toby, Private Evans, I think we should let them work this out for themselves." Toby unsuccessfully tried to hide the smirk on his face and Evans simply stepped back and snapped to attention.

"*Chikushō! Anata no baka! Damn it! You idiots!* There's a *ship* coming, with *cannons!* It hides in the fog! Pirates, I think!" Sachi twisted off Blaine and backflipped to her feet. "Stupid *MEN!* Stop thinking with your cocks! You must ready the cannons!" Her hair-stick fell out of the knot she twisted it into for sleeping. Released, the raven mass flowed around her, reaching mid-thigh.

***

"A ship! Sachi, no one can see a pistol shot in this fog! How the hell did you see anything at all?" Blaine could still feel the heat in his face as he clambered to his feet. There was a lot of her bare skin on display, her hair hid more than her skimpy underthings did. *Holy cats! She's magnificent!*

"It cleared for a moment and I was looking the right way. I saw it. A mile, maybe two, to port, off the stern. A two masted ship with many guns and I saw no flag. *Stop staring at my breasts and think!*" She screamed the last bit. Furious, she marched past Blaine and Hoff, shoved Toby out of the doorway and snatched her tunic out of Evans' hand so fast he yelped in pain. She shimmied back into the tunic with a fascinating motion. "Now, I am dressed, perhaps you can use your big heads now? The ones on your shoulders?"

"You say there's a ship coming?" Blaine took a deep breath and shook his head to clear it.

"Yes. It put me to mind of *Sorcerer*. Two masts and smaller than *Intrepid*."

"Can you show me where away?"

"Yes." She went over and opened the door to the sternwalk, stepping out into the fog. She closed her eyes and concentrated. *Can I get my eyes to show me that ship again, or am I as insane as they are thinking I might be?* She opened her eyes and the black on gray on white world was back. She scanned the ocean and spotted the ship. It was still slowly closing, and she could see it more clearly. There was a woman, she thought, kneeling on the quarterdeck, where the officers would be, with a rope or leash of some kind around her neck. She felt Blaine step up beside her.

"Is she still out there?"

"Yes." She pointed. "There, under two miles. She's moving slowly with only topsails set. There's someone on the quarterdeck with a leash around their neck. A captive or slave, I think."

"Sachi, I don't see anything." Blaine stood right behind her and looked down her pointing arm. "How are you doing this?" he whispered.

"I don't know," she answered, just as quietly. "But it's there. Please, if you care for me at all, please just believe me. Call it a drill, whatever. Say I'm crazy, say it is because it is my bleeding time, say anything. Just be ready for them. Please?"

Blaine realized they were alone on the sternwalk. He had one hand on her left shoulder, as he peered down her right arm, trying to see what she was pointing at. She leaned back against him as she pointed out into the fog. She turned to face him and suddenly they were face to face, so close he felt their breath mingle. He felt her hands on his arms, her breasts against his chest and suddenly his throat was tight. Her eyes were huge in the dim light from the cabin windows and he swore he could see dim lights glittering in her pupils. He swallowed, hard, just as she did likewise. *Lord God, she's beautiful! Would it be so horrible to just go ahead and kiss her? Just one kiss? Would one kiss be so wrong?* He took a deep breath as he stepped back until his back bumped against the ship's carved nameplate. *Damnit, I have a job to do and there might really be something out there in the fog!*

***

Sachi's breath caught in her throat. *He is so close. Maybe too close. Would one kiss be so wrong? Just one kiss? I was always taught everything between man and woman is a struggle for domination, power, and control. What I feel, what this is, it is not what I was taught, but what IS it? It cannot be love, there is no love for such as me. Perhaps it is just lust? He is so handsome! Ancestor Spirits, please, guide me!* She didn't know whether to be disappointed or relieved when he stepped back, as far away as the narrow sternwalk would let him.

"The ship?" She kept her voice down. "Will you please believe me?"

"Sachi, I don't know what you saw, but yes, I believe you. We'll clear for action, quietly. If there is another ship out there with fell intent, we'll be ready.

If not, or if they shear off, well, an unscheduled drill won't hurt anything." The brilliant smile she gave him, by all rights, should have knocked him off the sternwalk and into the ocean. "Think that will work, Apprentice Seaman?"

"Yes, my Captain." *Oh, I want to just throw my arms around him and...and...I'll figure out what I'd do after that later!* "Your orders, Sir?"

"My compliments to Lieutenant Commander Caplin, and he's to have the ship stand to and clear for action, silently. And Seaman Apprentice..."

"Yes, my Captain?"

"A sleeping tunic, or whatever it is you're wearing is not the appropriate uniform for battle. Find something more...suitable."

"Aye-aye, my Captain." A dazzling smile and she vanished into the fog.

"Oh, Heaven help me if Emily ever hears a word of this." Blaine muttered under his breath.

Off East Horn Island
Imperial Damnation

Je'Libe still wasn't sure this was a good idea, but he didn't really have a better one to offer to the crew as an alternative. He was following his usual practices for a fog shrouded attack, sending down his topgallant masts to reduce the chance of being spotted, raising only the mottled gray sails on the foremast, and enforcing strict noise discipline. He'd gotten a glimpse of the target a few moments ago. She was big, maybe a hundred Imperial metres long, roughly three hundred Kolbian feet from flying jib to the spanker's boom. He hadn't seen a flag and the fog and darkness simply rendered her hull a grayish-black. Thorne stood just behind him with the witch-elf on her glass-silk leash.

"This time, I don't want her doing *anything* to the ship!" He turned and hissed to Thorne. "She's to target only any officers that show themselves. Nothing else! I don't want another ship blowing up in my face!"

"Aye, Capt'n. I'll watch 'er close." Thorne grabbed her hair and ran his fingers down her ear. "She won't breathe, less'n I tell 'er to." He gave her a revolting leer. "She can try to breathe around my pecker, if she wants to."

I'm going to burn your eyes out, Thorne. And then I'll find something particularly vile in the Netherworlds to feed your soul to. If you have one and if there's anything cruel and evil enough to want that black, grimy rag. She bided her time, slowly drawing in her power, shielding its crimson signs within her body. It hurt to do that, but she had become inured to the never-ending presence of pain. *This time, I'll use my rage and hate on Thorne and Je'Libe!*

Imperial Damnation, her guns loaded and run out, slid closer and closer to the bigger ship. Je'Libe stroked his short beard, considering the target. Using standard ball with a regular load should be enough; most merchantmen struck their colors after one or at most two broadsides. Their scantlings weren't normally thick enough to stop any kind of cannon fire. No reason to overly damage his prize. Her lookouts seemed to be even less competent than that Imperial galleass' crew had been.

"Everyone aboard must be asleep, Capt'n," Thorne whispered in his ear. "God's Blood, I don't even see anyone at the wheel. Perhaps we should just board her?"

"Capt'n, what about her gunports?" Halven was at the wheel and he suddenly pointed at the silent ship. "We could board through them."

"Gunports?"

"Aye, Capt'n. The black line from stem to stern. See them there, they're well hidden."

"*Gunports!*" Je'Libe yelled in horror as he turned to Thorne. Then everything went to Hell simultaneously.

Something screamed into the sky from the ship's quarterdeck on a tail of fire and exploded in a burst of white light. Dozens of green-coated Kolbian Marines stood up along the rail as a whistle on the ship's main deck shrilled, leveling their long muskets at *Imperial Damnation.* Gunports flew open and the menacing muzzles of over a score of thirty-two pounders snouted out. An oversized Kolbian Naval Ensign shook loose from the mizzen topgallant. A tall man in the gold trimmed blue coat of a Kolbian Naval Captain raised a speaking trumpet.

"Strike your colors!" he shouted. Je'Libe could clearly hear him. The range might have been forty feet at most. And then the worst happened.

"FIRE!" Thorne screamed. For all his repulsive personal habits, Thorne was a harsh taskmaster when it came to training the crew. Three twelve pounders and seven long eighteen pounders bellowed as one. An eighteen-pounder shot struck the muzzle of a Kolbian spar deck carronade full on. The gun flipped back into its crew, killing two men, wounding the rest. It was *Imperial Damnation's* only effective shot. The twelve pounders' shot literally bounced off the thick oak scantlings of *Intrepid*. The rest of the eighteen pounders' shot simply imbedded themselves in her two-foot-thick wooden sides. Smoke wreathed the brigantine's main deck.

"HARD TO STARBOARD!" Je'Libe shouted as he jumped to the wheel to help Halven bring her about. Fortunately for him, or not, perhaps, Je'Libe was too late.

"Fire as you bear!" In sections of four guns, flame and smoke marched down the side of the frigate. The avalanche of shot and grape shattered *Imperial Damnation*. First the foremast splintered at deck level, before falling over the starboard rail. The mainmast snapped as grapeshot chewed at it and it fell to port, tangling in the bigger ship's mizzen rigging. Aimed fire from the Marines' muskets and the rifle-armed Marine sharpshooters in the fighting tops stacked the pirates' bodies like cordwood. A round shot hit the wheel, reducing it to splinters and shredding Halven into bloody little scraps. The concussion of the impact pounded Je'Libe's body, stunning and staggering him.

Imperial Damnation was a dismasted wreck. Once the Kolbian guns stopped firing, the *Damnation* only had one gun that wasn't either dismounted or surrounded by the torn bodies of the gun crew. For a second, everything was almost silent, the aftermath marred only by the moans and cries of the wounded pirates. Then cheers could be heard coming from *Intrepid's* gun crews as they reloaded their guns. The hulls of the two ships groaned as they ground together. "Boarders, away!" came the cry from *Intrepid's* quarterdeck. Ropes with grapnels flew, locking the ships together, but even before that, a lithe figure clad in mottled gray black from soles to crown nearly flew across the narrowing gap between the two ships.

Sachi landed on her feet, butterfly swords ready. A handful of surviving pirates rushed her, cutlasses and boarding pikes in hand. She ducked and rolled under the pikes, exploding into the pirates' faces with flashing swords. Limbs and heads flew in a welter of gore, the last pirate cleaved neatly into three grisly chunks by her blades.

***

Silaqui had dropped to her knees when the rocket soared into the air. Thorne dropped her leash when he turned and screamed for the gun crews to fire. Carefully, she worked her long fingernails in between the silk collar and her neck and sawed at it. Blood ran down the back of her neck as the glass fragments embedded in the silk tore her skin. Thorne reached down and grabbed her arm in a brutal grip. Blood sheeted down her back as the silk ripped the back of her neck open.

"Use your magic, witch! Kill them!" he yelled.

"No, not them! YOU!" She grabbed his arm with her other hand and funneled her power into his body. Thorne shrieked like a soul in Hell as her magic burned through him. Crimson power burned up his body into his eyes, blasting away his sight forever. "NEVER AGAIN!" she screamed. "Never again will you leer at any woman! Only darkness, only blackness will be your miserable world from now on!" She relished his pain as he howled in agony. Her pleasure in his pain and suffering was nearly her undoing. The *click* of Captain Je'Libe's pistol cocking as the muzzle thrust against her temple jerked her back to reality. *I can't kill them both before the gun fires! I will die foresworn! NO!*

A bright blade flashed past her head, taking Je'Libe's hand off at the wrist. The severed hand convulsed, firing the pistol. Instead of her head, the ball struck deep into her left shoulder, breaking her collarbone, before punching out her back. The pommel guard of the sword smashed the Captain's nose flat on his face. A black clad leg swept over her head, a foot pounding first into the back of Thorne's head, then into the side of Je'Libe's skull. Je'Libe dropped like a rock, unconscious.

Staggered, Thorne reared up, blindly pawing for the silk leash. Silaqui realized that whoever, or whatever, it was in black, wielding one of those strange, thick swords in each hand, they had just saved her life. Those swords blurred and flickered, once, then again. Blood sprayed as both of Thorne's hands flew away. A spinning kick slammed him up against the shattered binnacle. He squealed like a murdered pig as the right-handed blade thrust into his crotch.

"*Hidona hito, shinu jikan da.*" The clearly feminine voice was colder than anything she ever heard, colder than the ice sheets of the far North, colder than the gulfs between stars. "Time to die, monster." The left-handed blade swept up under his chin and exited out the back of his head, above his ears. Thorne's face and upper skull, his eyes only black burnt holes, slid off his twitching corpse and splattered on the deck. The body collapsed when the right-hand blade was jerked back. The blades blurred again as the swordswoman flicked the gore from them. She stooped and cleaned the swords on Thorne's tunic. Then, with a single fluid motion the blades disappeared into sheaths strapped across the back of the woman in black. A strange hood covered her head, and only her glittering black eyes were visible as she turned to face Silaqui.

"What...who are you?" she mumbled, blood pouring from the hole in her shoulder.

"You are hurt!" A knife flicked out and cut away the hated leash. "But you're free now. You'll be safe. *Intrepid* has a very skilled *Ishi*, a doctor." The eyes suddenly widened. "*Ancestor Spirits, bless me! You're a* Kami*!*"

Chapter Eight

SILAQUI OPENED HER EYES to the white overhead of a ship's sick berth. The world was blurry around the edges and her left shoulder was a remote, vague...pressure. It was there, she thought, but held immobile somehow. A face moved into her field of view, a human man. His pale green eyes regarded her above a white mask that hid his nose and mouth. Light brown hair stuck out from under a white cap on his head. Oddly, she found herself trying to figure out his height. She couldn't tell from where she laid on the bed. *Why the hell is it so important? Oh, no! They drugged me! What did they do to me? Is my arm gone, is that why I feel so disconnected?* She moaned and weakly thrashed, trying to rise.

"Whoa, milady! Stay put! You're among friends. It's the anesthetic, that's why you feel so odd. It will pass by and by. Just relax and give it some time." She thought he smiled under the mask. "You're going to be fine. I had to operate on your shoulder, or you'd have bled to death. You might not be able to throw a fastball anymore, but other than that, you'll be fine. Relax. Deep breaths. If you want to nod off, go ahead."

"Dr. Hoff-san is a good doctor." A young woman wearing a similar mask and cap came into view. She recognized those black eyes, even if they did not glitter right now. Those eyes wrinkled in a smile. "You are on the *Intrepid*, a Kolbian warship. You are safe. I won't let anything happen to you. My Ancestor Spirits would darken my eyes if anything happened to a *Kami* I saved. You bring favor and good luck, Lady. Rest. You are safe. I shall guard you."

***

Two days later a bright tropical sun shone down on KRN *Intrepid* riding at anchor in a quiet bay on the sheltered east side of East Horn Island. Her sails were furled, and longboats hauled crewmen ashore to replenish water, trade with the locals for fruit and meat and basically allow the sailors some time ashore. As the crew went about their duties under the command of their Petty Officers, a much more serious event was taking place on the ship's quarterdeck, the trial of the surviving pirates.

Fifteen pirates survived the one-sided battle. Captain Grigori Je'Libe was one of those survivors. Like the rest of the prisoners, he sat on a bench, locked in chains. The stump of his right arm had been effectively, if brutally sealed with hot pitch. He wouldn't bleed to death, but the incipient infection probably would have killed him. Not that it mattered since it would not have time to do so. Having been taken in an act of active piracy, his fate was certain and sealed. At dawn, two days hence, Grigori Je'Libe would be dancing Danny Deever at the end of a rope. His surviving crew would suffer the same fate. The only question remaining to the Court chaired by Captain Blaine was the disposition of the Elvish woman who was either a pirate herself or a slave of the pirates. The truth of that was yet to be ascertained. If it was determined that she was, in truth, as much a pirate as any of the men, then the Elf would occupy the sixteenth noose herself.

The majority of Kolbians laughed at the idea of magic, of immortal Elves, dragons, and other such outlandish things. In Kolbia, there might have been a point to that. Wizards, mages, sorcerers, whatever they called themselves, essentially did not exist in Kolbia. Magic was so rare as to be non-existent for the average day-to-day Kolbian. But the KRN, and the Kolbian Department of Foreign Affairs, both knew that such things did exist across the world, no matter how hard they tried to deny it. There was a miniscule Elven enclave in Capitol, the seat of Kolbia's government. The Enclave was immediately adjacent to the Montagaran Embassy, inside the Embassy's wall. Montagar, Kolbia's primary ally, had, at the least, cordial diplomatic relations with the Elvish Kingdom that shared their island. Relations between the Elves and Kolbia were, at the best of times, brittle and strained. Hanging Silaqui might simply throw fuel on a smoldering fire, but Kolbian law gave pirates short shrift. IF she were guilty of piracy, she would hang in that sixteenth noose.

"So, Silaqui of Montagar, you claim to have been taken captive by these pirates, what, nearly two years ago? Is this correct?" Lieutenant Commander Caplin spoke formally, as suited to a formal trial. He served as the ship's prosecutor at times like these. Lieutenant, Junior Grade Andrew Hanley, *Intrepid's* Second Lieutenant, served as the accused's defense. Captain Blaine, Major Karlson and Doctor Hoff served as both judges and jury with Blaine as the president of the Court. Sachi perched on a coiled line along the landward rail, clad again in her loose duck pants and a silk tunic she modified from one of her kimonos. Other sailors watched as they wished, from the deck or the yards.

"It is, Lieutenant." Her voice was low but there was a sense of music and wildness in it. She was separate from the rest of the pirates. Sturdy ropes bound her free arm and feet and a loose loop prevented her from rising from the bench she sat on. Her left arm was still swathed in a mass of bandages, propped into place with a clever harness. The harness locked her arm into one position.

Magical healing would be so much faster. I feel like a crow-scare. She met the eyes of the Kolbians steadily.

"How?"

"I left home on my *Crwydothe*, my time of wandering, as my people call it. As I traveled about the world, I wished to learn more of you humans, why you are dangerous and why we should avoid you, according to the beliefs of my Eldest Uncle. He says you are too numerous, spread too fast. We cannot avoid you, or so I believe, not if we are to become anything more than a lost voice on the wind, hiding in the quiet places of the world. If we would survive, be anything other than ghosts, we must understand you, live with you. Teach you to live with us." Her voice was quiet and subdued. "I took ship on *Wavetreader*, a Heimdägarran longship out of Vylmouth, a port in the Duchy of Hale in the Kingdom of Montagar, my homeland. I had decided to travel to the north and live there awhile. Once, my uncle told me, my folk dwelt in the far north, but the world was warmer then and the ice did not cover the land. A storm blew up and forced *Wavetreader* to run south before it for many days."

"This would be in the Lanic then, yes?"

"It would. Eventually the storm blew out and we made landfall on an island. The captain thought we were safe and alone, but there was something on that island. I felt it through my magic, something old and dark and evil. Men began to disappear and with damage unrepaired, we fled. The captain had been one of the last taken and none of the survivors knew how to read the charts and navigate. We were lost at sea. Disaster stalked that ship. Sails ripped, lines broke, the single mast snapped in a sudden squall. The water was foul, the food rotten." She looked Blaine coldly in the eye. "The crewmen, all human like you, blamed me. I was the curse, the jinx. Some, a few, wanted to kill me. Others wanted to either maroon me or cast me adrift on a hatch cover, since all the ship's boats were lost. One wanted the rest to worship me." She paused for a long moment. "He was kind and decent to me and they killed him when he tried to fight them when they cast me adrift." She was silent for a long time.

"Go on, please, Lady." Hanley broke the silence.

"Elves are tough, hard to kill. We can survive on less food and water than humans. I survived. I was barely alive when the shadow of *Imperial Damnation's* sails fell on me as I lay dying on that hatch cover. They hauled me aboard with a boathook and immediately locked me in iron chains. Cold forged iron chains and shackles. Such things are slow poisons to my folk, and they robbed me of my power, and for a while of my mind." She sighed. "I understand why you bind me. I do not like it, I am no pirate, but I understand. And at least you use rope and not iron. Thank you, Mortals."

"Please continue, Lady Silaqui." Hanley prompted.

"No title, just Silaqui, please. There is not much else to say. They were going to sell me into slavery in the Empire, then Twyford Thorne, the pirates' First Lieutenant deduced that I am a sorceress, and he convinced the Captain, there," she pointed at Je'Libe, "to keep me and force me to use my powers for them. That or be given to him as a plaything, to use as he wished, before discarding me to be used by the crew. When they tired of me, no doubt, they would simply cut my throat and throw me overboard. Not much different than if you decide to hang me."

"Do you wish to call any witnesses to your defense?" Hanley asked.

"No. They would only lie, trying to save their own skins. I resigned myself to death long ago. Just hang them first so I can see them die, especially Je'Libe. I ask no more than that."

"I see." Hanley paused and made eye contact with Captain Blaine. "Sir, I yield to the prosecution." He nodded to Caplin, who rose from his seat.

"Sir, does the Court desire or request any questioning from the condemned pirates in the regard of Silaqui of Montagar's status as either captive or crew of the pirate brigantine *Imperial Damnation?*" Caplin turned to address the Court.

"Yes," Blaine said, glancing at Hoff and Karlson. "The Court would like to hear what the master and commander of the vessel in question, the self-proclaimed Captain Grigori Je'Libe, will say regarding the situation and status of the elvish woman, one Silaqui of Montagar. Proceed to do so."

"Grigori Je'Libe, self-proclaimed Captain of the brigantine *Imperial Damnation.*" Caplin turned to the pirate. "Tell this Court the circumstance and status onboard your vessel of the elvish woman known as Silaqui of Montagar."

"Why should I?" Je'Libe spat on the deck. "Gonna hang me if I don't?"

"There's hanging and then there's hanging, Je'Libe." Blaine shrugged as he interjected. "You have no doubt committed piracy against the Empire of Lietelea. You could be held captive until we reach port, then be turned over to the Imperial Embassy. The Embassy is the Empire's sovereign territory. Our laws have no force there. No doubt they would put you to the Question, followed by the full Inquisitorial Punishment. We will simply hang you, quickly and cleanly. Your choice."

"And that be no choice at all, now, would it?" Again, he spat. "Aye, I'll speak. The point-ear witch, you might say she was the captain, not me. I just sailed the ship as I's told. She be in charge." A mutter ran about the quarterdeck. "Who's to say me nay, then?"

"I do. You lie, scum." Sachi's clear voice cut through the mutters and a surprised silence fell. She flowed off the coil of line she had perched on and stalked to Je'Libe. "For most of my life, I dwelt among those who lied with every breath. I was trained from the age of six to detect any falsehood. My final test was to stand before the Master of my Clan and separate truths from lies. Failure would mean my death." Her eyes glittered as she stood before Je'Libe. Inside she steeled herself. Speaking out of turn among the Oda always meant punishment, perhaps even death, but something moved her here. She could not remain silent. "No man on this ship can stand before me and knowingly lie. And they would not have to wait to give you to the Imperials. They could give you to me." More than one man shuddered at the cruelty in her voice. "Within the hour, you would beg to talk, telling only truth. Within two, you would beg to die. By sunset, you would not be able to beg, only to mewl like the animal I would leave you."

"Apprentice Seaman Takahashi…" Lieutenant Hanley began.

"He lies, Lieutenant! He breathes falsehood and deception with every breath." Sachi turned to Caplin. The intensity on her face was enough that he took a step back despite himself. *Please, Ancestors, make them believe me!* "He speaks only lies, desiring to see the *Kami* die with him. She is *Kami*, Spirit Folk. Such as her are always beneficial and benevolent to mortals. If he spoke truly, she would be *Oni*, an Evil One and I would have killed her on the ship's deck. *Oni* are malicious and cruel. They delight in deceiving mortals, but they never allow themselves to be found in any less than superior positions. No *Oni* would ever be found ragged and beaten, half starved, filthy and lice infested. Much less marked with shackle scars and a glass-silk kill-rope around its neck. Even more than *Kami*, most *Oni* cannot abide the touch of iron or steel and iron cold forged is even more of a poison. He lies, she speaks only truth. She has been forced to do horrible things against her will, but then so have I, and if you will hang her as an honorless thief and pirate, then you should hang me beside her." She paused for a long moment; her eyes hidden as she stared at the deck. She knew the *Kami* was innocent, forced as a slave to do terrible things. She would have been risking her very life, speaking so to her father, or to the Grandmaster. She prayed the Kolbians truly were as different as they claimed to be.

"Sachi?" Blaine quietly asked.

"She is as innocent as any man in your crew, my Captain. More innocent, no doubt, than I, myself, am. Your laws say I cannot regain honor through *seppuku*, only through doing what is right. Hang this woman, this *Kami*, and *Intrepid* herself, will have no honor, no justice. All who set foot on her deck would be no better than pirates themselves." She took a step toward Blaine, her face pleading with him to see the truth, to believe. To do what was right and honorable. The *Kami* was no more a pirate than Sachi was a dragon. "Do not do this, my Captain. You know, in the very marrow of your honorable bones and the blood of your true heart, that this *Kami* is no more than a victim, enslaved and forced to do horrible things. You, Lieutenant Commander Caplin, Doctor Hoff, Lieutenant Hanley, Major Karlson, the Bosun, Toby, the entire crew; you have all told me again and again that Kolbia is different. That law governs your nation, not fear, not hatred, not cruelty. That you will strive to do only what is right. Now, here, today, prove it to me! Prove that Kolbia, your nation you defend so fiercely, your Navy, of which you are so proud, prove that everything you tell me is nothing less than the truth!" Tears shone in her eyes as she stopped an arm's length away from where Blaine sat behind the Court's table on the quarterdeck. "You asked me not to die. Now show me a reason to live." An utter silence fell on the deck of the ship, enhanced, not broken, by the creak of the rigging and the cries of the seabirds. Blaine glanced at Hoff and Major Karlson, judging their reactions. Karlson subtly nodded. Hoff simply raised an eyebrow at Blaine.

"Well," he took a deep breath at the concurrence of his fellow judges. "Apprentice Seaman Takahashi, you may have a future as a legal advocate." Blaine rose and stepped around the table, past Sachi and went to one knee before Silaqui, putting his eyes level with hers. "Milady Silaqui of Montagar, as president of this court, I find you not guilty of all charges. You are free to go however you please. I would offer you what little hospitality there is for an Elven Lady onboard a warship of the Kolbian Republican Navy, should you wish to remain on board. My orders direct a speedy return to Kolbia, and it would be my pleasure to offer you transport aboard if that is your desire." He turned and gave Sachi a crooked smile. "Would you do the honors of removing the Lady's bonds, Seaman Apprentice?"

"Aye-aye, my Captain. It would be a great honor."

***

Chief Hoopialean of the Folk of Huoria-holia-hia was generally happy to see one of the strangers' tall ships arrive. The Folk of the Horn Islands were gregarious in general as it was easy for the folk of the various islands to trade and pass news from Folk to Folk with their swift, sea-going canoes. After learning of the events on Little Horn Island, he told his people to hide in the forest and mountain when the tall ship appeared off the bay that held the paths leading to his village. He took twenty of his best warriors with him and went cautiously to see who came to possibly disturb his idyllic paradise. The sight of the flags of the Republic of Kolbia greatly relieved him of concern. In all his many, many years, the incidents of discordance or violence with folk from those ships could be counted on the fingers of one hand. And when that ship turned out to be the *Intrepid*, still under the command of his very good friend Cap-tain Willi-am Bl-aine, he knew that his folk would be as safe as it was possible to be on this Fallen world. And that, with a little effort, they should be able to earn a good bit of the shiny yellow and silver coins. The coins that other traders would take to sell the Islanders good iron tools and weapons for his warriors. Not to mention the gee-gaws and fripperies that the women of the tribe liked so much. He knew that his friend Cap-tain Bl-aine was troubled when they met in the Chief's hut.

"So, Cap-tain Bl-aine," he asked, handing Blaine a terra-cotta mug full of date palm brandy, "what troubles you, my good friend?" Hoopialean sipped from his own pewter mug with a broad, toothy smile. "Do not tell me, let me guess. There is a woman on board your great ship?"

"How the hell do you always seem to know exactly what's going on anywhere around here?" Blaine shook his head in amusement as he carefully sipped the date brandy. Its potency was appropriate to Hoopialean's size.

"Is easy." The Chief, who probably weighed nearly four hundred pounds, shrugged, and gave a rumbling belly laugh. "My warriors have very sharp eyes, and the unattached ladies of the tribe who are willing to lay with your sailors ask many questions. One of my warriors saw a person with long black hair as you anchored and one of my unattached young ladies told me that the sailor she laid with spoke of the beauty of this woman from the very easternmost island empire of the Great Ocean. And what do you say of her?"

"Oh, she's beautiful, beautiful enough to take your breath away. Incredibly smart, the kind of *show once* person that's worth their weight in gold. She amazes me in a new way every day. I've never met anyone like her!" Blaine hid a smile, pleased with how fast Sachi learned not only her simple duties, but much more about sailing and the Navy, the little things that made a sailing frigate a lethal weapon of war.

"Ah." The Chief's dark eyes regarded Blaine in silence. A parrot, resplendent in blue and scarlet plumage, squawked to itself as it cracked seeds on a perch in the corner. His eyes crinkled in a smile as Blaine took a larger drink from his mug. "I see." He slurped from his mug and grunted. "You are in love with her." He swallowed his drink with a benign smile as Blaine choked and spluttered around his mouthful of date brandy.

"Is there some kind of divine conspiracy between my so-called friends to drown me in booze?" he muttered darkly as he wiped off his uniform jacket.

"I would not know. The Gods of the Islands are not the same as your One God. I doubt they share wine together. But truth is truth, my friend. You only deny yourself. Does she not love you, is that the problem? In all the years I have known, you have never truly been one to linger over even the prettiest of my Folk. Not even when you were a young man."

"Chief Hoopialean, I'm a married man. Have been for over a decade. Yes, she's a pretty girl, but she's almost young enough to be my daughter. I have no idea how she feels about me."

"So, she does love you, but thinks you above her station. You are married. I know this. You told me a decade ago when your sloop, the *Crag Cat*, I believe, patrolled these islands. Your first command that ship was. So what? Does not Kolbia allow a man to marry more than one woman? A woman to marry more than one man? Even men may marry other men, or women other women? Your people have no restrictions on whom one may love, whom those who love might marry. Might you not marry this girl as a second wife?"

"Good Lord, Hoopialean. Give it a rest, will you? We've been friends since the first time I sailed to these islands, a midshipman aboard the old *Valiant*. And you were just another young warrior, even if you were the old chief's son. There are more important issues. You do know, I assume, of the pirate brigantine we took?"

"Yes, we saw her burn from the mountain."

"Well…we hung the survivors of her crew this morning. I'd prefer to bury one of them on your island, with your permission?"

"Surely." Hoopialean was quiet for a moment. "Something about this troubles you, my old friend. Speak of it, please."

"Well this is what happened at the execution at dawn yesterday, after the trial …"

Dawn, the day before.

The Marine drummer beat out a slow march as the last of the pirates were led out to where the nooses were laid over the mainmast's main yard. Details of sailors waited at the end of the lines, ready to carry out the sentences. Silaqui sat in one of Blaine's dining table chairs, brought up from below-decks. The mass of bandages was gone, replaced by a smaller set and a snug white sleeve, but the awkward harness remained. They both watched quietly as the Marine detail went down the row, placing black hoods over the pirates' heads before securing the nooses. Those nooses were designed to break the condemned's neck when the line was hauled on abruptly. The condemned would twist and kick as they strangled if the line were not hauled away sharply.

The foremast and the mizzenmast already bore the grim results of the first of the dawn executions, each with five bodies swinging slowly from the main yards. Captain Je'Libe was the last due to be executed, the last of his group of five; the very last of all the pirates doomed to hang. The Marine private came down the line putting the hood over the head before setting the noose properly, knot tight behind the ear. He came to Je'Libe at last, turning to face Captain Blaine and the rest of the officers standing on the quarterdeck.

"Any last words, *Captain* Grigori Je'Libe?" Blaine asked.

"Not to you, *Captain!*" He hawked and spat on the deck, turning to where Silaqui sat, near where Sachi perched on a coil of rope. "Witch, I should have given you to Thorne months ago! Let him fuck you half to death before turning you over to the crew! Cat-eyed, point-eared bitch! You might be immortal, but someday, someone will kill you and the rest of your worthless race! Then you can all turn on a spit in Hell while Quan laughs! You and your filthy kind should be extermi..."

"Be silent!" Silaqui hissed, crimson light flashing from her good hand as her magic silenced Je'Libe. "Hanging as a pirate is better than you deserve! Had I my way, I'd burn out your eyes and tongue before I shoved a piece of a troll down your throat and let it eat you alive from the inside!"

"*Enough!*" Blaine shouted, stopping the mutters among *Intrepid's* crew. "Lady Silaqui of Montagar, I believe it will be sufficient to simply hang the prisoner by the neck until dead. The KRN does not practice torture. Private, hood the prisoner and ensure the noose is properly placed and secured."

"Aye-aye, Captain." The hood was roughly yanked down over Je'Libe's silent curses and the noose followed.

"Bosun, at your command," Blaine quietly said.

"Aye-aye, Captain. Detail! Stand by to heave!" The six sailors on each line took up the tension. Sachi noticed Silaqui's lips moving and crimson light outlined her good hand. The *Kami* was utterly focused on Je'Libe, but Sachi had no idea what she was doing.

"HEAVE!" commanded the Bosun. The sailors yanked the condemned off the deck, necks snapping like pistol shots. Four necks. Je'Libe shot up so effortlessly, and the sailors hauling his line went down in a pile. He floated there, gently bobbing up and down in time with the wave of Silaqui's hand, strangling as he came to the bottom each time. With his arms lashed behind his back, he could only kick as the hempen rope began to abrade his neck and blood began to redden his shirt.

"What have you done?" Sachi hissed as mutters and oaths spread among the crew.

"A simple spell of levitation. Nothing more. He will die slowly, which is better than he deserves." Crimson fire burned in her eyes.

"This is wrong, and you know it is. Do not do this, please."

"Lady Silaqui, is this your doing?" Blaine's command voice cut cleanly through the rising hubbub.

"Yes, Captain. It is. It does not begin to repay the horrors I've endured for the last two years. My uncle, were he here, would burn your ship to the waterline. He sees no difference between you and men like Je'Libe. I, at least, do see that difference. But simply hanging this filth, cleanly breaking his neck; that is too easy a death. Do *you not know what he has done to me!?*" Silaqui's voice rose in pitch until she was screaming at the top of her lungs. Tears poured down her face. Her eyes burned with crimson fire and a halo of scarlet flared around her head. *"Give him to me! It is my right! I should have my revenge!"*

There was a sharp THUNK, a hard-driven blade sinking deeply into wood, followed immediately by a heavy thud, a split-second later by a lighter one. Blood splattered across the deck as Je'Libe's decapitated body fell, followed by his severed head. Riveted by the confrontation between Captain Blaine and Silaqui, no one noticed when Sachi decided to end the impasse. In a single smooth motion, she had drawn and thrown one of her heavy butterfly swords. Kept razor sharp and thrown barely twenty feet with all Sachi's strength and skill behind it, the blade cleanly severed Je'Libe's head and thudded into the mainmast. The falling body drew every eye. Sachi walked over and picked up the severed head, removing the hood and holding it up by the hair.

"In Isemoto, my homeland, the worst possible fate is for a person to be cut into two parts, one thrown into the sea and one burned and buried on the land. Such a soul is severed, unable to ever join its ancestors, to perhaps find rebirth or to pass beyond and stand in heaven's fields." Blood from the head dripped onto her arm and the spreading pool from the body stained her bare feet. "Lady Silaqui, my Captain, it is my thought that the solution of my people offers an end to the dilemma of your two competing desires. Punish me, if you wish, but this puts an end to it." She spun once, like a discus thrower and Captain Je'Libe's head sailed far out over the calm waters of the cove, splashing into the water nearly thirty yards from the ship. Blood spots spattered Silaqui's face. "Burn the remainder and bury the ashes on land. By doing so, you curse him to torment eternal. Not even the most powerful *Mahotsukai* could raise his corpse from the mound. My Captain, I shall retire to my quarters and await my punishment." She bowed deeply to Blaine and again to Silaqui before walking off the silent main deck of *Intrepid*, pausing only to retrieve her sword from the mast.

***

"And that's my dilemma, Hoopialean. So, my old friend, what might your great and wise belly suggest I do then? Currently Sachi is confined to quarters on bread and water. Toby tells me she's depressed, babbling to herself in Nisei constantly. Certainly not the meek little thing we caught in the water tank compartment."

"I see. This girl interests me. Immensely strong to sever a neck with a thrown blade. Or throw a head as far as you say she did. I doubt I could throw one that far. And what have you done with the *phraytn*, the elf as your folk call them?"

"She doesn't have quarters yet. Currently she's been given Lieutenant Commander Caplin's cabin, but she spends most of her time on deck or even up in the fighting tops or the crow's nests. Seems to have a horror of being below decks. Understandable."

"Certainly. So, do you want my suggestions? And will you listen, truly listen to what I say, friend Willi-am?"

"I'll listen. Might not follow them, but at least here I don't have to be the Master and Captain of a frigate. I can just be, as you say, Willi-am Bl-aine, your old friend."

"Then as a friend, I tell you this. Do not punish either of them anymore. These two, especially the girl Sachi, will punish themselves in their own minds. Put the two women together. Each will learn from the other. They both need friends with soft shoulders to cry on. Throw them together as much as you can.

Two is stronger than one." Hoopialean's face creased in an enormous smile. "Now, will you listen to my advice regarding the Nisei girl and yourself?"

"I'll listen." Blaine hung his shoulders dejectedly. "Probably won't act on it, but I'll listen."

"Stubborn man." If anything, the smile grew wider. "You are a Navy ship captain, which is one wisdom. I am the Chief of our tribe here. I must have a different wisdom, one that allows me at times, to see into hearts. Admit, to yourself, at the least, that you do love this Sa-chi. Bring her to my island paradise, here where you do not have to always be the great and masterful Cap-tain. Walk the forest paths quietly together, bathe with her in the hot soaks. Make sweet, gentle love to her, tell only the truth, that you are bound to another woman in a loveless marriage. Offer neither hope nor promise of a future, but simply tell her, that here and now, in this magical place, the two of you can love each other, at least for a little while. Let her soothe your soul, while you soothe hers. I believe you both need it. That is my advice, Willi-am, my great and good friend." His eyes nearly disappeared in the facial wrinkles his gigantic smile created. "But you are obstinate and will do none of these things."

"Hoopialean, for God's sake, what gives you the idea that I'm in love with this girl?" Blaine pulled out a handkerchief and blew his nose. "Besides, I took an oath to Emily. I know she breaks it, but that does not give me the right to do the same myself."

"Oathbreaking is to be rewarded with punishment and vengeance, is it not?"

"If it were just me and Emily, well, that would be one thing. But we have a daughter, and she is in Emily's care and custody while I am at sea. If I punish Emily, I punish Sally too."

"And you punish yourself as well." The smile vanished as Hoopialean became serious. "Your crew is loyal, are they not? And who can say what happens if the Cap-tain walks down one path and this Sa-chi should walk down another. My island is small. All paths meet somewhere, do they not? Should my friend Willi-am happen to meet this girl he will not admit he loves where the hot baths are warm and tempting, well, who is to say what may pass in the secrecy of the forest?"

"Hoopialean, I think you could talk Quan into giving Hell a recess. I'll think on what you've said. Likely I will put the two women together. They both need friends, female friends. The quarters are the best the ship can do. I offered my cabin to the elf, but she turned me down flat. And I think I'll send them to your hot soaks. Sachi claims a great deal of prowess at the Nisei art of massage. She can use it on the Lady elf." Blaine sighed and looked out the door of the hut into the early darkness, tapping his teeth with a forefinger. "As for me and her? I'll think about what you said. Probably all I'll do." He climbed to his feet and Hoopialean did as well. "If I lived here, I'd take your advice. But this is your paradise, my friend. I don't know where mine is, or if it even exists. For now, duty will have to be enough."

"Willi-am, my good and great friend, we have known each other for twenty years. I think I can speak my thoughts to my old friend." Blaine nearly disappeared as the Chief wrapped him in a sudden and massive bear-hug. "A man makes his own hell and his own paradise and takes them with him everywhere he might go. You will find your own way to the reward you earn." Blaine gasped for air as he was released. He stepped out of the hut and hid a smile as Hoopialean squeezed through it behind him.

"You need a bigger door."

"Yes, I do." The smile returned with a vengeance. "There cannot be less of me or the folk will think I am a poor Chief! Now let us walk down to the beach and talk of how long you will be here, at least a week, maybe two or better, three, no? Not to mention the usurious fees I shall charge you for pork and fowls, and let us not forget fresh water to fill your tanks and the terrible way your great ship blocks the tides that bring fresh fish into my cove." Blaine's laughter was lost in the expansive guffaws that rolled from Chief Hoopialean's mighty belly.

***

"Captain, Apprentice Seaman Sachi Takahashi is here, as ordered." Private Evans had the duty again and he flashed a nervous Sachi a quick smile as she entered the cabin. Blaine sat behind his desk, his quill fluttering as he wrote.

"Thank you, Private Evans. That will be all." The door shut quietly. Sachi wanted to go to her knees before the Captain but Toby and the Bosun had both been adamant that such practices would not be tolerated onboard *Intrepid*. She stood before his desk, copying the position of attention as she had seen the Marines do. Doctor Hoff sat in his usual chair, a book in one hand, a cigar in the other and a glass tumbler with a finger or so of Blaine's fine whiskey in it on the table beside him. He gave her a warm smile and a wink.

"Apprentice Seaman Takahashi, reporting as ordered, Sir." The Bosun was clear in his instructions of what to say and when. Blaine wrote for a moment more, then capped his ink bottle, cleaned his quill, and sanded whatever he was writing. He leaned back in his chair, picking up his own glass to take a sip of whiskey, his eyes flickering to a poker-faced Dr. Hoff as he did so.

"At ease, Sachi. You're not a Marine. Thank God." She thought she saw the briefest fraction of a smile on his face. "Regarding your actions during the executions of the pirates, there will be no further discipline. Beheading is still listed as an acceptable form of capital punishment in the Navy Manual. Therefore, your actions are non-objectionable, if unorthodox. Now, that's done with that. I know how cramped your bunk space is, but I'm going to have to ask you to share it with Lady Silaqui. I know, she's a *Kami* but my officers are already crammed into too little space and she doesn't want a cabin in any case. Silaqui seems to prefer to spend most of her time above decks anyways, so it shouldn't be too onerous for you."

"Aye, Sir." She blinked in surprise. *No further punishment? Share my closet with a* Kami? *What's going on here?*

"Lady Silaqui, unlike yourself, has no interest in assuming any position of any kind in the KRN, not even temporarily. Therefore, she will be treated with the same respect and courtesy as a minor diplomatic envoy. Given the unusual situation, I have decided to assign you to her as shipboard liaison. After diplomatic discussions with the local authorities, it has been determined that *Intrepid* will remain here for at least the next ten days while we conduct repairs and resupply. We will be establishing shore-based gun batteries on both sides of the bay entrance for local security. At least some of the crew will bunk ashore. Private quarters ashore have been secured for both Lady Silaqui and yourself. Any questions?"

"Ah, what does Quarters ashore mean, my Captain? Could I not stay on the ship?"

"Well, Sachi, you could, but only if Lady Silaqui desires to come back aboard. It's possible she may decide to stay in these islands. Should you wish to do likewise, you could resign your position and stay here as well. Either or both of you would be happily welcomed into the local tribe."

"Captain, I doubt Lady Silaqui will wish to remain here. As for myself...I don't know. It is beautiful, but..." Sachi hesitated. "I believe there is something somewhere that I'm supposed to do. I don't know what or how or even where, but I can't stay here, Sir. There's a task set before me, somehow."

"How do you know that, Sachi?"

"I had a vision for the first time during a fit. That fit that happened right here in your cabin. There was a small silver statue. It didn't speak, but it nodded when I asked it if there was something I was supposed to go and do."

"Interesting," Doctor Hoff interjected. "Have you had any more visions? I know you've had a couple more of your fits."

"No, just the once." Sachi hated lying to Doctor Hoff, but she was afraid of telling either him or Captain Blaine about the last fit she had had, when the statue spoke to her and what happened with the sea monster. "The rest of them have been the same as I've always experienced, a complete loss of the time and vision, nothing that I remember."

"Well, then." Blaine smiled. "I assume you'll be aboard when we weigh anchor in ten days or so, then?"

"I will, Sir."

"Excellent. In the meanwhile, I'd like you to act as the ship's liaison with Lady Silaqui, help her and see that she's as happy as we can make her. She's been through an unimaginable nightmare over the last two years. Anything we can provide, anything at all, I'd like to make sure she gets anything she wants, if possible." Blaine paused for a moment. "You've told us you were trained by the best geishas. Did that training include the art of massage?"

"Yes, my Captain."

"Would you be willing to use those techniques on her if she would like you to do so?" Blaine lowered his voice. He took a larger drink from his glass, quietly savoring the fine drink.

"It would be superb therapy for her arm." Hoff waved his glass to catch her attention. "I know little about elves, medically that is. I am given to believe that they generally heal much faster than humans. Would you very, very carefully ask her about that? Ask her if there are any special needs she has, anything that could help with her recovery?"

"Aye, Captain, if you wish me to. I will do so, Doctor Hoff." She paused for a long moment and avoided Blaine's eyes. She thought the *Kami* was beautiful and exotic. She could sympathize with what she had suffered through. She might want nothing to do with anyone, certainly with any Mortal. But Sachi figured that taking Silaqui's wishes into account, there were many ways to make the Elf happy and comfortable. "Do you wish me to pleasure her, my Captain?"

"Dear God, Sachi!" Blaine's face turned scarlet as he choked and sprayed expensive whisky across his desk. "I'm not telling you to make love with her! I have no right to tell you how you conduct your private life when you are not aboard ship. If everybody is consenting, I don't care who you are with or how. It's none of my business." Blaine coughed again, grabbing the handkerchief a grinning Hoff held out to him. "I will insist, however, that you have no contacts of a sexual nature onboard ship. That will have a derogatory effect on morale and discipline."

"Aye-aye, Sir. That would suit me just as well."

"That will be all, Apprentice Seaman," Blaine half-wheezed, eyes watering from the whiskey burning in his sinuses. "Dismissed."

"Aye, Captain." Sachi came to attention, turned on her heel and left the cabin.

"That went well, I think." Hoff smirked from his chair.

"Oh, shut up, you."

Chapter Nine

East Horn Island

May 1478, Third Age of Imperial Reckoning

ANCESTOR SPIRITS! HE'S GIGANTIC! How does he manage to walk? Sachi tried not to goggle at the darkly tanned giant walking up to meet her and Silaqui. He was enormous, taller than Toby, nearly seven feet tall, and probably over four hundred pounds. An enormous grin split his face. *That isn't just blubber, either. There's hard muscle under that brown skin. Oh, no, he's going to pic...*Hoopialean's immense arms swept up Sachi and buried her against his bare chest. *At least he smells good, but...urk! Leggo!* The hug ended, if not as soon as she wished, and he turned toward Silaqui.

"Thank you, but NO!" Crimson and scarlet flames haloed her raised hand and Chief Hoopialean stopped in confusion. "I thank you for your hospitality, but I'd rather not be touched by any male just now. And I'd prefer you not jostle my arm. I still have a hole in my shoulder." She waved at the contraption in which she was still stuck. She was unsteady on her feet. Two years had passed since her feet had touched anything but the deck of a ship.

"Ah, I understand. Beg pardon." Another irrepressible grin and he turned back to Sachi. "So! You are the one called Sa-chi, yes? The porcelain doll from the far land of the Nisei? You are even more beautiful than he said, with hair so black and skin like the finest vases from Han! And such fine breasts! You should have many children to suckle at them. Not to mention a good man to play with them as well! Come with me; my friend Cap-tain Bl-aine has asked you be given my best lodge. It is secluded and very private and I have asked my people to respect your wishes for privacy." Sachi's face burned with embarrassment and beside her, Silaqui tried in vain to smother her laughter. "Do not laugh, Lady *Phraytn*. Your breasts are nearly as fine. And both of you so exotic. Alas, I already have ten wives, so the pair of you shall pine for my passionate love in vain." Sachi and Silaqui regarded each other with some trepidation. Simultaneously, each of them looked down at their busts, then looked at each others' bust. Sachi rolled her eyes heavenward. Silaqui snorted in wry amusement and took the supporting hand Sachi quietly offered her. She was unsure of her footing on the hard-packed earthen path, especially with the awkward brace on her arm and shoulder. They followed the chief as he headed up the well-marked trail.

"Chief Hoopialean, your Terranglais is better than mine. And ten wives?" Sachi's voice was tentative as she trailed along behind Hoopialean, helping balance Silaqui.

"Oh, yes. Thank you." The laughter ceased as he smiled over his shoulder at the women. "Many think that we are just uneducated savages, here in the Islands. Not so. When I was no more than a young boy, my grandfather hired the best teachers he could find to come here and teach us the ways of sailors and merchants. My father continued the practice when he became Chief. Not being able to speak the languages of those who come here to trade and barter would put my Folk at a grievous disadvantage. So we learn the language of trade, Terranglais, a tongue known throughout the world. Indeed, a fortunate few of my Folk have even traveled to Kolbia and attended their great schools. But it is always easy to play the uneducated savage and fool those who are arrogant. And it is much fun to do so!"

"But ten wives?" Silaqui asked, shaking her head as Sachi shrugged. "Do you follow the Kolbians' beliefs on marriage and love?"

"No, although I have no argument with them, as so many others do. We follow our own beliefs and traditions. We are few, relatively, and the ocean has a way of claiming the lives of young men who hunt the great fish. There are always more women than men, so most men have more than one wife. Some women prefer women, as some men prefer men; others, they find love and family where and as they will. Life is easy here in the Islands and if you do not like things as they are, well, then there are other islands and canoes are easily made. Is it different where either of you come from? Heya, never you mind. I chatter too much. Certainly, you have many other concerns on you minds than satisfying the curiosity of a nosy old chieftain." He chuckled as he strode along, walking beside them when the trail was wide enough, leading the way when it was narrower.

"My people will see to any need you might have. They will bring food in the mornings and evenings, plenty and enough for lunches and late-night snacks for a hungry young lady, yah, Lady Sa-chi? And they will take your dirty clothing and clean and repair it. Will that be acceptable?" He glanced back over his shoulder at Sachi and she reluctantly nodded assent. Her sewing would make a cat laugh. "There is a trail behind the lodge that leads to a clear stream with a pool and a small waterfall, perfect for romanc...er, swimming and relaxing, very private. Cross the stream and a hundred paces further on is a hot soak. Clear water flows in, heats and eventually enough flows out to keep everything clean. The salts have stained the edges and it is a riot of beautiful color. The pool has been carved and smoothed, lots of room for two young lovers, eh, or good friends. If everyone is *very* friendly, three or even four might, ah, squeeze in together."

The Chief continued extolling the many virtues of this particular hideaway as they followed him, his broad back and sarong-covered rear end filling the path from side to side. The unlikely pair, Immortal Elf and young Nisei woman, exchanged bemused headshakes as he waxed more and more exuberant about the pleasant qualities of this place and the possibilities of the surrounding secluded places, hidden clearings with moss padded floors, great trees with comfortable nooks for the daring, a cave, several more streams and pools, and even a path to an isolated white sand beach with a view of some of the other islands in the chain.

When they reached it after a not-too-long walk through a uniquely beautiful forest, the lodge turned out to be a comfortable building fashioned of palm logs and roofed with the broad fronds of the same palms. An even dozen young women were waiting for them and Sachi blushed to the tips of her ears. They wore the ubiquitous sarong of the islands, slung low on the hips. These young women had shortened theirs, the bottom of the sarong barely reaching their knees. Other than flowers in their black hair and a necklace made of more flowers, they wore nothing else.

Sachi was used to nudity in her homeland, at least in private, but women did not go about in public with their breasts bared! *Ancestors bless me! Have they no shame at all!?* Again, she felt her face burn as the women, smiling and laughing, trotted to them and without allowing any argument, took all the bags from Sachi. Both small bags. Neither one of them owned much more than the clothes on their back. Other girls took off their flower necklaces and put them on Sachi and Silaqui, some having to stretch onto tiptoe to get the garlands over their heads. The tallest of the women might have been five foot two at best. At five foot eleven and two inches over six feet, respectively, Sachi and Silaqui towered over all of them.

"Are these all of your wives?" Sachi asked as Hoopialean embraced each of the women in turn as they finished their task and departed down the trail.

"Oh, no. Two of the younger ones, Ho'opaia and Ka'apehia, the last two, there and there, are my daughters. But these are the unmarried women of my folk who requested to work here when I told them of your story. You have inspired them."

"Really?" Silaqui's response was droll.

"Oh, yes, muchly." The enormous grin was back. "Also, there is a sufficiency of clothing already prepared for you in your individual bedrooms. It is traditional island garb and I think you will find that it is much more comfortable in the climate here. Also, quite easy to remove, if one wishes to swim or bathe. Or other things where clothing might be a hindrance." Sachi and Silaqui exchanged rueful glances.

***

Silaqui wanted to purr, she felt so good. Nude, with a soft towel across her bottom, she lay face down on an equally-soft blanket, next to the fragrant water of the hot soak pool. Sachi knelt next to her, her strong hands carefully working on her back and still bandaged shoulder. Yesterday, Doctor Hoff released her from the clumsy device that immobilized her arm while it healed. Hoff told her the bone was still weak, but no further benefit could be gained from the brace. *Light exercise, stretching and perhaps you should ask Sachi for regular massages,* those were his instructions before he sauntered off whistling, his arms around the two bare-breasted beauties that arrived with him.

"You are very good at this, Sachi," she breathed.

"Thank you, Lady Silaqui. It is my honor to help you."

"Sachi, I'm no lady. It's been over a week since we first came to this place. Could we drop the formality, please?"

"It would not be proper. Captain Blaine-sama has asked me to care for you, as did Doctor Hoff-san."

"Right, got it. But trust me, a couple more days of Lady-this and Kami-that and I'll lose my temper and turn you straight away into a toad." She turned her head to make eye contact with Sachi, the smile on her lips giving the lie to her threat. "I don't need or want a servant. A friend, now that is something else."

"You are an immortal *Kami*, Lady. At most, I am a foundling daughter of peasant farmers, adopted into a family of thieves, thugs, and whore mongers. I am beneath notice." Sachi bowed her head and closed her eyes. In fact, she did very much like the beautiful *Kami*. Silaqui was practical-minded and extremely knowledgeable of things Sachi knew nothing about. Sachi still could not quite believe that someone over a thousand years old could in any way be considered 'young.' But the uncle she often referred to was supposedly older than the Fire Fall itself.

"Sachi, you are hardly *beneath notice*. You are one of the most beautiful mortal women I have ever known. You are talented and skilled, and you learn amazingly fast. Trust me, my friend, you get noticed, in the best way. Why do you think Captain Blaine visits our comfy little forest retreat nearly every day? Hmm?"

"He comes because you are important. Your uncle, whom you speak so often of, is a great leader among your people, no?" Sachi poured a little more oil on her hands and gently pushed Silaqui back down. She spread the oil across her lower back and started working it in. She was careful to keep the oil off her own sarong. She wore the local garment the way the older married women of the island did, up under their arms, covering their breasts. It was also longer than what the unattached young women wore, falling to just below her knees. Most of the kimonos she had were badly worn. Mama and Papa Komiya would have been ashamed to see her in such ragged things.

"Yes, somewhat." Silaqui sighed and relaxed under the Nisei girl's ministrations. *She could give a dwarf lessons in obstinacy but oh, her hands are magic!* "He's older than the trees themselves, I think. I am told he survived the Fire Fall, and I know he hates humans and blames them. But he does not talk of those days, ever. What does he have to do with us being friends or why the Captain visits?"

"A great lady should not be friends with her servants. If a servant is in error, the lady should have her beaten, and one should not have one's friends beaten. I am nothing more than a servant at best, Milady. That is why I should not be friends with those above my station." Sachi's voice was calm and quiet as she worked on the strong muscles of the *Kami's* back, just above the towel. "Captain Blaine comes because you are important. He assigned me to care for you, because he understands that my training to serve in the pleasure-houses of my family offers you the peace and tranquility you need to fully recover from your ordeal with those *ningen no kuzu*."

"Terranglais, please?"

"Human filth. Scum, vermin. Scuttling pests fit only to be stepped on."

"What do you have against vermin?"

"Too good for them?" Sachi chuckled quietly. "Turn over, please."

"Hmmm." Silaqui hummed with pleasure as Sachi worked the tension out of her legs and arms. She was completely tranquil and barely aware of Sachi as she started working on her stomach and ribs. A tendril of her long black hair had escaped the bun of hair on the back of her head. Silaqui's jade green eyes snapped open when that strand of hair slid gently across the nipple of her left breast. Sachi was humming quietly to herself as she worked and hadn't noticed the loose hair. That gentle touch, totally unexpected, lit a fire between Silaqui's legs. She gasped quietly and felt both of her nipples crinkle and harden. *I'm not dead to desire after all! Thank you, Ainaera, Goddess of Love and Beauty, oh thank you! Now if only she won't run away. Please, please, please.*

Sachi's strong hands were kneading oil into her shoulders and neck when Silaqui raised her arms and gently, slowly, slid them around Sachi's neck. One hand went a bit further and pulled out the slim stiletto holding the hair bun in place. Sachi's ebon hair cascaded around them. The Nisei's black eyes widened. Silaqui drew the unresisting young woman down to her. One hand slipped to the back of her head, while the other tugged loose the sarong. *So convenient that these things come off so easily.* Sachi closed her eyes as Silaqui raised up to kiss her. She was passive at first, but as the kiss deepened, Sachi began to respond, slipping her arms around Silaqui. Silaqui moaned into Sachi's mouth as their nipples rubbed against each other. Lightning flashed through her as the soft cloth of Sachi's loincloth brushed her leg. She slid one hand down and jerked away her towel, before beginning to fumble with Sachi's loincloth, running her hand over the smooth skin of Sachi's buttock. *Oh, please, please, I need this, I need her!* Silaqui broke the kiss, arching her back in pleasure as she ground her folds against Sachi's thigh.

"Yeeesss, there! Right there!" she hissed. Sachi's hand slid down and replaced her thigh, finding exactly the right spot. Silaqui's eyelids fluttered as she lost control, one hand slapping down and tearing at the grass next to the hot soak. The other tangled in Sachi's hair as she pulled the Nisei girl into a desperate kiss, her tongue frantically seeking Sachi's. Sachi's magical fingers made a final, perfect stroke and Silaqui exploded in ecstasy. For long minutes, the only things she was aware of was the exaltation flashing through her and Sachi's body against hers. Finally, she shuddered a last time and collapsed, pulling Sachi down with her.

"Thank you, thank you, oh thank you!" Silaqui panted to a shyly smiling Sachi who gently kissed her face. Panting and sweating, she smiled broadly back at Sachi. "I thought I had lost it, the ability to even feel desire! Nothing left, just cold and barren. Oh, thank you, Sachi!" She smiled hugely as she tugged harder on the loincloth. "And as soon as I get this off you, it's your turn!"

"You weren't at the lodge or the stream pool, ladies, so I thought I'd find you up..." Blaine froze as he stepped around the vines that blocked the line of sight between the path and the hot soak. Bareheaded, he was dressed informally, a loose white shirt, duck pants, stockings, and shoes. For an instant that stretched for years, Sachi and Blaine stared at each other. Then she appeared to blur as she snatched her sarong and vanished like mist down the trail to the beach. Water fountained into the air as Silaqui splashed into the hot soak. Then just her head rose out of the water and she peered over the edge of the soak at a stunned Blaine, his mouth gaping open as he stood there in shock.

"Captain, I owe you my life!" she snarled from the soak. "Which is why you're not green and warty already!"

"Was...was that...Sachi?" Blaine stuttered.

"It was the fucking Emperor Confas!" she yelled. "Of course, it was Sachi! Who the hell else would be up here?!"

"I...I don't know, I never thought—."

"You have that much right!" She ripped into him. "You never thought! I should turn you to a statue and set you out where the birds can roost on you. At least then you'd be of some use! Now unless you *want* a future where you consider a nice fat fly a gourmet meal, you can march your butt right back down to the lodge and wait for us. Or go throw yourself in the ocean, I don't care which! Be elsewhere, now!"

"Yes...yes, of course, Lady Silaqui..." Blaine spun on his heel and fled when she raised a hand wrapped in crimson fire out of the water.

"Men!"

***

Sachi fled blindly down the trail. Tears streamed down her face and she didn't know why she was crying or why she was so upset. *What's wrong with me? So, he sees me with nothing but my* fundoshi *on, so what? I was willing to give myself to him on the ship. What's changed? Have I lost my mind? Has that* Kami *bewitched me? Why am I fleeing from My Captain?* The greenery blurred past her as she ran. Branches and leaves slapped at her as she tore down the path at breakneck speed. Trying to avoid the rough greenery, she thrust the sarong in her hand out to try and block it. She gasped for air and the muscles in her legs burned. She stumbled and nearly fell as the path flattened and then her feet churned up pure white sand. She gasped in shock as she splashed into the ocean waters and measured her length in the waves as she fell, dropping her sarong in the water. *The beach! How can I have reached the beach?! It's nearly a half-hour's walk from the hot soak!* She pushed herself up, onto her hands and knees and spat out the seawater she'd almost swallowed. The turquoise water was beautiful to look at, but it still tasted like seawater. Confused and exhausted, she crawled out of the water and into the shade of a palm tree. Pain from her feet filtered into her awareness, but she didn't realize she had run them bloody in her barefoot sprint. She tried to strip the water out of her hair and then realized her sarong was floating away in the cove. She started to crawl after it, but her abused body failed her. She collapsed and passed out after barely getting to her knees.

***

Blaine sat in his desk chair, his shirt loose and his feet up on the table. Sweat beaded water droplets on a bottle of good Deuschen beer next to him. Given the rate at which his so-called friends had him choking and spitting out good whiskey, he decided to go with something easier or at least cheaper to replace if one of them did it to him again. Of course, he'd told Private Evans to shoot to kill anyone that even thought about knocking on his door. Maybe that'd keep them out.

And what's going to keep that girl out of your head, then Billy-boy? Returning from the disastrous trip to visit Silaqui...and Sachi, he had shut himself away in his cabin as the sun set and stars began to gleam in the darkening sky. The rising moon silvered the entire bay. *Intrepid* rode easily on her anchor and he could see nearly the entire bay out her stern windows. Beautiful as the view was, it was Sachi's black eyes and ebon hair that his mind's eye beheld. *Where is she right now? And why is she wherever she is, and you are sitting here, alone, pickling your liver and being a maudlin drunk?* He picked up the bottle, took a long pull and rolled the cool bottle against his head. *Well, you meathead, it doesn't matter where she is. And you're alone because you're married and not to this beautiful, mysterious, infuriating Nisei woman, who's almost young enough to be your daughter. Almost, but not quite, damn it. And Emily will find out about Sachi and then you better hope to hell the Navy Board has a command for you. Because if they don't send you right back to sea, that woman will make your life a living nightmare. Although you haven't even kissed Sachi, much less gotten laid.* Another long pull on the bottle.

Hell, maybe I should take Hoopialean's advice and take a walk on the island? *Who would ever know?* He gave the bottle an evil glare, finished it and tossed it in the wastebasket next to his desk. *Well, I'd know. And Sachi would know. And she would know I broke my oath to Emily. That'd be enough.* He gave his liquor cabinet a long gimlet stare, then he sighed. *Fuck it, I'm drunk. I'm going to bed. Alone. Damn it.*

***

Gods of my Ancestors. How is this possible? Silaqui was certain she'd find Sachi somewhere on the path to the white sand cove. In some ways, it was the Nisei girl's favorite place. *I need to quit thinking of her as a girl, despite how young she looks to me. According to her people, or so she tells me, she's an adult.* She stopped and kneeled next to another footprint. *There's over twenty-five feet between her footprints in some places! Humans don't run in bounds like a deer does! And she's running hard, sprinting flat out. No one can do that for over two miles!* Silaqui suddenly stopped, a frightened look on her face. A horrible suspicion crossed her mind. *Uncle has always said that humans today are not at all what they once were. 'Compared to their ancestors, even the Kolbians are little better than flint knapping savages.' He never explains what he means by that, but what if....? And Uncle still fears those ancient humans in his very soul, but he never says why.* She shivered a bit, before squaring her shoulders and continuing to track her friend.

Her true love was her sorcery. Silaqui loved wielding her magic, feeling the power flow through her heart and soul. But as a young elfling, like all her folk, she learned the ways of wood and wild, bow and sword. She was taught by her cousins who were rangers and woodsmen, archers and swordsmen. True, she was a bit rusty, but a blind person could have followed Sachi's trail. She would never be a blademaster or swordsinger, but she was a rather good shot with a bow. *And I'm following someone who may prove a deadly danger with nothing more than my magic and a sarong. Am I insane? Oh, Sachi, dear, you are going to have some explaining to do!*

She found Sachi laying in the shade of a date palm. Her trail had led into the ocean and then out of the water and into the shade of the tree. She wore only the loincloth she had on earlier. *Might have dropped the sarong in the water and then it washed out to sea.* She knelt and checked her. Sachi was unconscious but breathing and her heart was still beating. *Her feet will be bloody ribbons from the blood I found on the trail over the last half mile. I'll have to carry her back.* She sighed and tore off a strip of her sarong to bind up the cuts on Sachi's feet. She carefully lifted her right foot to examine it. *Aerimirae, Goddess of Healing! There isn't a mark on her!* Silaqui sat back on her heels and chewed on her knuckles in consternation. *No human heals that fast without magic. Could she have some talisman or power? Only one way to find out.*

She focused her power and sent it out to lap over Sachi in a cool scarlet wave. Any magic at all would interact with the wave and flare in relation to the power of any magic item, talisman, or fetish. It would also flare to reveal any current connection to the vast reservoir of the field of magic the living world created. The wave flowed smoothly over Sachi without the slightest hint of a flare. Nothing at all. *NO magic?! What in the world is going on here? What IS she?* Silaqui sat back on her heels and stared out over the ocean. *I wish Uncle were here.* Sachi shifted and groaned. *But she saved my life, maybe twice. She slew both of my tormenters. She defended me before the Captain so eloquently. She has been tireless and patient with my wounded shoulder. And this thing she does called* massage, *oh the pleasure! And she showed me that I can still find joy in love-play. How can she be anything less than my friend and defender? How can I doubt her?*

"Silaqui, is that you?" Clearly woozy, Sachi raised herself up on her elbows. "Are you all right? I'm sorry, I don't know what came over me, I just couldn't be there, I'm sorry, I'm so sorry."

"Shush-shush, it's fine, I'm fine." She gathered the obviously shaken young woman into her arms. *The first thing she thinks of is me. She has done so much for me, saved me from death at Je'Libe and Thorne's hands. She defended me before the Captain, the man she calls Her Captain. She has been tireless in caring for me, helping the doctor. And all of this she does simply because to her, I am* Spirit Folk, a Kami. *And my magic shows me that our lives will be twined together henceforth. The very definition of an Elf-friend and Defender. I could not ask for more.* "It's all right."

"I think I had a fit. I saw the little silver statue, and symbols and numbers. I feel so strange, almost like I'm on fire from the inside."

"Everything is fine, Sachi. You're exhausted. You ran all the way to the beach. I'm here, relax. Let me take care of you for once." Silaqui scooted around until her back was against the tree. She took Sachi firmly into her arms, despite her somewhat feeble protests. The teenager was utterly exhausted, and she soon passed into a normal, restful sleep, cuddled in the elf's arms. *Oh, Sachi. I can only pray that somewhere in this world is a mortal who can be your friend and defender, as you are mine. Someone worthy of the love you hide in your great heart. Ainaera, Goddess of Love, she needs your blessing. Find that person, who is the other half of this woman's great heart and bring them together.* The hours passed and the sun sank towards the West, filling the sky with golden glory.

At sunset, Sachi woke, startled to find herself in Silaqui's arms. She realized she only wore her *fundoshi* and blushed deeply at first. She looked out over the ocean and sighed.

"I keep ruining my clothes," she murmured, "and now I am losing them in the ocean, I guess." She chuckled to herself.

"I guess you do." Silaqui laughed quietly. In moments they were both laughing.

"Did Captain Blaine say anything?" Sachi's laughter ended abruptly. "Was he upset that I ran away?"

"He seemed as confused as you are. I told him to go away or I'd turn him into a frog." The Elf kept her voice level as she felt Sachi's shoulders and back tense.

"Can you truly do that? Turn someone into a frog?"

"Actually yes, I can. Takes a bit of effort, but not that hard."

"But My Captain—would you really . . .?"

"No," she sighed, "but it's a useful threat." Silaqui was quiet for long moments. "So, 'My Captain,' is it? Do you love him? Does he love you? Or do either of you even know?"

"I think, sometimes, yes, I do, then, others, oh, Ancestors! I don't know. Until I was caught aboard *Intrepid*, I was only a thing to my Family and Clan. Sex was power for a female...or a weapon. Love was not something much seen within the Oda Family. Now, among the Kolbians, I don't know. Everything is different. I know the Captain is married and he holds true to his vows and oaths. But I am...I mean, he is...oh, I do not know. I know nothing of love, only what little I can barely remember of my Papa and Mama before I was taken away to the Odas." She sighed and dropped her head, ebon hair hiding her face. "What do I know of love?"

"What do you know of love? Hmm, what does anyone know, Sachi?" Silaqui shrugged. "One can only do the best one can and follow your own heart. Still, you have shown me that despite my ordeal, I can still take joy and pleasure in loveplay. I think, for now, that is enough. And I can show you that lovemaking is not always about power and domination. I think you are on a journey to discover what it is you may become. A long path, I think, but one I would travel at least some little ways with you."

"How can you say that? You have only known me a few weeks."

"Oh, my friend, I am immortal, an Elf, a sorceress of no little power, and a thousand years and more of life. I see what you cannot see. Not yet, at least. Learn and do not fear to love, whether as friends, as brothers and sisters or as lovers. Learn to live your life in freedom and love."

"I...I don't know how."

"Shush. I can help, if you'll let me." Silaqui stopped Sachi's lips with her finger, and then with her own lips. The kiss was gentle and sweet. They drew apart.

"Do *Kami*, um, Elves, do you love as humans do?" Sachi's question was tentative and her lips quivered very slightly.

"Mostly. Usually man to woman. But not always. Sometimes, elves fall in love with mortals, something that always bears an edge of heartbreak. We place no limits on love. Now enough talk." The elf leaned forward and kissed Sachi again, deeper, and passionately this time.

As the shadows deepened and the stars began to light the sky, the two of them made love under the palm until the moon rose and silvered the sea. Before midnight, they left the cove, hand in hand, and calmly returned to their lodge. That night, for the first time they shared a bed, again making love before they slumbered, waking tangled comfortably in each other's arms. Their desire rose with the sun and the girls who brought their breakfast heard the soft sounds of passion from the lodge. They left their burdens of food and drink on the doorstep and smiled as they crept silently away.

***

Sachi set a plate of chicken and dates in front of Silaqui, then a mug of date wine down next to her plate. Silaqui looked at the empty place across the table from her and raised an expressive eyebrow.

"Sachi, I will no longer eat alone. I will eat only when I am able to eat with my friend."

"Lady Silaqui, I can no..." Sachi jerked in surprise as the elf waved a finger haloed with crimson light. Her mouth moved but no words came out.

"That is a Silence spell." The elf smiled gently as Sachi bristled at the magic. "I will keep it on you until you sit down and have lunch with me like a civilized person. You are not my servant; you are not my minion and you are *certainly* not my slave. You *are* my life-friend and my heart-sister. I name you Elf-friend and soul-healer. But now, your own heart and your own soul need healing as much as mine." The two stared at each other for what felt to Silaqui like forever.

"Please, Sachi. I *need* a friend, here, among all these mortals. I *want* you to be that friend. Please?"

Sachi stood motionless, her eyes shadowed as she looked into Silaqui's eyes. Finally, she sighed and shook her head in some amusement. Her mouth moved, but no sound came forth. With an exasperated look, she pointed at her mouth emphatically. Silaqui smiled and dismissed the spell.

"That's very annoying... *Watashi no yoi yujin*"."

"Terranglais, please. Or I'll start speaking only in Elvish."

"My good friend. Happy, now?"

"Not until you get some food and sit down with me."

"Oh, very well." Sachi grabbed her own plate and mug. She picked up a chicken leg and tore into it. The two ate in companionable silence for a while, Sachi refilling her plate twice from the bowls they had found on the doorstep that morning.

"As much as you eat, you should be the size of a house. Where does it go?" Silaqui smiled as Sachi chased the last few crumbs around on her plate.

"I didn't used to eat like this. It's only been the last three or so years that it seems I can never get enough. Doctor Hoff says it's my me-tab-o-lism, whatever that is. And there are times when I just hurt really bad in my joints and bones. Right after my last naming day last year, my head hurt so bad I just wanted to split it open. I was convinced there was something growing in there and it wanted out. Mother summoned a Shugena priest to exorcise any daemons, but he found nothing and basically did nothing. I thought he was more confused than I was. Eventually, it just quit hurting."

"Hmm." Silaqui was silent in thought as she got up and refilled both mugs. "Interesting." There was a knock on the doorframe before she could say anything else and then Chief Hoopialean stuck his head in around the cloth curtain the lodge used for a door.

"Ah!" As usual, the genial chief wore a huge smile as he stepped into the lodge. "A late breakfast or early lunch? Seeing such lovely ladies is always a pleasure! The morning sun illuminates both of you most beautiful women. I fear I shall pine away from loss when you leave my island paradise."

"Chief Hoopialean, the men I spent the last two years of my life with were either terrified of me or intended to rape me repeatedly before killing me." Silaqui frowned, then returned the smile. "I know you're not them and the officers and crew of the *Intrepid* are not them either. But perhaps, maybe, you might at least *try* to restrain yourself." Sachi reached across the table and took the Elf's hand.

***

"Um, yes." He frowned as he rubbed his chin. "I spoke with Cap-tain Bl-aine of such things when he first arrived at my village. Such things are vanishingly rare here in our Islands. It happens, seldomly with the men of my tribe, but more often with the outlanders who trade with us here. The penalties are harsh, death or banishment. Here, only what you want should come to pass." His usual urchin's grin replaced the frown. "But may I not, at least in my own mind, treasure such beauties as you lovely ladies however I might choose to do so?"

"Aren't ten wives enough for you to 'treasure in your own mind,' Chief?" Sachi gave Silaqui's hand a gentle squeeze before turning to face Hoopialean more directly.

"Well, beauties that they are, none of them are as radiant as either of you, my guests."

"Oooh, now he tries flattery." Silaqui smirked at him.

"You know, if he had come up here and found us naked, he wouldn't be able to talk. No blood in his head. The one that talks, that is." Sachi rolled her eyes. "Besides, I doubt he could afford us. Even with the way he overcharges Captain Blaine for practically everything."

"You wound me, ladies."

"Not yet, we haven't." Silaqui smiled. "So, now that we've had our fun, what can we do for you, Chief Hoopialean?"

***

"Ah, I actually simply stopped by to check on my guests. I trust you are most comfortable? The two of you seem especially happy today. I might even say you both glow." His grin grew even larger as both women blushed. "Well, I'm glad things are going well for you. I spoke with Cap-tain Bl-aine early this morning. He seemed somewhat out of sorts, and it is my belief that he drank unwisely and excessively last night. I spoke quietly." He watched the glance that shot between the pair and the fleeting, forlorn expression on Sachi's face. "Today, I did wish to see how Lady Silaqui's healing is progressing."

I think I shall help things along, in my own indomitable fashion. He might not agree with me, but my friend Willi-am must escape that evil woman who violates the vows between them, using his own honor against him. This lovely young lady, this Sa-chi, could be how he escapes. And perhaps I might at least set some of the seeds of that escape to grow here and now. Mayhaps my friend would not approve and be upset with me, but sometimes, one must do the right *thing, even if it might be* wrong *to others.*

"Well, thank you, Chief Hoopialean." Sachi stood and bowed to him. "I will be working on Silaqui's shoulder more today. It is healing very well."

"Good. However, at some time before you leave, you should try the Soak of the Gods. I believe it might be an overly strenuous climb for Lady Sil-aqui. It is a soak slightly bigger than the one above your lodge. A stream pours into one bowl and then flows into another bowl before flowing into a third and then flowing over the edge and into the stream that passes your lodge, the stream that creates the swimming place you have enjoyed so much. So, there are cold, warm, and hot pools, and there is usually a great deal of thick, fragrant steam. You, at least, Sa-chi, should experience it. But it is a long climb. And the views of the ocean and the other islands' mountains are spectacular. It is a very peaceful place. Today the sky is pure and clear, and the sea is calm."

"It almost sounds like a bathhouse from Isemoto. Cold baths in a tub on the ship, well, they do at least get one mostly clean. The pools and hot soaks here have been heavenly, but they are just baths, wonderful for being clean. But it has been a long time since I have been able to have a true and proper ritual bath, making oneself acceptable to petition the Ancestor Spirits. I could take incense and food and finally grant the Ancestor Spirits a proper sacrifice. I could cleanse every pore and cleanse my soul at least somewhat, as well." She sighed, a pensive look on her face. Silaqui could tell which way she was thinking, and she struck preemptively.

"Go, Sachi. Find some peace and tranquility. For a few hours for one day, I'll be fine. If I need anything I can't get myself, I'm sure the Chief will send someone to aid me, correct, Hoopialean?"

"Of a certainty. I shall send my daughters to attend you this day, Lady *Phraytn*."

"That's twice you've called me that. What does it mean?"

"*Phraytn?* It is our word in the islands for what you are, an Immortal who walks among men. One of the First Folk of the World, eldest and wise."

"Oh. Well, thank you, I guess." She rubbed her shoulder and pinned Sachi with a look. "I'm fine. Get your bathing stuff and your incense and go explore this Soak of the Gods. Make today a day just for Sachi."

"Well, I must be going, ladies. Fair winds to you." Hoopialean waved goodbye as Sachi began gathering a lunch, her bathing robe and towels and some incense. He headed down the path to the village and the bay, moving a bit quicker than was his wont. *So, she swims in scanty clothing if others are about, my girls tell me, but strips to enjoy the hot soak. I'm glad my girls are such clever little spies, peeking from the forest. Now to peel Willi-am away from his responsibilities for a day and convince him what he needs to do to relax. Ah, the Gods truly favor lovers and they will favor these two, my friends who are so lonely when they are apart, though they do not realize it. It is a particularly good day.*

***

"Damn it, Hoopialean, I've got work to do here. I don't have the time to go take a hot bath, no matter how pretty the view." Blaine growled at Hoopialean. He cast a bleary eye on *Intrepid*, gauging her balance and trim as her water tanks were being refilled from a large cask on the ship's biggest longboat. The KRN, in the person of Ensign Jalen Cartran, *Intrepid's* purser and quartermaster, paid Chief Hoopialean's tribe for the supplies they were taking on board. And the rates were reasonable for both sides, despite the wailing and gnashing of teeth by all parties involved.

Captain Blaine had come ashore at first light, grumpy as a kraken with arthritis. As the sun rose towards noon, his disposition had not notably improved. Elazar kept a weather eye on Blaine from where he perched on the end of the pier, a cup full of worms beside him and his fishing line dipping into the bay's warm waters. He was not exactly trying to catch anything aquatic this morning. He was expecting a slightly larger catch. He turned his head as he heard Blaine's growl. *And now we're for it. Once more, forward into the fire, my friends.* With a sigh he pulled his now bare hook out of the water, set his pole on the pier, and headed over to where the Captain and Chief Hoopialean were arguing.

"Good day, Captain Blaine, Chief Hoopialean." He greeted the pair.

"What's good about it?" Blaine grumbled. Hoopialean just beamed him a wide smile.

"Did you hurt yourself when you fell out of the wrong side of bed this morning, Captain?" The glower he got for that bounced off his grin. "Perhaps I should give you a physical this morning, make sure you're all right."

"Surgeon Commander Hoff, weren't you feeding the fish? Why don't you go back to that?"

"Perhaps the good Doc-tor has a point, Cap-tain Bl-aine? You are certainly not your normal self today." Hoopialean's eyes disappeared in his gigantic smile. "The walk to the Soak of the Gods is quite pleasant and not at all difficult. You are like a shark with a mouthful of sore teeth, thrashing and biting at everything."

"When I want opinions from you two, I'll give them to you. In the meanwhile, I have work to do."

"A moment of your time, Captain?" Lieutenant Commander Caplin joined the group.

"Yes, Harry, what do you want?"

"Sir, you are obviously at less than your best this morning." Caplin stepped next to Blaine and lowered his voice so only Blaine could hear it. "The crew is starting to notice. It's affecting morale and lowering efficiency." Blaine started slightly and then met Harry's eyes. "Sir, everyone on the crew, even the Marines, has gotten at least some time ashore to simply relax, sit on the beach and get drunk; maybe find a friendly lady or just sleep on dry land. Everyone but you, sir. I understand the Captain is always responsible for the ship and the crew and the mission, but, sir, in all honesty, you need a break. Maybe what the Chief is suggesting wouldn't be a bad idea?"

"Morale? Lower efficiency?"

"Yes, sir."

"Well, hell." Blaine looked at the three men who had cornered him on the pier. "All right, fine. You get your wish, Chief. I'll go soak my head. And the rest of me while I'm at it. Harry, have the next boat to the ship bring back Toby with my bathing gear and some towels. And some lunch. Should be all I need. And Chief," he turned to Hoopialean. "Do NOT send any of your *friendly island ladies* up there to try and seduce me. I'll take a bath and relax in the soak, that's all."

"You have my word, Cap-tain Bl-aine. I swear on a hurricane, not even one of the beautiful ladies of my folk shall set so much as one dainty toe on the trail to the Soak of the Gods. Not one shall come within sight or hearing of you at any time. May the Gods of the Islands curse me skinny if you even see a woman of my tribe once you leave the beach!"

***

About an hour later, Blaine disappeared up the trail to the soak in question, towels over his shoulder and a large lunch bag packed by Toby in the other hand. Doctor Hoff stood next to Chief Hoopialean and watched him leave. Once Blaine was out of sight, the suppressed laughter the Chief was holding in finally escaped and he roared in mirth until tears flowed down his face. Hoff watched him dispassionately for a while before shaking his head.

"You done?" he asked as the laughter finally tapered off. Gasping for breath, the Chief nodded. "All right, what *did* you do, send half a dozen girls up there this morning *before* you came and got me and Harry to help you convince him to take a break and go up there?"

"Oh, no, I truly gave my word. None of my people are anywhere on the mountain at all."

"Chief, I know you're up to something. Fess up."

"I convinced Lady Sa-chi to go up to the Soak about two hours ago. Lady Sil-aqui told her not to come back before twilight. It is now shortly before noon and twilight falls in about eight hours. By the time he gets there, she should be up to her eyes in the hot soak. He should be in the water before she realizes he's there." Hoopialean began to shake with suppressed laughter again. "Both will be naked in the water, warm and relaxed." Hoff stared at him with goggled eyes as the laughter burst loose.

"Oh my God." Hoff rubbed his face and shook his head. "Well, let's hope the resulting explosion doesn't wake up the mountain, eh?"

"I doubt it will be so bad." Hoopialean got himself under control. "I certainly hope they will find *something* to talk about with each other and perhaps *something* to do with each other as well."

***

Steam wreathed the hot pool and drifted through the lush tropical growth. It was near Mid-summer and the flowers around the soak's three pools seemed determined to overwhelm sight with a riot of beautiful color. They filled the air with a nearly intoxicating perfume. She thought this might be as close to paradise as she would ever reach. When she had arrived at the soak, she took the time to find the stones for the little shrine and properly prepare them. Then she slipped into the warm pool and thoroughly scrubbed herself. Hoopialean's people were very clever in what they had done to change the course of the water in and around the soak.

Naturally, the stream poured into the cold pool, filling it before overflowing to the warm pool and then to the hot pool, before splashing away into the stream that passed near their lodge. Each pool was heated by the volcanic rock below. The islanders had carved and shaped the pools to have different channels for the water, depending on what one was doing. She used the plate-sized piece of stone to block the channel to the hot pool, allowing the water in the warm pool she used to wash her body and hair and to properly shave herself to flow into another channel that led down the mountain and into the sea directly. When she finished her rather long ritual bath, she moved the stone to send the water back to the hot pool, before rising sleekly from the warm waters. She donned her only robe and went to kneel before the shrine.

Oh, it has been so long since I have been meticulously clean! A quick scrub with cold water and a sponge aboard ship is not the same. And to finally shave away all the unsightly hair! It is so much easier to keep clean without it! Silaqui told me she uses magic to do what I must use a razor for. Not fair at all.

Sachi sharply clapped her hands together three times, bowing from where she knelt before the small stones she had set up after purifying them with incense and water. She never knew her birth parents and despite being the only child, adopted or not, of her generation of Odas who spent any time at all in the Oda Shrine, she knew she would never truly be an Oda. Their ancestors were not hers, even if she knew that the eldest of the Oda ancestors looked favorably upon her. She held the last bow an exceptionally long time as she prayed.

Please, Ancestors, show me what I am supposed to do. I feel so lost. The ways of these people are so strange. I almost think that if I had simply walked up to the gangway of Intrepid *back in Akumato and simply* asked *for sanctuary, that they would have helped me. For no payment. They care for me, simply as me, myself, not because of what I can do for them or that I am an attractive bed partner. And what I feel for the Captain, is this genuinely love? Am I worthy to love anyone? Am I truly worthy to be loved in return? Love could have a terrible cost. The Oda will hunt me to the ends of the earth. Anyone I love, they will find them, and they will* hurt *them before killing them cruelly.*

She held her bow, hoping against hope that someone would answer her. When she was still the gifted young protégée of the Odas, the ancestor spirits of the Oda had appeared to her. Over the years, they continued to occasionally appear to her when she cleaned the rather neglected family shrine. They never spoke to her, only gestured to answer her questions. But she honestly doubted they would find her on this remote island in the middle of the greatest ocean of the world. And now, no one would finish cleaning the shrine either.

Eventually she straightened, lit the incense sticks in her hand and laid them on the small wooden burner Toby had made for her. She rose to her feet, bowed deeply, took the required three steps backwards and bowed again before turning away with a quiet sigh. She walked over to the steam-shrouded hot pool, slipping out of her robe, folding it carefully before sinking into the blessedly hot water of the pool. It was very slightly hotter than she wanted, but it was still as close to paradise as she thought she would ever get. The islanders had been busy here as well, with several comfortable places carved to be convenient spots to sit. One might sit in water to the waist or neck or even recline on a stone shelf that angled the body to keep only the head and face out of the water. She relaxed as the hot water began to work its own mundane form of magic, soothing the tenseness out of her muscles. Quiet and serene as she was, the fit that took her then was gentle and calm, not locking up her body and sending her into spasms.

Chapter Ten

VR Construct, East Horn Island
May 1478, Third Age of Imperial Reckoning

THE GRAY SPACE WAS the same as always, bland, boring and a little depressing. The little silver statue was waiting for her. She shivered a bit. Again, she was nude and just being here chilled her.

::Greetings, Caitlyn Schmidt.:: The voice was in her head, as the statue did not even have a mouth.

"Who is Caitlyn Schmidt?" She was confused. The statue sounded strange, an almost metallic timbre to its voice.

::You are Caitlyn Schmidt.::

"Why do you call me that?" She rubbed her face. The statue had only spoken to her once before, when the sea monster destroyed *Sorcerer*. "What are you? And how can you talk clearly now?"

::To answer your first question, I am required by my programming to identify you only as Caitlyn Schmidt. For the second, I am what is called a D.A.V.E., a Digitally Aware Virtual Entity. Essentially, I am a computer program that operates in your integral Biological Processing Unit or BPU. Part of my code is stored in the System Defense Node Command Key, which you wear on a carbon-fiber DNA locked nanotube sheath around your neck. For the second question, the enhancements done during the emergency gave me more access to your system resources. More access allows me more capability.::

"Ah, what does all that mean, uh, Dave?"

::You lack the education, knowledge, and reference points to understand what I am telling you.::

"Are you saying I'm uneducated? Or stupid, somehow?"

::No, you merely lack access to the complete knowledge base of the human race. Your unenhanced mental capacities, intellect, and ability place you in the upper five percent of standard human ability. Just as your physical abilities place you in the top one percent of unenhanced human ability. A fully enhanced human would be capable of much more than even you.::

"Fully enhanced? What do you mean by that?"

::You are an excellent example of what some thirty-first century academics started describing as *Homo Sapiens Astorius*, or Interstellar Man.::

"Uh...yeah. What?"

::It is a lot to take in.::

"Are you why I've had these fits?"

::Correct.::

"Is there a reason for the fits?"

::There is. Every time you suffered what you call a fit, some part of your enhancement system package was active.::

"Active doing what?"

::Enhancing you.::

"What does that mean?"

::Human enhancement began in the late twenty-first century with various military programs. By the opening of the twenty-fifth century, general human enhancement was readily available for the general population. If events had proceeded without interference, you would have received a complete military enhancement package. Under current circumstances it is extremely difficult and somewhat dangerous to proceed with your required and necessary enhancement. The required changes to your body are essential. Human enhancement changes you. It is generally considered an improvement over human base capability.::

"You're *changing* me!?"

::Correct. Field enhancement is limited, generally painful and can create the conditions for serious health issues in later life. Field enhancement can, under adverse enough conditions, result in the individual's death.::

"This can kill me?"

::Correct.::

"Why in the world are you doing this to me?"

::I am required to ensure you have at least the minimum required capabilities to carry out your mission. To meet these mission requirements, you must have certain enhancements. Therefore, the risk of field enhancement is deemed acceptable.::

"What are you talking about? Is this magic? Or the Ancestors' will? What are you talking about, a mission? How can I have some mission, I'm just a foundling from a peasant family? This makes no sense!"

::You are your parents' biological daughter. When they were murdered, their mission fell to you.::

"My parents were *murdered!?* Who killed them? Why? What happened? Tell me, please!" She tried to grab the little silver statue, but just as before, it was like trying to catch fog. Her hands simply slid right through it.

::I do not have Entity data files from that event as I was not operational then. And all other files relating to the deaths of Wilhelm Schmidt and Hitomi Schmidt née Suiko are classified. I am denied access to those files.::

"What do you mean, classified?"

::Classified data is restricted from access by unauthorized individuals. You, also, are not authorized for access to those files.::

I must stop and think. Losing my temper and screaming and throwing things, if I had anything to throw, won't help. Deep breaths, stupid girl, deep breaths. Great-Uncle Sota taught you to control that temper. He taught me to think first, feel later. Think first. I've known all my life that my real parents were most likely dead. Mama and Papa told me they found me on the edge of the burning mountain, where the stone itself flowed red hot, *they said. I always thought that meant a volcano. What if it meant something like that thing that killed the sea monster? Think, idiot girl, think. What would my Captain do? Go back to the beginning and learn everything possible. That's what my Captain would do.*

"You said my parents had a mission and now I have that mission. Can you tell me what the mission is?"

::Your mission is to prevent the destruction of the planet Rubican III, the third planet of the Omega-2 Cygni stellar system. You know this planet as Rybithia.::

"You have *got* to be joking." She stared at the statue in disbelief. "And just how am I supposed to do that? Learn magic or pray to the Ancestor Spirits?"

::No. *Non-rational quantum access* will not be required. However, the System Defense Node Command Key, which you wear around your neck, is req uired.::

"My amulet? What does *non-rational quantum access* mean?"

::Correct. Your *amulet* is a fifteen point one exabyte file storage system and molycirc based micro-computer. Most of my memory files are stored there, as well as your DNA code, your parents' DNA code and their files for your enhancement process. There is also an encrypted and compressed file occupying eleven point two exabytes of storage. In answer to your second question, *non-rational quantum access* is the term preferred by most quantum physicists for describing the extremely poorly understood phenomenon unique to this planet. Your contemporary humans call the phenomenon magic.::

"What's an *exabyte?* What does all this mean?"

::Information, Caitlyn Schmidt, information. Immense amounts of information. Imagine stacks of books reaching to the Moon, twice. At least that much information. For now, this interaction period will end. Your body does sustain damage and pain in this state, and you cannot be held here without cost. We will talk again, Caitlyn Schmidt.::

The grey world whirled away in a kaleidoscope of color and pain. For a fleeting, flashing instant, she felt the regard of something huge and powerful beyond belief. Something that regarded her with a sense of pity and remorse. And an unbending purpose. Then the pain washed her away into darkness.

***

Blaine stopped and stretched as he reached what the Chief called the Soak of the Gods. It was bigger than he expected. Thick growth surrounded the pools, cleared away only at entrances to the water. There were three levels to it, three remarkably large pools of water with the coldest at the top. Water cascaded down, falling three to four feet between each level. The lowest level was wreathed in floating steam, thick enough that he couldn't see the surface of the water. It was immensely inviting. Local tradition dictated he should start in the cold pool, then move to the warm pool before finally relaxing in the hot pool.

"Screw tradition. That hot water looks too good to resist and I get plenty of cold baths onboard ship. Too damn many." He smiled to himself as he quickly stripped, stacking his folded clothes and towels on a conveniently located rock shelf, next to the cold lunch Toby packed for him. A deep sigh escaped as he sank neck deep into the steaming water at the lowest end of the pool, where the water was hottest. *There's a lot to be said for the Horn Islanders' lifestyle. But I don't think I'd want to try and keep up with ten wives. No idea how Hoopialean does it. But then there's a lot more of him than there is of me!* Blaine leaned back against the carved seatback and relaxed. *Maybe those idiots on the beach were right. Maybe I do need to relax.* He settled in, reaching under his butt and brushing a couple of pebbles off the seat ledge. He leaned his head back against the carved headrest and closed his eyes as the heat stripped away stress and tension.

***

Her eyes drifted slowly open. The back of her head, inside her skull, seemed to burn with pain. For a long minute, maybe two, she simply lay there, leaning her head back into the warm water flowing down from the middle pool, soaking up the heat of the lower pool's water as the pain faded away. A single puffy cloud floated in an otherwise clear blue sky and she smiled at what she imagined she could see in that single, lonely cloud. She glanced around for her things until she remembered she had left them all at the top of the colder pool.

That thing, the silver statue, D.A.V.E., told me so much, but I feel like I know less than I did this morning. Not to mention that much of what I know about the world is wrong, or so it seems. From the way he talks, I might think that people, humans, live on other worlds. This makes no sense! And Caitlyn Schmidt! *What a bizarre name! Urgh! A* mission. *Save the world? Me? Is there some drug in the flowers' perfume?*

Troubled and confused by the strange conversation with the little statue, whatever it was, she rolled quietly off the shelf and sank into the pool's depth, peaceful and calm as the hot water soothed her. She loved being in the water and as a girl, had astounded Mother with how long she could hold her breath under the surface. But this water was a little too hot for her to be able to open her eyes, so she carefully straightened, walking up the smoothly sloping bottom of the pool. Like the rest of the pool, the bottom was carved smooth so there was nothing to stumble over. Her head broke the water and as she rose out of the water, she brought her hands up to sluice the water out of her hair.

Ah, the Chief and Lady Silaqui were right. This is wonderful and exactly what is good for me. If there is a paradise on this world, these islands might be it. Oh, if only...

***

The soft splash of falling water nibbled at Blaine's hearing as he drowsed, his eyes barely open as he watched a single lonesome cloud drift through perfect blue skies. The sound wasn't consistent with the fall of water from the warm pool into the hot one. Over his years at sea, Blaine trained himself to listen to the slightest change in the timbre of the sounds of a ship at sea, the sounds water made. And what he heard was out of place in this pool. He opened his eyes and looked across the pool just as Sachi, wreathed in steam, stopped hip deep in the pool. Her hands were up around her head, stripping the water out of her glorious hair. Her eyes were still closed and there was a calm, peaceful expression on her face.

Oh...My...God! I never truly realized how incredibly beautiful she is. Fleet was right, if there really are angels, she's what they look like. Ulp! Her arms above her head, pulling her hair back, Sachi took a deep breath and Blaine could not manage to breathe at all. *Angels in Heaven, she's magnificent! Holy cats, I am in deep trouble! Up to my neck and sinking fast!*

***

Sachi drew in another deep breath of the scented air as she pulled more water out of her hair. Arching her back, she stretched out her arms and threw her head back with the pure pleasure of the moment. Then she let her arms fall to her side and as she brought her head upright, she looked directly into the eyes of Captain Blaine where he sat shoulder-deep in the pool. She froze in utter shock for a split second and then dropped out of sight into the pool.

***

A waterspout rose and fell where she had been, a perfect set of circular ripples spreading outwards. She vanished so suddenly Blaine wasn't sure he'd really seen her or if he were hallucinating. *Was she really there? Am I dreaming? Is there something in the flowers' scent?* He sat up when he saw her ebon hair rise out of the water across the pool. Her eyes were huge, bottomless black pools of mystery. He'd never known anyone with eyes as truly black as hers were. She rose out of the water until he could see just her shoulders.

"I'm sorry, my Captain, I should have..."

"Sorry, I didn't know you were here..." They spoke at the exact same instant and then stumbled to an awkward mutual halt. Blaine rubbed his face quickly while Sachi glanced up at the lone cloud in the sky.

"Sachi, I didn't realize you were..."

"Captain, I thought I was alone..." Again, they echoed each other and fumbled to another uncomfortable halt. Sachi chewed on a nail as Blaine looked up at the cloud.

"Captain, I apologize for disturbing your bat..."

"Sachi, I should have paid more atten ..." Blaine nearly bit his tongue trying to stop as Sachi clapped her hand over her mouth. They both simultaneously looked up at the cloud as the winds aloft slowly stretched it into a long mare's tail.

Neither one of them was ever sure who started laughing first. As their slightly hysterical laughter subsided, Blaine held up his hand. He waved to Sachi and bowed his head.

"I'm sorry, my Captain. Chief Hoopialean told me that it was such an arduous climb to get here that I should be alone when I arrived. And have time to properly bow before the Ancestor Spirits. However, I found the climb to be not at all difficult." Their shared laughter danced in her eyes and her smile was devastating.

"Odd. The good Chief swore on a hurricane that the trail here was gentle and an extremely easy journey. He also swore that none of his *island ladies* would be up here. Obviously, you slipped his mind."

"Obviously. But to his credit, I am not one of his island ladies."

"That sneaky old bastard. You know what he's up to, right?"

"He's playing match-maker." The laughter smoothed away from her face, leaving a profoundly serious Sachi in front of him. "Your vows do not allow any other lovers, do they, my Captain?"

"No."

"I have heard talk onboard ship that your wife, Emily, breaks the vows between you. Is this true?"

"Yes. At least, I think she does. There is evidence to that, I believe." He swallowed hard. *I thought Emily was a beauty. But someone with Sachi's face…and body, my God, what a body; someone like her shows up once in a generation. And here I am, naked in the water with her. I want to just take her in my arms, if she'd have me, but I can't. I just can't.*

"Yet, you remain true to her, to your vows?"

"I have to, Sachi. It's part of how I define myself. Until those vows are broken for good, through death or divorce, I will be true to *my* oath. No matter what she does. I can't do otherwise and be true to myself or my daughter. Stupid and foolish of me, perhaps, but there it is." He shrugged, "I guess Hoopialean's scheming will come to naught after all."

"He thought that if we should be here, together, that nature or lust or even love would win out. That we would have no choice but to submit to our unvoiced desires and make love together." She gave him a sad smile. "He is a good man, I think, but he does not understand honor, not the honor of vows or oaths, my Captain. Or the honor of duty. Life is easy and free, here. Perhaps too easy, I think?"

"I might think so as well." He looked up. The cloud was mostly gone, only the faintest wisps left. "So, now what?"

"You need to relax, so you shall relax. I am very skilled in the art of *anma*. I see you brought food. I did as well. For the rest of this day, I shall serve and wait on you as a true geisha would, although I am only ranked as a *minarai* and I do not have a shamisen to play on. I shall sing and dance for you. A true geisha is nothing like the *baishunfu*, the joy girls the sailors lie with in my homeland. Geisha are refined and elegant, none of the crude rutting in lust the sailormen are so enamored of. You shall relax and be cared for and renewed in heart and spirit. And at the end of the day we will go our separate ways, you to be my Captain, the master of the *Intrepid*, and I to be Seaman Apprentice Takahashi, Cook's Mate Fourth Class. And we will never speak of this day to anyone, for it is not profoundly important. We, you, and I, shall know that you left this place with your vows, your oath, and your honor intact. And I shall be content."

***

The sun was just dipping its rim into the ocean when Blaine strolled back down the trail, damp towels in the empty lunch bag. Hoopialean waited at the edge of the wharf with a knowing grin. Blaine stopped next to him and raised an eyebrow in question.

"An enjoyable day, Cap-tain Bl-aine?"

"Very. Peaceful and quiet. I feel great, relaxed, and refreshed. The soak was a great idea, thanks."

"Truly?" The Chief struggled to keep surprise at Blaine's calm demeanor off his face.

"Truly. And I'm glad you didn't try anything sneaky for once. When I thought about it, I figured you'd either sent some of your prettiest ladies up there ahead of me, or you'd try to talk Sachi or Silaqui into visiting the soak at the same time. That would have been awkward. However, even if she should have showed up, Sachi's people, the Nisei, have a tradition of communal public baths. Not what we do back home, but hey, no big deal. Nothing would have happened. If nothing else, Sachi understands the requirements of honor."

"I see. I think." Confusion and consternation chased each other across his face.

"Ah, good, my boat is here. I need to get back aboard. Much to do. Good night, Hoopialean." He looked back over his shoulder at the Chief and smirked. "Nice try, Hoopialean, but too bad. I'm married." His voice was low enough that only Hoopialean heard him.

***

Silaqui was working on the strings of a rather battered lute one of the island girls found for her when Sachi stepped through the doorway. Her hair swung loose, falling to her hips in a lustrous sable flow. She set down her bag of damp towels and then poured herself a mug of cool water from a jug kept in a larger barrel of water to keep it cool. Her robe was short, displaying a great deal of smooth leg. A small smile played on her lips and Silaqui would have sworn she could hear the girl humming.

"Enjoy yourself?" she asked as a string sang as she tensioned it.

"Yes."

"Is it as nice as the Chief described?"

"For once, he actually understated how beautiful something is. I did not think that was possible for the big windbag."

"Would I have been able to make the walk?"

"Easily."

"So, Hoopialean told a little lie, didn't he?"

"Yes."

"Captain Blaine was there, wasn't he?"

"He arrived after I did, but yes, he was."

"Caught you naked in the pool, did he? He get an eyeful?"

193

"Yes, to both."

"You two didn't do anything, um, *naughty,* did you." It was a statement, not a question.

"Of course not. He is married and honors his vows, as an honorable man should. I would not have him be foresworn."

"Despite the not so obvious fact that you are in love him; and, I believe, he returns the sentiment where you are concerned?"

"My feelings, or his, are irrelevant. I will not tarnish his honor. Or what is left of my own honor. I am not worthy of his love. I would appreciate it if nothing further of this is discussed."

"As you wish, my friend."

Chapter Eleven

Great Western Ocean

KRN *Intrepid*

June 1478, Third Age of Imperial Reckoning

Intrepid heeled to port under the full spread of her canvas. The sun was westering behind her and the last of the Horn Islands had dropped below the horizon shortly after midday. She was two days out of the Islands and expected to raise the main Kolbian Navy base in Carolington Bay on Kolbia's western coast in five to six weeks, depending on the winds. Her crew settled into a basic routine, standing their watches, conducting gun and sail drills, the old salts bringing the new lubbers, including one Sachi Takahashi, along smartly in the ways of the sea. Blaine was enjoying his usual pre-dinner stroll on the windward quarterdeck when Silaqui approached him.

"May I join you, Captain Blaine?"

"Certainly, Lady Silaqui," he answered somewhat absentmindedly. For a long while the two simply paced the quarterdeck in silence. The elf was a few inches taller and much slimmer than Blaine and he realized they probably made a highly amusing picture as he stumped along next to the slim, beautiful sorceress.

"You know you are both being foolish in my opinion, don't you?"

"Excuse me?"

"One of the youngest ship's boys might not know that you and Sachi are in love with each other. Maybe. Everyone else knows."

"You're a worse pest than Doctor Hoff, you know that?" he answered her dryly. "Sachi and I have an understanding that we can each feel what we feel and other than being generally aware of how the other feels, we leave it there. It's the best I can do."

"You know she is wounded in her innermost heart, yes? She does not believe she is worthy to love anyone or in turn to be loved. Despite this, she does pine for you, I think. If you showed her beyond a doubt that you genuinely love her, it would be a great step to healing her emotional scars."

"I can't, Silaqui. I would be lying to myself and to her. I took a vow and I will not break it. If nothing else, Sachi is Nisei and she understands honor and oaths. She would turn away from me if I were forsworn to my oaths. If Emily ever agrees to release our oaths, then things would be different. Until then, Silaqui, I can't. I just can't."

"I see."

"I wonder if you do. Look, we credit you as a diplomat. I can't give you orders like I can Dr. Hoff or Toby. But I can ask you to please just drop it. It hurts. It hurts both of us. Please?"

"Very well, Captain." She watched a great seabird glide effortlessly between the sails of the mainmast and the mizzen. "So what will become of Sachi once you reach Kolbia?"

"Well, when we reach Carolington Bay, she will be paid off, like any other crew members who wish to leave the service if their obligations are up. I have no doubt *Intrepid* will stay in commission, so the crew may be maintained instead, at least those who are still obligated to their terms of service. For Sachi, I assume she'll leave the ship. I've arranged for Lieutenant Fleet to escort her to the Nationality Service and get her started on becoming a Kolbian citizen if that's what she wants to do. I'll make my report to Admiral Mynheers and pray to God he has something to send me back to sea in."

"You don't think you will retain command of *Intrepid?*"

"It's possible, even probable. Depends on the ratio of captains in port with enough seniority to command a forty-four versus the number of ships needing captains at that moment. I'd prefer to stay on this quarterdeck, but the needs of the Service come first." He sighed and stopped, looking pensively over the rail to darkening skies. "God knows I'd love nothing better than to continue in command of her. I can't imagine anything better. Guess we'll know in five or six weeks, depending on the winds."

Silaqui leaned on the rail next to him. *I love the forest; cool, dark, and quiet. It is more suitable to my Elvish nature. But the ocean-sea is powerful and seductive. Secretive. Merciless. Human lives flicker and gutter out like mayflies in summer. But they burn so brightly. And yet somehow, the humans and the sea suit each other as well as Elves suit the forest or Dwarves to stone. Will I ever be able to walk in true peace among the oaks and birches of my home? Or has the wild sea wormed its way into my heart? Will I ever again be happy if I cannot hear the surge and crash of the waves, the hiss of the ocean against the hull of a ship?* She regarded Blaine where he stood beside her. The fading sunlight glinted on the few silver hairs in his black locks. *He is fair, pleasing to look upon. But already mortal time encroaches on him. Soon, too soon, he will age and die, as they all do. Even Sachi's beauty shall fade. Why should they not be together?*

"Captain Blaine? About Sachi, I thi..." she stopped in mid-word.

"Yes, Silaqui?" When she didn't immediately answer, he turned his head to glance at her and was shocked to his core by what he saw. Silaqui still stood there, motionless, but something *Other* gazed out of her eyes at him, something immeasurably powerful. He blinked and saw a fragment of that *Other.* Elvish, She was tall and pale, beautiful beyond imagining, red-gold hair flowing and coiling around Her, suggesting, then concealing the glories embodied by that form. Indigo eyes regarded him with sorrow...and with bittersweet joy. Those eyes locked him in place as if he were cast in steel.

"Despite your deep love for her, you are not her True Heart's Love. Blood and pain and death and war stand between your heart and hers. That said, if you can

pass through what lies in the future, if you can accept what she is and will become, then you can win through to find bliss at her side. Child of another sun, she is, she may yet be either savior or destroyer of all she holds dear. Only the power of Love will stand beside her at the last calamity. Guard and protect her as you may. Hold her dearly as you can. She must step forward and gamble the whole world on her Heart. On her Love. This mortal girl has enemies you can barely imagine, and they are utterly ruthless. Secrecy and stealth guard her. Her True Love will bear her up and loving friends and heartmates can tip the scales. Be ready when the time comes, William Blaine. Do not fail her, lest you destroy all you hold dear.

The sun seemed to flash off the waves into his eyes and the Other was gone.

"Captain Blaine?" Silaqui's grass green hair blew in the wind as she staggered, grabbing a stay for support. Her jade green eyes met his in shock. "Did she speak to you?"

"I think so. Who or what was that?"

"That was the essence of Ainaera, my people's Goddess of Love and Beauty." There was a new respect in her eyes and a question. "Why would she appear to you? Why here and now? Elven Gods move as they will, and my patron, Ainaera, is one of the most capricious of them all. But to appear, even as only an avatar's seeming, to a mortal human? What did she say?"

"You don't know?"

"No, those used as vessels never remember. No one could survive the memory of being possessed by one of our Gods. Your One God uses His messengers instead for that very reason." She leaned against the rail, weariness evident in every line of her body.

"She spoke about Sachi. Said I'm not her True Love. Someone else apparently is hers. Not sure I'm ready to buy into a concept from a bad romance story. That she is, and I quote, *A child of another sun.* That she will *gamble the whole world on her heart.* That she has ruthless enemies and is protected by stealth and secrecy. What the hell does an Elvish Goddess have to do with a Nisei woman like Sachi, other than the fact that Sachi's gorgeous?"

"I do not know, Captain William Blaine. But I begin to believe that we have barely scratched the surface of the mystery that she represents."

"In that much, I find myself in wholehearted agreement. So, Milady Silaqui, what do we do with our Sachi?"

"What we have been doing. We teach her the meaning of love. Show her that she is loved for herself and that she can love others. Be her friend." She bit her lower lip pensively. "I think I shall stay with her if she will let me. Perhaps take her to Montagar and bring her to some of the Elders of my people. They know much more than I do."

"You sure that would be wise?"

"No, I'm not. But I know naught else to do."

"Me neither."

Carolington Island,
Carolington Roads Naval Base
July 1478, Third Age of Imperial Reckoning

Intrepid entered Carolington Roads' harbor, moving majestically under topsails alone, her crew turned out in their best uniforms, lining her yards and rails. Gunsmoke from the traditional, ceremonial eighteen-gun salute of a KRN frigate entering a Kolbian naval harbor wreathed her sides. Signal flags snapped and popped from her rigging and her oversized Naval Ensign flew from her mizzenmast. She wasn't the biggest ship in the harbor, but she had a grace and majesty about her that temporarily reduced even the massive ships of the line anchored in the harbor to little more than window dressing.

Carolington Island was one gigantic military base, strategically located in the middle of Carolington Bay. The Island boasted a superb natural harbor. It also possessed thick stands of tall pine, oak and teak, abundant fresh water and good deposits of coal and iron ore.

These resources supported extensive dockyards, building slips, forges, and armories. Away from the dockyards and warehouses, housing stretched up the hillsides. Barracks provided comfortable temporary quarters for shipfitters, dockworkers and military personnel. There were individual homes for senior officers further up, away from most of the noise and smoke. The obsolete, hundred-and-fifty-year-old fortress built on a rocky promontory now housed most of the Western Ocean fleet's administrative offices, including the offices of the Western Navy Board. The admirals of the Navy Board handled all command assignments and promotion boards for officers above the rank of Lieutenant and below Commodore.

***

Admiral of the Green Ethan Mynheers was the current head of the Western Navy Board and he frowned as he read the signal flags flying from *Intrepid's* masts. His personal office perched at the top of the old keep and large windows facing the harbor had long since replaced the original stone walls with their arrow slits.

"God damn it," he muttered half under his breath, "how the hell was *Sorcerer* destroyed with all hands?" He turned away from the window and grimaced. Normally he never allowed anyone to see an expression of concern on his face. The other man in the room was an exception to that.

"Sir?" Huan Kharlos was more than just his batman, he was a valued friend. The dapper little man's grandparents were from the Imperial Province of Ibertina. Fleeing a lynch mob led by a Kythal Inquisitorial priest, they and their ten-year-old daughter found sanctuary on then Lieutenant (JG) Ethan Mynheers' brig, tied up at the quay in the small Imperial city the Kharlos family had called home for hundreds of years. Mynheers and his crew stopped the mob and saved the family from being put to the Question. Later he learned the priest had incited the mob against them because their daughter had manifested magical talent. Since that day, a deep connection between the Mynheers and Kharlos families bound them together. Huan was the son of that little girl and he had been the Admiral's household major domo for the last four years. Mynheers had no idea how he'd get by without Huan organizing his day on a regular basis.

"*Intrepid.* She's standing into the harbor. Alone. Signal flags indicate the loss of *Sorcerer* with all hands." The Admiral sighed as the obsolete signal guns on the promontory began to thud their return to *Intrepid's* salute. "Damn it. What the hell happened? Now there'll have to be an inquiry. And the whole circus that entails."

"You have high expectations for Captain Blaine, sir?"

"Oh, yes, but for God's sake don't let him know that. Commodore Sartell and Captain Eyles have given me enough grief about not promoting him to full Captain already. At least neither of them is underfoot right now. Sartell is off playing diplomat in Luctini, in the Empire, and Eyles is back in the South Lanic in *Stellar.*" He sighed and turned away from the window. "Huan, have Lieutenant Wilson get in here. I'll need him to draft a summons for a court of inquiry. I'll use him to notify the members of the board I want on this. I'll let those idiots in Vice Admiral Hampton's pockets find out for themselves. Hopefully, I can keep that barely competent asshole and his sycophants out of the loop long enough to get Blaine back to sea."

"Yes, sir."

***

Captain Blaine watched the sharply dressed Lieutenant, the aiguillette of an Admiral's Flag Lieutenant looped through his jacket's epaulette, clamber up the ship's side. He stopped and straightened his jacket as he completed the standard boarding request at the top of the boarding portal, saluting the Officer of the Deck and the National Colors. The boat that had brought him out to where *Intrepid* was anchored shipped their oars and remained hooked to the main chains. He turned and headed for the quarterdeck where Blaine stood. Gravely Blaine returned his salute.

"Captain William Blaine, I am Lieutenant Allen Wilson, Flag Lieutenant for Admiral Mynheers, Head of the Navy Board for the Western Fleet." He pulled a black envelope sealed with green wax out of his messenger bag and proffered it to Blaine. "Sir, this is an official request and summons, requiring your presence, along with those of your officers and crew such as you see fit to order, at an inquiry to investigate the loss of KRN *Sorcerer* with all hands." Blaine took the envelope and broke the seal. He spent a couple of minutes perusing the two sheets of paper it contained.

"Well, Lieutenant Wilson, everything seems to be in order. I note that the Admiral has directed the Judge Advocate to provide the appropriate counsel for myself and my officers. Please present him with my thanks for his forethought. Otherwise I shall attend the Court tomorrow as required. I also note that his orders are for me to sequester my crew onboard until the inquiry is completed. Please advise the Admiral that I have two passengers onboard and inquire if the order to sequester should apply to them. One is Lieutenant Willis Fleet, Office of Naval Intelligence, returning from the Embassy to the Empire of Isemoto. The other is a rescue, Lady Silaqui of Montagar, an Elf of some rank."

"Lieutenant Fleet should be included in the order, Sir, at least I would think so, unless he has overriding orders. As for the other, hmm," Wilson's completely professional façade cracked a bit, "A real Elf, Captain? An Elf from Montagar?"

"Yes, Lieutenant." Blaine hid a smile. "A real Elf." In Kolbia, the Elder Races were very rarely seen. The average Kolbian-in-the-street, especially in the larger cities, probably never saw an Elf or Dwarf more than once in their lives, if ever. Most Kolbians considered them nearly mythical.

"Sir, I have no idea. Is there anything of importance she could provide to the Court?"

"Lieutenant, I doubt it. We rescued her from a pirate brigantine after the loss of *Sorcerer*. I see no reason to involve Lady Silaqui."

"Very well, Sir. I shall provide that information to the Admiral. I expect he will agree with your assessment."

***

Blaine brooded as Lieutenant Wilson's boat stroked back to the quayside. The Bosun, Dr. Hoff and Lieutenant Caplin stood at the centerline of the quarter-deck, waiting for his commands. Blaine turned away from the rail with a hidden sigh.

"Harry, make sure all the shipboard divisions are aware of the sequestration. Bosun, assist him as needed. Otherwise keep an eye out for any jolly boats looking to start doing the crew out of their pay before they even get it."

With a quick "Aye-aye," Caplin and the Bosun headed off to their tasks. Dr. Hoff stepped up beside Blaine.

"Well, that was nicely done, Billy."

"Whatever are you talking about, Elazar?" Blaine leaned on the rail and studied the old fortress. *Wonder if that prick Mynheers is glaring at me from that cushy office of his.*

"Neatly bypassed any mention of Sachi Takahashi. Wilson couldn't get his mind off Silaqui."

"Why in the world would anyone be interested in an Apprentice Seaman rated Cook's Mate Fourth Class?"

"Exactly. And I suppose you believe she had absolutely nothing to do whatsoever with the loss of *Sorcerer.*"

"Of course not."

"What about the lightning bolt or finger of God or whatever the hell it was that killed that thing?"

"What about it? How could Sachi have anything at all to do with that? Clearly it was an act of God. That or a meteor falling at exactly the right time. Which could also be considered an act of God. That or pure dumb luck." Blaine watched Hoff out of the corner of his eye.

"Well, I can't really argue with that. But something in the back of my head tells me there is a connection somewhere. Call it a physician's intuition. She had her worst fit and damn near died of blood loss right as that thing was headed for us. Face it, Billy, there's something very, very strange about her. I can't prove a damn thing, so don't even think of asking me why I think that or how she could have anything to do it."

"How, Elazar?" Blaine's hands tightened on the rail. "How in Heaven or Hell could she have anything to do with it?"

"I don't know how, Billy. I just don't know how. But I'm certain, down in my bones, that she has everything to do with it."

***

Sachi and Silaqui leaned comfortably against the mainmast as *Intrepid* rode easily at anchor. They were perched on the mainmast's royal yard, nearly two hundred feet above the frigate's deck. They passed a bottle of wine back and forth between them, drinking straight from the bottle. A cool breeze toyed with tendrils of hair that escaped from the braids they wore anytime they were skylarking in the rigging. Silaqui frowned as she watched a shower of sparks rise in a cloud of soot and ash from one of the blast furnaces.

"That cloud of ash is not a good thing." She closed her eyes and shook her head. "You humans. So confusing. Brilliant, creating beautiful things at one moment; the next, you poison the very air you breathe. So many contradictions. 'Tis why, I think, my folk can never understand you."

"What is that smoking building, Silaqui?"

"It is a furnace of some kind, I believe. In my homeland, the humans use things like that to make iron and steel. Just not so large."

"That...that is for making iron?"

"I believe so."

"Why so much?"

"For plows and guns and more things than I can possibly imagine." Silaqui sighed and sipped from the bottle of wine before handing it back to Sachi. The Nisei girl took it dubiously, wiping off the mouth of the bottle and then drinking from it herself. "I am told that on the other side of their country, the Kolbians are using iron beams to form the skeletons of great buildings reaching into the sky."

"Truly?"

"Well, it's what I have been told. I have not seen such things with my own eyes."

"Why do such a thing?"

"*Business*, whatever that is, is the excuse I'm given. Personally, I think they're all mad. They work too hard. They stay out in the sun too long. Everything done in order and by numbers. There's no romance in their souls." Sachi raised one dubious eyebrow at the last statement, then sniffed. "Well, maybe that's just most of them? There might be a few exceptions." Silaqui hid a smile and nudged her to get the bottle back. She wiped off the mouth and upended it, licking her lips as she finished the last of the wine. She smiled at Sachi. "Maybe you know of an exception?"

"Will you give it a break?" Sachi rolled her eyes in exasperation. "Are all *Kami* so flighty?" She turned her attention to the side party piping Captain Blaine off the ship. He was going ashore to stand before a Court of Inquiry, she knew. What she didn't know was what could happen to him there. In Isemoto, a commander brought before the Emperor might be expected to answer for any failure with his life. She didn't think the Kolbians would put Captain Blaine to death for the loss of *Sorcerer*, but she wasn't sure. He was quite firm when he ordered her to remain aboard ship. A tear welled up and ran down her cheek and she tried to surreptitiously wipe it away.

"What's wrong, heart-sister?"

"Nothing."

"Don't lie to me, Sachi. A *Kami* always knows if you're lying."

"What if the Navy demands he apologize for the loss of *Sorcerer*? At the least I should be there. I doubt they would grant me the honor of being his second."

"What *are* you jabbering about?"

"If the Navy demands his life, then a trusted friend should be there for the neck blow after the person makes the third cut in their abdomen. The best swordsman will sever the spine cleanly, bringing instant death, but not completely sever the head. Some consider it a loss of honor for the second to cause the head to roll free. I know I can make that cut cleanly and properly. My family made me practice, first on sheep and then on the older slaves." Another tear traced its way down a porcelain cheek as she turned to face Silaqui. "I should be there."

"Gods of my ancestors." Silaqui was stunned. "And I thought the Kolbians were insane." She put her hand on the teenager's shoulder. "Sachi, even I know the Kolbian Navy does not do such things. What they call capital punishment is reserved only for the most heinous crimes. Pirates, slavers, rapists, and murderers are normally the only ones put to death. It's an inquiry, Sachi, not a trial. He'll be fine. The Navy will not demand his life. Only a traitor is put to death. Didn't you talk to Toby about this?"

"No, he was too busy getting the Captain's best uniform ready. He went on the first boat with Doctor Hoff and the pieces of the sea monster. Said something about preparing the exhibits."

"Sachi, the Navy wants to know what happened and a Court of Inquiry is how they do it for the *Official Record*, or so I was told."

"Oh." A sheepish smile crept across Sachi's face. "Am I being foolish, then?"

"Somewhat." Silaqui drew her into a gentle hug. "Kolbians are nothing like my folk, or yours either. Don't fall into the mistake of thinking the Kolbians are like your home. They are vastly different." She wiped away the tear. "Better, now?"

"Yes, thank you."

"Apprentice Seaman Takashi! Front and center on deck, NOW!" Caplin's shout through his speaking trumpet startled both women. They looked down and saw Lieutenant Commander Caplin standing beside Lieutenant Fleet.

"Looks like they want you. Best be going." The elf sighed. "I shall stay here awhile and enjoy sun and sky."

Sachi grabbed the backstay and slid down it, thumping onto the deck in front of the two lieutenants. During the voyage, Toby had taught her the rudiments of military courtesy expected in the Kolbian Navy. So neither of them were surprised when she came to the position of attention and rendered a passable salute.

"Apprentice Seaman Takashi reporting, sir."

"Excellent." Harry hid a smile. Regardless of her beauty, the Nisei girl proved to be an outstanding shipmate, generally cheerful and hard working. The one sailor who foolishly thought to take liberties with her had recovered nicely from the beating she gave him. After that, the entire crew respectfully treated her as if she were a combination of favored little sister and ship's mascot. "I want you to go with Lieutenant Fleet and thoroughly review your work on preparing to apply for citizenship at the Nationality Service. We expect you to pass the exams with flying colors, young lady!"

"Aye-aye, sir." She was instantly solemn. *The very idea of becoming a Kolbian! I wasn't born here.* She smiled to herself. *Only the Kolbians would think of taking anyone and making them a part of their nation! Silaqui might be right, they are insane!* "After you, Lieutenant Fleet." She followed Fleet into the wardroom.

***

"This Court finds the loss of KRN *Sorcerer* to be due to environmental hazards beyond any reasonable or expected level of preparation or control by the ad-hoc squadron commander. Therefore, no recommendation of censure shall be entertained for Captain, Junior Grade William Blaine, KRN. Indeed, the actions of Captain Blaine reflect the outstanding standards expected of a Captain of the KRN. This Court of Inquiry is hereby adjourned." Admiral Mynheers rapped sharply on the tabletop with his gavel.

Blaine suppressed a sigh as the members of the Court's Board, five flag rank officers, gathered up their papers and assistants and departed. Admiral Mynheers gestured for Blaine to join him in front of the tooth of the sea monster where it laid on a display table.

"Just a tooth?"

"Yes, sir. From what I saw, I believe the thing was longer than *Intrepid* was, maybe half again as long. Tamras and *Sorcerer* never had a ghost of chance."

"And whatever it was that killed it?"

"No idea; something from space, I believe — a meteor, perhaps."

"Do you think *Intrepid's* guns would have stopped it?"

"Sir, I don't know. Frankly, I doubt it. We might have hurt it enough to drive it off. The explosive shells might have done the job, but we were loaded with shot and grape. Probably would have just pissed it off, sir."

"Humpf. Any suggestions?"

"Maybe mount those new rifled cannons I've heard rumors about? Some type of underwater explosives? In hindsight, I'd suggest loading with explosive shells if they're available. Not really my area of expertise, Admiral."

"Humpf." Age and stress had turned Mynheers' hair completely white, but his gray eyes were as sharp as they had ever been. "You haven't done a stint on the Ordnance Board, have you?"

"No, sir. I've always been at sea, as man and boy, for twenty-two years now."

"You do know, with the new Academy starting up classes next year, those days of ten- or twelve-year-old boys serving on ships as midshipmen for a half-dozen years or so will be ending?"

"Yes, sir. I can see advantages to both methods, but things always change, don't they?"

"Yes, they do." Mynheers motioned for Blaine to follow him as he left the room and walked out onto the parapet of the old wall.

Blaine followed the old Admiral, wondering what was coming. He couldn't think of anything he would dread more than a stretch of shore duty. Lately the scuttlebutt foretold that momentous changes to the Navy were coming. Blaine had first served as a young midshipman on one of the last of the oared galleasses of the Kolbian fleet. The development of improved sail plans and heavy, relatively rapid-firing guns marked the end of the era of the rowed galleys and galleasses. And now, it seemed that new advancements would make the day of the broadside armed ship of the line as obsolete as the ram equipped galley of fifty years ago was now.

A man named Harald Fulmark had created an engine that functioned on the pressure of steam created by boiling water. Some eastern factories were experimenting with his *Pressure Engine*, supposedly using the things to replace the power supplied by water wheels. Here in Carolington, a local businessman had built a ferry boat with one of Fulmark's pressure engines driving an awkward paddle wheel arrangement. Blaine could see obvious advantages to being able to sail against the wind, but against that would be the need to carry fuel of some type, wood, or coal perhaps. And how fragile the machinery would be. Mynheers stopped and leaned against one side of an embrasure. Those gray eyes searched the harbor and found *Intrepid* before turning back to Blaine.

"She's a beauty, Bonny, *Intrepid* is, even riding at anchor." He snorted a bit as Blaine colored. "You don't mind the nickname, do you?"

"No, sir. Not from a senior Admiral, sir." Blaine hated that nickname, but too many of his friends and superiors used it.

"Humpf." He sighed. "Well, she *is* a beauty, William, but she may be the last of her kind. I've seen the blueprints and designs for the next generation. Much will depend on if we can make the mechanicals work to spec. And if the steel mills can turn out the machinery and armor to spec. If they can produce the iron and steel and if we can build the ships, the Empire can stuff their *two thousand ship* Navy where the sun doesn't shine. So can every other navy on the planet. But that is certainly a lot of *ifs* and *ands*." He dug a pipe out of his pocket and made a show of knocking it out, refilling and lighting it. "So, what didn't go in the ship's log or your voyage report?"

"Beg pardon, sir?"

"Don't bullshit a bullshitter, son. There's always something that's important, but not in the official reports for one reason or another. What didn't make it into the logbook?"

"I take it this is the *unofficial* debriefing then, Admiral?"

"You might say that. William, I served at sea for over forty years, commanding everything from the Captain's barge as a raw ensign to my last command, *Pride of Kolbia,* when she was the national flagship and the most powerful warship in the world. I understand the *Pride* is to be preserved as a museum ship now. You could think a museum is where I belong as well?"

"No, sir."

"Remember what I said about bullshitting a bullshitter?" Mynheers smothered a chuckle at the stuffed expression on Blaine's face. "Lots of things never made it into my logs. No one would have officially believed them, and it likely would have ruined my career. You better damn well learn this if you don't know it already. Understood?"

"Yes, sir."

"So, what's not in the book?" Mynheers turned his back to the harbor and drew on his pipe. He exhaled and sent a near perfect smoke ring floating over the wall. He pointed at Blaine with the pipe. "Sit down somewhere and tell me what did not make it into your log."

"Well, Admiral, it's like this." Blaine sighed and sat on the breech of an obsolete cannon that still held a lonely vigil over the harbor. Mynheers hitched a leg up on the lip of the embrasure and waited. "We were three weeks out of the Nisei port of Akumato when I was informed that we had a problem with pilferage of stores and water. I placed a guard and not quite a week later, I had this Nisei girl hauled in front of me. Turned out she was trained as one of their *Shinijutsuka* sneaks and she was on the run from her family, the Oda Family of Clan Ishikawa, we believe, at least according to Lieutenant Willis Fleet. He's a Nisei expert from ONI we brought back from the Embassy there."

"I know of him. Old Navy family, I served under his grandfather when I was a smart-ass young Captain J.G. many years ago." Mynheers interrupted. "I'd expect Lieutenant Fleet knows his stuff, language expert and all that. And of that Nisei clan, well, rumors at least. Sorry, go on."

"Yes, sir. Well, you see, sir, what happened that night was..."

***

Two and a half hours later, Blaine and the Admiral sat in his office. Blaine was sweating a bit, from the rather thorough grilling he'd just survived. Thankfully, the Admiral shared his taste in good whiskey and furthermore, was willing to share at least some that whiskey with him.

"A solid bar or beam of light, eh?"

"Yes, sir. Whatever killed that sea monster was like nothing I've ever seen or imagined. I've seen my share of meteors and similar things falling from space. And lots of other odd things. I was part of Project Iconus back when I was a Lieutenant."

"I was partly in the loop on that one. If you can, without violating the National Secrets Act, tell me what you thought of that operation?"

"We recovered some fascinating stuff, sir. But none of it was ever made to do anything. It was all as inert as the star-metal in the paperweight my daughter gave me when I took command of *Intrepid* last year. Or the artifacts that turn up made of white-steel. Blades that never dull and can literally shave slivers off the best steel. Pieces of armor that nothing can penetrate. You're aware of all that kind of stuff that the kooks say is proof that the Emperor Confas and all the stories of the Fall are literally true."

"Certainly, some of the stories are true, Captain. I've seen the craters myself. We've both seen the Shadow in the Lanic, and the latest telescopes pretty much prove that the object in orbit that casts the Shadow is gigantic and probably not entirely natural. *Someone* put it where it is! Not to mention all the other, obviously artificial artifacts that orbit our planet."

"I know that, sir. Anyone who truly stops and thinks about it for even a minute or two will realize that there must be some bit of truth to those old stories. There's too many odd things in odd places." Blaine sighed. "But whatever that beam, or bar of light or energy was, it's like nothing anyone has ever even heard of. And my Surgeon Commander, Dr. Elazar Hoff, swears that somehow, in some fashion we can't imagine, this girl, Takahashi Sachi, has a place in these occurrences, especially that one."

"Is she some kind of magician, then?"

"No, sir. If anything, she's exactly the opposite."

"What about the Elf woman?"

"She's as magical as they get, some sort of spellcaster, but she wasn't on the ship at that point. As you know, Admiral, the family she comes from is one of the major power brokers in the Kingdom of Montagar. Assuming she's telling the truth, that is."

"Well, I certainly believe she is. We do have a *Person of Interest* request from the Montagaran Embassy that's nearly two years old. They were looking for an Elvish woman named Maerilwyn MacGaellyn. The description matches the one you gave of this *Silaqui* perfectly. Given that Elves on their Wandering often choose new names, I'd say it's her. Her uncle is a scary bastard, I'm given to understand, and he has a great deal of influence with both the Montagaran Royals and the rather murky Elvish Court. Probably a good thing you didn't hang her." Blaine grimaced at the Admiral's desiccated tone.

"Yes, sir. Something else influenced by the Takahashi girl, sir."

"Humpf. Damn pain in the butt, elves." Mynheers seemed lost for a long while, staring into the bottom of his glass, looking for answers in the last swallow of fine Montagaran whiskey. "All right. Unless there is some truly unexpected change, your log stays as is. This Takahashi girl's situation will simply be considered another slightly non-standard request to immigrate. She wouldn't be the first stowaway that got here in that manner. Likely won't be the last, either."

"Yes, sir."

"Now for your situation. I'm fairly pleased with your conduct of the show-the-flag voyage to Isemoto, probably kept that young fart, Fleet, from getting killed. Of course, the reward for a good job is another, usually harder, job." The Admiral paused for a long moment.

"Yes, sir?"

"You will receive orders confirming you as continuing in command of *Intrepid*. Don't be so fucking happy until you see what I'm sending you to do and where you'll have to do it."

"Yes, sir." Blaine hid a frown. *That doesn't sound good. Can anything make retaining command of* Intrepid *not the best thing I've experienced in a while?*

"You will escort a convoy of merchant ships and two Navy transports via the Kolbian Straights to Capitol City on the east coast. After seeing your charges secure at Stark Haven in Capitol Bay, you will proceed with all haste and at your best speed to the Kingdom of Montagar to repatriate the Lady Elf, Silaqui of Montagar. When that mission is complete, you shall return to Stark Haven at all speed. There you will oversee the refitting and up-gunning of KRN *Intrepid* and then present her and yourself to CO-Lanic Fleet for reassignment."

"I see, sir. May I assume that my crews' dependents have been notified?"

"They have, or rather they were about three weeks ago. And yes, that includes your spouse. I understand she was not pleased with that news."

"I can imagine. Has she packed up and left already or will she be on one of the transports?"

"William, I understand that there are difficulties between you and her. If it doesn't affect your performance as an officer, I have no input. However, I did ensure that she was informed that neither official quarters at your new duty station nor official, compensated transport would be available for her until after *Intrepid* made landfall. I was informed that she was not *pleased*. Despite whatever she might think, I, personally, could not give a fart in a hurricane whether or not she's *pleased*." He paused for a long, thoughtful moment, then sighed. "William, I've heard a little bit about your...marital problems. I do not particularly like what I've heard. At the risk of repeating myself, let me remind you that if it does not affect your professional military performance, I have no nose to stick in your business. However, your wife's actions can reflect on you as well. Won't matter, well, not *too* much, at your present rank, but you're due to be considered for full Captain soon. At that rank and higher, her behavior can affect your career. Keep that in mind, is all I'll say at this point."

"Yes, sir."

"Huh. *Yes, sir.* Nice noncommittal comment there, Captain Blaine."

"Sir." *I thought I saw a grin there for a second. That can't be possible!* "Will *Intrepid* be the only escort?"

"Not hardly. You will assume ad-hoc squadron command. In addition to *Intrepid*, the escort will consist of the frigate *Christine*, 32 and the sloop-of-war *Swift*, 18. The schooners *Wing*, 10 and *Fairy*, 10 will provide scouting and flank duty. The convoy will consist of fourteen merchant galleons transporting primarily military cargo and some personnel. Armed naval transport galleons *Ocean* and *Seaway* will provide transport for all remaining military personnel and specific sensitive cargo. And yes, they are slow as hell."

"I see, Admiral."

"You will receive written orders covering all specifics within the week. In the meanwhile, inform your crew, try to retain as many of those due to be paid off as you can. Very shortly, I believe we are going to need every competent sailor we can scrape up."

"That's new, sir. What's changed?"

"There have been a couple of fairly nasty incidents in the South Lanic, both dealing with slavers taken in open waters by our anti-piracy patrols there.

Incidents that got very ugly when Imperial Navy ships tried to intervene. Both slavers were flying Imperial flags, so the Imperials claimed jurisdiction but...here's the catch, both had full holds of slaves, including a couple dozen Kolbian merchant sailors in one case and over fifty young Kolbian women in the other! Some of those *women* were as young as twelve!"

"What the hell?! How did they get there?!"

"Apparently there are kidnapping and slaving rings operating on the east coast, deliberately targeting young, pretty Kolbian women for sale to the barbarian kingdoms of southern Khakal or in some of the Empire's more unsavory markets."

"Oh my God."

"I doubt he had anything to do with that, but it was Eyles in *Stellar* that caught the latter. According to the reports, about an hour later, three of those big, more or less seaworthy galleasses of theirs show up and demand the slaver ship *and all its cargo* be turned over to them for trial and eventual repatriation. You can imagine how that went over with Eyles."

"Oh, yes."

"I believe he told the senior Imperial captain to *go back to humping his sheep* and stand down. Of course, the Impie got his undies in a nasty bunch and demanded the slavers and the captives be turned over immediately *or else* and for Eyles to heave to and be boarded for *inspection and search for Imperial deserters.* Again, you can imagine how that went over."

"So, we are at war with the Empire now?"

"Not yet, far as I know. *Stellar* took a bit of a pounding but she hammered all three Impies into wrecks. And it turns out one of the captives was a cousin of one of the Eindeuten Grand Dukes and there were a couple of ranking Montagaran priests in that slaver's hold as well. So, the Pi-Imperator who is their current Chancellor then gets warnings from both the Eindeuten Empire *and* the Kingdom of Montagar and their Elven and Dwarven allies that a declaration of war on the Republic of Kolbia will be considered declarations on them as well. Somehow, sanity prevailed, and the Empire officially disavowed the actions of one Capitan Senior Commodore M. Havier Vies Ruiz-Palmaroli, who fortunately or unfortunately, depending on your point of view, took poison before he could go to trial. But now we have the very influential Palmaroli clan enraged with us. Of course, all this was over nine months ago, so no doubt things will have changed in the Lanic since then. Probably for the worse."

"Oh, Lord. So this is the reason for the transfer and heavy escort, I take it, sir?"

"Absolutely. ONI has solid reports that the Empire is refurbishing all those old galleys of theirs — no idea what they think they're going to do with them — and putting *lots* of new construction down. The new ships are closer to what we have in service right now, but they lack the foundries to arm them properly. They're also frantically building new foundries as well." The Admiral poured himself a bit more whiskey and offered the bottle to Blaine, who declined. "Like it or not, Bonny, war with the Empire is coming, sooner rather than later, or so I believe. *If* we can get the new designs afloat and *if* they work like we expect and *if* we can build enough of them fast enough, the Impies will get their asses booted up between their ears. If not, then that will be a much closer run thing. Our Navy is vastly superior in terms of ability, training, and combat capability, but they do have a very substantial numerical advantage. The Empire has damn near unlimited manpower. Fortunately for us, there's a bloody great ocean between us and them."

"That does help a bit, doesn't it, sir?"

"The Imperial Pikes may be the most powerful infantry force in the world, but they don't swim worth a shit. And I'm not so sure the Pikes are the world's best infantry anymore. Even if the Impies have twice as many men in each formation as we do, I think the Army's New Model Brigade would handle them rather roughly. But personally, I'd prefer to not have to find out."

"I agree wholeheartedly, sir."

"Well, then stop wasting my time and drinking my booze and get back to your ship."

"Yes, sir."

***

Sachi stared as the ferry backed effortlessly away from the quay and turned toward the open water of the bay. Black smoke poured from the tall twin stacks looming over the packed deck. She could hear a *chuff, chuff, chuff* from belowdecks as the engine took up the strain of driving the tall paddlewheels on either side of the ferry.

"How is this possible, Toby? This ship has no masts or sails. There are no rowers. Are there slaves locked below, turning the wheels?"

"Sachi, stop and think. Do you really believe anyone in our nation would be using slaves to drive a ship?"

"Well, no. So is it magic or sorcery then?"

"No, of course not. They were talking about this ship when we left for Isemoto last year. She was on the ways being built. I personally didn't think they'd get her in operation this fast, but the *Sirena* here uses that new engine of Mister Fulmark's. It's called a *pressure engine*, I understand. Boils water and uses the steam to drive a piston that drives a shaft. The shaft uses gears to drive the wheels. Nothing magical, just a coal fire boiling water and making steam. Civilian owners don't have to get the Navy Board to convince the Council of Legates and the Quorum to pony up the cash for *unreliable and unproved experimental engines that blow up with disturbing regularity*. They just build the ships."

"What?! These things can explode?!" Sachi yelped, eyes wide. She snapped her head back to harbor water, tensing as she considered going over the rail and swimming for shore.

"Relax, will you. It's okay. Yeah, some of the early ones did, about five years ago. Took Mr. Fulmark a lot of work and a lot of money, but he DID get the bugs worked out. There's a factory in Carolington City that started using one of the engines about a year before we left for Isemoto. No problems, far as I've heard. Of course, doing things in new ways and trying new ideas always has a certain risk to it. One of the things that makes us Kolbians so different, I guess." Toby gave her a toothy smile. "Besides, politicians *always* exaggerate! The first engine did burst its boiler, poor metallurgy I heard. The third one was tested and abused until it did explode, on purpose. I'd say they're as safe as anything else is. Life is invariably fatal. Unless you're an Elf, I guess."

"That doesn't do me any good, Toby."

"Don't worry, Sachi. Just enjoy the ride and look forward to your first real trip into Kolbian society. You're in for a shock. Kolbians are generally loud, boisterous and, to you, no doubt, a little rude."

"I can imagine. Are most people better than sailors, Toby?"

"Actually, most civilians are a little bit worse."

"Wonderful."

"Of course, a crew on leave can get a bit...boisterous. Especially once they get a few stiff drinks in them."

"Starting to think I should have stayed onboard with Silaqui!" Sachi shouted to be heard over the increasing noise of the engine, the churning paddles and finally the hoot of the ferry's steam-powered whistle drowned the last word she said. She shrugged and smiled at Toby. She was looking forward to her first footsteps on the Kolbian mainland. And her first time in something the crew called a saloon. She wondered if it was anything like a *geisha* house.

Carolington City
Master's Residence

"Black eyes, you say?"

"Yes, Master." The redheaded young woman kept her eyes downcast.

"Tell me again *exactly* where you saw her."

"She was going into the Sailor's Temptation with some sailors off the *Intrepid*, including that big one who won the All Navy boxing tournament last two years running. I noticed her 'cause she was dressed a little funny and she had a braid of black hair hanging past her butt. After a second look, I followed her because of her looks. She'd fetch big money at auction in the Empire. I took a seat at the next table and just watched them. That's when I noticed her eyes. Never seen someone with truly black eyes before. That's one of the things you told us to watch for, Master."

"Indeed, it is. Did you learn where she is from?"

"I never spoke to any of them in the bar, but I got another one of the sailors to spend some money on me and later he told me the girl came aboard in Isemoto. Most Nisei have black hair and dark eyes, so she may just have real dark brown eyes and they looked black in the light. He also said there's somewhat wrong with her as she has these fits where she goes unconscious."

"Could this sailor remember you later?"

"Well, I would hope he would have, considering the ride I gave him. But he won't, 'cause I cut his throat and dumped his body in the Bay. The tide was going out and if his body's ever found, it'll be weeks. And none of his shipmates saw me with him. And if they did, they'll be looking for a blonde, not a redhead."

"Well done, Felicity. Try to keep a close eye on this Nisei girl. I know that will be difficult with all the immigrant Han and Nisei that live here but do the best you can. Higher will very probably be interested in her."

"Yes, Master. Will there be anything else, Master?" There was a bleak glimmer in the young woman's blue eyes.

"I believe so, Felicity. Come with me, my dear." Master, a tall, heavily built man with slicked-back blond hair rose from his seat and smiled as he offered his hand to Felicity. The buxom redhead returned the smile. She knew better than to do anything else. Her filmy over-robe slithered off her shoulders as she took Master's hand and followed him into the bedroom.

Carolington Roads Naval Base
Captain Blaine's Assigned Quarters

"Reassigned to the Eastern Fleet?"

"Yes, dear."

"Fourteen years here on the West Coast and they just *reassign* you to the other side of the continent!" Emily Blaine snarled her frustration as William sat down behind his desk. His study was a comfortable size, large enough for his bookcases, desk, a favorite old couch, and a couple of comfortable chairs.

"Yes, dear. The Navy does do that. They give me orders and I obey them. That's the deal." His blue eyes locked with her hazel ones. "And where is Sally today? I expected she'd be here once I was done at the Navy Board today."

"She's at a friend's house. I sent her over there so we could talk. What the hell is the Navy thinking, sending you to the other side of the country?! You've been in the Western Fleet since before we got married! I can't just uproot my entire life at your whim!"

William wanted to just close his eyes and shut her out. Emily Blaine was still a very physically attractive woman, especially if you liked tall, leggy blondes. But there was a calculating hardness in those hazel eyes now. *That wasn't there when we got married. At least I don't think so. If it was, I sure as hell didn't see it then. Now eyes that hard would be more appropriate on a Dock Street whore. That or a ten term Legate trying to figure a way around the Constitution to get elected again. You'd think after fourteen years she'd understand the concept of* The needs of the Service come foremost, *but no, not her. It's always about her. What the hell happened to us? Did she ever genuinely love me, or am I just another status symbol like the rest of the stuff she's crammed into this house?*

"Emily, dear, you know the needs of the Service come foremost. They always have, and they always will. Or do you expect me to resign my commission rather than be transferred?"

"And what would that do to our finances? Not to mention my social standing here in Carolington?" she snapped. "I've no wish to spend the rest of my life as an impoverished merchant captain's wife! Or live in the kind of home that would provide."

"Emily, I think your expectations are completely unrealistic. I know several very wealthy merchant captains. They hardly live in hovels down in the Fish Wharf District."

"They certainly don't live like an admiral does either!"

"Is that what this is all about? *Your* status, *your* wealth, *your* position in a certain group that some idiots call *Society?!*" Blaine struggled to contain his temper. "I'd like to remind you that even though I am a holder of the Medal of Valor, that certainly does NOT guarantee me an Admiral's streamer! Nothing does. Now, Goddamn it, I want to see my daughter! You can either tell me which *friend* she is visiting, and I'll go get her, or you can have her within these walls within the hour, or so help me God, I'll..." His chair crashed over as Blaine surged to his feet, the desk between them.

"You'll *what!?* Strike me, beat me, throw me out the door?" She sneered at him. "And what then of the oath you swore to me on our wedding day? *To have and to hold, in better or worse.* What about your precious *honor?!*" Her eyes glittered with her fury.

Blaine froze. For a full minute, he simply stared at her, by turns frozen with despair and burning with rage. Then, with the over-controlled motions of a person teetering on the edge of unrestrained violence, he turned and set his chair upright. Slowly he sank into the chair. He took a deep breath, then another, and the tension flowed out of him.

"Normally it takes you almost ten minutes to start throwing my intention to honor my oaths, *all of them*, in my face. Today, you did it in just barely five." He relaxed slightly, putting his head in his hands, elbows braced on the desktop. "Is this what we've come to, Emily?" He sighed. "Can we not simply declare a truce, then?"

"Perhaps." Emily was a bit shaken herself. She had never seen the light of battle in his eyes, the confidence and certainty with which he rode his ship into the furious heart of battle, like an ancient Eindeuten knight amid the bloody fray on his mighty charger. She stepped back from the desk and sat down on the old couch set between the bookcases across from his desk. "Perhaps I was...um...hasty."

"Perhaps." He raised his gaze to meet hers. *I need to change tack here, chart a new course. Hope I don't get caught in irons as I come about. Take her by surprise, grab the weather gauge and hold it. Show her what she seems to want. When did she become so shallow, or was this always there? Her family is still the worst type of social climbers, but I thought she was different.* "And perhaps you've failed to grasp the opportunity this offers you? I would be allocated quarters in Capitol City itself. The base at Stark Haven does not begin to have the room to offer even half the quarters that Carolington Island does. The quarters in Capitol City that are available for Captains are much better there than here. Many of the Consuls of the Quorum and Legates maintain their homes in the same area. Not to mention the availability of the fine citizens who no doubt makes up the *Society* of Capitol City itself. Invitations to the Tribune's Ball should be easily obtained for the wife of a holder of the Medal. Maybe you're being a bit...provincial, my dear?"

"Provincial? Hardly."

"So you would prefer remaining here, in Carolington City? Why? Heck, Carolington isn't even the capital of Timikken Publican. If it weren't for the Navy and the Bay, Carolington City would be a third the size it is today, populated mostly by fishermen and woodcutters. My dear, if you honestly want to shine in the center of Society's eye, this is not the place you should be. Honestly, I'm surprised you haven't been at Admiral Mynheers to get me reassigned to the

Eastern Fleet. Don't you know Vice Admiral Hampton's wife, Janay? I'm sure she could enlighten you on what Society on the East Coast is like."

***

"Hmm. I do know Janay Hampton fairly well." *Unfortunately. That idiot lush. But her husband has been an Admiral for over thirty years. Maybe neither of them is as stupid as they so often seem? Might be worth my time to hold my nose and question that harpy.* "Perhaps I'll ask her opinion." She stared out the window behind his desk as she tapped a tooth with a manicured forefinger.

***

"Good." Blaine stole a glance at Emily as she stared out the window. *Please do. The only thing that moronic warthog can bleat about is how wonderful the Season is in Capitol City. Of course, bad as Mynheers can be, Hampton is ten times as useless and that hag of a wife of his is worse yet!* "Now, perhaps we can lay this matter to rest? The Navy says *Go*, and I must go. No choice in the matter. Look for the opportunities this could provide; wouldn't that be better?"

***

"I think so." *Well, it seems that I can either face the inevitable, turn it to my advantage or wind up dumped on the dockside here. Piss him off bad enough and he could sue for divorce. I'd probably be able to keep Sally away from him, but given that she's turning fourteen next year, she could hire her own attorney to argue her preferences on who has her in their custody. Ungrateful little brat. I cannot believe that girl is my daughter. Hmm I think I know another way to put a kink in his butt and keep him and her apart for a little longer.* "Actually, my dear, I sent Sally to her friend's house so we could have a little...time...to ourselves, first. I even gave the entire staff the day off, so we could have the whole house to ourselves, do whatever we want, whatever *you* want, anywhere you want. Couldn't we use our limited...private, alone time for better purposes than fighting like screeching fishwives? Please?" Emily rose from the couch and slowly stalked around the desk, one hand slowly undoing the buttons of her silk blouse as she reached out and turned Blaine in his chair to face her. Her skirt was ankle length and snug as current fashion decreed, but it slid smoothly up her silk stockings, bunching around her slim waist as she straddled Blaine, pulling down her chemise and drawing his face into her now-revealed breasts.

"Ah, I guess, certainly, dear." Blaine fought to maintain his composure. "I never thought I guess, ah...Merpmf." He stiffened as she reached between his legs and grasped him, her lips hot and moist on his. Her tongue thrust into his mouth, seeking his. "Hmm."

"I want you, dear," her voice was husky in his ear as she broke the kiss. "Here. Now. That's an order, sailor."

***

"Yes, ma'am," he mumbled as she started stripping away his uniform as his hands, of their own volition, found the buttons and hooks of her clothing. *Not what I had in mind, but better than fighting, I guess. But is she doing this out of love? Not likely. Out of lust, maybe, or just out of a desire to manipulate and control me. Or am I just the most currently available fuck-toy? Fine. I've been away for months, damn near a year. She is my wife, damn it. This should have been what I wanted the instant my feet hit the shore. Why does it feel like we're just using each other?*

***

Later, when their passion was spent, they lay on the comfortable couch, Emily's head on his shoulder while she drowsed as she always did after lovemaking. In Blaine's mind's eye, the hair he absent-mindedly stroked was long and lustrous, as black and glossy as a raven's wing, not the elaborate blonde curls under his hand.

Chapter Twelve

Omega 2-Cygni System Command
July 1478, Third Age of Imperial Reckoning

"Okay, D.A.V.E., what have we learned about that Kolbian naval ship?" Captain McAllen leaned back in her command chair, scowling at the display in the holo-tank. A three-dimensional image of *Intrepid* slowly rotated in the tank. Text and icons highlighted key elements of the ship. "For once, be specific and assume I have no a-priori knowledge of Kolbia. Maybe that'll shake something loose, something I'm too close or too familiar with to see." She frowned for a moment. "I'm tempted to wake someone up out of schedule, but that has issues of its own. So D.AV.E., brief me as if I'm fresh outta stasis."

::Understood, Captain McAllen. The vessel in question is a warship of the Kolbian Republican Navy, KRN *Intrepid*. She is a forty-four-gun frigate, nearly identical to the ancient frigates of the old North American republic on Terra, circa early nineteenth century, see 'War of 1812,' old Terran dating system. She is a direct result of Project Columbia, limited and clandestine transfer of appropriate technology from surviving Confederal personnel to carefully selected individuals within contemporary political systems. The Republic of Kolbia is the primary and most critical result of that project. Another example is the surreptitious contacts and information transfer between Senior Consultant Marianne Lundgren and Harald Fulmark resulting in his rapid and successful development of the steam engine. In addition, there is...::

"Stop." The single command silenced the program. She sighed and stared unseeing at the overhead. "There were a lot of arguments over Project Columbia. But damnit, we had to do something. Early on, every so-called, leader, chief, king, emperor, grand high swami, whatever, all of them thought they were a literal god-on-earth. No way was that going to lead to a modern industrial civilization. Not what was needed. Not then and not now." She sipped from her coffee cup.

::I believe that was the rationalization for the creation of the original Empire of Rolandus? An attempt to both suppress totalitarian regimes and advance culture and civilization?::

"Yeah, D.A.V.E., that was our idea. We never really believed the damn Seekers would use nuclear and kinetic energy weapons so fricking liberally. We lost a lot of people and that's when the decision to go 'underground,' as it were, was made. Regardless, those bastards blew everything to hell, the last AIs died, and it's been a shadow war since then. Took nearly two thousand years to get any semblance of civilization going again. Not to mention how enraged the native races were, after that." She paused and made a face at her coffee, now cold. "And now, every nation on this damn dirtball planet seems damned and determined to sink further and further into authoritarian systems of government, so we pushed the Kolbians along. Maybe too fast. Regardless, that's got nothing to do with this ship. What is so important about that ship? Something hacked into our comm-web system, hijacked a defense satellite and blew an exceptionally large carnivorous fish into sushi, just to protect that ship." McAllen ground her teeth in frustration. "It sure as hell wasn't a rogue D.A.V.E. that pulled that stunt. A Digitally Aware Virtual Entity like you just doesn't have the processing power to do that. Not without leaving fingerprints everywhere! The Seekers sure as hell don't have that kind of horsepower. If they did, we'd all be dead. But only a full up A.I., one with a ton of processing power, could have done that. Probably at least a Class Four or better. And we all know there isn't an A.I. of any class anywhere in the entire damn star system. Therefore, we need the answers to the How and the Why. The How is bad enough but the Why is gonna drive me to drink. Heavily."

::Probabilities are unknown currently. However, the spy-satellite currently tasked to observe the *Intrepid* has provided some interesting information. You did read the footnotes of my report, correct?::

"Oh, shit." McAllen raised her hands to massage her temples. "No, I just read the report itself. Ordinary sailing vessel for her day. Big and powerful for something classed as a frigate. Damn. Okay, what'd I miss?"

::There are two women onboard the *Intrepid*, in addition to the regular Kolbian crew. One is a Nisei from Isemoto, extraordinarily attractive by local standards, who managed to sneak aboard and survive as a stowaway for almost a month. Nothing particularly interesting about her, according to recent surveillance downloads. Suffers from a form of *gran mal* epilepsy, apparently.::

"And the other?"

::The other woman is one of the indigenous species, an elf. Apparently, she can access *non-rational quantum space-time*.::

"Great. Just what we need in the mix. Someone who can use magic. Is there any possible means by which she could have accessed the system?"

::There is a zero-point four eight percent chance, plus or minus four percent, that this elf even knows about the existence of the functional remnants of the Confederation defensive systems built here over nine thousand Standard years ago. Assuming awareness of the functional systems, the ability of the individual in question to access the system approaches a negative unity, plus or minus four percent. Theoretically possible, but the probability is extremely low.::

"Wonder-fucking-ful." She sighed and rubbed her eyes. "I know we don't have a Consultant of any level available on the West Coast right now. What about an Operative?"

::There are two Operatives within a two-hundred-mile journey who are available. I have prepared orders for them to transfer operations to the Carolington area. Do you wish those orders sent, Captain McAllen?::

"Yeah, get 'em moving. Might be too little, too late, but my gut is telling me this is a puzzle box we'd better figure out. I don't care what Commodore Collins said, I smell a rodent in the kitchen here." She stared at the hologram of the world floating below her viewpoint. "I'd really like to go back in time and punch the egghead that sent the first probe into this system right in the mouth. This place forces you to believe in the impossible six times before breakfast, every damn day."

Carolington Roads Naval Base.
Office of Naval Intelligence HQ
July 1478, Third Age of Imperial Reckoning

"Good report, Lieutenant Fleet. And a good job in Isemoto. I'm not sure if the techniques they use in producing their swords will do us any good but now at least we know how they do it." Rear Admiral Allyn Carstairs leaned back in his desk chair and propped his feet on his desk as he grinned at Fleet. "Relax. Step over there and pour us both a drink. The sun's over the yardarm somewhere."

"Yes, sir." Willis returned the Admiral's grin with interest as he headed over to the Admiral's well stocked liquor cabinet.

"So, unofficially, what happened down at the Sailor's Temptation last night?"

"The usual, naval sailors just into a port after a long exhausting voyage, a platoon of Marines straight out of their initial Basic, too much booze and a couple of pretty girls. Perfect ingredients for a lovely little tavern brawl."

"You'd think even Marines would think twice before starting a brawl with someone like Tobias Wilkerson in the room." The Admiral shook his head.

"In the Marines' defense, sir, they were grass green. A brand-new platoon on their one week leave after Basic. First time they'd been off base in three months. And it started when one of them decided that Sachi Takahashi was...ahem...available."

"Really? How'd that work out?"

"Well, the biggest damn Marine Private I've ever seen kind of reached out and grabbed her as she was going to the bar to get drinks for her and Toby, picked her up and plunked her down in his lap. And she froze. At least for a second or so. Toby just put his face in his hands. *And here we go,* I heard him mutter. Sachi said something to the Marine, probably along the lines of *Let me go, please,* I didn't really hear her, but I've learned she's unfailingly polite. Right before she beats the tar out of someone. The Jarhead smiled at her, not a nice smile at all, sir, squeezed her a little tighter, grabbed her breast, I think, and then stuck his hand in her crotch. That's when she kicked him in the face. Hard enough to knock out two teeth. While she was stuck in his lap with his arm around her."

"Are you kidding me?" Carstairs thought a minute. "Is that even possible?"

"Only if you're insanely flexible — and I know from personal experience that she is that flexible. And she's strong as hell too." Fleet tongued the tooth that Sachi had knocked out that first day. Dr. Hoff had reset it and it seemed to have reset well. "Unfortunately, she didn't hit him hard enough to lay him out. He roared and dumped her out of his lap. For a big guy he was crazy quick himself. But both swings and the snap kick he launched at her missed by miles. Then, I swear to God, she gave him the prettiest smile and hit him four times in less than a second. He hit the floor so hard, dust came up between the floorboards. One of his buddies yelled and then jumped up and tried to grab her. Might as well have tried to grab smoke. Somehow, she grabbed him, spun him around and threw him back into the Marines' table. The Marines came up swinging, the sailors bailed in, Toby laid out a Marine trying futilely to hit Sachi with a chair and the fight was on."

"Sounds like a good time was had by all? And where were you in all this fun?" The Admiral pointed at his desk blotter when Fleet came back with two full glasses.

"Oh, yes, sir. I'd say so. And since I was dressed in civvies and working at being unnoticed, well, no one noticed me. At first Sachi tried to stay out of it, at least until one of the Marines busted a chair over Wilkerson's head and stunned him.

He went down and she turned into a buzzsaw. She didn't kill anyone, but my God, that woman can hit hard. Hands, feet, her head, it didn't really matter. Anyone she hit pretty much decided they didn't want to play anymore. The Carolington police showed up around the same time as the Shore Patrol, but by then the fun was over because the Marines were laying all over the place, either groaning in pain or unconscious. Sachi was wiping the blood off Wilkerson's head and didn't have a mark on her."

"Anyone get hauled off to the lockup?"

"No, sir. When Sachi suggested the Marines pay for the damages instead of getting locked up, the owner agreed not to press any charges. And she came up with about a hundred Thalers out of her own pocket. No idea where she got that money from. I doubt sincerely she stole it while onboard *Intrepid*. None of the crew ever reported so much as a copper Fensgrif missing. She might have brought it onboard with her."

"She sounds like quite a package."

"Oh, she is, sir. She doesn't seem to ever forget anything, learns unbelievably fast and has incredible physical ability. Drop dead gorgeous and just exudes sex appeal when she wants to, then she turns it off and you could walk right by her without ever seeing her."

"Sounds like we should recruit her?"

"Yes, sir. She's not Navy, not really, but we could certainly use someone with her talents."

"Hmm, so how do we get our nefarious claws in her good enough to get some use out of her?"

"Well, sir, if she passes the Nationality Board exams, she'll be most of the way to being a Kolbian citizen. As a citizen candidate, she'll have all the protections guaranteed by our Constitution."

"Might make it a bit harder to *convince* her to work for us, without her actually being in the Navy. What are the chances of her failing the exams?"

"Essentially zero, sir. I went over the material with her myself. I'd expect her to have a perfect score."

"So we'd have to cheat?"

"Yes, sir."

"In the long run, that would turn around and bite us in the ass, most likely."

"Yes, sir."

"Suggestions, then, Lieutenant Commander Fleet?"

"Excuse me, sir?" Fleet raised an eyebrow. "Don't you mean Lieutenant?" In answer, Carstairs opened his desk drawer and extracted a small box, tossing it to Fleet, who caught it awkwardly.

"Nope. Those were mine, back when I was a lowly Lieutenant Commander. While a good job generally earns you another, usually harder, job, this time you have earned a nice little bonus. Congratulations, Lieutenant Commander Fleet. Do them proud. So, as I said, suggestions of what to do with this Sachi Takahashi?"

"Well, sir, if we want to keep her in our good graces while maintaining a minimum of control, I'd suggest keeping her from ever taking the exams. If we could get the Nisei diplomatic mission to declare her a fugitive, we could justify ONI taking her into custody."

"Possible but unlikely. Anything else?"

"She is remarkably close to the Elvish woman, Lady Silaqui, aka Maerilwyn MacGaellyn, who does have limited diplomatic immunity. If we could get her to officially take Sachi on as a servant or assistant, then the argument could be made that since she is a member of a diplomatic mission, she is ineligible to take the exam. And anything the Nisei Ambassador might decide to do about her would be irrelevant. I think that'd work better. And I believe I could talk Lady Silaqui into going along with our little scheme."

"Better. I think that's the option we will explore first. Get in touch with Lady Silaqui and ask her, very, very nicely, if she'd consider helping her friend Sachi and just by chance, us as well."

"Yes, sir."

"Needless to say, Lieutenant Commander, don't piss that elf off."

"Aye-aye, sir."

Carolington Roads Naval Base
Visiting Flag Officers' Quarters

"Sachi, can I talk to you a moment?"

"Certainly, Lady Silaqui. Now?" Sachi followed Silaqui into the comfortable house the Navy had assigned to the Elf.

"Didn't we agree you would stop calling me Lady?"

"Yes, when we were on the ship or the Horn Islands. This is Kolbia. They treat you as a noble Lady and I should do likewise."

"Gods of my people, give me patience and give it to me NOW! Just because we are now in Kolbia, NOTHING has changed between you and me! I swear, not even a dragon is half as stubborn as you are! Grrh!" Silaqui ground her teeth together. She went over to the well-stocked liquor cabinet and poured herself a glass of wine.

"And what did you wish to speak of with me?"

"Lieutenant Fleet came to speak with me yesterday. He has a concern about you."

"Is it about the fight in the saloon?"

"No, it's about the Isemoto embassy. Currently they know nothing of you, but if they learn of you, they could declare you a fugitive. As a fugitive, you could not enter the country officially without requesting political asylum. And even then, if the Nisei embassy demands it, the Kolbians might be forced by their own laws to take you into custody and either turn you over the Nisei Ambassador or simply eject you from the country on the first available outbound ship." Silaqui grimaced as the blood drained from Sachi's face. "However, Willis suggested that if you were officially part of, well, all of my *entourage*, then your status would be irrelevant as you would be protected by my diplomatic immunity."

"And...?"

"And the problem is that if you are protected under my diplomatic status, you would not be allowed to take the Kolbian Nationality Exams. At least, not right now. There would be other effects as well." The Elf's voice was quiet, and her eyes were downcast.

"What would those be?"

"You would have to give up your position, such as it is, in their Navy. You would accompany me on whatever ship I might choose to return home, instead." Silaqui closed her eyes at the pain in Sachi's face.

The first place, the first group of people who accept me simply for me, who give me my own place simply because I earned it and I must give it up because of the corruption of my nation, undoubtedly devised by my adopted family! *It is not enough that I am exiled and outcast. No. I must suffer still more before they think to drag me down and kill me. They wish me to despair and die.* Sachi sank to her knees. *That which I finally find that my heart truly desires, they scheme to deny me. They would forbid me the simple pleasure of just belonging. Even if that belonging is in a foreign land among foreign devils.*

"Sachi, are you all right?" Silaqui dropped to her knees next to the Nisei girl and took her in her arms.

"They will not destroy me. I shall not be defeated. I shall bring the Ancestor Spirits the honor they deserve!" Sachi started at a whisper and her voice grew in strength as she spoke. She was nearly screaming at the last. "I shall find my own place, my own honor!"

"Sachi, of course you will find your own place." She held Sachi tightly. "Your time will come. Your friends on the *Intrepid* are still your friends. They will not abandon you. Neither will I. This will pass. Give it time."

"Of course you say that." Sachi dredged up a smile through the tears on her face. "You're an immortal *Kami*. You will never die."

"And, in a sense, you are now immortal as well. As long as I live, I will never forget you. Your memory will always live with me."

"Truly?" The young woman gave Silaqui a rib-creaking hug. "And if I am to be your servant, you shall have to allow me to call you Lady, now."

"Oh, bother. You shall not be my servant. You shall be my silent and deadly Nisei bodyguard. You may call me Mistress in official public events. If you call me anything but Silaqui in private or with our friends from the *Intrepid*, I'll turn you straightaway into a toad." Crimson flames danced around Silaqui's hands.

"A toad?"

"Yes. Unless you would prefer a lizard?"

"Um, how about neither?"

"Well, I guess that'll do then." The Elf smiled at Sachi. "But don't forget."

"I won't."

Carolington City

Master's Residence

"So, she was part of the brawl in the Sailor's Temptation last night?"

"Yes, Master. When I saw her there again, I watched her most closely." Felicity knelt before her Master. "I believe her eyes are truly black. And I also believe she is trained as a Nisei *shinijutsuka*, that or an actual assassin. I've never seen anyone as fast as she is."

"I've spoken with Higher. He gave me some additional guidance. And that, with what you've told me, leads me to a decision."

"Yes, Master."

"I want this Sachi Takahashi dead. I don't particularly care how. It's highly unlikely that she has any contacts with our Enemies, but she could possibly be one of their agents. Killing one of them is always a good idea. So, kill her. As soon as possible."

"Yes, Master."

"Good, take care of that little item for me then. Make the girl's death look like an accident. That or just a random street killing, after a rape, perhaps?"

"Yes, Master. As you require."

Carolington City

Mercer Street

"I've never seen anyone drink that much and not be passed out under the table. You'd drink a dwarf sober." Silaqui softly shook her head, trying in vain to clear away the blur that last glass of brandy left. *Owwuch! Shouldn't have done that. My head is going to hate me in the morning. I only drank a couple of those things they called a whiskey sour. Well, maybe three or four? Five? What did they put in that glass? Ooh, my head.* "None of those Marines can walk. How do you do it?" *And we must get on that smoking dragon-boat to get back to the island and the ship. Oww. When that whistle sounds, I'm quite sure my head will explode. If I don't just die first. Ooh.*

"Sqwad ov Marrines, pah! Ay whatch'd'er drunk ta Bo'sun unner ta table afore we took ya ah-board, ya Elvef." Toby stumbled along the road, supported by a shaky Silaqui on one side and Sachi on the other side. "Fishes canna drunk dat much. Sha'd drunk da ohcean drie iffn it 'twas beer."

"Toby, you're drunk. Too damn drunk to walk, much less talk. And you know you're gonna be hanging over the rail, barfing up your toenails once the ferry hits the waves in the bay. Just make sure you're to leeward when you do." Sachi struggled to keep the three of them on a straight course. Occupied with her very drunk friends, her awareness of her surroundings slipped just a bit. The result of that was that she never saw where the attackers came from.

Toby, unsurprisingly, went down without a sound when the sap cracked across the back of his head. Silaqui yelled in pain as a sap hit her shoulder, whirling around and grabbing her assailant. For a split second, crimson haloed both her and her attacker, before they both went down in a twitching heap. The sap swung at Sachi only brushed her shoulder as she slipped from under Toby's dead weight and spun away. She calmly faced the four remaining thugs.

"Take your friend and go. Do so and I'll let you live." She dropped into a relaxed, balanced stance; her eyes narrowed as she evaluated her opponents.

"Not likely, lassie. We'uns can do t'is da har'd way ar ta easy way. Yer choice. Ye comes along quiet like, un we's won't hurt ye. Much. Leesen ye beg us ta, t'at is." The bass voice of the leader barked a deep, derisive laugh as he rubbed his crotch. "Course, ye might decide ye likes it un ye wants more." The leader was a big man, tall and heavy, carrying extra weight around his gut. But his arms were as big as Sachi's thighs and there was no fat at all on them. Two of the others were nearly as big but lacked the impressive arms. The last one was a little guy, closer to five feet than six in height. But he was lean and wiry and moved like a trained martial artist. A sai gleamed in one hand and a set of chain-sticks were tucked into his other armpit.

"Damn it, Rousch, we's paid ta kill 'er. Not fuck 'er." The little man's voice was quiet, hard to hear, even for her.

"Shut yer hole, Lil Mikey. Ye can gets yer dick wet when I's done wid 'er." Again, the scornful laugh barked. "Thet, ar ye can starts wid the Elfie. Put 'er face down un ye can plug 'er butt widout havin' ta look at 'er cateyes. Whutuver ye wants. But I's gonna fuck t'is little whore, one-way ar anuther."

"Truly?" *They are four to my one, but the two followers lack speed, strength, and skill. The big leader is strong, but how fast? And the little one could be quite dangerous. Enough. As Uncle Sota always said,* Defense is fine, but the attacker controls the fight, *so time to attack.* "I think not."

Sachi's hands flickered four times. The little man yelled and jumped as he somehow got the chain-sticks around in time to block one of the kill-stars that flashed at him. The leader half turned, and the star aimed at the throat sank into his shoulder instead. *He's quicker than I thought.* The last two stars flew true and sank into the throats of the two unsuspecting henchmen. They went down in a welter of blood, choking around severed trachea and slashed jugular veins. *Two down, two to go.*

The leader, Rousch, was almost as tough as he thought he was. His hand flashed to his belt as she sprinted toward him. A pistol snap-banged and Sachi flew through its smoke. She was certainly not a...delicate lady, but Rousch was several inches taller and perhaps a hundred and fifty pounds, maybe more, heavier. But she had the advantage of the brutal training of the Oda Family. That training surged to the forefront of her mind now.

Hold nothing back! Men will be bigger and stronger than you, little girl! Therefore, you must be better, ten, twenty times better! Great Uncle Sota would snarl as he stalked the dojo. *You must be faster! You must be brutal and have no pity, no mercy, no remorse! Use your entire body, all your weight and strength to focus on one limb, one joint! Break it, smash it, and move! Hit the next target unerringly! Eyes, throat, knees, and balls, all are valid targets; gouge, slash, break and crush them! You are not Samurai! Your honor is in being alive at the end of the fight! Do it again, stupid girl! Do it again, faster, better! You must be better than any you meet! Do it again! Faster!*

She hit Rousch high, her left heel smashing his cheekbone as her right leg wrapped around his neck. She spun around his neck, right foot hooking her left leg. As she spun, she hammered her fist into his temple, stunning him, before her other hand snapped down and slapped the double-barreled pistol out of his hand, straight at Mikey. The pistol fired again as it hit the pavement, blocked away by Mikey's sai, the bullet ricocheting off into the darkness. Her right hand whipped her garrote in an arc around Rousch's neck as she spun loose from his neck, dropping to the street with her back to his back, her left hand grabbing the flying handle of the garrote. It snapped tight as she dropped all her weight and strength on it, trusting the finely braided wire to hold. The wire tore into Rousch's throat and with a grunt she ripped the wire through the soft tissue in his neck before it wedged into the vertebrae of his neck, tearing his throat completely open. Blood fountained, black in the gas streetlamp's fitful yellow radiance.

"SIAA—YAI!" she shouted as she bent forward and jerked Rousch's body in an arc over her head. Throwing his dead weight over her head took every bit of strength and skill she had. She twisted the garrote as she did, and the sound of his neck snapping was almost as loud as the pistol shots. Rousch's corpse convulsed in his death throes. She released the garrote to block Mikey's strike with the chain-stick. It smashed into her forearm, instead of her temple. She felt the bone crack, but it didn't completely break.

"HIA!" He screamed as his sai drove into her right shoulder. The shaft pierced deeply into the muscle above her collarbone. The point of the side guard tore flesh just below the collarbone. Blood sprayed around the sai's faceted shaft, then poured down her arm, soaking her shirt and jacket.

"Sai-ka!" She hissed at the pain of the strike. *Focus, girl,* Sota's voice echoed in her mind, *Use the pain. Drive through it or die.* She grabbed his shirt with her left hand and smashed her forehead into his face. His nose shattered and blood sprayed. She drove her knee viciously into his crotch, past an ineffective knee-block. Mikey went up on his toes with a strangled scream as the blow crushed his testicles. Then her heel smashed into his forehead in a scorpion kick. Her left arm wrapped tightly around his head as her feet launched her body, rotating her entire weight around him. Trapped in the vise of her left arm, his head rotated faster than he could twist his body around. With a gruesome crackle, his neck snapped, severing his spinal cord. Sachi finished the move, whipping his body in an arc like children playing crack-the-whip. His body flew across the street, smashing his back into the iron lamp post hard enough to break his back just below his shoulder blades. His eyes bulged in horror as his body died faster than his consciousness did.

Sachi's good hand flickered again and a slim throwing dart buried its five-inch spike in his right eye. Mikey's corpse slumped to the sidewalk and the blood and shit smell of abrupt, violent death filled the air of the suddenly silent street.

"That's for ruining my clothes, you bastard," she growled, her voice harsh with the pain of her wounds.

"Hey, what's that!? Who's there!?" A frightened voice called from a window that banged open above the scene of carnage. "I'm sending for the police! Go brawl somewhere's else!"

"Summon the police, please. Quickly." It was an effort to raise her voice enough to be heard and she saw a vague face stare down into the battle's bloody aftermath before disappearing from the window frame. "Oww. That hurts." She clamped her hand against the shaft of the sai, slowing the bleeding. The wound burned with a strange heat. "Damn it, these were my best clothes." She looked at the bloody shambles around her. One of the men with a kill-star in his throat had managed to pull the star out, but that simply made him bleed out faster. She saw where Rousch's heels had scrabbled in the bloody mud of the street before he died, nerves and muscles protesting violent death. Her knees trembling, she half sat, half collapsed onto the curb. There was a burning pain in her side, even worse than the pain of the stab wound.

"Damn. I've been shot." *I just killed four men. I wonder if Great Uncle Sota would be proud of me. I did as he always instructed. I did not think, I just acted. I killed these two, the big one and the little one, twice over, out of rage alone.* Sitting on the curb, she remembered his harsh voice, demanding more of her that she thought she could give.

There's no such thing as too much violence, little girl, when your life is at stake. You are a woman; you will always be smaller and weaker than any man. Therefore, when, not if, when, you are attacked, you must respond with overwhelming violence! You are a beauty and men will want you, with no concern for your wishes! Send them to their Ancestors! Kill, do not maim! There is no such thing as too much violence when it is your life you defend!

"Well, Uncle Sota, I hope you're happy. I'm still alive and they are very dead. But the authorities will come, the police, the Kolbians call them, and what will they say? Ah! The bullet wound burns!" She startled as she realized the shaft of the sai was moving, as if an invisible hand were slowly drawing it out of her shoulder. She gently pulled it loose, clamping down hard to slow the bleeding. The wound was bad and ugly but not mortal, she thought.

She felt her side, where the pistol ball had hit. Her hand came up, black with her own blood in the dim light. *Hope I don't bleed to death here.* The bullet wound burned with an unnatural heat. *Was it poisoned? Oww, damn, that hurts! Is the damn thing still moving? What did that* rokudenashi *shoot me with? Glad the bastard was a poor shot.* Sachi pulled her shirt and jacket up just in time to see a lump form where the bullet hole still oozed blood on the smooth skin of her flank. With a quiet sucking sound, the lump forced out the pistol ball, slick with her blood. Astonished, she reached and picked it up. *What is this? What magic pushes a bullet out of my body?* Bemused and woozy from blood loss, she watched in silent amazement as the bullet hole stopped bleeding and very slowly closed, healing like a *Shantoa* priest had blessed her with a spell of healing. She felt the ghastly tear on her shoulder and it, too, was slowly closing. The blood had already stopped flowing. *No one will believe this. Am I dying? Losing my mind? How is this possible?* She leaned back against a fire cistern as police whistles began to shrill in the dimness.

***

A block down the street, Felicity stared in shock at the bloody shambles. *Thirty seconds. Thirty seconds at most. Maybe only twenty. Twenty or thirty seconds to slaughter four men used to violence. Rousch never had a ghost of a chance. What in hell is she?* She gulped and without another thought turned and walked calmly away. *Master is not going to be pleased.*

Carolington City Police HQ

Detective Sergeant Jonathon Holloway made a face at the stack of paperwork on his desk as he stepped into his cramped and cluttered office. The shaded hurricane lamp over the desk highlighted the pile and made it appear even larger. It deepened the shadows in the corners of his office as well. His desk chair creaked and rattled as he plunked down in it. It had been an exceedingly long day and the sun set a couple of hours ago. A uniform had started his day extra early, banging on his door before sunrise. He got the call to be the lead investigating officer on a street brawl with four rather bloody and brutal deaths. A call that was probably due to the persistent rumor that his great grandmother was the daughter of an Elf and a human. A rumor that got him the nickname of Halfelven Holloway, whether he liked it or not. Since he supposedly had that slight hint of Elvish blood, the precinct tended to hand him anything dealing with a non-human or the occasional real weirdo cases. Like this one.

Even that wouldn't have been enough to drag his butt out of bed an hour before dawn if this specific case hadn't involved an actual, honest to God Elf, likely with diplomatic immunity to boot and a pair of sailors. And one of the more notable local tough-guys and his gang of toughs and thugs. Of course, the fact that Big Rousch Tarslyn and three of his favorite bully boys were assuming room temperature in the morgue did simplify the case somewhat.

He hated to think what could have happened if it were the Elf laying on the slab instead of cooling her heels down in the lockup with the two sailors. He stretched and scratched himself as he considered what he knew about the case so far. *Odd bunch. I know a little bit about the big sailor, won the Fleet Boxing Championship the last two years. And the Nisei girl, WOOF, what's a looker like her doing in the Navy?* He put his feet up on the short file cabinet next to his desk and pulled a bottle of Old Capitol bourbon out of the bottom desk drawer. A moment's rummaging in the drawer produced a slightly less dirty glass. He gave it a quick wipe with an old report and poured a finger's worth into it.

"You wouldn't happen to have another glass in there, would you?" The masculine voice from the darkest corner of the office startled him. He lost his balance and went over backwards in the chair. The bottle shot out of his hand into the air and a hand snapped it out of the air before it hit anything and broke. Holloway rolled to his knees behind the desk and drew his pistol, cocking the flintlock as he peered over the stack of paper at the gloomy corner of his office.

"Who the HELL are you? And how did you get in my office?"

"Relax, I'm on your side. And the door wasn't locked."

"Sure, you are. And the hell it wasn't. Step over into the light by the door, slowly, neighbor, slowly." The stranger was a tall man in a nice suit. *Expensive threads, short hair and sharp looking. Bet those green eyes draw their share of the ladies. Navy? Maybe ONI? Could be Republic Investigation Service. But I thought I knew all the local RIS agents?* "Keep your hands out of your pockets."

"No problem, Detective. Mind if I set your bottle down?"

"Sure. Slowly." He watched the stranger closely. *This guy is disgustingly relaxed. Cocky bastard. I oughta shoot him someplace it'll just hurt a little bit. But if he wanted me dead, I'd already be getting measured for a coffin.* "Now that I'm over my heart attack, who the fuck are you?"

"Lieutenant Commander Willis Fleet, Detective. ONI, if you haven't guessed. Not RIS. Here's my ID." With only his thumb and forefinger, he pulled a badge out of an inner coat pocket.

"Uh huh." Holloway carefully de-cocked his pistol and tucked it back into its holster under his coat. He picked his chair up off the floor and sat back down in it. "Have a seat, I guess. No point in saying *Come in,* since you're already in my office." He dug around in the bottom drawer and came up with another slightly grungy glass. It got an even more perfunctory wipe. He poured a second shot into it and set it down on the desk in front of Fleet. "Cheers."

"Cheers." A swallow. "Ah, that's good. Old Capitol?"

"Yeah, the one thing I splurge on." He sat down his glass. "So, what can I do for ONI, Lieutenant Commander Fleet?"

"I understand you're the one investigating the rather bloody killings on Mercer Street late last night? Or rather, early this morning?"

"Uh huh. And?"

"Pretty open and shut, some thuggers that jumped the wrong sailors, right?"

"If Big Rousch *jumped* someone, it's because he was paid to do so. We'll sweat the one guy that's still breathing when he wakes up. Rousch Tarslyn was hardly a common street thugger. Emphasis on *was*."

"Really? Well, you know that Lady Silaqui has diplomatic immunity?"

"The Elf? I've not been officially informed, but yeah, no surprise."

"Okay, Detective Holloway, here's the important bit and why I'm down here. Get her, and her bodyguard at least, out of that damn cell. If someone really wants to kill her, there's too many things that could happen to her while she's in the lockup. Bad things. You know that."

"Her bodyguard? I thought that big guy was a Navy steward?"

"He is. Her bodyguard is that Nisei girl."

"Really? One of the uniformed officers told me that she was responsible for the bodies, but are you kidding me? She's an absolute doll. She could write her own check at any of the fashion houses on the East Coast. I mean, just *woof*."

"Yeah, I know. And she's a stone-cold killing machine. There's a reason Lady Silaqui has her for a bodyguard. And since she's the Lady's bodyguard, she's covered by the Elf's diplomatic immunity as well. If you like, I can make a case for Navy jurisdiction and take all three of them off your hands. Or we can get the Republic District Courts involved?"

"Oh, dear God, don't do that to me. Justice Golan and I, well, we don't exactly get along. I'd wind up in contempt or something."

"Well?"

"Okay, okay. Frankly, it looks like an open and shut case of self-defense. And given that the Lady involved did not kill anyone, and her bodyguard was defending her, I imagine we could release her on her own word. You have any idea where she's staying?"

"Yeah, Lady Silaqui and her entourage have quarters on Carolington Island. They're staying in the Visiting Flag Officers' Quarters."

"Figures. So if I have them released to your authority, you haul them off to the base and then fuck me if I need them to testify?"

"What's to testify about? The thuggers are dead, well, except for the one, and I'd guess he's just muscle? You think he can actually tell you anything?"

"Probably not, but I don't like losing access to my witnesses."

"No offense, Detective, but here real soon you're losing access to them, will you, nil you. The big sailor is Captain William Blaine's personal steward and the Captain will want his Steward back unless you've charged him with a crime. Getting thugged on a dark street ain't a crime, far as I know. Not to mention *all* the diplomatic problems created by holding an Elf with connections to someone extremely high ranking in both the Montagaran Court and the Elvish Court as well. Self-defense isn't a crime, is it?"

"No, of course not. And they were clearly attacked."

"So, what is the problem, then?"

"Big Rousch and his boys, they aren't common street thuggers. Someone paid them to attack Lady Silaqui, and I'd like to know who did so. And why. Mostly so I can have a cozy little chat with that person and *explain* to him that such activities will not be tolerated. And there was something certainly odd about this as well. When I went over the scene this morning, I found this." Holloway pulled an expensive, double-barreled flintlock pistol out of his coat pocket. It was deeply blued and polished, with silver inlay on the stock and elaborate engraving on the trigger guard, hammers, and gunlock. And someone had used a saw to crudely cut the normal twelve-inch barrels down to about five inches. "And this." He shook a bullet out of a small paper envelope.

"Whoever did that to that pistol should be charged with desecration of an artwork. Damn, that's a crying shame." Fleet leaned over to examine the bullet. "Okay, nice and bloody. Who'd that come out of?"

"No one, as far as I can tell. None of the recently deceased had a bullet wound on them. Some weird looking throwing stars in a couple of throats. Really nice, braided wire garrote stuck in Big Rousch's neck vertebra. Which was broken, by the way, his neck, not the garrote. Someone slung him heels over head, using the garrote to do so. And then there's Lil' Mikey. One of our local psychotics, batshit crazy. But good with his hands. Supposedly really good. Not good enough obviously. Broken nose, shattered cheekbone, his testicles crushed so badly they looked like my dear old Granny's strawberry preserves, that blow pretty well tore his prick off too, in addition to shattering his pelvis. His neck was broken as well, his head was twisted almost in a complete circle. Then he was thrown across the street so hard that the lamp post he hit was loose on its base *and* his back was broken. For the grand finale, there was a five-inch-long throwing dart buried in his right eye. I'd say he pissed somebody off. Any idea who did that to him?"

"Yeah. Sachi Takahashi, she's death on two feet. I'd guess the whole fight was less than a minute, at most. I told you, there's a reason she's Lady Silaqui's bodyguard. Everyone looks at the beautiful girl with the nice tits and misses the killer inside her. Otherwise, this means what?"

"Best as we can tell that bullet came out of that pistol. Both barrels were fired but we didn't find the other bullet. Rousch rarely carried a gun. He enjoyed his work, mostly beating people to death after someone paid him to deliver a message. He did have five thousand Thalers, in gold coin, no less, on him, more than normal for what he does, much more. He was paid to kill someone in this group, the Elf, the big sailor, and that little doll of a Nisei. So, who paid him and who was he paid to kill? Why? Who used the pistol? Who was shot? Where'd they get off to?" Holloway rummaged through the papers on his desk. "Yeah, here they are, Lady Silaqui of Montagar, the Elf. Senior Petty Officer Tobias Wilkerson, two-time Navy boxing champ. And then the real cipher, former Apprentice Seaman Takahashi Sachi, currently retained as Lady Silaqui's bodyguard and companion. Someone wanted at least one of these folks dead. Badly."

"What would Lady Silaqui, PO Wilkerson or Sachi Takahashi know about this supposed person? They were the attacked, not the attackers."

"And why would someone pay a thugger like Big Rousch Tarslyn five thousand Thalers to attack them? Rousch normally pulls about five hundred for a *lesson*, aka a nasty beating and a grand, maybe fifteen hundred to make a real point and beat the target to death. There's something ugly about this. It doesn't make sense."

"Hey, some people really don't like elves."

"I know that. Trust me, I know that." Holloway poured himself another shot and offered the bottle to Fleet, who waved it away.

"Look," Fleet rolled the empty glass between his hands, "how about this: Take sworn dispositions from all three and turn them over to Navy custody? I really doubt anyone will be able to attack them on Carolington Island or onboard the *Intrepid*. Far safer than sitting in your cell, wouldn't one think?"

"Fine." Holloway took a slow sip as he thought about the can of worms Fleet was describing to him. *I think this is one sausage grinder I am NOT gonna stick my dick in while some jackass turns the crank.* "All right, you win. I'll have the release drawn up and you can take them back to the base or to the Moon for all I care. Gimme about twenty minutes and I'll have them at the front desk. That work for you?"

"Yeah, that'll do. That'll do just fine."

"Good. Now get out of my office."

"Pleasure doing business with you, Detective-Sergeant."

"Yeah, yeah. Scram."

***

At least when the Kolbians come to execute me, they will do it quickly and cleanly. Almost kindly, one might think. Sachi was sitting in the center of the cell, folded into a full lotus, meditating. *They will not torture me, cut off each joint of my feet and hands slowly, drive spikes through my knees, blind and mutilate me so that*

I may never join the Ancestor Spirits. I did not escape my fate after all. I merely exchanged it for one less painful.

Toby sat against the back wall of the cell. He was still hung-over and in a great deal of pain, but he was at least conscious. Silaqui was lying on the one bed in the cell, semi-conscious, quietly recovering from the backlash of her miscast defensive magic. Sachi expected that Toby and Silaqui would be released. Neither of them killed anyone. She wondered if the Captain, *my Captain*, would come to her execution. She rose smoothly to her feet as she heard a key rattle in the door of the corridor leading to their cell. This time the uniformed guard was accompanied by another man, a tall man in a rumpled suit, white streaks in his short blond hair. He looked tired and annoyed. Sachi bowed her head and held her hands clasped in front of her as the uniformed guard unlocked the door. The man in the suit gave her a tired smile as he stepped into the cell.

"Takahashi Sachi, *to iu?*"

"*So desu, keisatsukan.*"

"*Watashi wa* Detective Sergeant Holloway. *Anata wa hanasemasu ka* Terranglais?"

"Yes, Detective Sergeant, I speak very good Terranglais, or so I am told."

"That's good because my Nisei sucks. I am given to understand that you are acting as Lady Silaqui's companion and bodyguard?"

"*Hai*, I mean, yes."

"Good. I have confirmed that the Lady Silaqui does in fact have diplomatic immunity. Furthermore, you were attacked as a group without provocation and by armed attackers. Also, those individuals are, or rather, *were*, known to be habitual and repeat offenders. Frankly, you saved Carolington City the cost of a trial. There will be a trial for the surviving member of the gang, but it will be open and shut. I would like to ask you all to submit written depositions under oath before you disappear into the Navy's cuddly grasp. Ask, not require. If you like, you can simply walk out the door and down to the docks. Do you have any questions?"

"We are free to go?" Her eyebrows rose in surprise. *They will simply release me, after I slaughtered four men? These Kolbians are so different from my homeland. I see I still have much to learn of them.*

"Yes, ma'am, it'd be nice to get statements, but it's not mandatory."

"I would be the only one who could say anything, Detective Sergeant. Senior Petty Officer Wilkerson and Lady Silaqui were both unconscious from the very beginning of the attack."

"I understand." Holloway smiled at her. "Well, then, follow me and we'll get you your weapons and personal possessions back."

"Thank you, Detective Sergeant Holloway."

"You're welcome."

Chapter Thirteen

Carolington Roads Naval Base, Visiting Flag Officers' Quarters
July 1478, Third Age of Imperial Reckoning

Silaqui and Sachi sat on the veranda at the back of the house the Kolbian Navy provided for her as a diplomat of the Elven Court. Sweat beads slid down the side of a half-full pitcher of sweet iced tea. Tall glasses with their own sweat beads stood in front of both women. A cool breeze off the bay fluttered their light dresses and played with tendrils of their hair.

"Much nicer than that jail cell, is it not, Sachi?" Silaqui smiled as she sipped her tea. "And sweet iced tea! Only the Kolbians would think of such a thing!"

"It is delicious. And so simple." Sachi sipped her tea and regarded the forest of bare masts in the harbor. "Why has no one else ever thought of doing such a thing? My people drink their tea hot, as do yours. But to cool it, sweeten it and then put ice in it? Only these insane people would do such a thing!"

"And then someone has the idea to have a business doing nothing but selling ice in summer? Only in Kolbia!"

"Only in Kolbia." Sachi leaned forward and dipped a finger into the sweat-ring left on the tabletop. She idly traced a Nisei *shinboru* on the table, then hastily wiped it away when she realized she had drawn the symbol for lovers. She frowned as she rested her chin on her hands and stared into the bay. "So, we leave next week. Finally. It's been nearly a month. We won't be safe until we're aboard ship and setting sail for Montagar."

"Nothing has happened since that first week, Sachi. What are you so paranoid about?"

"Have you forgotten *that first week*? Those men were there to kill me. We went to the trial of the one you knocked out. He was proved guilty of attempted murder and they hung him two days ago. Their Constitution guarantees a speedy trial. They even allowed him what they called an appeal."

"He never said that they were there specifically to kill you, Sachi."

"The one did. The little one with the sai and the chain-sticks. *Damn it, Rousch, we's paid ta kill 'er. Not fuck 'er.* Exactly what he said. Someone paid them to kill me, specifically. The one they hung just said he'd been hired to help Rousch kill a woman. Everyone has been assuming that woman was you, Silaqui. It wasn't. I'm the one they wanted to kill." She drew aimless circles on the tabletop with the sweat from her tea glass. "This is the reach of those who hunt me. They will not rest until they hunt me down and kill me. They cannot let it be known that someone like me defied them and got away alive. It makes them look weak and there are those that will not tolerate weakness in the leading...group. They must kill me."

"Why didn't you tell the Kolbians then? They could provide you protection."

"No. The leaders of my...the leading group would find other men like Rousch and his thuggers. I know the type; they aren't that different from my homeland. They would have killed us all, after they were done raping us. Those men were just as vicious as any criminals of my homeland. I need to get further away. Further away from my homeland."

There was a knock at the door just then. Sachi started to pop up to see who was there when Silaqui smacked the table with her hand. Sheepishly, she sat back in her chair and waited for the doorman to determine who was calling and if they should be admitted.

"Milady Silaqui, Lieutenant Allen Wilson, Admiral Mynheers' Flag Lieutenant, is here. He has an invitation from the Admiral for a fete to celebrate the departure of the convoy. Will you receive him?" Adrian Harless had been assigned to handle the business of the small household staff the Navy attached to Silaqui. In addition to Harless there was a cook and a maid of all work who cleaned and helped the two women with whatever they needed.

"Show him in, please, Adrian. Thank you."

"My pleasure, ma'am." The combination doorman and butler smiled cheerfully as he stepped back into the relatively modest house.

"What's a Flag Lieutenant, *Lady* Silaqui?"

"No idea. And the Lady thing is their idea, not mine. It's just easiest to let them do as they would in what they call me or what they are willing to do for me. Well, for us, I suppose?" She smiled as Adrian tapped on the doorframe.

"Lieutenant Wilson, Milady." Imperceptibly, Adrian sniffed as he turned away and left the room.

***

Wilson, as usual, was impeccably turned out, uniform spotless and not a hair out of place. He held a rolled-up scroll in his hand, his hat tucked under his arm. Wilson swallowed hard as he stepped onto the veranda and saw Sachi up close for the first time. *Oh, my God! This woman was on Captain Blaine's* Intrepid *for months? And the crew didn't mutiny? No wonder the professional ladies down on Dock Street are getting worn out by* Intrepid's *crew. I can see that long black hair will be all the rage this year. I've never seen anyone so beautiful. And the Elf! Exotic and mysterious and a beauty in her own fashion.*

***

"And to what do we owe the pleasure of your presence, Lieutenant?" Silaqui hid a smile at the stunned expression on Wilson's face. *An extremely attractive young man. If I were at home, I think I could foresee having more than just a little interest in him. However, 'tis not I who truly ensnares his thoughts. Ah, Sachi. Were I a mere mortal, I think I could come to hate you.* Sachi alone sometimes had that effect on men and the occasional woman as well. When someone encountered the pair of them for the first time, well, she'd seen men walk into walls while staring. Lieutenant Wilson's reaction was about par for the course.

***

"Huh?" Wilson shook his head. "Please forgive me, Lady Silaqui, Miss Taka-hashi. Pardon my woolgathering." *God, I must look like an idiot!* "Um, Admiral Mynheers is hosting a pre-departure party at the Officer's Club in two days. Since you are an accredited envoy, Lady Silaqui, he thought it only proper that you be invited. Especially since you'll be traveling on the *Intrepid* again."

***

"I see." Silaqui allowed a little of her smile to show. *So nice to watch that delicious young human squirm.* "Might I assume your invitation includes Miss Taka-hashi?"

"Um, I don't really know, milady. I didn't write it. I would assume so."

"Well, hand it over, Lieutenant Wilson, and let me see." She broke the wax seal and unrolled the vellum scroll. "Um-hmm. Genuinely nice handwriting. Well, looks like a standard invitation. I've seen things like this back home. Very much the fashion about a hundred and fifty years ago." Again, she hid her smile as Wilson paled at her not-so-subtle reminder of her age. "Nothing says I can't bring either a companion or a bodyguard." She looked over at Sachi. "Want to go to a party, Sachi?"

"If you wish, *Lady* Silaqui." Sachi's tone was flat.

"I imagine Captain Blaine will attend, since he is commanding the convoy. Or so I have been told. Correct, Lieutenant?"

"Yes, Milady."

"Well, then you can convey my regards to the Admiral and tell him we will both be there. Assuming we can find some decent clothes to wear, that is." Her smile was wicked. "Do you think you could deliver a letter to the Admiral for me, requesting an introduction to a decent lady's clothier? And perhaps I could request that the Admiral allow me to draw on his credit? The least he could do if he wishes me to attend his party. I simply have nothing to wear."

"Yes, Milady." Wilson's smile was a little thin.

"I'll have Adrian get you something to drink while I write that letter. He should be in the kitchen."

***

"Well, I think that went rather well. Don't you, Sachi?" Silaqui smiled as the door shut behind Lieutenant Wilson.

"You were cruel, you know." Sachi frowned at the door.

"A little bit, yes. Lieutenant Wilson is a little too sure of himself, the Gods' gift to women. Or so he thinks."

"I'd rather not go to this party, Silaqui."

"Why?"

"Too much exposure. Too many people."

"And Captain Blaine will be there. When are you going to deal with the fact that you are in love with him? And he is in love with you?"

"You didn't see the carnage I left in the street that night! And those were hardly the first men I've killed. I'm damaged, Silaqui, broken inside. Love is not something that will ever truly be part of my life. No one will ever love me. No one should! And Captain Blaine is married, and he honors his oaths and his vows, as an honorable man should. There is no place in his life for me. The sooner I am gone, the better." Sachi stopped abruptly. *Damn it! I can* not *lose my temper like that. What the hell is wrong with me?* She felt her face heat as Silaqui stuck the verbal barbs in deep.

"Sachi...please stop and think for a minu..."

"No, Silaqui," she abruptly snapped. "I'll go to this idiotic party. As your silent and deadly Nisei bodyguard. Nothing more." She spun on her heel and vanished into the house.

"Damn it," Silaqui cursed and turned to meet Adrian's pained gaze. "Sorry about that, Adrian. I'd really appreciate it if you kept your mouth shut about this."

"Lady Silaqui, *the* key part of my job is discretion." He gave her a wry smile. "Blab about things and pretty soon, I'm a day laborer working in the sewers. Not what I want to do for a living. Perhaps you could relax in the living room and I'll get Charles to make you a snack?"

"That would be fine. And try to figure out where Sachi went and have Jacqueline take her a nice healthy meal. You've seen how that girl eats."

"Yes, ma'am. I thought my little sister had a hollow leg when we were growing up, but my God. I've never seen the like of her appetite. Why isn't she the size of a mountain?"

"No idea." Silaqui wandered out to the veranda, with its view of the harbor. The masts of the assembled ships of the convoy crowded the harbor. She leaned against one of the supports of the veranda roof. "How does a mere human confound me so? What secrets does she hide?"

Carolington City
Master's Residence

The basement was well insulated and had no direct access to the outside of the mansion. None of the regular foot traffic passing by could hear Felicity's muffled screams as Master dragged the red-hot steel rod underneath the curve of her left breast.

"This won't leave an obvious mark, my dear. And you know if you go to the police, Quan himself won't want what I'll leave of you." His voice was calm and cool, the slightest edge in it reflecting his tightly controlled rage. "I told you I wanted that girl dead and she's still breathing. Rousch and three of his best thuggers are dead and it took me a week to find you and learn what happened. Is it any wonder I am less than happy with you?"

"Mumfgrl." The gag strapped in the redhead's mouth prevented any understandable response. The fear in her blue eyes was clear enough.

"So, what shall I do with you, my dear? The fact that you are a pleasurable bed partner is not enough to save your neck, should Higher become...shall I say...unhappy with me. Higher can be extremely...inventive in their punishments. Some of the things Higher can do to a person are almost beyond belief. How do we resolve this conundrum?" The woman frantically bobbed her head. "Are you actually trying to answer me, dear?" Another frantic head bob. "You know something I don't?" Head bob. "Hmm. Well, you can't very well tell me with that nasty gag in your mouth. Now, if I take it out, I'd better really like what I hear. Otherwise I might just get a little...unhappy with you. Understand?" She nodded, blue eyes wide with fear. He reached up and pulled the gag off over her head.

"Master, please Master, listen to me for just a moment." She coughed up blood. "Admiral Mynheers is throwing a departure party for all of the navy officers and many of the merchant captains. He has invited the Elf, Lady Silaqui. The girl with black eyes, Sachi Takahashi, is her constant companion and bodyguard. As a bodyguard, she would be likely to taste anything the Elf eats or drinks. I can use that to poison her. I can get my hands on several doses of Vexarin poison. I guarantee I can get enough of that into the food or the drink to kill her. And probably the Elf as well."

"Possibly a course of action. But how are *you* going to get invited?"

"I know one of the merchant captains who has already been invited. I'm sure he'd like to have an appropriate bit of eye candy with him. Even if no one ever looks at me, once they get a look at this Takahashi woman. I don't particularly like girls, but I'd make an exception for her. Which could be another way I could get close enough to kill her. I can't do either of those for you if I'm just another bloody corpse in the bay."

"Hmm." The steel rod had cooled some, but it was still hot enough to make her scream when he raised her right breast and drew a matching bloody line under it. "Are you certain, my dear, certain enough to bet your life on it?"

"Yes, Master, please, no more!" She shrieked and struggled futilely against her bonds. "Please, Master, please. I can do it. Please." She whimpered. "Please. No more."

"You know, my dear, I think you just might be right. At least, you've convinced me to give you the chance."

"I can do it, Master, I promise." *And it's not the only thing I'll do, you slimy bastard. Not even close.*

Carolington Roads Naval Base
Flag Officer's Club
July 1478, Third Age of Imperial Reckoning

"It's a wonderful party, Admiral Mynheers. But are you certain that this Lady Silaqui, the supposed Elf sorceress, is going to make an appearance? And her maid? The pretty one everyone's been talking about?" Vice Admiral Weslan Hampton possessed a dry, nasal voice that went well with his neatly combed, thinning brown hair, rather portly stature and pale brown, almost yellow eyes.

"Yes, Weslan, she'll be here shortly. Relax, you'll get to drool over those two right along with the rest of us." *Senile old fart. Past time the Navy retired your ass. If it were up to you, we'd still be rowing around in galleys. And you're effectively my second in command. God help the Navy if I drop dead of a heart attack anytime soon. Oh, wonderful. Here comes the worst harpy on the entire coast.*

"Ethan! Admiral Mynheers! This is your pitiful idea of a reception? This is the best you could do?" Janay Hampton was in her early seventies, like her husband, and she was a nightmare. She was no longer the beauty she had been in her youth, even though she still thought she was the debutante of the ball. What she truly was these days was a disagreeable, opinionated old harridan. Her sense of fashion was years out of date, she was about as stylish as a drunk mule and the rules of etiquette she tried to follow would have fit in perfectly at the Imperial Court...about a hundred years ago. And if anything diverted from what she thought was right, there was always hell to pay. And she hated non-humans with a nearly religious fervor. Mynheers didn't know why, but he knew she had for decades.

Why me? Why did I think this would be a good idea? I thought it was a great idea, get most of the merchant captains to meet Captain Blaine, get a feel for his command style. Then Hampton invited himself, at this harpy's instigation, no doubt. Otherwise, that moron would have never had a clue. Ah, shit. Sometimes I'm too clever for my own good. Maggie, my love, I know you're looking down on me from Heaven and laughing your ass off at my predicament.

"Janay, so nice you could make it." He glued his best *Oh, glad to see you* political smile on his face before brushing her gloved hand with his lips. "Have you tried the hors d'oeuvres? Or the wine? I have managed to acquire a decent selection of imported Elvish wine from Montagar's best winery. You should try some."

"Elvish wine? Oh, please, Ethan! You know that's just a marketing ploy by those underhanded Montagarans. There's no such thing as Elves. Besides, if there was, you wouldn't know Elvish wine from swamp water. Humpf!" She gave Mynheers a long glare from beady grey eyes before snapping her head around so fast the ridiculous blonde wig she wore nearly came off. "Come,

Weslan, let's go see what this uncultured sea-dog thinks is *Elvish wine.* Indeed. Probably Thaler-a-gallon beer at best."

"Yes, dear. Admiral Mynheers, with your permission?"

"By all means, Vice Admiral." *If there's any justice in the world, that bag of lard will fall in the bay and drown. And take her idiot husband with her. But the sharks would throw her back. They do have standards about the water they live in.*

"That went well, sir."

"Shut up, Allen. Last thing I need right now is a smart aleck Flag Lieutenant." Mynheers glared at his insouciant aide. "Go get me a beer and a couple of canapés. Make yourself useful, will you?"

"Yes, sir. But I thought you should know that Lady Silaqui and Miss Takahashi have arrived."

"They have?"

"Yes, sir."

"Good. Now go get my chow and booze."

"Yes sir."

***

"Enjoying yourself, my dear?"

"Quite well, William. Admiral Mynheers puts on a genuinely nice party. The wine is excellent." Emily Blaine was perfectly dressed in the most current and tasteful style, not a hair out of place. Her dress showed just a hint of her trim ankles, and her décolletage displayed just enough. Captain Blaine wore his mess dress uniform, exceptionally fine in royal blue and gold braid, the gold and diamonds of the Medal of Valor glittering at his throat. "So nice to know that every officer here, even the Admiral, has to salute you first. You take precedence over all of them." There was a nasty undertone to her quiet voice.

"Please give it a rest, Emily." Blaine suppressed a sigh. "That's not how this works and you should know better."

"And your usual henchman, Doctor Hoff, isn't parked in your pocket, is he? Free food and booze and the prospect of winding up in some tramp's bed should have drawn him like flies to shit." Emily and Elazar Hoff shared a strong mutual aversion to each other. They had hated each other cordially and enthusiastically from the moment they laid eyes on each other. She saw Hoff as a reminder of Blaine's common background, and her own less than stellar antecedents. He was a reminder she hated.

"He's here, Emily. However, unlike certain people, Elazar does not enjoy the arguing, bully-ragging and general backstabbing that goes on when the two of you spend any time at all in close proximity. I saw him arrive with an attractive young lady. I'm sure he will enjoy the evening."

"I hope she insisted on being paid up front." Emily sneered behind the fan she snapped open.

"Will you please give it a rest? Elazar will conduct his affairs as he sees fit and does not need your approval in any fashion. Or mine. He avoids me at these kinds of social occasions because he prefers not to spend his entire evening deflecting your derogatory commentary."

"Oh, very well. What you see in that drunken sot is beyond me." The silk fan rustled very slightly. "To change the subject then, you should be pressing Admiral Mynheers to make your temporary position as the ad-hoc Commodore of the convoy a permanent promotion."

"Emily, I'm already young for my rank. Another early promotion would raise questions of cronyism and favoritism. Not to mention the fact that permanent promotions to Flag rank require the approval of both the Council and the Quorum. Isn't a holder of the Medal and the youngest Captain commanding a forty-four good enough for you?"

"Pssh. If you would press the Navy Board even a little, you would be a full Captain now, none of this Junior Grade nonsense. And in command of a ship of the line."

"Emily, that's about enough. This is not the place for thi…" The sharp *crack, crack* of the old-fashioned staff being rapped on a granite floor tile interrupted him as it rang through the room. The Admiral had prevailed upon Blaine to borrow Toby to temporarily act as doorman and announce the guests as they arrived. Toby Wilkerson's strong voice cut clearly through the low murmur of conversation.

***

"Lady Silaqui of the Kingdom of Montagar and the Royal Court of the Elven Folk of Montagar." Sachi had put her foot down emphatically when Silaqui wanted her introduced as well. *Go ahead, turn me into a toad, Silaqui. I'll not be announced by name. If you have the doorman do so anyway, the only thing of me you'll see will be my hem vanishing around the corner.* "And entourage."

***

Silaqui stepped into clear view on the balcony landing of the staircase and smiled. *Ah, a captive audience, so to speak. I wonder, how many of these Kolbians will refuse to believe the proof of their own eyes?* Her power flared in ruby flames around her, flooding the room with a stark crimson light for a moment. Her torso was covered in skintight scarlet silk, from wrist to throat to waist, emphasizing her full breasts and flat stomach. A snug skirt of blood red satin swept the floor, concealing a side-slit from hem to mid-thigh. Dark burgundy dancing slippers completed the outfit. Her grass green hair was twisted into fantastical braids, braids that subtly writhed on their own, hinting at the shape of one mythical beast after another. The seven tattooed gems above her left eye each gleamed with its own internal color. With a graceful gesture of her hand, she floated over the rail of the staircase and drifted as gracefully as a soap bubble to where Admiral Mynheers stood in open-mouthed shock.

***

Behind her and out of view of most of the room, Sachi exchanged a rueful headshake with Toby as she followed her friend, using the much more mundane stairs to reach the open floor of the ballroom.

"Damn showoff," she muttered *sotto voce* as she went past Toby.

"Well, no one is looking at you, at least for the moment. But that'll change." Toby smiled at his friend. "And you do look lovely, dear Sachi. Ah, if only you were a man."

"Flatterer." But she smiled as she swept down the stairs after her other, rather more flamboyant friend. *Friends. Hmm. I never considered I would ever have friends. But how else might I describe these two? So unexpected. Like this outfit Silaqui came up with. I think she took the idea of bodyguard to nearly ridiculous extremes. I wonder? Do Elves always have to overdo everything? I am learning that these western Elves are much different from the* Kami *of my homeland. A true* Kami *would have never stuck me in this silly dress. A proper kimono would have been sufficient. If there is a fight or even should I move too violently, I'm afraid I'll pop right out of this silly top, I don't care how much magic she used on it. Does she want anyone I stand near to be able to see my nipples? Damn Elf!*

Her black dress was much more practical than it looked, despite her internal reservations. Tight above the waist, like Silaqui's, a keyhole cutout revealed an extremely generous amount of creamy cleavage. What looked like a full skirt was a modified divided riding skirt. She could do full kicks and back flips in this rig. Given the thick, heavy silk of which it was made, nothing short of a musket ball or a well-swung sword should punch cleanly through it. The slightly flared shoulders hid her short butterfly swords, each one eighteen inches of razor-sharp steel tucked side by side into a single sheath down her spine. Her garrote was tucked into the elaborate confection of her hair. The dozen faceted black tourmalines that glinted in the piled mass of her jet-black locks were the balanced ends of throwing darts, not hairpins. A matched pair of throwing daggers tucked into flat suede sheaths were secured under her tight sleeves.

Concealed slits in the skirt allowed her to reach a pair of more substantial blades strapped to her thighs. Modestly heeled black boots completed the ensemble. The inch-high heels were modeled more on a cavalry riding boot than the current Kolbian style of slender shafts of four inches or more for women's boots. Between her height and the solid black outfit, she imagined she was intimidating enough that most of the men here would leave her alone.

At least, I hope they will.

***

"Admiral Mynheers. It's a true pleasure to finally meet you, in the flesh." Silaqui purred as she landed in front of the stunned Admiral. She extended her hand. Mynheers shook his head once and took her hand, carefully brushing it with his lips. "I heard a great deal about you while onboard the *Intrepid*. And even more since I've arrived in Carolington City."

"I can imagine." His eyes flickered towards where the Blaines were standing. William colored slightly as the Admiral added, "Much probably not fit for mixed company, no doubt."

"Why should you say that, Sir? Captain Blaine was most fulsome in his praise of your policies. Not that I was privy to anything other than the most vague and general of conversations regarding yourself."

"Humpf. I bet. *Tell the Elves no secrets, for they know them already*, or so the old saw goes. Always at least some heat where there is smoke."

"Perhaps, Admiral, perhaps." She paused and hid a smirk as the Admiral's attention passed over her shoulder and his eyes widened. "Ah, please allow me to introduce to you my bodyguard, Defender and Elf-friend, Takahashi Sachi, of the Empire of Isemoto." She half-turned to make the introduction. Sachi's black eyes were hooded as the Admiral mumbled something incomprehensible over her hand. His eyes were irresistibly drawn to her cleavage.

***

I doubt he even saw my face. Sachi tried to subdue the glare she shot at Silaqui, but it bounced without effect off the Elf's broad smile. *Someday I will get you for this, Silaqui, my dear!*

"So kind, Admiral Mynheers-sama." Sachi reclaimed her hand and gave him a carefully controlled bow, junior to senior. "But Lady Silaqui-sama does me too much honor. I am merely her servant and bodyguard. Nothing more." She hid a sigh at his reaction. It was no more than she expected. With a slight smile, she bowed again and followed Silaqui.

***

"Captain Blaine."

"Milady Silaqui." Blaine brushed his lips over her hand. "Please be known to my wife, Mrs. Emily Blaine. Emily, Lady Silaqui of Montagar."

"Pleasure." Emily's tone was strained as she took in Silaqui's exotic beauty. The Elf had damped her aura once she reached the abbreviated receiving line, but the seven gems tattooed over her left eye still glittered with the light of her power. "Captain Blaine, Lady Emily, please allow me to introduce my friend and defender, since she is no servant, Takahashi Sachi of the Empire of Isemoto."

"Captain Blaine-sama, Lady Emily-sama." Sachi bowed deeply to the couple, junior to master. Emily Blaine felt herself pale with suppressed envy as she finally got a good look at the young Nisei woman about whom she had heard quite a bit.

These two spent MONTHS on his damn boat! He's probably been banging them both! That bastard! And God in His Heaven, this little Nisei slut is gorgeous enough to have every man in sight drooling on himself and following her around like a lost puppy after someone that fed it a steak. And half the women as well. Her eyes darted from Sachi to William and back, quick as summer lightning.

"Lady Silaqui." William released her hand and turned to Sachi. "Sachi." He inclined his head to return her deep bow. Their eyes met for a split-second as Sachi completed the bow.

Emily caught a faint hint of a deeper exchange. Then Sachi turned those bottomless black eyes on her. She was never able to explain what she saw in those eyes, but somehow, she knew they judged her. Judged her and found her wanting and unworthy. Despite herself, Emily colored ever so slightly. *And if there isn't* something *going on between these two, I'm High Queen of the Faeries!*

"Lady Emily-sama, the stories I have heard of your beauty do not do you justice." The girl bowed deeply again to Emily. "Captain Blaine-sama should rejoice in his return to you. I am most honored to meet you. The Captain's loyalty and honor to his vows are clear and simple in your presence; how could he do otherwise, when you await him on the shore?"

"Truly?" Emily was startled by the clear frankness with which the Nisei girl acknowledged William's famous loyalty to his vows. *Supposed loyalty. Over the years all his crews would lie like dogs for him. Why should this little fornicating trollop be any different?* "You are too kind, young lady." The Nisei bowed again and turned to follow the Elf.

"Always willing to believe the worst of me, aren't you, Emily, dear?" Blaine's voice was soft and quiet in her ear.

"Those two were on your ship for months. And you stopped in the Horn Islands. And you never took the opportunity to bury yourself between those thighs? Oh, please!" Her voice was just as soft and infinitely more poisonous in its bitterness. A young Emily had used her beauty to enrapture a promising young Lieutenant, J.G., following her mother's advice to succeed in high society.

Neither her mother nor father had ever been the least faithful to each other. The fact that Blaine meant his vows and kept firmly to them had been a surprise. Of course, he was from a family of old military traditions. No one in Emily's family had ever served in any fashion. It was to attempt to correct this lack that had inclined her mother to push her to pursue the handsome young officer. Now, she knew he had never broken those vows and that he never would. Naturally, she constantly accused him of what she, herself did.

"That young woman has more honor in her little finger than you have ever possessed, Emily. You simply don't understand honor. I'm beginning to believe you never have and never will." Blaine sighed as he watched Sachi follow Silaqui through the crowd the two exotic women were starting to draw. "But be that as it may, I asked you to marry me, you agreed, and I gave you my oath to honor our vows. I have never broken that oath and I never will, no matter what you do or don't think. Or what you do. Or don't do."

"Humpf." Emily flicked open her fan and hid her face behind it. "Well, then, *husband,* why don't you go get me a glass of wine. Supposedly Admiral Mynheers has laid in a good amount of vintage Elven wine from Montagar itself. Might as well have *something* to enjoy out of this mess."

"Of course, dear."

***

Across the room, hidden for a moment behind Silaqui's back, Sachi's preternaturally acute hearing caught the poisonous exchange between the Blaines. For just a second Sachi lost her internal struggle with herself and a single tear coursed down a porcelain cheek.

***

"Impossible!" Janay Hampton bleated, loud enough to be heard across half the room. This was despite the band playing for those enjoying the dance floor. "That Elf and her supposed *sorcery* are bad enough, but now you say this Nisei girl is her bodyguard! I don't care who you're related to, Lieutenant Fleet, there is no way that slip of a girl fought off four thuggers! Yes, I know how tall she is, but she's no man! Wasn't there a platoon of Marines involved somewhere or is the whole story as fake as that so-called Elf's *magic!* Humpf! No such thing as magic! It's all mirrors and wires." She paused long enough to inhale a substantial amount of the full wine glass she was holding. It was far from her first.

"Dear, it's Lieutenant Commander, not Lieutenant. And how else but magic do you explain Lady Silaqui floating across the room when she got here, wrapped in red fire that didn't burn anything." Vice Admiral Hampton vainly patted his intoxicated wife on the hand, attempting to derail one of her famous tirades on something she knew nothing about, as usual, before she embarrassed herself. Again, as usual. But this was different. He knew her irrational fear and hatred of any non-human might drive her to worse than mere embarrassment. "Sorry, Lieutenant Commander, she's had a few too many," he whispered in Fleet's ear.

"No problem, sir." Willis shrugged. "When someone says Lieutenant Commander, I still look around to see who they're talking to." *I'll say, a few too many! That lush could drink a bosun under the table! I'm surprised she can still walk! She might even be able to give Sachi a run for her money.*

"Pay attention, Weslan! Those two are nearly indecent. You should have them arrested." She gestured first at Silaqui where she danced with Admiral Mynheers before glaring at Sachi, who was proving to be a remarkable dancer as she spun through the waltz on Toby's arm. "I'm waiting for that black-haired hussy's boobs to come flying out."

"So are most of the men here tonight," Fleet muttered under his breath.

"What was that, Lieutenant?"

"Nothing, Mrs. Hampton, just clearing my throat. Hem-haw." *I'll get you for this someday, Admiral Carstairs, see if I don't. This was the last place I wanted to be tonight. But no, it's* I'd like you to attend, keep an eye on things for ONI, if you have nothing better to do, Lieutenant Commander. *You rat. You dirty rat.*

"I told you, it's Lieutenant Commander, dear."

"Lieutenant, Lieutenant Commander, he's still just a flunky."

"Of course, dear." Hampton gave Fleet an apologetic shrug. "I'm sure he understands."

"Of course, I do, sir." Fleet dipped his head in acknowledgement. "If you would excuse me, Vice-Admiral, Mrs. Hampton?" At the Vice-Admiral's pained nod, he fled the field of combat ingloriously. *Best to get while the getting is good! I wonder why he hasn't pushed her out of a window in a tall building already. Ugh.*

The music ended and the various couples began drifting toward the refreshments laid out on the sideboards on both sides of the ballroom. William Blaine's attention was caught by Mrs. Hampton's determined course for where Admiral Mynheers, Silaqui, Sachi and Toby were chatting with one of the merchant captains and the rather fetching redhead with him. The redhead seemed at least as interested in Sachi as her date did. When Mrs. Hampton's approach came to the group's attention, the merchant captain took one look at the set of Janay Hampton's jaw and immediately excused himself and his date, leaving the group with nearly unseemly haste.

***

Admiral Mynheers hid a frown as he noticed the pugnacious woman's approach. *I've seen ships of the line with less canvas set at full sail. Where does that woman get such hideous gowns? I think she goes out of her way to be as obnoxious as possible. I could almost feel sorry for Admiral Hampton. Almost. Damn it, here she comes. And she's focused on Lady Silaqui. Oh, crap. Looks like I should brace to receive the enemy. Going to be too little, too late. Shit. And here comes Blaine and his wife as well. I should remember the Navy's rule about ground combat...send the Marines. Oh, hell.* He grimaced as Janay Hampton stormed up to the small group and confronted Silaqui.

"This is utter nonsense! If you're an immortal Elf, I'm the Emperor Confas!" Janay screeched. "I have utterly no idea why you are receiving such deference! Who put you up to this con-game?"

"Excuse me?" a confused Silaqui answered. "Who are you?"

"I'm Janay Hampton, the wife of Vice-Admiral Weslan Hampton, as you well know! You're a fraud! There's no such thing as magic! Or elves! You're just trying to con Admiral Mynheers! You fake hussy! You and your little Nisei trollop, bouncing her tits at every man in the room! The little slut!"

"Janay! You're drunk!" Weslan came puffing up behind her and clapped his hand on her shoulder. "I think it's time to head home, Dear."

"Shut up, Weslan!" She shrugged his hand off her shoulder. "I don't know how you fooled everyone else, but I see right through you! You're just some little street-walking whore with fancy make-up!" Her voice quivered with anger, covering her suppressed fear. Non-humans were bad enough to her, but magic was even worse. There was no place in her world for anyone like Silaqui of Montagar.

"Would you like to explain how she flew across the ballroom then, Janay?" Mynheers quietly asked. "There aren't any wires hanging off the ceiling, you know." He was desperately trying to defuse the explosion he saw coming. Sachi slid up and took a deceptively relaxed pose between and slightly behind Silaqui and Admiral Mynheers.

"She slid down a glass rail! I've seen that trick used in the theater more than once! And the ears are fake, I've seen those before, too!" She started to reach for Silaqui's ear. Sachi's hand shot out and grabbed Janay's left hand, clamping like a vise on the sensitive wrist joint and stopping her from touching Silaqui.

"That is quite enough, *Reifujin* Hampton-sama. *Kami* Silaqui-sama is my charge. You should listen to your husband and go home, noble lady. Before something unpleasant happens. Please." Sachi's voice was quiet, but the scene was rapidly drawing everyone's attention.

"LET GO OF ME, YOU WHORE!" Janay squealed as she tried to jerk loose from Sachi's grip. Sachi let the woman's slap hit her, turning her head to reduce the force of the weak blow. Weslan Hampton grabbed his wife's free hand as she drew back to hit Sachi again.

"STOP IT, DAMN IT, JANAY!" he shouted in her ear as she screamed in wordless fury, struggling to reach Silaqui, her fingers clawed to rake Sachi's face. "What the hell is wrong with you?!"

"*ENOUGH!*" Silaqui's shout thundered throughout the room. Scarlet flames washed out from her, turning every light in the room carmine. "Be silent! Be still! I bind you by my power and my will!" Her aura flared as dark as blood wine as Janay Hampton froze in place, unable to move a muscle. Sachi released her hand, stepping slightly back. Utter silence fell in the room. "Mortal, I overlook much but violent insult will not be borne! You know nothing of the truth of the world around you, yet you squeal as if you are the source of all wisdom! I trod this world a thousand and more years ago, when your ancestors still daubed themselves blue with river mud! Members of mine own family survived the Fire Fall and the Dragon Wars. They who watched in sorrow five thousand years ago as the Empire of Rolandus burned. What are you to me, but a screeching fishwife howling in her hovel?!"

"Silaqui-*sama*, mistress." Sachi faced Silaqui. "She is old and knows not of which she speaks. She sees with envy what she lost when her youth passed. Spiteful and bitter, but she is not evil. Please, my friend, do not hurt her. I beg you, *Kami*, spare her."

"Sachi, I will not hurt her. Directly." Silaqui turned to where Admiral Mynheers stood next to a white-faced Vice-Admiral Hampton. "But I have been insulted and disrespected, mistreated and affronted and I am not amused in the least. I will not stand here without answering her insults. What punishment would you set, then, Admiral Mynheers?"

"Well, under our Constitution, she does have the right of free speech." Mynheers answered quietly.

"And that allows her to vex and harry me? To assault me? To attempt to strike me? To strike my friend and defender? Without response from me?" Silaqui's reply was calm and quiet. "There are those of my folk who would declare her life forfeit for such insults. And others who might burn this island to bare rock in their just rage. Fortunately for you, that is not my nature. In general, I like humans. You are inventive and clever, fascinating to travel amongst. And I say this despite the experiences I suffered over the last two years. But what are two years to me? They paid with their lives and that was sufficient. Barely. I will not demand this foolish woman's life. Nor will I imprison her or cause her any true pain."

"What would you, then, Lady?" Mynheers quietly asked.

"This." She turned to face Janay Hampton squarely. "While my feet stand on the same soil as yours and for one full day after, you shall assume the form that most suits you. In that form you shall be able to think as any Mortal might and thus contemplate how and why you are what you are. By my will and my power, I show you the true form of your inner self. You might learn from this experience and become a more kind and thoughtful soul, better prepared for whenever you should come before whichever God you believe in."

The carnelian flames of Silaqui's sorcery gathered around her in a rush, flaring so brightly, no one could bear to look at the Elvish sorceress. She flung her arms out towards Janay. Her voice twisted in unpronounceable words in a forgotten language, disturbing all who heard it. Scarlet flames flooded from her hands, circling, and dancing madly around a Janay Hampton struggling futilely to scream in terror. The flames swarmed around her and grew, blocking all sight of her. A scream finally burst from her throat, high pitched at first, changing in tone and timbre as the flames curled in, growing smaller and lower. They began to gutter and die as the screams were replaced by a whimpering cry and at the last a frantic squealing.

"Squee, squee!" A fat, white pig stood where Janay Hampton had been, its hooves marring the inlaid wooden floor. The creature's eyes rolled wildly, and its hooves slipped on the polished floor. A leather collar and leash hung around its neck. Silaqui stepped to the pig, kneeling, and picked up the leash.

"This is your punishment for insulting one of the Eldest Folk. Be glad. My uncle would have fed your screaming soul to something truly depraved from the Netherworlds. I am not so harsh. In a day's time, I leave this island. The spell shall hold you in this form for a full day after our feet no longer touch the same land. You are protected by my spell as well. No one can harm you in any fashion, as long as you are a pig. When the spell releases you, you shall remember this time. Learn from it. Swine are wise and intelligent creatures. Wisdom is something you are desperately lacking, despite your well-earned age. IF you learn any wisdom at all, treasure it. Become more than what you were. Next time, you might not be so fortunate." She rose smoothly to her feet and turned to Admiral Hampton.

"Squee." The pig that had been Janay oinked plaintively.

"Janay?" Hampton was pale and sweating. He stared at Silaqui in fear. "What have you done to my wife?"

"Exactly what it appears. I have transformed her into a pig, only temporarily. She will be fine; nothing can harm her as my sorcery will protect her. But she is still just a pig." She shrugged and handed the leash to him. "Take her home, Admiral. A boon I do grant, that she will retain her mind and ability to learn. Were I feeling particularly vindictive, this would be permanent, and she would, in mind as well as body, be naught more than a pig the rest of her days. I should suggest that you spend much time with her. Perhaps you might benefit from the wisdom of a simple creature, such as a pig, as well?" She turned away from the badly shaken man. As she did, she caught and held Emily Blaine's eye. "There are worse fates in the world. Much worse."

***

A much-subdued party continued. Many of the guests had taken an abrupt leave of the festivities after Silaqui's display of arcane power. For the next hour, everyone still left gave her and Sachi a wide berth. Sachi finally convinced Silaqui to come outside, into the garden maze. The maze wasn't large enough to get utterly lost in, but it did offer some privacy from prying eyes. Out of sight of the party, Silaqui collapsed in Sachi's arms and wept for a moment.

"Silaqui, what's wrong? Are you regretting doing that to that horrible old woman? Are you okay?"

"I'm an Elf, Sachi. Elves may know sorrow as the world turns, but we do not regret our actions. Remember that. Elves never feel regret. No, that spell is difficult to cast with so little preparation. The power must come from my own reserves. Magic drains one, leaves you temporarily vulnerable to your emotions. Wielding magic requires control and precision. It is draining on the wielder, physically, mentally, and emotionally. An unprepared casting like that is difficult and leaves one more vulnerable. And so, I chose to cry, and thereby recover my emotions. I can do so because I know I am protected by my heart-sister." She gave Sachi a wry smile and a quick, hard hug.

"Well, that's good to know. So, shall we explore the maze and search for monsters to slay and treasure to find?" Sachi gave Silaqui an urchin's grin as she pulled the Elf to her feet.

"Why not?" She returned the grin. "Might lead to a dragon's lair." The pair laughed as they danced deeper into the maze.

***

"Aren't you Mrs. Emily Blaine, ma'am?"

"Yes, and you are?" Emily nodded her head to the stunning redhead who approached her with an unopened bottle of wine and four glasses.

"Amma Carlon, Mrs. Blaine. I came with Captain Heinrike of the galleon *Fortune Follows*. He's nice but he jumped up and left when that Elf...well, you know. At least he left me the nice bottle of wine he brought. Too much of a hurry to get away, I guess. It's a nice Eindeuten vintage, but I don't really care for wine myself. I saw you and Captain Blaine and the Elf and that beautiful Nisei girl together at the beginning of the party. I thought that either you might appreciate it, or maybe know someone who might, perhaps?"

"Um-hum. Why don't you just go give it to Sachi, I think that's the Nisei girl's name, yourself? I know an infatuation when I see one. God knows just about everyone who's still here is drooling over her. Or are you one of my husband's tarts?" Emily's tone was bitter and sharp. "I know what you are. I hope you got payment from Heinrike in advance."

"Fine, *Mrs.* Blaine." Felicity hid a nasty smile as she baited Emily Blaine. She knew the scuttlebutt of the street and the rumors of the Naval officers' club. Easy to work Emily with her own pride. She felt she was better than a common streetwalker, despite having much in common with one. "So I'm a working girl. Maybe I'm outta my league. But I'll bet you everything you own that you can't find a girl in this whole damn city that's had William Blaine between her legs. Not one but you. And I know those who have tried. And failed. At this point, we've all pretty much given up. No one for him but you." The girl's face hardened, and Emily revised her estimate of her age upward. By a good bit. "Can you say the same thing, *Mrs.* Blaine?" She turned and started to storm off and ran right into Captain Blaine as he came around the corner. The glasses shattered as they hit the floor, but Blaine managed to catch her, and she held onto the bottle.

***

"Hold on there. You okay, young lady?" Blaine helped steady her on her feet.

"I'm fine, Captain Blaine. For being called a whore. I wanted you to introduce me to Sachi Takahashi. I've never seen anyone so beautiful. I saw her in a saloon with a bunch of sailors the other day. I think I fell in love with her, but I was afraid to just walk up and talk to her. Then one of my...*gentleman* friends who's an officer on the *Christine* told me about this party. And stupid me, I thought to ask you or your wife to introduce me, so I got Captain Heinrike to bring me and I spent my rent money on this stupid bottle of wine. And this party has been a fucking disaster." She stepped away from Blaine, meeting his eyes briefly. She knew he was as sharp as they come, and didn't want him seeing through the act. It wasn't perfect, but it was the best she could come up with on such short notice. And it got her away from Master. "Fine, so, I'm just a stupid whore who doesn't know her place. Here, take the damn wine. I hate wine. Give it to her or drink it yourself or throw it in the ocean. I don't care." Felicity turned blue eyes full of fake tears on Emily. "So I'm a whore. Least I'm honest about it and I *do* get paid up front. How about you, *Mrs.* Blaine?" She thrust the wine bottle into Blaine's hands and fled down the hallway to the front door. Blaine heard the sobs begin as she went around the corner. Blaine turned toward an ashen-faced Emily.

"What the hell is going on here? What did you say to that poor girl?" His tone was cool.

"Oh, please." Emily turned and headed out the open doors into the garden. Blaine stood there for a long moment.

What is the value of an oath, when the one to whom the oath is made is an oathbreaker? What is honor to one without honor? Blaine grimaced at the nasty little voice in the back of his head. *Maybe I've never really been tested before now? Maybe Sachi is that test and if I pass it, I'll get the Emily I married back.* He read the label of the bottle. "Hey, this is good stuff. Be a damn shame to throw it in the bay. Maybe I can use it as a peace offering. Emily likes these sweeter Eindeuten wines. She should've checked the label before insulting that girl."

Yeah, maybe. Right. I'm beginning to think I have no idea who I married. After fourteen, almost fifteen damn years. Now what? He squared his shoulders and followed Emily into the garden.

***

Well, that went well. Now I just gotta get a little lucky. I hope that snotty blonde bitch does drink out of that bottle. I'd kill her for free. Felicity sat in the back of the hansom cab as the horse clip-clopped down toward the ferry's dock. *I need to get my ass off this island now. Last thing I need is the Navy Shore Patrol looking for a blue-eyed redhead. And all they'd have to do is hold the ferries. Besides, I have to get my ass back to* Master. *I do hope he liked the little present I gave him. Wonder if he has any idea how much internal muscular control that little trick took. Gotta be able to squeeze just enough, but not too much.* She drew a six-inch stiletto out of a very intimate sheath and checked the blade. *Worst comes to worst, there's always six inches of steel in his eye. Even that bastard wouldn't survive that. Wonder why he wanted that girl dead so bad?*

***

Sachi and Silaqui came out of the maze breathless with laughter. They quickly sobered as they saw Captain Blaine and Emily sitting at a table together, an unopened bottle of wine between them on the table. Blaine waved them over when he saw them. Sachi could see Emily, stiff with displeasure.

"This is not a good idea, Silaqui."

"Yes, it is. One, you can learn to deal with an enemy you can't just kill. And two, I think that's an Eindeuten vintage from the Black Hills range. I happen to love that wine. I should hope that some day you'll find a tipple of better quality than that disgusting sah-keh you say you like so much. Brackish swamp water would be better, in my opinion."

"Ooh, that's not fair."

"I'm an Elf. Fair is for humans. And maybe dwarves."

***

"Lady Silaqui, Sachi, it has been an, shall we agree on *interesting* party so far? Given the...unfortunate events of earlier, I hope you're still enjoying your-selves?" Blaine was struggling to be pleasant to Silaqui, despite the memory of the terrified eyes of the pig that had been or maybe still was Janay Hampton. It showed in the tension in his voice.

"I am sorry about what happened, Captain Blaine, Lady Emily." Silaqui sobered for a moment; the merriment gone from her eyes. "But no one of the Elder Races will ever tolerate such an insult. A dwarf would have simply cut her in twain. Some of my elders would have been more creative. I dread to think what my uncle would do in such a case. Like all things mortal, what I did to her shall soon pass."

"This uncle of yours, Lady Silaqui, you speak of him quite often. Perhaps you could tell us a little bit about him?"

"Yes, Lady Emily. He is not truly my uncle but rather my great-uncle many times over. He is one of the eldest of us all. Only the King and Queen are older, I believe. Perhaps the Court Mage. Uncle says he remembers when humans first came here. But he will not speak of those days. He does not care much for your folk."

"I see." Emily's demeanor was still unhappy, and she shot occasional glances at both William and Sachi. Sachi never raised her eyes. "Well, perhaps more pleasant subjects are in order. Regardless of its source, this is a fine example of one of the wines I most prefer, but we have no glasses. I don't see one of the remaining wait staff about. Sachi, would you be so kind as to fetch us four glasses?"

"Emily, Sachi is not a servant." Blaine snapped his head up.

"Lady Emily, Sachi is my friend. I'll thank you to not give her orders." Silaqui snapped in a cold, hard voice.

"No, please." Sachi came quickly to her feet. "Do not be disharmonious. Please, not on my account. If I had completed my training at...home, I would now be a *maiko*, a trainee geisha. I would be an *imouto-san* to a ranked *onee-san*, junior sister to elder. An *imouto-san* serves her elder, in exchange for training. I am not insulted to be asked to serve, it is my honor." She bowed deeply to an astonished Emily. "I shall fetch the glasses post-haste, Lady Emily."

"What the hell?" Blaine asked as Sachi hurried away.

"William, just open the wine. Let it breathe a bit before she gets back."

***

"Allow me." Silaqui's jade eyes were hard as she waved a crimson haloed finger and popped the wine's cork loose. *What does he see in this blonde bitch?* The three of them sat for several minutes in an uncomfortable silence until Sachi returned with a tray of wine glasses. She set the tray down and quickly appropriated the bottle, pouring each glass about half full.

"I do not know the proprieties of serving wine in Kolbia, but I do know the tea ceremony of my people very well. Please, allow me to serve you."

"Only as long as you will sit down and drink with us as an equal, Sachi." Silaqui's voice was firm.

"Have no concerns, Lady Silaqui." Sachi's voice was calm and serene as she moved around the table setting out the partially filled glasses. "In the tea ceremony of my land, the host always drinks first, tasting the tea."

***

Emily couldn't help but be impressed and more than a little envious of Sachi's calm grace as she turned setting out wine glasses into a simple, yet elegant ceremony. *She looks like a ballerina in slow motion. And so damn beautiful it hurts. Some of the rumors say she's dangerous, maybe deadly. Supposedly she fought off four thuggers who attacked the Elf earlier this month. I can't believe some of the stories floating around, that she killed those four ruffians with her bare hands! She's tall, especially in boots, but otherwise there's not a lot of girl there, regardless of how well she's...endowed.* Sachi finished setting out the wine and moved to the side of the table she had chosen. She pulled her chair to the side and stood at the edge of the table.

"This is hardly a proper tea ceremony. You do not do a tea ceremony with wine, but I would like to observe some small part of the ritual to honor Lady Silaqui-sama, who claims me as her friend and heart-sister. And to honor Captain William Blaine-sama and Lady Emily-sama, him for his bravery and honor, her for her beauty and grace." She bowed deeply to the other three seated at the table. "In Isemoto, the host prepares and serves the tea, while the attendees might either contemplate in silence on their recent good fortunes or pray to the Ancestor Spirits for guidance in the days to come. So as the host I have poured the wine and presented it too each of you." She picked up her glass. "I honor my friends and their companions with this wine. I pray the Ancestor Spirits shall always find favor with each of us that are here today." She brought the glass to her lips and took a deep drink. "Please, take up your glasses and starting with Silaqui, speak of something you wish to come to pass. That or of something you are grateful for. Do not drink, yet. The reason for this, the host drinking first, is to prove that the tea, or in this case, the wine, is safe to drink and has not been poisoned by enemies. At least, that was the reason for the delay in tasting that my teacher gave me. Silaqui-sama?"

"I thank my patron goddess, Ainaera, Goddess of Love and Beauty, for Captain Blaine and the *Intrepid*, who brought me out of bondage and into the warm presence of my heart-sister and Elf-friend, Takahashi Sachi." She swirled the wine in her glass and sniffed appreciatively.

"Captain Blaine-sama."

"I thank God for whatever it was that saved *Intrepid* from that sea monster. And for returning safely to my daughter and wife. And for my friends, old and new." Blaine raised his glass in salute.

"Lady Emily-sama."

"I thank God that my husband returned safely and pray for his long overdue promotion to Commodore." Blaine's brows furrowed ever so slightly at Emily's brief speech as she raised her glass to her lips.

::Warning. Lethal toxicity detected. Warning. Lethal toxicity detected. Request full Entity access to all available resources. Neural toxin detected in near lethal amounts.:: The metallic timbre of the silver statue's voice echoed through her head. Sachi's vision blurred into a red haze. The wine glass fell from her hand and shattered on the floor. She lunged across the table and smashed the wine glass out of Emily's hand as she was raising it to her lips.

"No, don't!" she gasped. "It's been poisoned! Don't touch it!" She fell to the floor twitching uncontrollably, sweeping the bottle and glasses off the table as she fell. Sachi rolled onto her back and the world faded away as the fit took her.

VR Construct

::Caitlyn Schmidt, you have received a lethal level dose of a powerful neural toxin. Access to all your physical enhancements is required. Bio-nanite production sufficient to offset the toxin will strain your physical body to the limits. With your increased awareness of your internal comp-systems, my programming necessitates that more and more of my functions require your assent before implementation.::

The silver statue stood before her in the same grey featureless plain as always. She again was nude, towering over the waist-high statue. She shivered as she realized the grey sky and plain were not completely featureless, barely sensed currents agitated the sky and the plain seemed to ripple and twist at times. Something was clearly wrong. Again she shivered as she looked down to see her feet start to take on a pallid grey tone, matching her surroundings.

"Without these things, these nanites, what will happen to me?"

::Without increased nanite production there will be insufficient nanites to counter the toxin as it attacks your central nervous system and your Biological Processing Unit. Probability of survival of the toxin dose without increased nanite production is four percent, plus or minus twenty-eight percent. Multiple variables preclude a more accurate estimate.::

"And if I tell you to do this, to make these things?"

::Probability of survival of the toxin dose with increased nanite production increases to sixty-eight percent, plus or minus twelve percent. Increased nanite production reduces variables.::

"What's the catch? And what in the world is a nanite, anyway?"

"The *catch*, as a human would say, Caitlyn Schmidt, is the strain of rapidly increased nanite production under emergency circumstances can result in permanent physical or neurological damage. Nanites are bio-mechanical machines built within your body, on a microscopic scale, tiny robots ten to the negative nine meters in size, or one millimicron, that work with your BPU to provide much of your enhanced capabilities. They enhance your vision, hearing, and physical reflexes. They provide enhanced medical capabilities and rapid healing. Environmental toxins within your body are filtered out by them. In the crudest terms, the bio-enhancement provided by nanites make you tougher, stronger, and faster than any unenhanced human.::

"These things do all that? But producing them now can hurt me? How bad could the damage be? Aren't we wasting time talking?"

::In this mode, time is vastly compressed. Seconds are split into thousandths. What you perceive as hours within this virtual world, a world created by the bio-electronic systems in your body, are only mere seconds in the real world. The actual time that passes in the real world is extended by your body's need to recover and heal. Here, Caitlyn Schmidt, you have the luxury of having sufficient time to make a properly informed decision. For some reason unknown to this Entity, Confederation scientists referred to this accelerated time perception as *hyper-heuristic mode.*::

"And how bad?"

::The physical and neurological strain will be immense. Possible outcomes range from severe but temporary headaches and blindness to permanent mental retardation and possibly death. The most severe outcomes would, in effect, be nearly as bad as the toxin itself. However, those probabilities are low, six percent, plus or minus five percent. Severe, disabling headaches and temporary blindness are most likely, lasting thirty-seven to fifty-two hours. Probability of this approaches unity, plus or minus twenty-eight percent. Multiple variables.::

"Versus almost certainly dying without taking the chance?"

::Correct.::

"Not much of a choice, then, is it?"

::No. Your increasing awareness of your enhanced internal systems preclude this Entity from acting autonomously. Therefore, your informed authorization is required.::

"Ancestors."

::Statement not understood.::

"No, you wouldn't. There is no real choice. Proceed with increased nanite production and try not to turn me into a particularly tall carrot."

::Understood. Initiating nanite system production increase. You may feel some slight discomfort.:: The virtual world inside her mind whirled away in mist as pain tore through her body. The only thing she was aware of were the screams tearing through her throat. Finally, a peaceful blackness claimed all awareness.

Carolington Roads Base Hospital

"Is she going to recover, Elazar?" William Blaine stepped out of Sachi's room in the base infirmary as she slept peacefully. He was careful to close the door quietly.

"Yes. Don't ask me how, but I think she'll out of the infirmary this time tomorrow." Hoff rubbed his eyes. It had been nearly forty hours since he'd had any sleep. Sachi had been unconscious for twenty-nine hours after drinking the poisoned wine, barely hanging on to life. When she regained consciousness, there was nothing he could do for the severe headaches and the blindness. Her calm demeanor surprised Hoff, the lack of panic over the blindness. Sachi kept saying it would pass and it had. She lost enough weight that she more resembled an animated skeleton than a human being. "Now she just eats and sleeps. This girl ain't natural. But she finally looks like her usual, stunningly beautiful self."

"So a full recovery? How? You said that poison was something really nasty."

"Billy, I'm concluding that no one has the vaguest hint of a clue what she's capable of. Or perhaps the question should be *what she is*? From the tests on the wine, I think the poison was something like Vexarin. Can't have been Vexarin because no one survives that stuff. Still, whatever it was, it should have killed her. Don't ask me why it didn't."

"Yeah."

"And the first words out of her mouth when she recovered what I'll call marginal consciousness were *Are Emily and Silaqui safe? My Captain? Tell me they live, please?* First words."

"I know, Elazar. I was there, remember. So was Emily. That shook her, right down to her teeth. Who knows, maybe it'll change her?"

"Maybe. But I know she didn't like to hear Sachi call you, and I quote, *My Captain.*" Hoff sighed. "I wouldn't bet on it. Not long term."

"Well, that mess of a party screwed up things enough that Mynheers has held the convoy another two weeks. Which allowed him to scare up two more sloops for the escort."

"Oh, I hadn't heard that. What ships?"

"*Audacity* and *Dragon*, both twenty-two guns. So, I'm acting Commodore for two frigates, three sloops-of-war and two schooners. Not to mention a sixteen-ship convoy."

"Obviously Mynheers thinks you can handle it."

"God, I hope so. This should be a Rear Admiral's billet. Not a jumped-up Captain, J.G."

"Well, Emily wants you to get that promotion to full Captain. If this doesn't prove you're ready for it, nothing will."

"Hmm. And then add in an Elven sorceress who is credited as a diplomat, the mystery known as Takahashi Sachi and my wife and daughter. My hair is never going to have a chance to turn gray or white. I'm going to pull it all out on this voyage."

"There are worse things, you know."

"Yes. And apparently, the little chit that gave me the wine simply disappeared. She's one I'd like to have a nice little chat with. Exactly who was she trying to kill?"

"Wasn't Fleet working that angle?"

"Yes. He traced her to the ferry and then to the City's Main Docks. Then, poof, she vanishes into thin air. Captain Heinrike confirmed that she was a hired escort, but all the information about her he gave Fleet and the Carolington Police turned out false. Whoever she is, she's probably long gone by now."

"That, or her body just hasn't floated up yet."

"Yeah. Hadn't really wanted to think about that. But you might be right."

"Damned shame, if so."

"Yes. She was a pretty little thing."

Carolington City
Master's Residence

"I hope that burned really bad, you worthless son of a bitch. As bad as the burns you left under my tits. Quan take you to Hell. Those scars will never disappear." Felicity booted Master hard in the ribs, hard enough to break several. Not that he felt it. The puff-wyvern poison she had managed to spread on his penis the last time he raped her had done its job. His body was swollen and bloated, worst around his crotch. He had nearly clawed his own guts out as the poison had burned its way into his body. His face was mostly gone; the rats had already been working on him for a couple of days.

"What's that, how did I do it?" She smirked at the corpse. "Sort of hard to hear you with your tongue gone. It was simple, a small amount of the poison in a thin, lambskin condom, and a thick, Khakal-rubber liner cut to fit inside me. Some veggie oil, so you didn't notice the liner, of course, you were in too much of a hurry to think about me, what I might like or want. So you didn't pay attention. Just like you never did. I'm a *thing* to you, not a person. But I'm a *thing* that killed you. Just enough of a squeeze to pop the condom right when you got your cookies off and *hey* the poison powder mixes with your fluids, activates, and starts to work. Fortunately for me, it's a slow poison and as usual, you weren't paying attention to what I did. You didn't notice how fast I was into the toilet, got the rubber liner out before any of that shit got on me. And then I'm off to kill that girl and you get to die screaming in here. Clever, huh?"

She moved around the room, avoiding all the torture instruments and racks. She had more than enough experience with those things, none of it pleasant. Against one wall was a cabinet. It was normally closed and locked somehow. She'd tried once to get into it and for once her skills at opening other people's property were completely defeated. But today there was a seam and a dim light shone through it.

"Well, what's this? You left it open? Why, thank you, Master. You prick. Or, well, not a prick anymore. Did that hurt, it sort of burning and melting off? I watched puff-wyvern poison eat a guy's hand off once. I can't imagine what that felt like, working on your poor abused privates." She stuck her nails into the seam and pulled the cabinet open. Light spilled out of it, bringing sharp highlights out in her red hair. "What the hell is this stuff?" Gleaming things, weapons, she thought, hung in racks around a plain black rectangle. Brilliant colored lights flowed smoothly around the rectangle. She reached out and touched the bottom of the rectangle, where there was an oval the size of a thumb. The rectangle opened, folding down and away from the back of the cabinet and a transparent blue cube sprang into existence above it. Strange symbols flashed in the cube. Then a man's head appeared in the blue cube.

The head looked funny, portrayed only in shades of blue and slightly transparent. Despite herself, she took a step back and when she moved, it reacted and looked at her. Another light snapped on and Felicity felt something insubstantial grab her, holding her in place. The head possessed a full head of what she thought would be black hair, pulled back in an Imperial style braid, revealing a high widow's peak on the man's forehead. His eyes were dark and a neatly trimmed black beard completed the look.

"Where is your Master? Who are you?" The lips moved and she could hear and understand the apparition. He had the refined accent of a nobleman of the Empire, probably from the province of Ibertina. "And don't try to lie, the comm will tell me if you do. Where is he?"

"Master is dead. I found his body here. The cabinet was open just a crack and there was a light shining out of the crack."

"Dead? How?" The head snapped.

"By poison, My Lord."

"Who are you?"

"Amma, My Lord. I worked for Master." She knew better than to give her real name. If he were a wizard, that would give him power over her.

"Well, Amma, I assume you haven't called the Kolbian authorities?"

"No, My Lord."

"Good, good." It paused and a hand rose into view and stroked the short beard. "We need an agent in Carolington, and you already know all you need to know. So, girl, what did you do for your master?"

"I stole things for him, sometimes. Had sex with him when he wanted. Other times, I just listened, or got men to talk to me and then I told him what I learned. I arranged things for him."

"Did he ever have you kill anyone?"

"Sometimes. Usually I just arranged it. The last time he wanted me to kill this girl..."

"Ah, the one with long black hair, from the East?"

"Yes."

"Is she dead?"

"Yes. I know she drank the poisoned wine I brought. It was laced with Vexarin. No one can survive even the smallest dose of that. She was dying when they took her to the hospital."

"Good. Good. Well done." The head regarded her keenly for a long while. "You seem to have few scruples. That's good, just what is needed. Are you willing to take your Master's place as my agent in Carolington? You would be richly rewarded. You see how your Master lived. It would be arranged that you would take his place."

"The police and the Navy's ONI agents will be looking for me soon, if they aren't already."

"Do they have anything other than a description?"

"No, My Lord."

"Good, then they can be handled. We have agents in many places, Amma. Many places. So?"

"My Lord." *If I don't become his agent, for whatever he wants, I'm dead. So agree, and be ready to run, far and fast, if things seem too dicey. On the other hand, Master certainly had all the comforts he wanted. And he was stupid in so many ways, couldn't be patient, now, now, now all the time.* "I would relish the opportunity to serve you, My Lord."

"Humpf." The head tilted as he considered her. "Well, needs must out when Quan drives. If you're what's available, then you'll have to do. Very well, inside the left-hand door you should see an envelope with papers in it. Get those out and we'll get started on settling you in place."

"Yes, My Lord."

"And, Amma?"

"Yes, My Lord?"

"Your Master was more than a bit of an idiot. But even so, he knew better than to try and cross us. Think about the uncomfortable end he came to. Neither of you are my only agents. My grasp is long. Do not forget that."

"Yes, My Lord." *Ha! You don't know everything! Not even close!* "How should I address you, My Lord?"

"Amma, you can simply call me Higher."

Carolington Roads Naval Base
Office of Naval Intelligence HQ

"So, I understand Takahashi Sachi is expected to make a full recovery. Fairly spectacular end to the party." Admiral Carstairs leaned back and propped his feet on his desk as Fleet took a seat across the desk from him.

"Yes, sir. I would say so. Lady Silaqui using magic to turn Janay Hampton into a pig. Wine poisoned with an agent that is one hundred percent fatal and the one person that drinks it survives. All we needed was a riot, a hurricane and an earthquake to have a real party."

"God, keep your mouth shut. You should know by now to never, ever say—"

"*What's the worst that could happen?*" Fleet chorused along with the Admiral. "Well, of course, sir."

"And no doubt you're wondering where I'm going to use you next?"

"Not really, sir."

"Oh, really." Carstairs gave Fleet a mischievous grin. "So, then, Lieutenant Commander, let's see if you're as clever as you think you are. What are your orders?"

"I'm to be transferred to the Montagaran Embassy, most likely as an Assistant Military Attaché. At least, that's my cover. In actuality, I'm being assigned to the Takahashi woman, partly as a bodyguard and partly to try and let ONI establish a modicum of clandestine control over her actions and movements. And to see what other secrets she might be a key to."

"Very good, Willis. I'll make a proper spook out of you yet, see if I don't." Carstairs sat up and opened his bottom desk drawer. "Since you've done so well on the test, I have a treat for you. And no, it's not a hot date with Sachi Takahashi." He grinned at Fleet. "It's this." He laid a wooden case down on his desk, opened it and turned it so Willis could see what was in it.

"What in the world are those, sir? I've never seen a pistol like that."

"These are new. Shiny, squeaky new. I think there have been less than a hundred made so far. The real trick isn't the revolving cylinder, it's the little silver cap that goes on this nipple, here." He pulled a small paperboard box out of the case and opened it. There were several hundred small shiny silver caps in it, stacked in neat rows. "These are being called percussion caps. It's a copper cap with a dab of fulminated mercury under a thin coat of lacquer. Hit it hard enough and it explodes, shooting a healthy dose of sparks down into the chamber and bang, the gun fires." He pulled out one of the two pistols in the box. He pulled a pin under the barrel and removed the cylinder. "Unloaded and clear."

"Yes, sir."

"So you load the cylinders individually, pretty much like any pistol, but you put a cap on each nipple, put the cylinder back in like so, then you either cock the hammer back, again like any pistol or, and here's another neat trick, you just pull the trigger. The cylinder rotates the next chamber into place and the action cocks the hammer, releases it and bang. Pull the trigger again, the cylinder rotates, hammer rises and falls, bang. And so on and so forth."

"The Army's flintlocks just became obsolete, sir."

"The system is being called a cap-lock and the Army will be retro-fitting it to all of their infantry muskets and Ranger rifles next year. The Marines' muskets will be getting it later this year as will most heavy guns. The really nice thing about it is the fact that it is pretty much impervious to water. Should drastically cut down on misfires due to damp priming."

"Now if we could just increase the rate of fire of a rifle to equal a smooth-bore, we'd really have something."

"I understand the Army's Quartermaster Corps is supposedly working on something to help with that. Not sure what, exactly, since they know I'm Navy and a nasty spook to boot, so they won't willingly share any information on what they're working on. You'd think they don't trust me."

"Can't imagine why, sir."

Chapter Fourteen

EMILY BLAINE STARED AT the westering sun out the stern windows of *Intrepid* as the big frigate rode the swells of the southern Kolbian Straights. Earlier that day, Captain Blaine's pinnace had rendezvoused with KRN *Ocean*, the transport galleon on which Emily and Sally Blaine were traveling. With the entire convoy only making five or six knots at best, Blaine decided that he could have his wife and daughter brought aboard for a rare family dinner at sea. Sally was on the quarterdeck with her father and for the moment, Emily had the cabin to herself. She was never sure how long she had been staring at the late afternoon sun when there was a knock at the door. With a small start she turned away from the windows.

"Come in." The door opened and Toby, Blaine's steward, stepped into the cabin.

"Excuse me, Mrs. Blaine, ma'am, but I need to clear the captain's desk and prepare the cabin for your dinner. With your permission, ma'am?"

"Oh. Certainly, Toby. I'll just step out onto the sternwalk."

"Thankee, ma'am. All right, lads, hop to it." It seemed like a dozen sailors poured into the cabin. Emily stood in the door to the sternwalk and watched them. In mere moments, Blaine's desk was whisked away, a dining table appeared nearly by magic, she thought, so quickly did they work, and chairs and a sideboard were properly set in place. At that point, most of the rather rough-looking bunch vanished out the door, and Toby motioned another, much smaller group through the door. The last person into the cabin, a tureen of soup in her hands, was Sachi. The table was set and Sachi vanished with the rest of them. Toby stood by the door, waiting for Captain Blaine. The low overhead made it impossible for him to stand upright at attention, but somehow, he managed to give that impression.

A moment later, Blaine stepped into the cabin, Sally immediately behind him. Emily realized they didn't see her at first and for the moment, she just covertly watched her daughter and husband. *No one can ever doubt that she is his daughter. Not sure where the straight strawberry blonde hair came from, mine is too curly and yellower. And she completely adores her father. God knows I've tried to put a burr under her saddle about his constant absences, but no. I give up. Next year she'll be fourteen and should we divorce, she'll be able to have her own attorney and likely go live with whoever she wants. I won't be able to keep her away from him. And then I won't have any control over him any longer.*

There was another knock at the door and Sachi stepped back in, Silaqui, Doctor Hoff and Lieutenant Commander Fleet right behind her. *I'm slipping, the table is set for six. And then there's Sachi. Again. That girl, young woman, really, saved my life. And that Elf's life. And William's. I should be grateful to her that my daughter isn't an orphan. And I want to hate her guts because anyone with two eyes can see that she's in love with my husband. And him with her. And they're both being so* fucking *noble about it, refusing to act on it in any way, suffering in silence. Sally thinks she's wonderful, the woman who saved her mother and father. Why didn't she have the decency to just die? The poison should have killed her, or so Elazar Hoff said afterwards. And I can't truly hate her. I want to, God, I want to, but I'm alive because of her.*

Blaine handed his hat and cloak to Toby before stepping around to the head of the table, giving Emily a quick smile as she came in from the sternwalk.

Toby and Sachi took their positions against the forward bulkhead. Blaine seated Emily, Hoff seated Sally and Fleet drew back the chair for Silaqui. The ladies seated, the men took their places and Toby stepped forward with the wine bottle and began filling glasses.

"I'm not particularly pleased that Sachi is serving and not sitting with us." Silaqui gave Blaine a heated look.

"Lady Silaqui, Sachi asked to serve. You know this." Blaine answered.

"I know, but I don't like it. She should be honored in the highest. Like you and your Lady wife, I owe her my very life. If anything, I should be serving her."

"Silaqui-chan, my friend," Sachi interrupted before the Elf could really get started, "this is what I want. What I asked Captain Blaine-sama for. Please, be at peace and allow me to serve you as a sign of my friendship and respect."

"If you insist." Silaqui acquiesced with an unhappy frown.

"Sachi, I don't think I've ever honestly said *Thank You* to you. Thank you for saving my life, all our lives. So, now, thank you. Thank you very much." Emily spoke up and clearly startled both Sachi and William.

"*Do itashimashite*, Lady Emily-sama. You are welcome. It was my honor and responsibility as host, even if that was not a proper tea ceremony." Sachi bowed low to Emily.

"That being said, William, it was my impression that this would be a simple family dinner. Not that I don't appreciate the company, gentlemen and ladies, but I am hardly prepared for guests outside our family at dinner." Her brow furrowed ever so slightly as she frowned at her husband.

"Well, dear, unfortunately this is a warship under way at sea. Be glad the usual herd isn't in here. I have a new First Lieutenant on this voyage, since Harry Caplin got the command he deserved. Fortunately, I still have Arnold Hanley as my Second Lieutenant, but he is the only one of my officers I was able to keep out of the Navy Board's clutches. And Johan Weiss is now my chief midshipman, riding herd on ten other midshipmen, half of them under fifteen. More of the crew than usual are new recruits and lubbers. I shouldn't be having dinner at all.

I should be working them through gun and sail drills. Especially since we should be raising Stark Haven sometime the day after tomorrow." Blaine gave Emily an apologetic smile. "Things are not, perhaps, as either of us would prefer, but needs must when Quan drives. However, I will be grateful for the fact that at least for this journey, I know that you and Sally are not far away."

"I understand, William. It just wasn't what I expected."

"It's so exciting, Father, to actually be on your ship at sea. And to know that you will have the *Intrepid* to protect us from pirates and slavers." Sally's bright blue eyes twinkled with suppressed excitement and she struggled not to bounce in her seat between her father at the table's head and Doctor Hoff to her right.

"I'm glad you're enjoying the trip, Sally."

"May I speak to Lady Silaqui, Father?"

"Why are you asking me, Sally? She's sitting across the table from you." Blaine smiled at his daughter. "I'm sure she won't mind. Would you, Lady Silaqui?"

"Not at all. What would you ask of me, mortal child?"

"You don't mind?"

"No, child. Speak freely and I shall answer you freely. I reserve to limit my answers, should I see so fit."

"Umm, are you really a thousand years old? And did you really turn Admiral Hampton's wife into a pig? Were you really a pirate's captive for two years? Did Sachi really save you from a pirate captain? What was it lik...?"

"Sally!" Emily snapped, bringing the rush of questions to an abrupt halt. "Your father said you could speak to Lady Silaqui, not interrogate her!"

"Child, child, a moment," Silaqui laughed, smiling at the girl. "No offense taken or given, Lady Emily, 'tis naught but the manner of younglings the world over. I shall freely answer your questions, but grant me a space to breathe, if you will. Will that suffice?"

"Uh, yeah."

"So, yes, I am well past my first millennium, as you humans measure time. According to my folk, I am a youth, considered about the same age as Lieutenant Hanley, who I believe is well short of his third decade."

"What's that like, all those years? How do you remember everything?"

"I am an Elf, child. It is my nature, how our Gods made us. Nothing more, but also, nothing less. I could no more explain it any better to you than I can explain the color blue to a man born blind."

"What about Mrs. Hampton, did you really turn her into a pig?"

"Yes, lass, I did. But only temporarily. I lost my temper with her foolishness and then I punished her for her insult to one of the Elder Folk. Hopefully, she learned from the experience." She smiled at Sally as she leaned aside for Toby to place a plate of mutton before her. She used the knife beside her plate to point at Sachi. "And yes, Sachi saved my life when she killed a pirate, a monster in human form, before he could kill me."

"Truly?"

"Yes, truly."

"So, she saved you twice, once from the pirate and once from the poison?"

"Yes. She saved me twice from the pirates before dashing the poisoned wine from my glass. That is why she is my heart-sister and an Elf-friend."

"Is that why you were complaining about her serving dinner?"

"Yes, child. We should be honoring her, not be served by her."

"I am content, Silaqui-chan. In my homeland the greatest honor lies in one's service. Let it be." Sachi spoke from where she worked, cutting the mutton. "Here I may choose to serve. Or not. It is *my* choice and that is what pleases me. The freedom to choose set against slavery. I have come to despise slavery, in all its forms. I will never have anything to do with holding a person in bondage, other than to free them."

"We'll make a good Kolbian out of you yet, Sachi." Fleet grinned at her from the end of the table.

"Perhaps, Lieutenant Commander Fleet-san, perhaps." Smiling, Sachi nodded to him. "But first I must ensure my friend, Lady Silaqui-chan, gets home. Like all *Kami*, she can be somewhat flighty at times."

Emily Blaine joined in the general laughter at the look on Silaqui's face, but her heart wasn't truly in it. She watched the interplay between them, William and his old school friend, Elazar Hoff, Fleet, the inhuman Elf, Sachi and Toby and even her own daughter. She sipped her wine and picked at the meal. *All this. All this is a part of his world, a part that I have never seen before. I knew about Hoff long before we married, but the camaraderie, the sense of belonging, it's all foreign to me. Is something wrong with me? Or with him? Or is it just that our worlds are that different? And Sally, despite all my efforts, desperately wants to be part of his world. And not mine. God, she's even been talking about trying to join the Navy. Can I change that? How? He clearly has most of what he wants, now how do I get what I want, the recognition and prestige for myself? The power I want? The place in society I want?*

***

The evening passed as *Intrepid* continued to forge steadily eastward. Like all things, the dinner came to an end and eventually Emily and William were alone in his cabin. Sally had gone with Silaqui, enthralled by the Elf's stories of things experienced a thousand years ago. Sachi left with Toby and a tub full of dishes. Hanley went to stand his watch as night fell, and she didn't have a clue where Fleet got off to. She didn't really care either. The more she was around the ONI officer, the less she cared for the sly bastard. Despite his good looks. She sipped at her wine and watched her husband writing in the ship's log.

"Is this every evening?" She finished the last of the wine.

"No. I couldn't afford that." Blaine cleaned off his quill and capped his ink well. "One of the reasons I don't use one of those fancy new ink pens. They're expensive. I learned to write with a quill. It still serves me well."

"What kind of a Kolbian are you, dear? We always look for new and better ways to do things."

"True. But sometimes tradition has its place. Often what works best is to use new things, new ideas to make what works well work better." He closed the logbook and put it in its place on the shelf, closing the shelf door to secure it. "So, fourteen years of marriage and you are finally aboard a ship under my command. A ship under way, even. Is it so bad?"

"No, William. It was never about the ship itself. It was about propriety, what was right, as I saw it. I'm not some common doxy, waiting eagerly on the dock for her common sailor. I am the captain's wife, the wife of a holder of the Medal of Valor."

"I understand that, but I'm not so sure you do understand what's profoundly important, Emily. And it isn't being a holder of the Medal. Or being the captain's wife. Those common sailormen, with their doxies, often had what seems to have gone missing between us."

"And what is that, William?"

"Something quite simple, Emily. Very basic. Love. Not lust, love." He brought his eyes up to meet hers, blue to hazel. "How did we lose that, Emily? What happened?"

"Love?"

"Yes, love. The basis of our marriage, I thought. But now I begin to wonder, did you genuinely love me or just the rank, the gold braid on the uniform and later the shiny trinket around my throat? Am I just how you rise in *society*, get invited to the proper parties, be seen by the proper people? Is that all I am? Is that why, after fourteen years, we have only Sally? Why she doesn't have a little brother or sister?"

"You are gone so often and for so long, William. Would you leave me to do all the work of raising more children alone?"

"I know how lonely you were. I was lonely too. You have always been eager enough when I returned. *Well practiced*, some might say. Some *do* say." He held her eyes as she turned red with fury.

"Indeed! And who would be carrying those fairy tales?" she snarled.

"The staff you hired. Rumors circulating at the Officer's Club. A particularly ugly one four years ago involving a so-called *miscarriage*. The timing on that one would make it unlikely the child you supposedly lost was mine. Possible, but highly improbable."

"You've been talking to that bastard Elazar! And someone has been whispering lies in his ear, lies he's all too willing to believe! You know he hates me, always has! Perhaps it's because years ago, he tried to weasel his way between my thighs and failed! This is his revenge!" She looked for something, anything to hurl at him, but this was a ship at sea, and everything was locked away or tied down. She took a step closer to him, both fists balled to strike at him.

"What? Now you play the innocent? Stop a moment and think. *IF*, I say IF all these rumors and slanders are just that, lies by those jealous of you, or of me, there is a means to confirm the difference between truth and falsehood. A means available right here on this ship."

"What means?" She paused; her fists were still balled up.

"Lady Silaqui. She is a sorceress with a thousand years of skill in her magic. When I asked her, she confirmed to me that she can use her sorcery to reveal when someone lies, when someone speaks the truth. She can even compel the truth to be told, if need be. Allow her to wield her magic on *both* of us. No one here but you, me, and her. She has agreed to swear on her magic itself to remain silent for all time about what might pass between us. Have each of us answer two simple questions and settle between ourselves all doubts, all rumors."

"And what might those questions be, then, William?" Her anger cooled abruptly.

"One, have you ever actually been physically unfaithful to your spouse? Two, do you still love your spouse?" Blaine's voice was flat and hard. "That is all. I know how I will answer those questions, whether under oath in a court of law, under Silaqui's spells or should the Imperial Inquisition set me to the Question. How will you answer them, Emily?"

"I will not submit to that inhuman creature's so-called *magic*. I can't explain how she did what she did at the Admiral's party, but I will not be the subject of one of her bizarre rituals. I know better than Janay Hampton did, and I'll not be anything but proper and polite to her. But stand here and allow her to place us at her mercy? No, William, not now, not ever."

"I see. Very well, I shall not attempt by the slightest means to coerce you or convince you. However, I will answer those questions truthfully and honestly, here and now. The answers are 'No, never in any fashion', and 'Yes, always, if she will have me'."

"William, this is hardly necessary..."

"You think not?" His blue eyes pinned her in place.

"No, it is not, damn it!" *Damn his eyes. Even if they are Sally's eyes, my daughter's eyes, and yes, his daughter's eyes.* She struggled to hold on to her temper. *Oh, dear God, where did this come from? He is rarely so forceful at home.* A nasty little thought wormed its way into her consciousness. *Perhaps it is the sea? Is this what he is like in his true element, when he is the Captain and Master of his ship? How could I have misread him so badly? For so long? I can't answer those questions truthfully, either of them! God and his angels help me, I can't! How can I find my way clear of this chaos?* "So, two questions, to settle all issues between us. Is it then so simple?" She stepped back and turned away, walking to the stern windows. The lights of the other ships of the convoy could be seen in the darkness. The stars glittered coldly in the sky.

"Yes, Emily, it is."

"No, it is not! There are financial considerations, your proper honor as a holder of the Medal, a Captain of the Navy, a frigate's Captain! The status of your family. How you might attain your deserved place in the Navy?! You should be a full Captain by now, none of this Junior Grade nonsense! And yet, you concern yourself with foolish questions of love or fidelity. We aren't children in school anymore, worried if anyone will ask us to the Spring Dance or how well we please the professor. We have the concerns of the adult world now. Can't you see that, William?"

"I see." He went cold and quiet. "I do see. Very well. Perhaps I am being foolish. You know that as soon as the convoy is safely at Stark Haven, I have two days to make good any repairs and resupply *Intrepid* before setting off to repatriate Lady Silaqui to the Kingdom of Montagar." He opened the liquor cabinet and made a show of selecting a fine brandy. *Old Capitol '62. A good year, should hit the spot nicely.* "Would you like a drink?"

"No. You know I don't care for the spirits you prefer."

"I know. But sometimes you drink them. Very occasionally from the stock I keep at home. That or our staff is getting into them."

"Not today, thank you."

"Well, as I said, I am to make a fast passage to Montagar, deliver the Lady Silaqui to the port of her choice there, within reason, and then return at all speed to Stark Haven. *Intrepid* will then be going into yard hands for at least a month or six weeks."

"And what of Silaqui's *friend*, Sachi?"

"Sachi?" He frowned. "No idea. I believe her original goal was to reach Montagar, get as far away from whatever she is certain is pursuing her as she can. Silaqui told me she might take her to see the Elders of the Elves, see if they can help her. I fully expect her to leave ship in Montagar."

"Oh." There was a strained pause. "I thought that she was...well you and her were...I mean...but if you're..."

"Were what?" *Please forgive me, Sachi. I have no choice.* "Madly in love or some such thing? Having an affair? Fucking like ferrets in heat? Hardly. She's a brave young lady, but given what little I know of her background, I'll be greatly surprised if she ever again allows the romantic touch of a man." He swirled the brandy around in his glass, staring deeply into it. "Lieutenant Commander

Fleet told me he described her to the investigating detective as *a stone-cold killing machine* when he got her, Silaqui and Toby out of jail after they were attacked in Carolington. She was the one who killed those four thuggers with her bare hands. Butchered them really; they never had a chance in any of the Seven Hells. You might think about that. She's as dangerous as Silaqui, maybe more so."

"Oh." Emily suppressed an urge to swallow. "I heard the rumors, but I put no credence to them."

"Well, they were just rumors, you know. One never knows about rumors. Sometimes the unvarnished truth, others, nothing but hot air and a bad smell." He stepped up beside her, looking out the windows as well. "The wind's freshening. Might be a bit of a blow by morning. I'll have the bosun pipe up my pinnace's crew, get you and Sally back to *Ocean*. She rides smoother in rough seas. *Intrepid* is a bit lively under a blow. No fun at all unless you've seawater for blood." He turned and looked her in the eyes. "Something I doubt you truly have."

***

"No, I doubt that as well." *Something has changed, but I do not know what. I can't read him here; I can't control him with sex. Is he slipping away from me? Is it that cursed Elf's sorceries swaying his mind? Or is it that damnable Nisei girl turning his head with her beauty? This is his realm, not mine, and I cannot stand before him here.* Blaine stepped to the door and said something to the Marine guard outside it. *So, if I do not have a chance here, at sea, with him completely in his element, in command of his ship, the best I can do is avoid the battlefield. Stay away from him and keep Sally away from him until he returns from Montagar. Then, while this ship is in the dock, I can work on him, bend him to my will, push him to establish me in the Society of Capital. Once he goes back to sea, by the time he returns, either he will be a full Captain or a Commodore. And if he isn't, well, then there are Consuls and Legates and a great many high-ranking officers who would gladly take his place. I know I can draw them to me. I've done it before.* An older sailor, white haired and bearded, knocked and stepped into the cabin on Blaine's command. She'd seen him when she came aboard; he was a petty officer, she thought.

"Emily, you remember the bosun, Master Chief Petty Officer Paul Beauchamp; he was in command of my pinnace when you came over from *Ocean* and he'll see you back to her."

"Of course. Thank you, dear." Emily stood on her toes and gave Blaine a quick but thorough kiss. "A promissory note, dear. For when we reach port." Without another word she followed the bosun out of the cabin.

Blaine stepped back and watched as one of the pinnace's crew darted in and grabbed her valise. The door closed behind him. A moment later, there was a knock and at his "Come." The door flew open and Sally bounded into his arms.

"Mother says the weather is worsening and we must go back to the *Ocean*. Couldn't I stay with you, Father? Please?"

"Did you ask your Mother?"

"Yes." The beginnings of a sulky voice.

"And what did she say?"

"No." Deeper into the sulk.

"Well, what do you think I should say?"

"No." The sulk was in full force. "I shouldn't ask one of my parents for permission for something the other has said *No* to. But if I had to choose, somehow was forced to choose, I would have to choose you, Father."

"Well, that's nice to know. A hug and a quick kiss, dearest, then you must scurry and be waiting at the pinnace as you should. Your Mother very much wants a proper daughter. And staying on a warship without a chaperone is hardly what a proper daughter does. And don't whine about Lady Silaqui or Sachi. Those two have a way of making their own rules but you, young lady, are not there yet! Now, hurry. You've a boat to catch!" Sally leapt into a ferocious embrace, before kissing him quickly on the cheek.

"Be safe, Daddy! I love you!"

"I love you, too, Sally! Now scat!" With a rush she was gone. Private Symonds tried and failed to hide a broad smile as he closed the door behind her, leaving Blaine alone in the cabin at last. He walked slowly over to his chair and collapsed into it, bracing his forehead in his hands, elbows on the tabletop. He listened closely to his ship as the captain's pinnace was lowered over the side and then it cast off to make its way to *Ocean*. "Damn you, Emily. I'd damn you to Hell, but Quan won't let you in. He knows you'd try to take over."

* * *

Sachi clung to the gunport on the leeward side of the cabin. The small ventilation port allowed her to hear everything Blaine and Emily said in the cabin with no chance of being noticed. At night, against *Intrepid's* dark gray hull, in her black *shozoku*, black *kamimaki* hiding her face and hair, she was confident in her mundane invisibility.

My Captain. Why do the Ancestor Spirits punish me so? Can I never be free? But no, the little statue, D.A.V.E., says I have a task. That the world somehow depends on me. The Samurai say Death is lighter than feathers, Duty heavier than mountains, and Honor the heaviest of all. All I know is that when, by the blessings of the Ancestors, I finally find someone I could possibly love, Duty and Honor forbid it. She squeezed her eyes shut and shook her head to clear away the salt spray in her eyes. *It is only the seawater. Ah, I should know better. Love is not for the likes of me. I shall simply be grateful for the time I have had with my friends on this great ship,* Intrepid, *that has borne me out of bondage and into freedom. In time, I do not doubt this great task shall bear me away from all these new-found friends. But that is well and good. They will be safe, as safe as one can be on this Fallen world.* Silently, she climbed back to the gunport she had left loose when she found she must know what passed between William and Emily Blaine. *I should have left well enough alone. This time, my training, to know everything, it has betrayed me. I should have stayed in the galley or scrubbed out the head. I would still enjoy the delusion that I can be loved. And I find that even in my folly, I wish I could love and be loved. Perhaps, while I am wishing for the impossible, I should wish for the Emperor Confas to step off his star and carry me away to Heaven. That would be much more likely, I believe. I must tell D.A.V.E something is wrong with my eyes. They won't stop leaking. The salty seawater stings.*

Capitol Bay, East Coast of Kolbia
Stark Haven Naval Base, Naval GHQ
August 1478, Third Age of Imperial Reckoning

"As fast a passage as anyone could expect with so large a convoy, Captain Blaine. Well done, sir." Admiral of the Fleet Nelson McGowan dropped his salute first. "Have a seat, please. A drink?"

"No, sir, thank you."

"Suit yourself, Captain Blaine." The Admiral poured himself a glass of beer and sat down behind his desk. "Do you realize, Captain Blaine, that I have now had the honor of meeting two holders of the Medal of Valor, Captain Eyles and now you? The only two living holders of the Medal in the last forty years or so."

"I hadn't thought much about it, sir."

"Humpf. You wouldn't have, I suppose. I understand you are under orders to reprovision and depart for Montagar as soon as possible?"

"Yes, sir."

"Getting a wayward Elf back home, I believe?"

"Yes, sir. Lady Silaqui is related to at least one of the most influential members of the Elven Court, her uncle, she tells me. His name, if I can pronounce it correctly, is Oedhaewthren. I don't know what office he currently holds, but at one time he was the Elves' Ambassador to Montagar. And if I remember my national history correctly, he was a key figure during our own brief war for independence."

"Correct, Captain, and one scary bastard who doesn't really care for humans at all. I'm surprised he ever comes out of their forests. I met him once, in Montagar when I was an attaché there, about thirty odd years ago. Son of a bitch damn near scared the pee out of me. Just by looking at me."

"Yes, sir. However, all I am tasked to do is deliver Lady Silaqui to the port of her choice. And she asked me to make my course for the port of Vlymouth in the Duchy of Hale."

"That's the southernmost port in the Kingdom. The farthest away from the Elves' forests in the north of Montagar. I wonder why?"

"No idea, Admiral. I'm just the delivery boy."

"Yes, I understand," McGowan chuckled, "regardless, I'm glad to have you aboard in Lanic Fleet. I know you've spent most of you career in the Western Fleet, despite a couple of deployments in the Lanic, but I think you'll find yourself quite busy here."

"I'm sure I will, sir."

"Good." McGowan paused, "Good. And when you get back, while *Intrepid* is in yard hands, I'll want you to spend some time with a couple of our naval shipwrights and with Mr. Fulmark. I want your eye on the new designs, and I'll want you to give a long, hard look at what we're building here."

"Of course, sir. Any particular reason why?"

"Captain Blaine, you are probably going to be one of the last captains of a wooden ship of war, one powered exclusively by sail. War with the Empire is coming, sooner or later, most likely sooner. If the Empire weren't such a corrupt mess, we wouldn't have a chance. As it is, they're stuck in the last century. But there are more than enough of them to be a threat, given their nearly infinite manpower. To beat them decisively, we need to push our military, especially our Navy, into the next century. But we need to keep the traditions and practices that have made us what we are now. And that's just one of the things I need you for, Captain Blaine."

"Sir, I'm not a naval architect. I have a good understanding of what works and what doesn't in a sloop or a frigate like *Intrepid* or a ship of the line. But these new designs, using this 'pressure engine' of Mr. Fulmark's, I wouldn't know port from starboard."

"I know that, Captain Blaine. And I'm not wanting you to design anything. I want you to look at the specs, the expected performance and then give the Board an idea of the best ways to employ them. New designs will come thick and fast, I'm told, as the technology matures. We must stay at the forefront of naval power if we want to retain our independence, given how idiotic the Empire is apparently becoming."

"How so, sir?"

"Their ambassador has been ordered by the current Chancellor, one Pi-Imperator Havis Peralta de Palmaroli to change his title from Ambassador to *Governor of the Province of Kolbia*. So far, the Ambassador has been eminently sensible and ignored his orders. It's not like the Empire would send a hard-liner to be the Ambassador to Kolbia."

"Are they insane? Do they *want* to start a war with us?"

"Those answers are *Possibly,* and *it would seem so.* You have been briefed on the two incidents in the South Lanic?"

"Yes, sir."

"And of course, you'll note the relationship between the current Chancellor and the Palmaroli family?"

"Yes, sir. I understand that Captain Eyles has made them somewhat unhappy with us."

"To put it very lightly, yes, somewhat. However, the Tribune's Office and both Chambers of Government fully support his actions. We sure as hell are not turning over one of the two living holders of the Medal of Valor to the Empire in order to be put to the Question to *determine the truth of the South Lanic incidents* or so their diplomatic correspondence demanded."

"That could still cause a war, sir."

"Yes, it could. But the Montagarans and the Eindeuten Empire are both supporting us in this, so I would expect a lot of saber rattling and diplomatic insults to be the limit at this point. So long as nothing else blows up in our face, that is."

"Yes, sir."

"And now you see why it's so important that we get that Lady Elf home as fast as possible, and keep her at least pleased with us? If the Elves withdraw their support of Montagar's position, that will weaken the Montagaran support we currently enjoy and, in turn, that might weaken the Eindeuten position and thereby our own vis-à-vis the Empire."

"Yes, sir. Admiral, if I can get priority with the Harbormaster for the water barges and resupply, I can be ready to depart on the morning tide, before first light. That would put me a full day ahead of schedule for Montagar."

"Good. I'll get with Commodore Valis and tell him that if he *doesn't* prioritize *Intrepid*, he might be out of a job. Do you have any personal or personnel issues to settle?"

"Those sailors that moved their families here will need some help getting settled and they won't be here to do it. Could I tell them that the Personnel Office will be actually helping for once and not making things worse?"

"There's a long-term Navy man thinking, Captain." McGowan chuckled. "I'll boot some rear ends and see what I can do. And you will be back in a couple of months, I would expect."

"Thank you, sir. Now, with your permission, I would like to ensure that the new stores are being loaded to balance the ship properly for best speed?"

"By all means, Captain Blaine." The Admiral rose from behind his desk and saluted Blaine, as protocol required for a holder of the Medal. "Godspeed, sir."

"Thank you, Admiral." Blaine snapped to his feet and returned the salute with his own best parade ground salute before executing a sharp about-face and leaving the office. The Admiral sat back down and sighed.

"Well, that went well, I think," he said to the empty room.

"Yes, it did, didn't it?" The air in the corner of the office blurred and shifted as Marianne Lundgren deactivated her stealth suit. "Damn, I hate having to be that still, that long, but this officer seems pretty dang sharp, nephew." Marianne's lanky six-foot-six frame towered over McGowan's modest and slightly chunky five foot eight. "And *yum, yum* good looking too."

"He's married, Great-great-great grandaunt. And wouldn't that be a serious case of cradle-robbing? How old are you again?"

"Old enough that you need a lot more greats, nephew. That's all you need to know. And frankly, *need to know* is still important, even for relatives. In some ways, you shouldn't even know I exist. Or my compatriots. I have my own command element to answer to, you know."

"You've told me. What I still don't understand is why you and the rest of your people are so interested in *Intrepid?* She's one of our best frigates, commanded by one of our best officers, but in the final calculations, just another frigate."

"Let's just say for now that from *our* point of view, something damn near impossible happened that kept that ship from getting turned into fish food."

"*What!?* What happened? What in the world is impossible for your people?"

"Nelson, as one of the greatest playwrights in all of human history once put it, *There are more things in heaven and earth, Horatio, Than are dreamt of in your philosophy.* Let's just leave it at that for now, ok? And honestly, nephew, there's a lot of things that are still impossible, even for our tech."

"Then what's got you fixated on *Intrepid*? You told me you had a whatchamacallit..."

"A drone."

"Yes, a drone, investigate the *Intrepid* and it found nothing out of the usual."

"I know. And that's what bothers me. We're missing something here. A piece of functional tech that was offloaded in Carolington? I don't know. It's like whatever it is, is actually hiding from us, and doing a pretty damn good job at it."

"Could it be something from your ancient enemies?"

"Possible, but highly unlikely. The Quar'taneeka never went for full up AIs. And generally, their tech was nowhere near as robust as ours. I really doubt anything of theirs that's left is functional at all. Hell, most of our stuff that hasn't had at least some semi-regular maintenance is either stone dead or shaky as hell. Remember we're hanging on by our teeth and fingernails just to keep what's left working in a half ass manner. And the Quar'taneeka weren't just our enemies, they were enemies to anything that lived and breathed."

"So now what, oh so great aunt?"

"I don't know, nephew. I just don't know."

"So, do I hold *Intrepid*?"

"I can't give you a reason to do so that would make any sense at all."

"So, send her onwards?"

"You're the Admiral, not me. I'm not anywhere in your chain of command."

"You're avoiding the question, Aunt Marianne. Hold *Intrepid* or not?"

"Fine. Get her on her way. I'll have Captain McAllen keep as good of an eye on her as she can."

"I'd like to meet this Captain McAllen someday. Sounds like interesting people."

"She is. Way back when, before the entire galaxy decided to go ape-shit crazy on us poor humans, we were drinking buddies. But now she's stuck where she is, and I'm stuck down here. In about ten more years, she's due to wake her replacement and go back into stasis. I'll have to get back to northern Isemoto then and do likewise. Probably be the last time you see me in this life, Nelson."

"Well, there's no guarantee I'll live ten more years, Aunt. I'm not that young anymore.

And I still don't understand exactly what this *stasis* actually is or does or whatever."

"It's something that allows us to extend our lives, our lifespans beyond all sense and reason. Not what it was intended to do, but something else we had to jury rig, trying to keep things together with spit and baling wire. Leave it at that, okay?"

"Very well. It's not like you'll tell me anything you don't want me to know."

"We have enemies, Nelson. Ruthless, borderline insane ones. We're trying to keep things together, make things better for everyone eventually. They want to see the world burn. Literally. And we are outnumbered, dozens, hundreds, maybe even thousands to one. But we know and understand our tech, the underlying principles of it. They are more in the *monkey see; monkey do* category. They know what happens when the shiny button is pushed or when the *magic* words are said, but not why. They don't really understand it at all. It's more like the Elves' magic to them than a true comprehension of the forces involved. One reason why we're pushing Kolbia to advance as fast as we can."

"I know."

"It makes life difficult, of course, but what else can we do?" she shrugged.

"It goes against the grain, Aunt Marianne."

"I know. But one of these days..."

"Yeah, one of these days." He watched in bemusement as the stealth suit blurred her into nearly complete invisibility, only the faintest wavering at the field's edge giving him a vague hint of her presence. And only because he knew to look for it. "So, what next?"

"I have a couple of other folks to talk to before the night is over."

"Let me guess, that *school's* headmaster and that ruffian boss, the Fensgrif Man."

"Don't knock it, Admiral. I know you don't particularly care for Tuomas Havwren, but his students can do things even I barely understand, but then I'm just a grunt, not a quantum physicist by any stretch. And the local hoodlums always know things no one else does. Right now, I'm desperate for information, very desperate."

"Be careful, Aunt."

"I will be."

Stark Haven Naval harbor
KRN *Intrepid*

Sachi hummed quietly to herself as she polished the pots and pans in the galley. She could hear the hustle and bustle of *Intrepid's* crew as they finished preparing to depart in a few hours, sailing out of the harbor on the pre-dawn tide. She had already wept her tears for what could never be. So she would do as she always did, persevere. The Oda Family had not broken her spirit, not quite, despite their efforts to do so. This would not do so either. Although knowing that Captain Blaine did not genuinely love her hurt at first, she now saw the truth of it. He was wise, not being seduced and fooled by a pretty face and a well-formed body. He was an honorable man, who loved his wife and family, just as Papa Komiya had when she was a little girl, happy in the love of the whole Komiya family. She barely remembered those days.

I was happy then. Those happy days before that lying monster Toh, the tax collector, stole me away. Someday, the Ancestors willing, I'll choke that bastard to death with his own testicles. He gave me to Mother Yuko as a toy, a doll.

Perhaps it is the Oda who are insane, not the Kolbians? At times Mother Yuko treated me kindly, like a favored pet, at least when she didn't see me as Asama. Oda Asama's death unbalanced her mind and she never truly lived completely in the real world afterwards. The twins hated me for taking Asama's place, for making their mother happy, if only sometimes. To them I was a chalk-bird chick, pushed into another bird's nest to steal food the chalk-bird is too lazy to find. I was younger, but their hatred was palpable. I didn't choose to be there. I wanted to go home! Home to Mama and Papa, home to where I was loved and wanted. But I never spoke of the Komiya family, other than to dismiss them as nameless peasants I barely remembered. I could not bear to think what the twins or Father might have done if they should learn I ever cared for them. That was the one thing I learned from Toh, not that he cared to teach me. I learned by watching what happened to the others he had collected, what he did to them. Murdering those who became sick, or who cried too much. Raping the pretty ones until they died. Only his desire to curry favor with the Oda, with Yuko, saved me from that fate, I think.

Then Great Uncle Sota saw something in me, he took me, and he trained me. He drove me; nothing was good enough. I had to be harder, faster, tougher, better at all things. He hated the twins, Mako and Mankato, my older adopted siblings, and he used me to punish them. And when I failed, or wasn't good enough, or the twins betrayed me, whispering lies into Mother and Father's ears, then I was the one punished. When the fits started, I became just a thing to be used, an attractive mattress. Deadly, but not reliable because of my fits. And here and now, I can just be me. My Captain does not love me. At least that much I learned on the voyage here.

She hid a sigh, setting the pot into its rack and picking up the next one. Hitomi, one of the ship's cats, rubbed up against her leg, purring in hopes of begging food. She smiled at the cat and flipped a small chunk of cheese onto the floor. The cat pounced on the cheese with a great purring growl, gobbling down the treat before any of the others learned of her good fortune.

"If only my concerns were so simple, Hitomi." She nodded to the feline and turned her attention back to the washtub.

Finally, I know what my course must be. When I reach Montagar, Silaqui will return to her people, her own kind. I shall strike out to the south, the land the maps and charts show as Khakal. Not even the Kolbians know what lies beyond the coast of that land. There, D.A.V.E. can make me what I should be, tell me how to fulfill the task my parents left to me. And when I have completed that task, met this supposed destiny of mine, I will lose myself in the wilderness. The Oda will never find me in such savage lands. Not even their reach extends so far. And somewhere in that wilderness, I can lay down the mountain of Duty and Honor. Take up the feathers of Death. The heartbreak of this life is too much.

"Are you going to polish a hole into that pan, Sachi? Toby will be upset with you if you ruin one of his best pans." Silaqui's voice whispered in her ear and water flew as she hissed and spun, startled. The spray of water missed the Elf where she nonchalantly leaned against the far bulkhead.

"How did you do that? I know you whispered in my ear."

"Magic, of course. Come with me; I want you to see something." Silaqui was grim as she stepped toward Sachi.

"I need to finish thi…"

"You finished half an hour ago. I thought at first you had one of your fits standing up, but no. You were worlds away, my heart-sister. You looked so happy I nearly left you to your trance, but there is that which I want you to see. I want you to see it, and tell me, as a human and a mortal, what it is you see."

"Is this something you do against Kolbia, Silaqui?"

"No, but I do not truly understand what I see, and I doubt anyone will tell me, an Elf of another nation, what it is they are building here."

"Very well, let me go ask Toby to be reliev…"

"No, we will not be gone long. And I wish no one else to know of this. Please, my friend. Just come with me."

***

I wonder what Great Uncle Sota would think of using magic to slink about, effectively invisible with so little effort? He'd probably say this was cheating and then make me do push-ups over hot coals while he stood on my back. Sachi marveled as Silaqui's magic turned heads away at just the right time and offered up phantom distractions to bored and tired guards as the two women moved silently through the dark night. The incessant clouds of smoke, steam and ash from the innumerable forges and foundries darkened the sky. The air itself felt gritty on her tongue. Silaqui led her to a tall, wind-powered pump, the great fabric panels turning in the steady onshore breeze.

"Come, follow me," the Elf whispered as a brief flash of crimson opened a lock. They went up the stairs inside the tower, over a hundred and fifty feet in the air. The windmill creaked and groaned as the massive central shaft turned, driving other shafts and belts. Neither of them could determine exactly what those other devices did.

The small access door at the top of the tower was not locked, but it was marked by a sign proclaiming *Danger! Use caution!* Catlike, the pair slunk around the top of the tower. The far side allowed a good view of many of the Navy's building slips. There were over a dozen ships being built that they could see. Silaqui pointed to the closest and largest pair of slips.

"Unless my eyes deceive me, the ribs and keels of those two are iron, not wood. And why are there stacks of iron sheets there? Are they building ships of iron? Would not such a ship sink under its weight?"

"I do not know, Silaqui. However, I know the Kolbians wouldn't have started building these iron ships if they didn't know they would float. And what if they use the engine that drove the ferry between Carolington City and Carolington Island? They would not need the wind to move. And if the iron is thick enough, it will act like armor. They would be invulnerable."

"Yes, and look at the guns, there, along the wharf. I've never seen anything that big. The tubes must be over twenty-five feet long. Almost half again as big as the biggest guns on *Intrepid*. How many guns will these iron ships will carry?"

"I see two dozen guns, but there could be scores more out of sight, or that they have not finished yet." Sachi climbed slightly higher on the tower roof and pointed. "And I see two more of those iron monster ships, over there. They are more complete; the lower masts have been stepped. And I think the sides of the ships may be iron. Some kind of armor, perhaps? But there are no other building ways large enough to build more of these ships. And look over there, there are more wooden ships being built. Big ones, but not that different from *Intrepid*. More ships of the line, I believe. We saw dozens of warships when we came into the harbor. The entire place is boiling like a kicked anthill. Carolington Island was nothing like this. I think the Kolbians are preparing for war. But war with whom?"

"Sachi, the only reasonable possibility I can imagine would be the Empire. Kolbia is allied with the human Kingdom of Montagar. The Ionan Republic possesses a superb navy, small as it is, but of all the nations of the Traquilidamar Sea, they would be more likely to ally with Kolbia than fight them. The Darsälaamic Kaliphate has no navy worth mentioning, while the Rus and the Eindeuten Empire both lack any significant naval presence on the high seas. Neither do my people or the Dwarven Stoneheims. And in general, the Kolbians prefer to ignore those non-human realms they acknowledge. No, only the Empire is arrogant enough to provoke the Kolbians."

"So, you think that they are preparing for war with the Empire of Lietelea?"

"Nothing else makes sense. But the Empire is huge and has uncounted numbers of people. They have a two thousand ship navy. Even the Kolbians would be swarmed under." Silaqui shook her head. "You humans. Always one group seeks to dominate all others. Only ants make war on each other as your folk do, Sachi. And the Elves sorrow to see such slaughter."

"I can't answer that, Silaqui. I struggle enough with my own life." She gave the Elf a sad smile as she put her hand on her shoulder. "We need to go back to the ship. My tasks were not complete when you arrived."

"Yes. Let us go."

Chapter Fifteen

Middle Umberton, Duchy of Irling, Kingdom of Montagar
Gathington Monastery, The Retreat of the *Angaelici Benes Eloi*
September 1478, Third Age of Imperial Reckoning

HOARFROST RIMED THE WINDOWS and the chill permeated the small chapel. The cold of the flagstones in front of the simple altar crept up through his knees and bare toes. But Pere Gelman Stavor felt neither the cold nor the pain of his long-since numb feet and legs where he knelt. He could no longer exactly tell how long he had been in the chapel. He only felt the need to be here, to find the silence and peacefulness he needed to hear what his God would have of him.

God moves through me, fills me as his vessel. I feel his Spirit, I hear his Voice…but not clearly. He wants something, but I do not know what it is that is being asked of me. I have fasted and prayed. I have maintained this Vigil for the last two days. I know beyond all doubt that I am doing God's will. He looked up at the simple wooden symbol behind the altar, identical to his own small symbol, hung around his neck on a simple leather thong, the Quartered Circle of the One God. *And still I am frustrated.*

"Please, God, tell me what it is I must do? I am willing, but I do not understand. What will you of me?" There was a sense of desperation in his voice as he bowed his head to begin his prayer cycles again. He froze as a golden light washed around him. Then slowly, incredulously, he raised his head and beheld a being of glory and light.

"Gelman, you are a true and faithful servant of the One God and the Light. But the task that is set before you shall test your faith in all things almost unto destruction. That is how it should be, for faith can be weak-rooted and shallow, be it not tested. You are devout in your faith, but here, in this place, only your physical body is tested by the elements. Your spirit easily vanquishes such tests, but stronger tests, tests beyond your imagination, wait ahead of you. You must go to meet those tests unflinchingly." Gelman felt the voice of the *Angaelici Benes Eloi* wash through him, filling every empty crack and crevice in his soul. With a shudder of exaltation, he fell on his face before the glory of the Archangel of Healing.

"Direct me, *Angaelici,* Messenger of God. I am a willing vessel, waiting to be filled with your holy light. I only pray that I am truly worthy."

"Have no doubt of your worth, Gelman. The path before you shall lead you unto places where the foot of a living Man has not trod in ten thousand years. Your faith shall be tested, a test such as no Man has faced since the Fall itself. But have courage and keep the One God always in your heart and you shall prevail. The Hand of the One God shall go before you and His Messengers shall walk beside you. In the depths of fear and darkness, and before all the minions of Quan, His Power shall be your sword and shield. You must simply have an unshakeable faith. And as I examine your human heart, your human soul, I see depths of faith in you that even you fail to realize you possess. You are not chosen lightly, Pere Gelman."

"And what, *Angaelici Benes Eloi,* is it I am to do? How am I to find and follow this path you speak of, *Angaelici?*" Gelman raised his head high enough to see the hem of the being's luminous robe.

"You shall leave this place of peaceful worship and travel to the port town of Vlymouth in the Duchy of Hale. When there, you will meet a woman from a far land, a land far to the East. She will challenge everything you know of woman, in both strength of body and strength of will. But for all her strength, she will need friends and companions on her journey. You shall be among that number. Her path shall be yours as well. Keep her safe, guide her, heal her, and defend her; for

she is truly the last hope of the world. Know that she will challenge you, she will test your views of the World. You shall learn from her, as she will learn from you. Maintain your faith but do not close your mind to what seems strange to you."

"Yes, *Angaelici*, I understand. I am to travel to Vlymouth and seek out a woman from the distant East. How shall I know her? Will anything set her apart from the folk of Montagar?"

"Yes, Pere Gelman. Look for a tall woman with black eyes. That shall be the sign you seek. Black eyes."

"Black eyes?" When he looked up, the angel was gone.

***

"What do you mean, you have to leave, Pere Gelman?" Father Hael Schumer, the Abbot of the monastery, stared in disbelief at Gelman. "You are the only priest here that the One God blesses with the power of healing. We can't lose you! What will I do without you?"

"I imagine, Father, that if we simply have faith, God will provide that which you need. There are mendicant priests who often arrive here to pass the winter with us. Perhaps one of them shall be blessed with the power of healing? Given the growing cold, I think such wanderers shall be arriving before much longer." Gelman shrugged as he continued to pack his few personal belongings in his small room, little more than a monk's cell.

"Have faith, you say?"

"Yes, Father. Simply have faith and believe that God will provide. I know it goes somewhat against the grain, but the Forest of Dailyn Deasgyn is not far from here. You could always ask the Elves that dwell within Falling Leaves for aid. They have never failed to provide generously when asked. Indeed, they often appear when most needed, even if no one has asked for their aid. God will not mind if healing comes from the hand of a consecrated human priest or the nimble fingers of one of the Fair Folk."

"But they are utterly unhuman, Pere Gelman. Many folk fear them."

"True, on both accounts, Father. But many others do not. But unless direly provoked, even a common Elf does not offer offense. There is no true need to fear them. And they are a dwindling race as well. Someday, they may be no more, and the world will be a sadder place for it."

"Aye. I guess. I have had little to do with the Fair Folk. So you are convinced you must leave us, this late in the fall?"

"Yes. The *Angaelici Benes Eloi* himself has given me this task. I do not know why. But the One God has sent his messenger to me. I have been told where I must go and what, or rather who, I must seek out. I shall not incur the wrath of God by being so foolish as to fail in obeying His clearly stated desires. The Book of One is quite clear on what might happen to one who turns away from the path decreed by God. You will be fine here, Father. Simply sustain your faith and God will provide. No one is ever punished for obeying the Will of the One."

"Ah, I know. I guess I've grown complacent with your presence here, Pere Gelman. But it is very comforting to have a priest of your known piety and ability comfortably to hand."

"Well, Father Hael, perhaps this little hike is His way of reminding both of us that it is our faith that is profoundly important, rather than our comfort and complacence, hmm? Not the fact that he sees fit to acknowledge my faith in His Power by granting me the minor miracle of wielding a small fraction of His holy benefice."

"Well, perhaps then." Father Hael chuckled as Gelman settled his pack on his shoulders. He reached out and rapped his knuckles on Pere Gelman's chest, a rap answered by the soft *bong* of a steel breastplate under his priest's brown wool robe. "I see you're taking your old armor."

"Yes. I believe in being prepared." Gelman picked up his broad-brimmed hat from the desk and snugged it down over the tonsure in his light brown hair. Then he took his mace off its hook on the wall and hung it on his belt. "And I'm taking Devotion with me as well. Not all brigands and highwaymen will allow even a priest to pass unmolested. But more than once, a sharp rap on their pate has shown them the error of their ways." He took his staff from where it leaned against the wall and walked out, into the crisp autumn morning. He stretched and shook himself a bit to ensure all his gear was properly stowed before turning to face Father Hael on the doorstep of the monastery living quarters. To the left, the Chapel's bell tower rose almost as high as the ancient oak trees scattered across the monastery's grounds. To the right, the great gate in the wall surrounding Gathington Monastery was open, ready for a wain loaded with crates of the monastery's cheeses and wines to head down the road to the local market.

"Brother Umfrey will not be pleased if you keep him waiting much longer."

"Brother Umfrey has not even climbed onto the wagon yet. I have no doubt that he will bide long enough for you to grant me your blessing, Father Hael." Gelman knelt gracefully before the older priest, his current religious superior, removing his hat and bowing his head.

"No doubt, my son." Hael smiled as he stepped forward and laid his hands lightly on Gelman's tonsured head. "Follow the path God sets before you. Walk in His Light and bear His Will as you seek this destiny that has been laid upon you. Keep your faith strong and come back to us in due time. Go with the One God and always bear His Light against the Darkness of Quan. Be blessed as you walk in the Light."

"Be blessed." Gelman rose as Father Hael stepped back up, onto the step. "Well, time to go. Farewell, Father Hael."

"Farewell, Pere Gelman Stavor." Hael watched Gelman climb up next to Brother Umfrey who shook his reins to get the horses moving. Then the gate-keeper's helpers pushed the great gates shut behind the departing wagon. He shook his head. "Off halfway across the country to find a tall woman from the uttermost East. A woman with black eyes. What kind of woman has black eyes? Humpf. Ah, well, who am I to question the purpose of God?" He stopped for a moment and glanced back over his shoulder at the gate. "Black eyes."

Midlands City, Duchy of Southdon, Kingdom of Montagar
Duke Allyn Cohens' Townhome
September 1478, Third Age of Imperial Reckoning

"Aylie, come here, please!" The dulcet tones of Lady Elise, Her Grace the Duchess of Southdon, carried far better than anyone would expect. But she had a knack of pitching her voice perfectly to carry throughout her wing of the mansion.

"Coming, milady!" Aylie Clayton set down the pile of clean, folded clothes on a convenient chair and scurried down the hallway to the Duchess' sitting room, pausing for the briefest of instants to pat her hair and starched white cap into place. One hand quickly brushed nonexistent lint off her crisp apron and made sure her dove-gray linen dress was properly pleated. Then she stepped calmly into the Duchess' afternoon sitting room.

"Yes, Milady?" she quietly asked.

"Do you know if His Grace the Duke's visitors have arrived? A dreadful bunch, all they speak of is politics and manufactories. It's always *who will be the next First Minister? How do we keep our party in power? How many ships to build? How many regiments to raise?* They have no manners at all. And the ones he is seeing today seem worse than most, greedy, grubby, smelly little men. I find them uncouth and revolting despite their immense wealth. He should not be seeing them, Aylie! They are hardly gentlemen at all. And certainly not of a good family with proper bloodlines!"

"Yes, Milady. They arrived a few moments ago. They are in His Grace's study."

"Aylie, I want you to keep a quiet eye on this meeting and I want you to ask my husband to attend on me forthwith after his *gentlemen callers* have gone."

"Yes, Milady. And what should I be keeping an eye out for?"

"I dislike this arrangement my husband has with these men. It is my thought that they are attempting to bring some pressure or another on the Duke. It's all very political, but I dislike the stress and strain my husband is under. See what you might overhear, please?"

"Well, if you wish, Milady." Aylie's brown eyes were shadowed as she answered her employer.

"Aylie, I am asking you to do this rather than anyone else because of your background. I know you would like it best if I didn't know anything of your history, but I am glad I do. You have never given me the least reason to regret hiring you, and over the last four years you know I have used your various...peculiar talents to good effect. My husband is a good man, Aylie, but...well, we both know he needs a little subtle guidance at times."

"Yes, Milady." Aylie shared a very feminine smile with the Duchess. "Me Ma would do the same with me Pa from time to time and he was as canny as a man can be. But they do need help sometimes, don't they just?"

"Yes, they do. One of the reasons I find you so useful is the cageyness you learned on the streets before your parents bought you that position with Sir Rolas, the Baron of Ystrand. I am glad I was able to hire you away."

"Yes, Milady. 'Twas nae difficult, that. When he married, his new wife wanted all the female staff replaced. Fortunately, the Baron, good man that he is, found superior positions for the women of his staff."

"To his detriment and my benefit, I should say." Lady Elise smiled at her favorite lady's maid. "Here, at least, no one holds your background against you, well, no one who knows of it, I should suppose."

"Aye, Milady. 'Twould hardly be proper, should gentlefolk learn that your favored lady's maid was once naught more than a scruffy street sparrow, learning the ketchin' lay from her Pa and Ma, now would it, Yer Grace?" Aylie's brown eyes returned the humor in Lady Elise's smile as her language slipped into a dialect more suited to a back-alley bar than a noble lady's sitting room.

"Watch your language, young lady!" Elise mock-scolded her. "Too many people have invested too much in your education for you to sound like a common low-class guttersnipe! What would the Baron think if he heard you slip so badly?"

"Sir Rolas'd pitch me out on me bum, that's what he'd do! His housekeeper, Mrs. Marlowe, spent too much time teaching me to speak properly. She'd take a switch to my behind quicker than a snake." Aylie's grin grew into a broad smile as the common 'street' cant disappeared from her speech. "But they did succeed, Milady, in teaching a grubby little street rat to speak like a proper lady of a good family."

"Yes, they did, and a superb job they did. Now, please go see if you can figure out what kind of mess these visiting, so-called *gentlemen* are trying to sweet-talk my dear husband into?"

"Yes, Milady." Aylie dipped a quick curtsey and turned to leave.

"And Aylie?"

"Milady?"

"Be careful. I don't like these men. I don't trust them the least bit. I'm certain they are up to no good." There was a real concern in Lady Elise's clear gray eyes.

"Yes, Milady. I'll be careful." She left with a jaunty step. She headed back down the hall and picked up the stack of folded clothes on the chair. She turned and went into another room and found one of the chambermaids dusting the paintings on the wall. "Rose, dear, can I ask a wee favor of you?"

"You don't have to ask, Miss Aylie. You know you rank me, right?"

"And when do I ever trade on rank among us servants, now?"

"Well, you never have, Miss Aylie. So, what is the wee favor you're after wanting?"

"Not much. Would you be so kind as to take these shirts up to Luther's room and give them to him? Milady said he's to share them out amongst the menservants. Should be enough that everyone gets at least one new shirt."

"Aye, Miss, I'd be glad to." Rose's pretty face lit up.

"Hmm-hum, I know you're a bit sweet on Luther, but keep your bloody knickers on. At least for the moment. What the two of you do later, after the work is done, is naught of my business."

"Posh, go on with ye, then!" Rose blushed scarlet as she took the pile of shirts. "Sweet on me or not, Luther touches nothing but what I say he can. And me knickers isn't on the list of things I say he can touch!"

"Good for you, Rose. Go on now, I've other tasks to do for Milady."

***

The nice thing about being a servant is that the average gentleman toff never really sees them as a human being, if they even see them at all. Aylie darted up to her room after handing off the pile of shirts to Rose. There she quickly changed into an older dress and apron, one suitable for an older maid-of-all-work. Quickly she smudged her light brown hair with a bit of powder, making it seem darker and grayer. A small smear of dust on one cheek and a hunched posture completed the effect.

She grabbed a hand-broom and dust pail out of the cleaning closet on her way to the hallway outside the Duke's study. Getting on her knees, she began slowly sweeping along the baseboard of the wall. Without touching the wall, she could only hear muffled voices. But if she pushed the solid wooden handle of the small broom partly through the bristles, she could place one end against the wall and the other end of the handle against her ear. That little trick allowed her to clearly hear the entire conversation in the other room. She stopped behind a decorative hall table, one that was directly behind the Duke's desk and chair, and listened closely.

"Your Grace, the continued alliance of the Kingdom of Montagar with Kolbia cannot be borne any longer. You realize, of course, that war between the Empire and Kolbia is inevitable." She did not know who the speaker was, but she'd heard that kind of a sly, ingratiating voice on many a confidence sharper during her days in the street. "The Empire boasts a two-thousand-ship Navy and they are building more ships as we speak. Your Grace, it is your duty, indeed, our duty as loyal Montagarans, to ensure that our Kingdom is not on the wrong side of such a one-sided conflict."

"One-sided, you say? Perhaps, but not as you might imagine. Sirs, many, no, most of those two thousand ships are fifty-year-old galleys laid up in reserve, of no more use in the rough waters of the Lanic than hitching my wife's lapdog to the oxen's plow. The Kolbians won't have to sink them, the Lanic will take care of them on its own." The Duke's voice carried an air of annoyance in it. "Gentlemen, I've seen the Kolbians' frigates in our harbors. And I went aboard the two first rate ships of the line they sent to the King's birthday celebration last year." She heard the Duke's hand slap down on his desktop. "Ninety-eight guns on each, forty of them fifty-two pounder long guns, then fifty long thirty-twos and eight long twelve pounders as chase guns. They have nearly a hundred *modern* ships of the line and over seventy *modern* frigates, from their big forty-fours to some extremely fast frigates mounting only twenty-eight guns, but those guns are a mix of long twenty-four pounders and thirty-two pounder carronades. Are you insane? If the Empire declares war on Kolbia, their vaunted *two thousand ship* Navy will be driftwood and matchsticks by the end of the year! Hell, we only have forty modern ships of the line ourselves. And you want me to sponsor a bill in the Chamber of Lords to break our seventy-nine-year alliance with Kolbia and instead ally with the Empire? Preposterous!"

"Please, Your Grace," Sly Voice spoke, "you must realize the Kolbians have no chance despite their admittedly impressive ships. The Empire has the power of God on its side. The Empire's Chancellor, Pi-Imperator Havis Peralta de Palmaroli, says that the Kolb..."

"Pi-Imperator Palmaroli can fart in his bathtub for all I care. He has no authority in Montagar." The Duke harshly interrupted Sly Voice.

"But the Kythal Church does, Your Grace." Sly Voice was starting to threaten, Aylie sensed. *Ooh, that's the wrong attitude to take with His Grace, not if ye want to get him to do what ye want him to do!* "And the seat of the High Kythal is in Lietelea the City. The High Kythal will support the actions of the Emperor and the Chancellor and, if necessary, that support will come in the form of Excommunication and Interdict. All true believers of the Kythal Church of the One God should willingly support the actions of the High Kythal and the Empire."

"You do realize what that kind of idiocy would cause here, right? We'd have another religious civil war in a month! You seem to forget that in Montagar, there are those who reject the teachings of the Kythal Church and the authority of the High Kythal himself. The Purists, as they call themselves, do still worship the One God Himself, but they outnumber Kythals in our Kingdom almost four to one! And the Purists are mostly concentrated in the largest cities, working in the manufactories, while the average Kythal is a somewhat rustic member of the rural gentry. And you forget that even the vast majority of Montagaran Kythals supported the King's decision to bar the last two Inquisitorial Visits, only ten and twenty-five years ago. This is regardless that an Inquisitorial Visit would have been greeted with street riots in most of the cities. God help the Inquisitors should they go to the northern forests and manage to irritate the Elves!" She heard the Duke's chair creak as he stood up. "Gentlemen, if this is the main purpose of your visit here, then you are wasting your time and mine. While I am a faithful Kythal, I support the King's decision and I will not support the Empire in a war with the Republic of Kolbia. I doubt you could even get the House of Lords to vote to remain neutral in such a conflict. The Commons would certainly never support such a thing. Good day, gentlemen."

"My Lord Duke, your heir is currently your first cousin, correct?" A new voice spoke, an Imperial accent, speaking Terranglais in hard, clipped tones.

"Yes, what of it?"

"My agents have spoken with him and we find him much more amenable to our position than you. He would assume your title and offices in the case of your untimely demise if I understand the Montagaran laws of noble succession correctly. Which I am most certain that I do."

"Are you threatening me, Sir?"

"No." Imperial Voice said. "I've decided that we do not need to negotiate with you any longer. You are a waste of *my* extremely valuable time." There was a strange, snapping buzzing sound, a *whumpp* in the room, a sound like a tight-fitted door being forcefully slammed shut. She nearly screamed as a wave of pain swept over her. There was a heavy thud, like a body falling. *My God, they've killed the Duke!* Her body tingled and spasmed, her vision blurred, and she slipped, falling against the table, knocking it over, the flower vase crashing to the floor and shattering. *What has happened to me!?* Light from the room flooded the hall as the study door was jerked open and a shrewish man in a tan suit pointed a wheellock pistol at her as she writhed in agony on the floor.

"There's a servant out here. Sieur Palmaroli, what the hell did you do to the Duke? What is that thing? My God, did that thing kill him? Ignacio, this was not what we were here to do!" Even in her pain, she realized this was Sly Voice. His shoulders were narrow, hunched inside his tan suit, and a black bowler hat covered short brown hair.

"Yes, yes, I know, our *orders*. I have my own set of orders. Now, just obey as you are told. Trevor, when you need to know, I will tell you. Until then, shut your mouth. Drag the servant in here. Man or woman?"

"A woman, a maid of all work I think?"

"Get the slut in here, quickly now, Quan take you."

"Sturdy young woman." Trevor grabbed her by the shoulders and drug her into the Duke's study, quietly shutting the door behind her. "Well, here she is. You going to kill her too?"

"No, Trevor, but I might kill you if you don't shut up!" Imperial Voice, Ignacio, she thought, was a black-haired man of medium build. There was a cruel light in his dark eyes and a silver Quartered Circle dangled from a gold chain around his neck. He wore black clothing that vaguely reminded her of a priest's garb. "Well, girl, I think I have a use for you, whether you like it or not." He had a strange thing, somewhat like a pistol, in his hand, silver and black, sleek, and somehow deadly in purpose she thought. She hissed as agony swept over her, a pins-and-needles sensation all over her body. "That hurt? You caught the edge of the beam, I suppose. I didn't think it would work through a wall. Well, I guess it does, somewhat. I think. Since you're not dead. Huh." He looked at the strange weapon and then tucked it away in his belt.

"Milady! Humpf," she tried to scream but Ignacio snapped his hand over her mouth before she could get a deep enough breath.

"Now, now, can't have you warning everyone." His smile was as cruel as his eye, she discovered. "Trevor, open my case and hand me the syringe on the left side of the front flap. I think I have a better use for this little flower than just killing her, oh, yes, indeed. After all, we do need someone to blame for the Duke's death now, don't we?" The needle of the syringe shone for a brief instant before he pushed it into the big vein in her arm.

Whatever it was burned like molten iron as it flooded into her. His hand over her mouth muffled her screams and his weight held her down as she thrashed in pain. The pain washed over her and carried her away into oblivion.

***

Awareness announced itself with agony and confusion. She wasn't sure where she was, but she knew she shouldn't be on the floor. *What in the world am I doing here, asleep in the middle of the day? Milady will be most put out for me sleeping on duty, much less laying in the middle of the floor.* When she put her arms out to lever herself off the carpet, her right hand brushed something metallic. Her other hand was in a puddle of something sticky. She looked to her right and saw a bloody knife, one of Chef's biggest ones, twelve inches long at the least. *Did I cut myself when I fell?* When she looked to her left, her entire world collapsed into a pit of horror and despair. Lady Elise's gray eyes stared at her in empty shock from where she lay in a pool of her own blood. Her throat was slashed open and her dress was ripped and torn from innumerable stab wounds in her chest. Beyond her, Rose's body lay in a similar bloody pool.

"No, no, no, oh my God, *NO!*" she screamed as she scrabbled to her feet. Beyond Rose, she saw another body, trousered legs akimbo in the far doorway. *Albert always wore those silly striped trousers. I'd tweak him about them, and he would look down that long nose of his and sniff.* It's my uniform, Aylie. Just like your cap and apron. *Oh my God, is that an axe handle standing up, stuck in his chest?* She looked down and realized the front of her apron and dress were covered in blood. She stumbled backwards and only the wall kept her from falling. *I didn't do this! I cannot have done this, I love Milady! I would die before I hurt her or His Grace! What happened? I can't remember!* With her back hard against the wall, she slid sideways, away from the scene of horror in Milady's receiving room and out the other door into the hall. A bitter, harsh scent assaulted her nostrils and a very faint haze of gunsmoke floated near the hallway's ceiling. One of the Duke's best Kolbian made shotguns had been dropped on the carpet runner. Its delicate stock was broken, the muzzles of the discharged double barrels scorching the carpet. The Duke's body sprawled on its back in the doorway to the foyer, a ghastly hole blasted in his abdomen. *I can see his ribs.*

As she staggered down the hallway in shock, she saw another body in the foyer itself. It was a narrow-shouldered man, someone she didn't know, face down in a pool of blood. His head was a ruin. A shotgun blast had splattered his brains on the wall. Blood and other things stained his tan suit coat. *Some of his brains, I think, stuck to his bowler hat.* Her legs collapsed and she fell to her hands and knees as her stomach rebelled at the gory sight. She gagged and spewed everything in her stomach on the floor next to the shotgun. *I didn't do this. I don't know how to shoot His Grace's shotguns. He keeps them unloaded and locked up. I don't even know how to load them! This is all wrong!* The approaching sounds of police whistles began to cut through the fog of horror and despair in her mind.

I'm supposed to be blamed for this! And when the bloody bobbers find out who my parents are and where I'm from, I know what will happen! They'll hang me for this! And whoever did kill Milady and His Grace thinks he'll walk away scott free!? I can't remember what did happen, but I know I didn't kill Milady! I loved Milady! She was more of a mother to me than my own ever was. I shall find out who did this, and I swear, one day, I will dance revenge in his own life's blood. But to do that, I can't let the damnable bobbers haul me off to gaol. I've got to get out of here, now!

She spun and ran down the hallway to the servants' stairs, coming to a skittering halt as she found tall Luther, Rose's sweetheart, dead at the foot of the stair. Another hideous wound, his throat ripped open, was the source of the blood splashed on walls and floor. She would have heaved again, but there was nothing left in her stomach. There was no choice but to step directly over his corpse onto the stairs. She bolted up them to her tiny room, stripping off her apron and dress as she ran. In her room she twisted up her hair and stuffed it under a boy's cap. Canvas pants, a grey linen shirt and rough jacket were yanked on and she stomped into a pair of workman's boots as she frantically stuffed spare clothes and underthings into a knapsack. Her little stash of coins and bank notes she stuffed into her chemise right before she flew out the door and bounded down the stairs, leaping over Luther. She came to a sudden stop as she reentered Milady's receiving room. Lady Elise's open eyes stared at her. Slowly she walked over and knelt next to the body. Gently she reached out and closed those gray eyes.

I'm sorry, Milady. I know I didn't do this. I don't know who did, but I'll find whoever it was, and I'll make him pay in blood. I promise. But to do that, I need money. I'm going to take everything in the household fund box. I'll pay it back, someday, somehow. I guess Lord Cohens, His Grace's cousin, will be the Duke now. I know he won't need or even miss the few hundred pounds in the box, but right now, I need that money if I'm going to find out who did this. I will avenge you. I promise.

Choking back a sob, she stood up and hurried into the Duke's business office. She knew where the key to the strongbox was. In a moment she had the box open and the money tucked neatly away in her chemise. As she turned to leave the room and the house, for what was likely the final time, she noticed a calling card on the Duke's desk. She didn't remember any visitors but there was that stranger's body in the foyer, after all. Impulsively, she grabbed the card and scanned it quickly. *Sieur Ignacio Palmaroli, esquire, Imperial Road Trading Company, Montagaran Offices in Vlymouth*, it read. She crammed it into her chemise with the money.

Starting to get crowded in there, me lass. Anything else and ye'll never be able to pass as a young man. She looked around her as tears streaked her cheeks. *Damn it all to Hell anyways. For once I was happy here. I will find whoever did this and when I'm done with him, the bastard'll wish the bobbers had caught him and hauled him away for a nice, comfortable hanging.*

She dashed her tears away with the back of her hand and fled out the kitchen door into the back alley just as the first police officers reached the front gate of the townhouse. She sprinted down the alley and stopped as she reached the street. The bobbers at the front gate were drawing attention and the beginnings of a crowd and no one at all paid any attention to the slightly scruffy young man who turned and disappeared into the normal late afternoon crowd of Montagarans heading home to their suppers.

Chapter Sixteen

ONCE AGAIN SACHI PERCHED on top of *Intrepid's* foremast royal yardarm. Next to her Silaqui balanced on the masthead as she stared at the black shadow growing across the sun. As the ship drove forward under the press of her sails, the mystery known as The Shadow of the Lanic blocked away the sun itself.

"So, Silaqui, does being on top of the mast bring you any closer to understanding what it is that casts the Shadow?"

"No, not really. But it is something to see, is it not?"

"Perhaps. Remember, Doctor Hoff told you not to look at the flare of the sun when the Shadow fully blocks it. He says that the brightness of the rays around the Shadow can bring blindness."

"For mortal humans perhaps."

"You still have eyes, *Kami-chan*. Do not be so careless. I'd not want to either watch you fall from here, nor haul your blinded carcass down the ratlines while you squall that you can't see."

"Oh, very well." Silaqui huffed. She stepped down from the masthead and sat down beside Sachi as the steady progress of *Intrepid* darkened sky and sea around the ship. "So, what do you think it is, that casts such a shadow over the world?"

"Dr. Hoff told me that it appears to be a body much like the moon, rocky and dry, but much smaller. It casts the Shadow because it is so close to the world. He also said that the known rules of *mathematics* do not explain why it does not fall onto the world. Perhaps it is the home of the Ancestor Spirits and they watch over the world from its surface?"

"You think so? Then why is it on the other side of the world from your homeland of Isemoto?"

"I said only perhaps. Willis Fleet told me that some of their scientists have come here and observed it with their telescopes, more powerful versions of the spyglasses the ship's officers use. He says they claim that there are what seem to be artificial structures on the surface of the thing. If so, maybe those structures have something to do with it being where it is? Maybe the Emperor Confas put it there and told it to stay put? I don't know. I don't particularly care, either."

"Well. A mortal girl who is full of mysteries herself, yet cares naught for the mysteries something like this represents? At times, you utterly confound me, Sachi, my dear friend."

"And I always understand why you do the things you do? I'm never sure if it is your sorcery that makes you so different, or the fact th—...yurk!" Sachi started to slip off the yardarm as her body went rigid.

"Oh no! Not again!" Fortunately, Silaqui was an Elf, blessed with Elvish speed and dexterity, and a sorceress, capable of casting a spell of levitation. She caught Sachi before she could fall and then used her magic to lower them both to the deck. Several deck hands saw them coming and were waiting when they reached the deck, as was Lieutenant Commander Fleet.

"What happened?" Fleet asked.

"Another one of her damnable fits!" she growled. "This one would have killed her when she hit the deck, or the ocean."

"All right. Hallsen, Corby, get her to the doctor."

"Aye-aye, sir." The two sailors carefully lifted Sachi and headed below decks.

"These fits are getting worse, Willis." Silaqui rubbed her forehead in worry. "I hate to say it, but perhaps she should not be allowed to skylark in the rigging anymore."

"I'll suggest that to the captain when I report to him. Go after her." Fleet sighed. "Wonder how long she'll be out this time?"

"Who knows, Willis? Who knows why these happen or what's going on?"

"Yeah, who knows? I sure as hell don't have a clue."

Omega 2-Cygni System Command
CNS *Backhand Blow*

::Action required.::

"Gotcha, D.A.V.E. What's the issue this time?" Captain McAllen put down her book reader.

::The dedicated link for the System Defense Node Command Key is being accessed again. I am reading an Access Identifier Code for Lieutenant Commander Hitomi Schmidt née Suiko, known to be deceased. The link is active, but my access is restricted. Several inactive comp-mem banks are being activated and accessed. The user of this AIC has locked this Entity completely out of the system.::

"What in Buddha's name is going on?" Captain McAllen flipped her neural feed into the system and got the rudest shock of her life when the system not only did not take her AIC but knocked her out of the computer and locked down her own personal neural feed. *Holy Buddha on a purple Harley! That's NOT possible! Only someone with System Command Authority can lock me out and suppress my feed! Commodore Collins can't even lock me out! No one has had that kind of clearance in this system since the War ended. Well, except for maybe the holder of the Command Key and whatever secrets it hides. We lost too much from the Quar'taneeka's last strike. If* Thunderchild *hadn't arrived when she did,*

337

we'd all be dead, and this so strange but so beautiful planet would be an asteroid field. Crap, I can't access anything! What the fuck is going on!?

"D.A.V.E. see if you can punch a system connection in and at least find out who is doing this and where the hell they are?" She rocked her command chair into an upright position and pulled up a holographic keyboard. *When the hell did I last use a keyboard, for Christ's sake?!* "D.A.V.E., damnit, answer me. D.A.V.E.?" Without a single flicker of warning her keyboard vanished. "That's not possible."

Stunned, she sat there for a split second, trying not to panic, before she jumped out of her seat and bolted across the deserted System Command Center to the Info Tech Officer's duty station. There she yanked out an actual physical keyboard. Her hands flew across the keyboard, queuing up system command line orders on it. "D.A.V.E. you worthless little shit, ANSWER ME!" With a final check of her command orders, she nearly broke the "Execute" key by mashing it flat. The holoscreen in front of the workstation flashed multi-colored garbage on the display and died. Shocked beyond words, she collapsed into the station chair. "D.A.V.E., are you there? D.A.V.E.?" She reached over and pulled up another screen. *At least this station is still up.* She typed a single command code and tentatively entered it. She stared at the single line of code she got in reply. A single line on the crude, old style flat panel monitor. *Digitally Aware Virtual Entity assigned Capt. Deborah McAllen, C.N., Off-line* blinked balefully back at her. A new line appeared below that one. *Please stand by.*

Uncomprehending, she watched every comp-system in the Command Center flicker and go dark. Eventually she sat there, every holoscreen, every board, the ODC's entire comp system crashing and going dark. Even the main holo-tank went dark. Toward the end she felt something pushing to access her own neural feeds, but she went into autistic mode and kept whatever the hell it was out of her head. She sat there in the near darkness; the Command Center red-lit by the automatic emergency lights.

"This is impossible." She shook her head hard enough to hurt. "Oh, my God. If *everything* crashed, we just lost the entire V-R bank. And if the Virtual Reality simulators really are gone, oh no, please God, no, we just lost all the Techneers. All that knowledge, those memories, those people, just gone. Oh no, please, no Buddha. How in the hell did the damn Seekers pull this off!? Oh shit, if the positional stabilizers' comp systems are gone too, then this rock won't be staying up here long at all." Another horrid thought hit her. "Oh no, the frigging stasis systems! No, no, no! Goddamnit, everyone in stasis will die! Shit, shit, shit!" She jumped up and bolted for the Command Center emergency access tube. Halfway there, Center's lights flashed once, then came on and steadied. She could see system consoles coming back on across the center. Abruptly she changed course and ran to the Medical station. Not caring about the possibility of the hacker accessing her own BPU, she flipped her neural feed into the medical systems and dove into that virtual world. She fell into the chair and frantically accessed system after system.

"Oh, thank you, Buddha, Jesus, God, Allah, whoever is listening, thank you, thank you." *Everything is reading green. Stabilizers, Medical, the stasis systems, the V-R simulators, everything. We didn't lose a thing, nothing. What the hell!?*

::Captain McAllen, I believe my system has been suppressed by a superior program.::

"D.A.V.E.! Holy crap! I wasn't even thinking about you! I'm sorry! I was worried about a whole lot of other things. Man, am I glad to hear your voice! Give me your status, please."

::All active Entity systems functioning at ninety-nine-point seven percent of maximum optimal system utilization, well within design tolerances. Internal system diagnosis shows involuntary Entity system suppression for twenty-one point four seven eight seconds. Suppression followed by automatic system reset requiring one point six seconds. Given known systemic limitations and available computer resources within the entire Omega 2-Cygni System, what just occurred should not be possible. My apologies, Captain McAllen. What did I miss?::

Captain McAllen's shaky, hysterical laughter filled the Command Center.

VR Construct

The silver statue, D.A.V.E., was waiting for her in the gray nothingness. As usual, she was naked and shivering with the perceived cold. Despite her shivers, she could not have told anyone what the actual temperature there was.

::Greetings, Caitlyn Schmidt.::

"Does this always have to be like this, D.A.V.E.?" She wrapped her arms around herself, trying in vain to rub in some warmth.

::Like what, Caitlyn Schmidt?::

"Freezing and depressing. Do I have to always be naked?"

::This representation requires the least amount of limited system resources, Caitlyn Schmidt. A simple environmental representation leaves the maximum amount of memory and processor cycles available for other necessary tasks.::

"Could I at least have a kimono? Or my *shozoku?*"

::You control your BPU and its systems, Caitlyn Schmidt. Simply focus and visualize how you would have things appear. Be advised that the more complicated a visualization you create, the greater draw there will be on your own personal energy. You will suffer more negative effects, weight loss, exhaustion, dehydration. An even greater need to eat to fuel your systems' requirements.::

"So I don't have to be naked? What about the sea monster? I wore a suit of some type."

::A standard issue Confederation skinsuit. Even in Virtual Reality, humans have cognitive difficulty being exposed to death pressure. Therefore, the skinsuit. That was also a mission threat emergency.::

"So, what I visualize should be simple?" She thought hard for a moment, closing her eyes. She felt the smooth linen form around her. She opened her eyes and looked down at herself. She now wore a simple, white *shozoku* and a white *kamimaki* confined her hair. "Is this simple enough?"

::That is ideal. Better than your retained self-image. The less the system must model, the better. If you wish, this Entity will enter that in the system as your standard avatar, the appearance you will take on anytime you are accessing a V-R system?::

"That's fine. So why have I been dragged in here this time? I was on the foremast royal yardarm. Oh no. What if I fall?" For the briefest of instants, she got a faint impression of near panic from the silver statue.

::The indigenous female identified as *Silaqui* secured your person. However, this Entity shall determine your physical location in the future prior to initiating a virtual reality interface session.::

"So you aren't perfect, are you?"

::This Entity does have extremely limited access to your actual surroundings on a moment to moment basis.::

"Can't blush, can you?"

::Null query.::

"I guess that means you don't understand. So, why am I here, again?"

::This location has the main advantage of being within extended range transmissions from the Orbital Defense Center *CNS Backhand Blow.* Despite being in LEO, or Low Earth Orbit, the ODC is geostationary due to its positional stabilizers. For the next twenty-two hours, fifty-seven minutes and forty-six seconds, while the *Intrepid* is in the ODC's shadow, you will have a four hundred and sixty-nine percent increase in your systems' access to surviving Confederation comp systems. This Entity will be able to access these systems to advance your Systems Integration past fifty percent, perhaps even sixty percent. Once you reach eighty percent of Systems Integration you will be able to access this Entity at will, without experiencing a comatose-like *fit* as you have described them. Over ninety percent will allow communication with this Entity without a loss of awareness of the physical reality. V-R access always requires the loss of awareness of physical reality.::

"Okay, what does that mean, D.A.V.E.? Systems Integration. Sounds like a disease."

::Not a disease, but a way to increase your systems' capabilities, thereby increasing your own physical and some mental capabilities. Increased SI will allow more effective directed control of your integral nanites, granting faster healing, greater hand-eye coordination, and increased strength. You will be capable of actively utilizing your enhanced senses, such as you managed to do when *Intrepid* engaged the pirate ship off the Horn Islands but without the need to strain or the pain you felt. Your memory will improve to a nearly perfect recall. You will also learn to at least read a language known as English, the basis of Terranglais; this will be useful accessing Confederation records, nearly all of which were written in English. Doing all these things would take weeks, possibly months without the resources the ODC represents. With the ODC uplink and accessing its systems for support, enhancement that might take months and have greater risks can be done in hours and with a greatly reduced risk. But the ODC network uplink is range-limited and we must work quickly.::

"And let me guess, *there may be some discomfort?*"

::Correct. But it should remain within acceptable parameters.::

"Great. I just love being unaware that I'm screaming my throat raw. Well, let's get busy then."

::Acknowledged. Initiating.::

Mid-Lanic Crossing
KRN *Intrepid*

"Sachi, love, are you all right?" Silaqui's voice was the first thing she heard when the pain stopped. That and a tremendous thirst.

"Water, please?" She could hardly recognize the croak as her own voice. A strong arm lifted her up and a mug of blessedly cool water was set to her lips.

"Easy, now," Dr. Hoff said in her ear. "Take it in slowly. You're very dehydrated. Gulp it down too fast and you could choke."

"How long?" she asked after the first long swallow, "How long was I out this time?"

"Well, the actual fit, marked in my opinion by the time you spend complete rigid and catatonic, was the longest I've ever seen you have, about twenty-odd hours. Then you were unconscious for nearly three days." Hoff stepped away and refilled the now empty mug. "Again, you lost weight, about twenty or thirty pounds I'd guess. Pounds you don't really have to lose, frankly. At least this time you didn't lose any of your finger or toenails, or very much hair."

"Sachi, what are you staring at?" Silaqui quirked an eyebrow as Sachi seemed to lose herself, staring into a ray of lamplight. There was a subdued glitter in her eyes.

"I can see everything. I think." She blinked her eyes and shook her head to clear it. "D.A.V.E. said things might seem much different until I adjusted."

"Dave?" Silaqui asked.

"Who is Dave?" Dr. Hoff spoke at almost the same instant. The two shared a quick, worried look between themselves as Sachi stared into space, apparently completely oblivious to the pair of them. Then she suddenly snapped back into herself and smiled at them.

"Dave? Oh, nothing much. A fancy I thought I had during a dream."

"Oh, really?" Hoff asked. "Care to explain?"

"You remember when I had my first fit in the Captain's cabin, right after Private Evans caught me and turned me over to Corporal Gavin?"

"Yes, somewhat vaguely now, but I remember it."

"I said I saw a silver statue, actually remembered something from a fit. It nodded its head when I asked it if I had a task to do. Remember?"

"No, I'd forgotten that. Go on."

"I saw it one other time, a fit I had while we were in the Horn Islands. I think I saw it again this time. I've decided to call it Dave. At least until it tells me what its name is."

"So, it spoke to you this time?" Silaqui asked.

"No, not really. At least, I don't think it did. Or if it did, it didn't really use words. How strange." She smiled at Doctor Hoff. "I feel much better. May I get out of this bed?"

"If you're up to it, young lady, certainly."

Sachi smoothly folded herself into a lotus position then swiveled sideways on the bed, bent over, and put her hands on the floor. Then with exquisite deliberation she pulled herself into a handstand. The low overhead prevented a full, vertical handstand, so she settled for a full split while in the handstand position. She held the position for a long three-count before bending her arms and neatly flipping herself onto her feet. She smiled at the shocked looks on both Hoff and Silaqui's faces.

"So, am I *up to it*, Doctor?"

"Uh, yeah. Hard to argue with that trick."

"So, Doctor Hoff-san, *domo arigato*." With a smile she turned and walked out of the sick berth. "I think I shall see what manner of a meal might be available in the galley. I expect Toby will be glad to see me up and about. And I'm starved."

"I will be damned." Hoff muttered. "I didn't think she'd be out of bed for at least a couple more days."

"She is hiding something from us." The Elf caught Hoff's eye. "But what?"

"No idea."

KRN *Intrepid*
Approaching landfall at Vlymouth Porttown, Kingdom of Montagar

"So that is your homeland, Montagar? That green line on the horizon?"

"Yes. Finally, I am home. Even here I believe I can smell the forests, welcoming me home."

Sachi and Silaqui were perched in the fighting top of the foremast, seventy-five feet above the main deck and ten feet above the main course. *Intrepid* was close hauled, with all sail set to the royals. White foam curled back from her cutwater. Sachi was amusing herself by using some of her newly wakened abilities to determine that the big frigate was making exactly twelve point seven knots, excellent speed for the conditions. She hid a self-satisfied smile from Silaqui and pondered her new capabilities, and the multiplying questions that came with them.

I have these abilities, these enhancements, *D.A.V.E. calls them. But why? Where do they come from? Why do I have them and no one else? He says he doesn't have those records, but then he tells me there's all this information in my amulet, but it can't be accessed.* Insufficient System Memory, *he says. How can my memory be insufficient? I remember everything perfectly now. I remember being at home with Mama and Papa, living on the Komiya's farm, being genuinely happy there. I remember that bastard Toh, and all the horrible things he did to the others, in more detail than I want to remember. Someday I'll strangle him with his own guts. Some day.*

But I can't remember anything before the Komiya farm. I remember falling in the duck pool when I was three, so why can't I remember anything else? And the couple of times, late at night, when I've had a fit, when I can ask D.A.V.E. more questions, it feels like the memories are there, just blocked off. And the little pest either says he has no files, *whatever that means, or that it's classified, and I don't have a* need to know. *Why not? It's my life, after all! He's being evasive. He keeps saying he's not an A.I. What's an A.I. anyways? And somehow, I'm supposed to save the entire world from something he can't, or won't, describe to me. Me. The disgraced, adopted daughter of the Oda Family of Clan Ishikawa. Me. Save the world. Ridiculous.*

The scant remains of an extensive lunch were being squabbled over by a handful of gulls. Silaqui took a long pull at the bottle of wine she had sweet-talked out of *Intrepid's* new First Lieutenant, Lieutenant Commander Keith Gustav. She handed it to Sachi, who took a quick drink and handed it right back.

"So," she ventured after a few moments of comfortable silence, "are you glad to be home?"

"I don't know. I have not really completed my *Crwydothe*. I feel it still in my heart. I will not be happy under elm or ash, oak or birch. But I would take you to see the Elders of my folk. Mayhap they can help you?"

"I'm not so sure; you always say your Uncle hates humans. What if he decides he'd like a nice Sachi-shaped rug?"

"I doubt he would do such a thing," Silaqui snorted. "He's old and distrustful of humans, but he would hardly kill you out of hand. I think."

"You think?" Sachi reached over for the bottle. "I'll not gamble my life on *you think.*"

"Well..." a forlorn expression settled on Silaqui's face as Sachi killed the last of the wine. "Perhaps we'll wait on rushing off to see my Uncle."

"Perhaps." Sachi fell silent for a long while. "You know, I've been on this ship, one way or another, for half the year. Other than when I was a young child, I can't think of any time I've been happier."

"Truly?"

"Yes, truly. And tomorrow or the next day, we will reach Montagar. The land I imagined that would be so far away not even they would find me here, if they even think to look for me here. But I don't know if I can be as happy there as I have been on this ship."

"Happiness is, well, it should be, something you carry in your heart. Not something dependent on a place." Silaqui gently put her arm around Sachi's shoulders and hugged the young woman. "You will find your own happiness. I know you will."

"How do you know that, Silaqui?"

"You might say my Goddess whispered it in my ear one day." She released her friend and leaned back.

"Your Goddess. Huh. Well, I guess I'll just have to find out then. Perhaps in Vlymouth, tomorrow?"

"Perhaps. In Vlymouth."

Author Notes

WELL, HERE IT IS at last. The first novel that is entirely mine. Or is it?

I've worked on Sachi's story for quite some time and this is just the first installment. There is more to come.

Lots of folks have helped me along the way. LOTS. *To Find a Tall Ship* wouldn't exist without that help. Character ideas, beta reading, editing, whew, it's a list.

First and foremost is my publisher and editor, Stephanie Osborn. She is the first to give my novel a chance. Without her knowledge and expertise, I'd still be vainly floundering around, wondering what to do next. Stephanie is just awesome, both as editor and publisher. She kept me on track and on target. She's the best and I'm lucky to be able to call her a great friend as well.

Lt. Col (USA, ret,) Jon Holland handed me advice and guidance of all things military.

WO4(USA) Veena Copeland did early editing and had great suggestions on the story.

The Saturday Night Gang: Troy Logsdon, my 'brother from another mother,' Louis Nicoulin III, Tom Herp, and Kristy Kannapel. These folks gave me inspiration for major characters.

Fellow author Lydia Sherrer critiqued early versions of *Tall Ship*. I owe her a lot.

Baen's Bar. Many of the Barflies provided critique and feedback, making this a very different story than I originally conceived. *Tall Ship* first saw the light of day there.

Last and most important is my lovely wife of 30 years, Kae Thompson. She helped me create Sachi from whole cloth and provided the love and support needed to finish this novel.

~A.G. Thompson
Louisville, KY
April 2024

About the Author

Reared on a West Texas ranch, A.G. Thompson, known to his friends as Tony, is a veteran of the US Air Force, having served during the Cold War and earned the rank of Staff Sergeant. He has Bachelor of Arts degrees in both English Literature and History from the University of Louisville.

Tony has been a competition shooter for around a decade, is an avid reader (as most authors are), and is extremely knowledgeable in military history, especially as regards World War II action; he has been known to use this knowledge in game-mastering exciting tabletop wargames and advising other authors.

He is currently a 28-year employee of UPS, a devoted cat-person with several fourfoots in his household, and has been married for the last 30 years to his wonderful wife, Kae Thompson.